PALACE
CIRCLE

PALACE CIRCLE

REBECCA DEAN

Broadway Books
New York

Copyright © 2009 by Rebecca Dean

All Rights Reserved

Published in the United States by Broadway Books,
an imprint of The Doubleday Publishing Group,
a division of Random House, Inc., New York.
www.broadwaybooks.com

BROADWAY BOOKS and its logo, a letter B bisected on the
diagonal, are trademarks of Random House, Inc.

Book design by Nicola Ferguson

Library of Congress Cataloging-in-Publication Data
Dean, Rebecca.
Palace circle / by Rebecca Dean. —1st ed.
p.   cm.
1. Young women—Virginia—Fiction. 2. Marriage—Fiction.
3. Nobility—England—Fiction. 4. Nineteen tens—Fiction.
I. Title.
PS3604.E1537 2009
813'.6—dc22
2008021188

ISBN 978-0-7679-3055-0

PRINTED IN THE UNITED STATES OF AMERICA

1 3 5 7 9 10 8 6 4 2

First Edition

For all those who work for, and support,
the Brooke Hospital for Animals

Part One

DELIA

1911–1930

ONE

The first rays of the rising sun filtered through the half-open shutters of the vast bedroom. Eighteen-year-old Delia Conisborough stirred slightly, her tumbled hair a glorious flame-red against the pristine whiteness of lace-edged bed linen.

The man beside her, snoring gently, didn't move and, much as she loved him, she didn't want him to wake. This was the morning that, as a bride of five days, she was to leave her childhood home and embark on the long journey to England and a lifestyle so different from anything she had previously known. There were goodbyes to be said. Not to people. They would come later when the Chandler clan descended on Sans Souci to wave them off as they left by train for Richmond. From Richmond there would be a longer journey to New York and then, most exciting of all, the five-day Atlantic crossing aboard the RMS *Mauretania,* the most luxurious liner afloat.

Still trying to come to terms with the realization that her surname was no longer Chandler but Conisborough and that she had a title, Viscountess—though Ivor had explained to her she would generally be referred to as Lady Conisborough—she swung her legs to the floor, her silk nightdress swirling about her ankles. It wasn't yet six o'clock and she had at least two hours in which to say private goodbyes to all her favorite horses and all her favorite places—as well as to Sans Souci itself.

The bedroom she had been sharing with Ivor for the last four nights was not the bedroom she still regarded as being hers. That bedroom lay in the opposite wing of the house and she padded barefoot along the corridor toward it, plaiting her hair into a single waist-length braid as she did so.

"Mornin', Miss Delia," said one of the servants, who had been at Sans Souci for as long as she could remember, as she passed him outside her father's room. "Ah sure am sorry you be leavin' us."

"I'm sorry too, Sam," she said, not at all abashed at being clad only in her nightdress. "But my husband has promised we'll be back for visits."

She flashed Sam a dazzling smile and, if she had been dressed, would have hugged him. No one ever stood on ceremony at Sans Souci. The easygoing intimacy between family and servants was taken for granted, though Ivor had been shocked by it.

"Great Scott, Delia!" he'd said disbelievingly when first witnessing the way the Chandlers treated their staff. "You won't be able to behave like that in England. They would think you had taken leave of your senses!"

Now in her old bedroom she smiled at the memory, pulling her nightdress over her head and then dragging her ankle-length riding skirt and her riding jacket from the closet.

Though she was only eighteen she had enough sense to know that it was her American ways that had captivated her new husband. He certainly hadn't married her for her money. A handful of other aristocratic Englishmen, those with vast estates and little money to maintain them, had married American heiresses, but Ivor Conisborough did not fall into that category. Twenty-two years her senior, he not only came from an exceedingly distinguished family; he had also been a financial adviser to King Edward VII, who had died a year ago, and was now financial adviser to the about-to-be-crowned King George V. As a consequence of his position and his aristocratic lineage he was very much a part of the royal circle. A royal circle of which she, as his wife, would also soon be a welcomed part.

As she pulled on her riding boots, excitement and anticipation flooded through her. Ivor's visit to Virginia—and his subsequent acquaintanceship with her father—had changed her entire future. As daughter of one of the leading families of Virginia she would, of course, have married well and always lived comfortably, but there could be no comparison between the life she had expected and the life she was now about to lead.

Chandlers rarely saw any reason to leave Virginia and it was a foregone conclusion that if she hadn't married Ivor, her future husband would have been a distantly related Chandler cousin, perhaps Beau Chandler, who was a cousin twice or three times removed. She could never remember which. Beau was handsome and fun into the bargain, but as his interests didn't extend much beyond drinking and gambling it was always fun of short duration. With Beau there would have been regular trips to White Sulphur Springs, a fashionable spa, and maybe even the occasional trip to Niagara, but there would certainly have been no Atlantic crossing and most certainly none of the sophisticated social life that lay ahead of her in London. A social life that would, in a few weeks' time, include attending a coronation in Westminster Abbey.

In the stables she took her time saying goodbye to her father's horses. Her father had always been a keen horseman. A member of the Deep Run Hunt, he had taught her to ride before she could walk. When Ivor had asked her to marry him, it had been her only query. "I shall still be able to ride?" she had asked, her heart slamming hard against her breastbone.

"You'll be able to ride every day in London," he had said reassuringly in the clipped English accent that sent tingles down her spine. "Many of my late wife's friends ride daily on Hyde Park's Rotten Row. It's a bridle path with stabling nearby. And if you want to hunt—"

"I shan't," she had said, before he could finish. "Pa hunts. I never have."

"You may change your mind when you find friends disappearing to Leicestershire every November," he'd said drily. "We'll wait and see. One thing is certain: once people see how you take a horse over a five-foot gate fence, everyone will know what a superb rider you are."

She had wanted to ask how far Shibden Hall, his family seat, was from Leicestershire. She knew it was in Norfolk but had no idea how far both counties were from each other, or from London.

"But London is where we shall be spending the most time," she said now to her horse, Sultan, mounting him unaided.

Riding bareback, she cantered out of the cobbled yard and past the paddocks. It was a glorious spring morning, the air thick with the scent of summer. On mornings like these it seemed to her that the lush rolling Virginian countryside was as vast as all eternity. The softly rounded peaks of the Blue Ridge Mountains were hazy in the distance and nearer were belts of thick woodland edging a swift-running river and half a dozen creeks. She knew the names of all the trees. Red maple, tulip, black gum, sassafras, hickory, dogwood, and sourwood. In autumn their leaves were a blaze of color. Now, in April, it was wildflowers that were at their best.

By the edge of the nearest creek she could glimpse the delicate pale mauve of wild geraniums and, beyond them, flashes of maroon-red trilliums and swath after swath of marsh marigolds, their deep-yellow petals glinting like gold.

She reined in Sultan and with the reins slack in her hands she stared at the landscape she loved. The trouble was, she also adored Ivor and Ivor's life was in London—and not only

London. He was just as familiar with Paris and Rome and St. Petersburg as he was with New York and Washington.

That she was the wife of such a distinguished cosmopolitan man thrilled her. The moment she had been introduced to him she had been bowled over; but he was of her parents' generation, not hers. Even when her father told her that their visitor was a widower it had still not occurred to her that he might show romantic interest in her.

It had been her aunt Rose, her mother's spinster sister, who had set out to catch his eye. Her mother, when Ivor had extended his stay in Virginia, had thought that perhaps Rose had a chance. Her father had always been far more perceptive.

"Lord Conisborough's marriage was childless," he'd said when Delia had ever so casually brought up the subject of her aunt Rose's hopes and aspirations. "When Conisborough marries again it will be to a woman much younger than Rose. He'll want an heir and, because of his age, he'll want one fast. Poor Rose. I'm afraid she's going to be out of luck again."

Her father was right, but when it became known that Lord Conisborough had asked for Delia's hand in marriage, Rose had been poleaxed.

Delia, too, had hardly been able to believe it.

Her father had believed it, though, and had done so gleefully. "An English viscount! A peer of the realm! Dammit, girl! I *told* you he'd be looking for a young wife! Wait until *The New York Times* gets hold of this! They'll have to describe us as Virginian aristocracy!"

Her mother had been far more restrained. "He's been widowed for only such a short time, Delia," she had said, seated beside her on the edge of her bed, her hand holding her daughter's. "And he is so much older. I'd hate to think you were marrying because your head had been turned by the thought of an English title."

"It hasn't," she'd said adamantly. "I'm marrying him because I'm in love with him. I'm marrying him because he's different to any other man I have ever met or, living in Virginia, am ever likely to meet. He's cultivated, sophisticated, intelligent—and *very* good-looking. Don't you think he is very good-looking?"

Her mother thought of Ivor Conisborough's chiseled features, the aquiline nose, the faint hollows under the cheekbones, the well-shaped mouth that betrayed an arrogance that could never be wholly hidden, the dark-blond hair, arrow-straight and silkily smooth, and had, with a marked lack of enthusiasm, agreed with her daughter.

As Delia now turned Sultan's head in the direction of Sans Souci, she hoped her mother's lack of enthusiasm was because Ivor was the complete opposite to her father. Always chewing on a plug of tobacco, her father was on the short side, no more than five foot eight or nine, with broad shoulders and a barrel chest. Most comfortable in shabby, well-worn riding clothes, he seldom wore anything else and wherever he went there was a ruckus of talk and laughter.

Ivor was tall, at least two inches over six foot, favored Cuban cigars, and was accompanied on all his travels by a valet. His starched collars were higher than anyone else's in Virginia and he always wore either a homburg or, in deference to the Virginian heat, a straw hat with his fashionable lounge suits. Exquisitely tailored though they were, Delia privately thought he never looked quite at ease in them. He was a man who suited formal clothing. In the frock coat and top hat he wore whenever they visited Richmond, he looked superb.

Unlike her father, he never spoke unless he had something pertinent to say, and there was something in his manner that commanded immediate respect. Even Beau, who had volubly declared he had no intention of fawning to English nobility, had referred to him as "Your Grace" on first being introduced to him.

By then Delia had been conversant enough with the way

to address and introduce Ivor to know that Beau had made a social gaffe.

"Refer to me as Ivor or as Conisborough," Ivor had said, tired of giving the instruction to Delia's army of relations. "Only dukes are addressed as 'Your Grace,' and then only by servants or anyone with whom they are having nonsocial communication."

Unused to Ivor's clipped way of speaking, Beau had interpreted the remark as a put-down and, refusing to let Delia persuade him otherwise, had vowed he would never forgive it. When she had married Ivor a month later in Richmond's St. James's Episcopal Church, Beau had been noticeable only by his absence.

Despite the sumptuousness of her silk-and-satin wedding gown, with its high bodice encrusted with seed pearls and its slim skirt and lavish train, it hadn't been quite the extravaganza she had always imagined her wedding would be—or the wedding her mother had always planned for her to have—because it had all been so sudden.

"It is impossible for me to return to England—which I must do almost immediately in view of the forthcoming coronation—and then travel back to Virginia for a spring wedding," Ivor had said to her father in the tone of a man accustomed to getting his own way. "And it would be highly inappropriate for Delia to accompany me to England without doing so as my wife and it is not what she wants."

It wasn't what her father wanted either; hence the speedy wedding that had set tongues wagging all over Virginia.

As she neared the hill that gave a perfect view of Sans Souci, Delia urged Sultan into a canter, still thinking of her husband and the intimidating effect he had on people. Sometimes even she felt a little intimidated by him, but common sense told her that it was natural when her respect for him was boundless and when he was, in so many ways, still a stranger to her.

Cresting the hill, she reined Sultan to a halt. This was the view she most wanted to remember.

Set against a background of evergreen trees, Sans Souci lay cradled in a circle of lushly green hills. Near to the house were the paddocks and then, a little to one side, the stables and the various barns for the yearlings, the broodmares, and the winter foodstuffs. Beyond them lay the neat precision of apple orchards.

And dominating everything was the house.

It was a three-story brick-built colonnaded manor, its elegant Georgian windows flanked by pale-yellow shutters, a flight of stone steps leading up to its double front doors. The sun shimmered on its slate roof and honeysuckle fragranced the porch where her father and his friends liked to sit in the evenings, frosted mint juleps conveniently to hand.

It was the only home she had ever known and suddenly the prospect of leaving it caught at her throat. Sans Souci meant, in French, "without a care," and her mother had ensured that since the day she had entered it as a young bride, it had lived up to its name.

Delia's hands tightened on Sultan's reins. Though Ivor had told her they would be spending most of their time in London, she was sure that Shibden Hall would begin to play a large part in their married life once she had given Ivor an heir, and she was determined to turn it into the kind of home her mother had created at Sans Souci. A home that however impressively splendid, was also welcoming with fresh flowers in every room. A home where everyone who entered it instantly felt at ease. Most of all, a home where Ivor would want to be whenever he could get away from London and his court commitments.

As she gazed across the open meadowland, the double doors to the house opened. For a heart-stopping moment she wondered if she would see Ivor's distinctively tall figure. She had been gone for nearly two hours and he would be up and dressed by now and wondering where she was. The thought of him walking into the meadows to greet her, as impatient to be with her as she was to be with him, filled her with excitement.

She dug her heels into Sultan's flanks, but even as she did so she saw that it wasn't Ivor stepping out onto the colonnaded porch: it was two of the servants hauling black traveling trunks.

Her disappointment was intense, but swiftly overcome. Any moment now the luggage would be loaded into one of the many horse-drawn buggies that would accompany them when they left Sans Souci for the local train station. It meant she hadn't much time in which to bathe, eat breakfast, and change into her traveling clothes. And though Ivor wasn't yet in sight, somewhere within Sans Souci he was waiting for her.

At full gallop she jumped the treacherously high split-rail fence that marked the beginning of Chandler land, eager for the opportunity, aboard ship and away from the prurient eyes of her family, to get to know her husband better. Eager to embark on the new, exciting life awaiting her in England.

TWO

The country that was to be her home wasn't remotely what she had expected. When the *Mauretania* had neared land after a windy transatlantic voyage she had expected to see white cliffs topped by springy green turf. Instead she faced a forbidding-looking city of stone. The grayness of Liverpool was something she had never experienced, not even in New York.

The train journey to London had also been a disappointment. She had seen no picturesque houses with thatched roofs and doors framed by roses; no children skipping around May-poles; only distant church spires and fields of cows huddled miserably together in heavy rain. By the time their train steamed its way into King's Cross Station she realized that the reality of England was going to be far different to her naïvely idealized picture-book expectations.

Her new home, however, was far from disappointing. Tall and imposing and with a splendid portico, it was situated in an elegant square only a few minutes away from Buckingham Palace. Her first surprise was the stiff etiquette she immediately was met with.

The staff—a veritable army of white-capped maids and liveried footmen—had lined up to greet her and when she stepped out of the Conisborough Rolls-Royce, their reaction was one of unanimous disbelief.

Ivor had already warned her what to expect. "Be prepared to meet with a little bemusement, sweetheart," he had said as they neared the house. "Whatever the staff are expecting, it won't be an eighteen-year-old with flame-red hair who uses expressions such as 'a cracking good one,' 'I'm mighty glad,' 'real soon,' and—don't deny you've said this, because I've heard you—'shucks.' "

"I'll have you know," she had replied archly, "that I've been tryin' real hard to drop all my Virginian speech and slang. I just haven't gotten to replace it yet with an acceptable cut-glass English accent."

Beneath his blond mustache his austerely straight mouth had twitched with amusement and she had squeezed his hand lovingly.

Nothing could have been farther removed from the easygoing atmosphere of Sans Souci than the formality of the Cadogan Square house. Over the next few days Delia made a determined effort to inject a little Virginian friendliness into her new home. There were occasions when Ivor cleared his throat or pursed his lips in disapproval, but she took no notice. Bellingham, the butler, soon became her adoring slave and wouldn't allow a word of criticism to be said about her belowstairs. As she had arrived at Cadogan Square without a personal maid she had rejected Ivor's suggestion that she hire a suitably experienced young woman and instead, having taking a great liking to Ellie, one of the young parlor maids, had asked her to fill the position.

Ellie was a chatterbox, something Delia was grateful for, since she still knew no more about Ivor's first wife than she had on the day he proposed.

"Lady Olivia spent very little time in London, my lady," Ellie had said when Delia had pressed her for information. "She much preferred being at Shibden Hall."

It was a piece of information that had startled Delia. Somehow she had never thought of Olivia as spending a great deal of time away from Ivor.

Then there was the mystery as to why, among the many family portraits adorning the walls of the Cadogan Square house, there wasn't one of Olivia.

Again, it was Ellie who told her.

"There used to be one, my lady," she had said as she brushed Delia's turbulently fiery hair until it crackled, "only it's been taken down."

"Taken down?" Delia had turned away from her dressing table. "But why, Ellie?" she'd asked. "For what possible reason?"

With an awkwardness she rarely displayed Ellie had said, "I think, my lady, his lordship thought it best. I think he thought you wouldn't constantly want to be reminded that he had once been married to someone else."

That Ivor should have been so sensitive to her feelings had taken her breath away and she had instantly forgiven him for the long hours he spent away from her at the palace, the House of Lords, or his gentlemen's club in Pall Mall.

One friend, Sir Cuthbert Digby, had even ushered Ivor away to Buckingham Palace only minutes after he had escorted her into the house. She had tried not to be cross about it, but she had been alarmed at the realization that if the aged Sir Cuthbert was typical of Ivor's friends, then their wives were all going to be as old as her mother or, even worse, her grandmother.

Gwen, Ivor's elder sister and his only close relative, was nearer to fifty than to forty. Though she had speedily become deeply fond of Gwen, Delia very much wanted to make friends with people of her own age—and thought it unlikely she was going to be able to do so. A comfort was that Ivor left her in no doubt that his friends had all taken her to their hearts.

"Cuthie thinks you're a delight," he said, preparing to leave in a hurry for the palace. "And lovemaking on a morning is going to have to come to an end, sweetheart, if this is how late it makes me."

She laughed, knowing he was teasing, and helped him into his frock coat.

He reached for his top hat, gave her a swift kiss, and was gone.

She was just about to ring for Ellie when she saw that in his hurry Ivor had left his appointments diary behind. She picked it up, about to run after him with it. A photograph fell from between the diary's pages and as she knelt to retrieve it, she saw that it was of a woman far too young to be Ivor's mother and far too old to be a niece or a godchild.

She sank back on her heels, knowing the photograph could only be of Olivia. She had expected Ivor's late wife to have been lovely and dignified. What she had not expected was for her to have been shatteringly beautiful.

Dark-haired, dark-eyed, and dazzling, she was wearing a diamond tiara on her upswept, intricately arranged hair. Her eyebrows were strongly marked and dramatically winged. Beneath them, heavily lashed eyes stared out boldly with an expression of sultry insolence. Her cheekbones were high, her darkly lipsticked mouth sensually curved. The evening gown she was wearing was low-cut, revealing a full bosom and a wasp waist. In addition to the diamonds in her hair, there were diamonds at her throat, her ears, her wrists and on her fingers. Even in a photograph she glittered and shone, the epitome of exotic, *soignée* glamour.

Trembling violently she turned the photograph over. *All my love, darling Ivor, is for you and you alone* was written in an extravagant flourish in mauve ink.

That Ivor had obviously loved his first wife was something that had never troubled her. She had been too confident of his love to allow herself to become jealous of a much older woman who was now dead.

But that had been before she had realized how staggeringly beautiful Olivia Conisborough had been. And before she had realized that though Olivia's portrait had been taken down, Ivor still kept her image where he would see it frequently.

As she heard the front door close she placed the photograph back into the diary with unsteady hands and then put the diary back where she had found it.

It was something she knew she would never be able to speak to Ivor about and, no matter how deep her shock, it was something she was determined to come to terms with.

A day after her arrival in England she met a friend of Ivor's that she instantly liked. They were walking along Piccadilly when Ivor came to such a sudden halt, she almost tripped. A second later a man she judged to be in his mid-thirties walked up to them. As toughly built as a heavyweight boxer, he was wearing a dove-gray lounge suit and his matching gray homburg was tilted at a rakish angle. There was a devil-may-care air about him that reminded her of Beau and that she found unexpected in someone who was obviously on friendly terms with her statesmanlike husband.

"Jerome, I would like to introduce you to my wife," Ivor said, an odd note in his voice. "Delia and I were married a little over a fortnight ago in Richmond, Virginia. Delia, Sir Jerome Bazeljette."

Something crossed Bazeljette's handsome swarthy face that was as indecipherable as the expression in Ivor's voice.

"My congratulations, Lady Conisborough." He shook hands with her and raised his hat, and as he did so, she saw his hair was black as a Gypsy's and thick and curly as a ram's fleece. "And to you, Conisborough, as well, of course," he added.

To Delia's mystification the conversation then came to a standstill.

Delia, who could launch into conversation with anyone, beggar-man or king, said pleasantly, "Have you ever visited Virginia, Mr. Bazeljette?"

"No." He was clearly startled by her disarming directness. "I haven't. Is it one of the states south of the Mason-Dixon Line?"

There was genuine interest and friendly feeling in his voice and she responded to it sunnily. "It most certainly is. And Virginians never forget it. We still fly the Confederate flag at Sans Souci."

"Sans Souci?" There were gold flecks in his brown eyes.

"Sans Souci is the name of my family home, Mr. Bazeljette," she said, thinking what a very attractive man he was.

Ivor put a quick end to the conversation by saying, "We must be on our way, Jerome, before Piccadilly Circus is treated to a rendering of 'Dixie.' "

It was a remark that could have been taken humorously, but there was a hard edge to his voice that caused Delia to gasp.

"Perhaps I will have the pleasure of hearing 'Dixie' sung at another time," Jerome said, and something in his voice indicated that he too had caught the undertone in Ivor's voice. Turning his attention to Ivor, he said crisply, "Sylvia is on the Riviera, as I think you know, Ivor. I'm not sure when she intends returning," and without waiting for a response he raised his homburg once again and sauntered on his way.

The minute he was out of earshot Ivor said tightly, "It isn't up to me to tell a man when his wife intends returning to London, but I can promise you, Delia, that Sylvia will be here in time to present you at court." A pulse was beating at the corner of his jaw and there were white lines around his mouth. "And Jerome is a baronet," he said as they again began walking in the direction of the Ritz. "Anyone bearing the title of 'Sir' is either a baronet or a knight. Referring to him as Mr. Bazeljette was a great solecism. In conversation the surnames of baronets and knights are never used, except by their men friends. Only their Christian names are used with the prefix of 'Sir.' "

Delia bit her lip, not because she was distressed at being spoken to in such a way but because she was so furiously angry that she wasn't sure she was going to be able to control her voice.

"And just how," she finally said as they entered the Ritz, "was I supposed to know that? And how am I to address Sir Jerome's wife when I meet her?"

"Until you are on intimate terms with her—which I hope you will be very quickly—you address her as Lady Bazeljette. Wives of baronets and knights are never formally addressed by their Christian names as doing so indicates that the lady is the daughter of a duke, a marquess, or an earl."

It was all so ridiculously complicated that Delia rolled her eyes.

Fortunately Ivor didn't see her.

As they were led across the opulent dining room to a table overlooking the terrace, she took a steadying breath. "Why is it Sylvia who is presenting me at court, Ivor?" she asked, hoping to put the conversation on a friendlier footing. "I'd much prefer it if you were to present me."

The change of subject had the desired effect.

He gave a slight smile. "A presentation can only be made by a lady who has herself been presented. And as Sylvia has no daughters of her own, presenting you will give her great pleasure."

Delia didn't protest any further. If Lady Bazeljette was as amiable as her husband, then Delia was only too happy to put herself into her hands.

———

Two days later her hopes that she was already pregnant were ended. For a few hours she was plunged into gloom but then common sense reasserted itself. Not everyone was like her cousin Bella, who had become pregnant on her honeymoon. It might well take two months, maybe three, before she was able to give Ivor the news he so wanted to hear. For the moment though, he was, she knew, going to be disappointed.

He wasn't just disappointed. He was devastated.

"I thought young women your age got babies easily," he said, staring at her as if perhaps she had made a mistake. "Dear God, it isn't as if we haven't tried hard enough, is it?"

The crudity was so unexpected—and so unlike him—that she gasped.

"I'm sorry, sweetheart." He pulled her down onto his lap, hugging her tight. "It's just that I was so hoping for good news. Perhaps next month, eh?"

"Yes," she said, her head against his chest. "Perhaps next month." But as his lips brushed her hair, she felt as though she had let him down—and letting Ivor down was the very last thing in the world she wanted to do.

A week later and she was at Madame Colette's, the dressmaker Gwen had recommended.

"It's a great shame Sylvia is still not back from the Riviera," Gwen said as she watched Madame Colette adjust the white satin gown Delia was to wear at court. "She always leaves things to the last minute, but as Ivor said she was so thrilled at having been asked to present you, I really do think she should have kept us *au fait* with her travel plans."

Already nervous at the thought of appearing at Buckingham Palace before King George and Queen Mary, Delia became even more tense.

"If she don't arrive back in time, could you present me, Gwen?" she asked anxiously.

"No, darling, I couldn't." Gwen's voice was filled with regret. "All the paperwork for your presentation is already with the lord chamberlain." As an afterthought she added, "And it's 'doesn't,' Delia, darling. Not 'don't.'"

Unlike the occasions when Ivor corrected her speech, Delia was unperturbed. Ever since their first meeting Gwen had shown nothing but maternal-like affection toward her, and when Gwen corrected her Delia knew she did it to be helpful—and that the helpfulness was always meant in the kindest possible way.

When the pinning and tucking were done to her satisfaction, Madame Colette asked for Delia's white satin embroidered train to be brought out and temporarily attached to the gown so the full effect could be appreciated.

"Lady Conisborough's fan will be the one I carried when presented." Gwen, majestic in a dress of gray silk worn with a wide-brimmed black hat decorated with a red rose, eyed Delia's hand-span waist with satisfaction. "And also," she added as an afterthought, "Delia will be wearing the family tiara."

"Any other jewelry?" Madame Colette asked, not wanting anything to be chosen that would fight with the purity of the gown's neckline.

"A three-strand pearl necklace," Delia said, "and pearl drop earrings."

"Ah! Another family heirloom, Lady Conisborough?"

Delia shook her head. "No. They were a honeymoon gift to me from my husband when we were in New York."

"And a perfect choice for a presentation at court, if I may say so, your ladyship."

When the fitting was completed, Gwen insisted that the two of them have tea at Fortnum & Mason.

Delia walked into the St. James's Restaurant conscious that she was looking her best in a royal-blue walking costume, the short bolero jacket worn over a high-necked, heavily flounced white chiffon blouse, the ankle-length skirt skimming prettily buttoned shoes, her wide-brimmed, blue-and-emerald peacock-feathered hat at a seductive angle.

Gwen exchanged pleasantries with several other ladies taking tea and then, within minutes of their sitting down, Jerome Bazeljette strolled up to them.

"Good afternoon, ladies," he said, oblivious of the many female heads that had turned to admiringly watch him as he crossed the room.

Gwen's middle-aged face flushed.

"Do please join us, Jerome," she said in a manner that indicated he was a far closer family friend than Delia had thought. "I believe you have already met my new sister-in-law?"

"I have indeed." He took a seat at the table and smiled. "Though sadly these surroundings are no more suitable for a rendering of 'Dixie' than our previous encounter."

Gwen blinked in bewilderment and giggles fizzed in Delia's throat.

"I'm curious about Virginian high society, Lady Conisborough," he continued. "Is it very different here, in London?"

Delia fought down a rush of homesickness. "Yes, totally different. In Virginia nearly everyone in polite society is somehow related to everyone else. And no matter how distant that relationship, everyone knows it. Genealogy is a very popular pastime in Virginia. And because of that, class doesn't matter in the way it does here."

"Good heavens!" Gwen straightened her napkin, hardly able to believe that things were so different on the other side of the Atlantic.

"And we're Republicans," Delia continued, thinking it was something Gwen might need reminding of. "Our public life doesn't revolve around a monarchy. Here, in London, Ivor's life and those of nearly all the people he meets are centered around what is happening at court. And if it isn't court affairs that are being discussed, it's politics."

"But, my dear, that's only natural." Gwen ignored the decadent-looking pastries on the cake stand. "Ivor's position as a financial adviser to King Edward puts him right at the heart of British political life, isn't that so, Jerome?"

Jerome nodded and in the light of the chandeliers—fully ablaze even though it was a sunny afternoon—his curly hair gleamed blue-black.

"King George, however," Gwen continued, "is far more conservative than his late father—and far less cosmopolitan. You won't find His Majesty gamboling at Biarritz and Monte Carlo, or visiting fashionable spas such as Marienbad and Carlsbad."

"Though you will find me at them," Jerome interjected.

"That's true," Gwen said scoldingly, but with much affection, "and why Sylvia condones such behavior I can't imagine." She turned to Delia. "Sylvia is the most scintillating creature, Delia. As a society hostess no one can hold a candle to her—not even Margot Asquith."

Margot Asquith was the prime minister's wife and having met her at a dinner party the previous evening, Delia had realized that she was a woman who neither tolerated fools nor anyone not fiercely intelligent and bitingly witty. The prospect of acting as her hostess—which Ivor had told her she would have to do in the not-too-distant future—filled Delia with terror.

"Tell us more about Virginia," Gwen said. "Do Virginians eat very strange food?"

Grateful for the change in the conversation, Delia took a sip of tea and said, "Some of it may seem very strange to you, Gwen, but it ain't strange to Virginians. We eat soft-shell crabs and shad roe and fried chicken and watermelon and home-cured ham—and it's all absolutely delicious. And compared to life here, everything is easy and informal."

She told them about the glorious Virginian countryside; about how, in May, the scent of flowering dogwood filled the air and of how, from Sans Souci's shaded porches, there were hazy distant views of the Blue Ridge Mountains. She told them about her father's horses—particularly Sultan—and she told them of the sultry summer heat that was so different from anything she had so far experienced in England.

"Though today is delightfully balmy," Gwen said in defense of English weather. "May is often the loveliest month of the year in England. And now I really do have to go. I have a beauty appointment at the House of Cyclax in twenty minutes' time. I'm so sorry, Delia, because I'd thought we could take a cab together and that you could have been dropped off at Cadogan Square, but now there isn't enough time for that and I'm going to have to go straight to South Molton Street."

Delia smiled, not at all put out. "That's no problem, Gwen. You can take a cab and pop off to your appointment and I'll walk home."

Gwen's china-blue eyes widened in horror. "Good gracious, you can't do that, Delia! It's way too far—and even if it wasn't, you couldn't walk there alone!"

Delia was just about to protest that she most certainly could when Jerome said in a voice that brooked no argument—not even from Gwen—"No need to worry, Gwen. I'll see Delia safely back to Cadogan Square."

"That would be wonderfully kind of you, Jerome." Vastly relieved, Gwen allowed him to usher her out of the restaurant and out of the building, saying to both of them as she stepped into one of the horse-drawn cabs that were lined up outside Fortnum's, "And I'll see both of you this evening at dear Cuthie's birthday party."

As the cab began to pull away she leaned out of it in order to call to Jerome, "Only please don't allow Delia to walk all the way to Cadogan Square, Jerome! It's much too far!"

Jerome merely waved until the cab was lost in a sea of other horse-drawn cabs, horse-drawn buses, and a scattering of open-topped motorcars and then said to Delia, "Is it too far? It's about three-quarters of a mile, maybe less."

She flashed him a wide smile, saying teasingly, "That's nothing to a Virginian. We walk that far to get from the house to the stables."

He chuckled and then, in happy companionship, they set off in the direction of Hyde Park Corner and Kensington.

"How are you settling into life as part of the palace circle?" he asked as, on their left-hand side, they reached the park that backed onto Buckingham Palace.

"I ain't"—she corrected herself swiftly—"haven't met Their Majesties yet. That won't happen until I've been presented at court. I've been to a dinner party at which the prime minister and his wife were fellow guests, though. And I've met Sir Cuthbert a few times and Lord Curzon."

"Cuthie can be a bit of a fusspot but Curzon is a splendid fellow. He was viceroy of India until a few years ago—and that made him one of the most powerful rulers in the world. Can you imagine it? At thirty-eight he held the destinies of millions in his hands."

"He must have looked magnificent in viceregal robes mounted on an elephant," she said, laughter in her voice. "Just think how he must miss them."

"The robes or the elephants?"

"The elephants."

They were both laughing now and suddenly the homesickness that had never quite vanished, did so. She had, at last, found a friend, and it was a good feeling.

As they cut across a corner of Green Park he said, "And who will be presenting you at court, Delia? Gwen?"

Her eyes flew wide open in startled surprise. "No. I'm to be presented by . . ." She came to an awkward halt. Ivor had told her that she must address Sylvia—and presumably speak of her—as Lady Bazeljette until they were on terms of good friendship, but saying she was to be presented by Lady Bazeljette, when Lady Bazeljette was his wife, seemed far too awkwardly formal, especially as she and Jerome had somehow slipped so comfortably into first-name terms. "Your wife is going to present me," she said, amazed that he didn't already know.

He couldn't have looked more shocked if she had said that the Dalai Lama was going to present her.

"Sylvia?" he said. "Ivor has asked *Sylvia* to present you?"

"Yes." Her amazement was fast turning to alarm. "There's nothing wrong with that, is there, Jerome?" And then, assuming his incredulity to be due to the fact that Sylvia was probably still on the French Riviera, she said reassuringly, "Ivor is confident that she will be back in London by the time I am to be presented."

"Is he, indeed?" His voice sounded almost as grim as Ivor's had been when Ivor had said that it wasn't up to him to tell a man when his wife intended returning to London.

Seeing the consternation in her cat-green eyes he said swiftly, "And Ivor is right, of course. If Sylvia has said she will present you, nothing on earth will prevent her from doing so."

For a minute or two there was silence between them and then, as they skirted Hyde Park Corner, she said, unusually subdued, "I'm findin' English titles and just who is connected to whom—and how—quite difficult, Jerome. And if I'm findin' it difficult now, what is it goin' to be like when I'm in the company of royalty—as Ivor tells me I often will be?"

"Just remember that King George is addressed as 'Sir,' as is the Prince of Wales. Queen Mary is addressed as 'Ma'am.' And you never speak to royalty without having been spoken to first. You also never leave any function that royalty are at, until they have left first. And if the King and Queen should visit

Shibden—and they did when Olivia was alive, for Ivor is on very close terms with King George and Sandringham is close to Shibden—then from the moment they enter the house until they leave it, they are regarded as being the owners of it."

"But what on earth does that mean?" she asked, her alarm spiraling.

He flashed her an amused grin. "Well, for one thing it means that you and Ivor will relinquish your seats at the top and bottom of the table and sit at the side with the rest of your guests. Don't worry about etiquette around royalty. Ivor will see that you don't come to grief. Other things are a bit trickier."

She groaned and his grin deepened.

"You need to understand that London high society is a complex web of cliques and sets, Delia. Some are intellectual. Some are more rackety and bohemian. Ivor, for instance, belongs to the former and I belong to the latter. And while we are on this subject, there is something I need to warn you about."

She waited expectantly and he said, suddenly serious, "I'm telling you this because I prefer to tell you myself rather than for someone else to tell you—and once you begin making friends in London you will most certainly be told. I have the reputation of being a philanderer—a rather notorious one, I'm afraid. And before you protest the reputation can't possibly be deserved, I have to tell you that it is."

"Oh!" She couldn't think of anything else to say, but suddenly a lot of things made sense, for it explained the tension that so clearly existed between Jerome and Ivor, for Ivor, so upright and honorable, would quite obviously find Jerome's reputation one hard to come to terms with.

She knew she should be shocked and outraged by his disclosure, but what she said was: "I *knew* you reminded me of my cousin Beau!"

His crack of laughter was so loud that people walking nearby turned to look at them disapprovingly.

Neither he, nor she, cared.

"Someday," he said, "you'll have to tell me about Cousin Beau." He quirked an eyebrow, suddenly serious again. "I don't know about marital fidelity in Virginia, Delia, but marital fidelity among the British aristocracy is not a highly esteemed virtue. It's accepted practice to marry for commonsense reasons and to find love afterward, and that goes for wives—once they've produced an heir—as well as husbands."

"But that's . . . that's outrageous."

"I'm rather glad you think so. However, it happens and everyone knows it happens. At every weekend house party in the country, bedrooms are allocated with a nod to who is presently involved with whom—long walks down corridors in the middle of the night not being popular. There is only one fundamental requirement and it is that though everyone knows about it, one mustn't be caught out."

"Or the jig will be up?"

He burst into laughter again. "Yes, Delia. Or the jig will be up."

The frank nature of their conversation prompted her to ask something she'd longed to ask, but had previously thought might be too personal. After all, Ivor had said that Sylvia had no daughters. It was equally possible she had no sons, either, and that the Bazeljettes' marriage was as childless as Ivor's marriage to Olivia had been. "Have you children, Jerome?" she asked. "You haven't said."

"I thought you were never going to ask. Yes, I do have a child. I have a son, Jack."

He stopped walking and reached into his waistcoat pocket and withdrew a small snapshot. "He's three. Do you think he looks like me?"

Though small, it was a formal studio portrait. Standing on an Oriental rug by the side of a decorative Chinese pot holding an aspidistra, was a confident-looking little boy. His hair was dark and curly and, still being worn long, hung in ringlets any girl would envy. His eyes were as dark as his father's and full of bright intelligence. He was wearing a sailor suit and knee-high white socks and shoes.

"Oh, he's a *cracking* little boy!" she said sincerely. "You must be very proud of him."

A doting expression crossed his face as he said, "I am," and slid the photograph carefully back into his waistcoat pocket.

They were now at the corner of Cadogan Square and as he walked her to the foot of the steps leading to the Grecian-pillared portico of the Conisborough mansion, she said, "Ivor may be home from the House of Lords by now. Would you like to come in and say hello to him?"

He shook his head. "No. I'll catch up with him this evening at the Digbys'. Goodbye for now, Delia."

She wished him goodbye, impatient to know if Ivor was home, and when Bellingham opened the door to her with the words "His lordship is in the drawing room, your ladyship," she dragged off her peacock-feathered hat, sent it spinning onto the first available surface, and ran for the drawing room, eager to have her husband's arms around her once again.

THREE

Despite the fact that a maid or a footman was likely to walk in on them at any moment his kiss was deep and passionate and she slid her arms up and around his neck, responding to him ardently and with all her heart.

When at last he raised his head from hers he said, "I have good news, sweetheart. Sylvia arrived back in London an hour or so ago. She'll be at Cuthbert's birthday festivities this evening."

"Oh, what a wonderful surprise for Jerome!"

"A surprise? Probably not, Delia. He most probably went to meet Sylvia from the boat train."

Still held in the circle of his arms, she shook her head. "No, he didn't. Gwen and I met up with him unexpectedly while we were having afternoon tea at Fortnum's and then, because Gwen had to leave rather hurriedly for an appointment in South Molton Street, he walked me home."

Ivor raised his eyebrows, his slate-gray eyes startled. "He walked you home? From Piccadilly? What an extraordinary thing to do. And since when have you and Jerome become on first-name terms with each other?"

"Since he joined Gwen and myself for tea at Fortnum's. I'm not quite sure how it happened, Ivor, but as it's mighty comfortable, please don't be cross about it."

His arms dropped from her waist, but with relief she saw that though he was exasperated, he wasn't cross. "It's the sort of thing I should have expected from Bazeljette," he said disparagingly. "He's far too bohemian for truly polite society."

Suspecting Ivor was referring to Jerome's faithless private life and not wanting her husband to put an immediate end to their burgeoning friendship, she made no response, merely tucking her hand lovingly into the crook of his arm.

His light-colored eyes darkened with desire. "I've told Willoughby I won't be needing him for the next hour or two." Willoughby was his secretary. "And if you have already had afternoon tea you will not be wanting more. It's a situation I think we can take advantage of, don't you?"

Heat flooded through her. Even though it was only late afternoon he was going to take her to bed. Her response was one of immediate willingness—and amusement. For in making love to her when it was still light, her handsome and oh-so-correct husband was himself behaving in a bohemian fashion.

The mint-green satin evening dress Ellie helped her into a few hours later had not come from a London—or a French—fashion house, but was one that Ivor had bought for her in New York before they had sailed. The three strands of enormous pearls he had bought on the same day were precisely the right length for the daringly décolleté gown. Her soft-flowing skirt was fashionably straight, barely skimming her feet.

Ellie had brushed her Titian-red hair in a center parting then, allowing the deep waves to frame Delia's face, had coiled the rest high into a chignon.

"I don't think I want any jewels in my hair," Delia said as Ellie reached for a diamond hair ornament. "There is an arrangement of white roses in the drawing room and I think one tucked in my chignon will look far better than jewels."

It did. When her toilette was complete and Ivor walked into the bedroom dressed in white tie and tails, his stiff-fronted shirt fastened with mother-of-pearl studs, his blond hair shining, his expression at the sight of her was one of deep satisfaction.

"Will I do?" she asked, as she had always asked her father before going to a ball at White Sulphur Springs.

"You will be the center of attention and I shall be the envy of every man there," he promised as he escorted her out of the bedroom and along the broad corridor to the head of the magnificent, brass-balustraded staircase.

As they began to walk down it she noticed, for the first time, that on a prime position overlooking the stairs there was a faded area where a large painting must have once hung.

Her hand tightened involuntarily on Ivor's arm for she had no doubt at all that the painting had been the portrait of Olivia.

"All right, sweetheart?" he asked, flashing her a quick glance.

She nodded, forcing a swift bright smile, grateful that the portrait had been taken down, knowing how disconcerting she would have found those brilliantly piercing black eyes.

Sir Cuthbert and Lady Digby's house was in Fitzroy Square, a half-hour drive from their own home. "And not as convenient for either Buckingham Palace or the House of Lords," Ivor said drily as the Conisborough Rolls-Royce crossed Oxford Street in the direction of Regent's Park.

Ivor's chauffeur made a couple of right-hand turns and as they neared Fitzroy Square, Delia could sense Ivor's increasing tension. That he was impatient to show her off thrilled her and her nervousness ebbed into pleasurable anticipation.

Once they had been received by Sir Cuthbert and his elderly wife, she quickly realized that the term "birthday party" had been a complete misnomer, for the "birthday party" was a full-scale ball. In Virginia, the balls held at White Sulphur Springs were regarded as incredibly grand, but they were nothing in comparison to this gala.

Beneath a sea of glittering chandeliers several members of the royal family had gathered, though not the King and Queen, who she had quickly learned rarely attended private functions in the evening. There was a scattering of foreign royals—she recognized a Montenegrin prince and a Russian grand duke whom she had seen at the unveiling of the Queen Victoria Memorial. The rest of the guests were British aristocrats and politicians. A vast number of men were wearing military decorations—the Montenegrin prince was as heavily festooned as a Christmas tree—and all the women were sumptuously bejeweled.

Across the crowded room she caught sight of Jerome in conversation with the prime minister and was relieved that there was at least one person present whom she knew well enough to be able to have a friendly conversation with.

She waltzed with Ivor. She waltzed with the Montenegrin prince. She waltzed with Lord Curzon. When she wasn't dancing, Ivor introduced her to so many people that her head spun. Just when she thought she might be able to speak with Jerome, Ivor's hand tightened on her arm and he said with a throb in his voice, "Sylvia has arrived. It's finally time for me to introduce you to her, Delia."

She allowed him to lead her through a throng of people to a dark-haired woman who was seated on a spindly legged gilt chair, one hand languidly holding a fan of ostrich feathers.

She looked like a queen holding court, for though she was seated there was a semicircle of gentlemen around her, all paying her avid attention. Her gleaming hair was drawn to a flat coil on the crown of her head. Her midnight-blue sequined gown was very slim-fitted, very *soignée*. Even before she turned her head at their approach, Delia knew her face would be spectacularly beautiful.

Ivor cleared his throat. "Sylvia . . . I would like to introduce my wife. Delia, Sylvia, Lady Bazeljette."

As Sylvia Bazeljette turned, Delia was aware of two things.

The first was that she had been right in her assumption, for Sylvia Bazeljette was the most beautiful woman she had ever seen.

The second was that Ivor had been wrong. Her worries were not now at an end. They were escalating with such speed she could no longer breathe, for the face of the woman now regarding her with mocking amusement was the face in the photograph that had spilled from Ivor's diary.

Jerome's wife was the woman whose photograph Ivor needed to see on a daily basis. Jerome's wife was the woman who had written on the back of the photograph that her love was for him, and him alone.

It was all too bewildering for her to take in.

"How lovely to meet you at last." Sylvia's husky voice was like cracked ice and the smile on her beautifully curved ruby-red lips was patronizing. "Ivor tells me you are to be my protégée."

Delia gasped, bewildered no longer.

With utter certainty she knew that Sylvia Bazeljette had been Ivor's mistress. The knowing expression in those sloe-dark eyes told her so as clearly as words. Ivor's barely suppressed impatience in the Rolls-Royce had not been because he was impatient to show Delia off. It had been because he was impatient to see Sylvia. When Jerome had warned her of the lack of marital fidelity among British aristocracy, he had done so in order to prepare her for this moment.

The realization was so earth-shattering that she swayed.

Jerome, not Ivor, steadied her.

Out of nowhere he gripped hold of her elbow, saying nonchalantly to Sylvia and everyone around her, "It's devilish hot in here, isn't it? I think the heat is proving too much for Lady

Conisborough. It might be as well if I were to take her outside for a breath of fresh air."

And without waiting for Ivor to answer he propelled her away from the group. Only when they had stepped through open French windows onto a blessedly empty balcony did he swing her toward him, saying fiercely, "How, in the name of God, do you *know*?"

"Her photograph is in Ivor's diary." She began to shiver. "I thought it was a photograph of Olivia."

He swore beneath his breath and she said, "I don't understand, Jerome. Was it after Olivia's death that . . . that . . ." She wanted to say "that my husband and your wife became lovers," but she couldn't.

He didn't finish her sentence for her. Instead he said brusquely, "You're cold. I'll go get your evening cloak."

"No!" She put a hand on his arm, appalled at the thought of being left alone on the balcony. "I'm not cold, Jerome. It's the shock. I thought Ivor kept the photograph where he could see it every day because despite his being so much in love with me, he was also still grieving for Olivia. And I could understand that . . ."

"Stay here," he said, his voice charged with emotion. "I'm going back to give your apologies to Lady Digby. I shall say I'm escorting you home as you have a headache and that I am doing so, instead of Ivor, as the King has asked him to speak in an unofficial capacity to one of her guests. The Montenegrin royal will be a good choice as it's common knowledge he returns to the Balkans tomorrow."

"What about Ivor?" she said, knowing she couldn't possibly face her husband until they were in the privacy of their own home.

"I'll give him the same message, and publicly, so that there is no gossip about you leaving with me. He'll pick up straightaway on the Montenegrin red herring. And when we leave there's no need for us to walk the length of the ballroom. There's a small side staircase just to the left of the French windows."

Without waiting for any kind of a reply, he was gone.

She closed her eyes, knowing that the very worst thing about what had happened was that there was no question of her having put two and two together and having made five. Though Jerome hadn't said so specifically, that he knew his wife had been Ivor's mistress was too obvious for her to have made any mistake about it.

The sound of laughter and the buzz of animated conversation drifted through the French doors. And then the orchestra struck up into a deafening Strauss waltz.

She dug her nails into her palms, knowing that she was going to have to come to terms with the fact that she would regularly be meeting with her husband's ex-mistress. Even worse, that it was Sylvia who would be presenting her at court.

She bit her lip so hard that she tasted blood. She had thought Ivor sensitive, yet in having asked Sylvia to present her at court he had behaved in a way that was unimaginably cruel. She remembered Jerome's shock—the way he had said, "Ivor has asked *Sylvia* to present you?" when she had told him the arrangements.

She tried to think how she would feel, being accompanied to Buckingham Palace by a woman who was as intimately acquainted with Ivor's body as she was; a woman who knew exactly how he kissed, how he always shouted at his moment of climax.

It was a situation so far removed from anything she had ever experienced that she didn't have the slightest idea as to how she was going to handle it. All she wanted to do was go home and wait for Ivor to return. When he did, he would, she was sure, make everything all right. He would explain about the photograph and how he had presumably forgotten it was still tucked in his diary. He would explain how, after Olivia's death, he was so stupendously lonely that he had embarked on an affair with Sylvia. She tried not to remember that Sylvia was Jerome's wife and that his having an affair with her was the action of a cad. She would come to terms with that later. For now, all that mattered was that Ivor reassure her that she was the one he loved with all his heart and that his feelings for Sylvia were in the past.

The French windows opened and Jerome stepped onto the balcony again, her cloak over his arm. "We can leave without causing gossip, Delia," he said, slipping the evening cloak around her shoulders. "Clara Digby sends her sympathy and will call on you in the morning. Are you ready to make the short walk to the side stairs?"

She nodded and he took her arm, the anger he felt toward her husband and his wife so intense he thought he was going to explode.

Jerome's motorcar was parked in the square; there was no chauffeur. He opened the front passenger door for her. "I always drive myself," he said, knowing very well that Ivor never did so. "I hope you'll feel safe."

"I will." She managed a wobbly smile and something terrible trembled within him.

As she huddled deep in her warmly lined cloak he cranked up the car.

A few minutes later they were driving out of the square and into Fitzroy Street and she said with touching simplicity, "Is it because Sylvia has been unfaithful to you, that you are unfaithful to her?"

He crossed Howland Street and continued into Charlotte Street fighting the temptation to say yes and gain her sympathy, knowing that if he did she might, in a little while, even turn to him for comfort.

With any other woman—especially a woman so overwhelmingly desirable—it was a ploy he wouldn't have thought twice about using. Delia, however, was different. In the short time they had known each other she had become a friend and, unscrupulous as he was about many things, he was always punctiliously truthful to his friends.

"No," he said. "I'm unfaithful to Sylvia because being unfaithful is in my nature. I'm sorry if I disappoint you, Delia."

She shook her head to show that it didn't matter to her; only Ivor mattered to her. Ivor, whom she suddenly felt she didn't know at all.

Jerome changed gear. "Would you like me to take you somewhere so you can get your thoughts in order before going home? We could drive out to Hampstead if you'd like?"

She shook her head. "No. I want to be in the house when Ivor arrives. I want him to explain about the photograph to me—and I want him to tell me that I need never spend time with Sylvia again after she presents me."

They were driving down Park Lane, Hyde Park dark and mysterious on their right side.

He frowned, his face grim. He had thought that she understood—and he now knew that she understood barely anything. He said unhappily, "If you need me, you've only to telephone my club, the Carlton, and leave a message for me there."

"Thank you—and thank you for bringing me home," she said, as he turned into Cadogan Square. "And don't worry about me, Jerome. You once told me that marital fidelity wasn't a virtue highly esteemed among the British aristocracy, but my marriage is far different. Whatever the situation that existed in the aftermath of Olivia's death, it isn't one that will continue. Ivor loves me now and he will be as faithful to me as I will to him."

He brought the car to an abrupt halt, knowing that he should say something.

With the breath hurting in his chest he walked around the car and helped her step from it.

She squeezed his hand tightly and then, before he could speak, ran across the pavement and up the steps.

If Bellingham and Ellie and the rest of the servants were intrigued seeing her arrive home without Ivor they gave no indication. Bellingham was as imperturbable as ever and when Ellie removed the white rose from her hair and unpinned her chignon, she did so swiftly and silently.

Later, when Ellie had left her, Delia seated herself at her dressing table and stared at her reflection in the mirror. The face looking back at her was not the face of the carefree young girl who had left the house three hours ago.

White lines of tension edged her mouth. She had told Jerome that whatever the situation that had existed between Ivor and Sylvia after Olivia's death, it was one that existed no longer, but as she remembered the expression in Sylvia's voice, fear flickered in her chest.

Sylvia's demeanor had not been that of a woman whose lover had fallen in love elsewhere. Her expression was one of a woman whose lover's marriage was of no consequence whatsoever.

It would, though, be of consequence to Ivor. Of that she was sure.

She looked toward the small clock that stood on her dressing table. It was now an hour since Jerome had escorted her home and with luck he had already told Sylvia that no matter what her expectations to the contrary, her affair with Ivor was over.

Fraught with tension Delia began brushing her hair hard. Then, from the street, she heard the sound of a car door closing. She held her breath, the hairbrush motionless in midair. Moments later the front door opened.

Slowly she laid the brush down.

There was a sound of muted male voices, though whether Ivor was speaking to Bellingham or to his valet she couldn't tell. She heard his tread on the broad sweeping staircase.

She remained where she was sitting.

The door opened and their eyes met in the mirror.

He smiled and closed the door behind him. "I take it you've recovered from your headache," he said, walking toward her, undoing his tie. "It was a great shame it attacked when it did. Sylvia was most concerned."

She didn't believe that for a moment, but she said, surprised at how steady her voice was, "I didn't have a headache, Ivor. I left the ball because I'd had a shock."

"A shock?" He tossed the bow tie onto her dressing table and said, intrigued, "What kind of a shock?"

"The other day when you left in a hurry for the palace, you forgot to take your appointments diary with you. I picked it up, intending to run after you to give you it, and a photograph fell from it. I thought it was a photograph of Olivia and that despite us being so happy together you were still grieving for her. But tonight . . . tonight I realized the photograph wasn't of Olivia. It was of Sylvia."

"I have photographs of lots of my close friends in and among my personal possessions, Delia. The photograph I have of Sylvia isn't one that need cause you concern."

Not rising from the vanity stool she turned around to face him. "There was a very personal message on the back of the photograph," she said, her voice no longer so steady. "It said, 'All my love, darling Ivor, is for you and you alone.' "

She waited.

A pulse began to throb at the corner of his jaw.

She licked lips that were suddenly dry and said, "And so . . . and so I know that she was once your mistress and though I wish that you had told me so . . . and that you hadn't arranged for her to present me at court . . . I do understand. Or at least I think I understand."

Despite his sophistication he had the look of a man who was cornered, who couldn't decide on what was the best course of action. With sudden certainty she knew she had to assure him she wasn't going to let Sylvia destroy their happiness. She had to let him know that she was mature enough to understand.

Speaking very fast, she said, "My uncle Ellis Chandler was widowed when in his early forties and he almost immediately began a most unsuitable relationship with a showgirl from White Sulphur Springs. One of my aunts was very angry but my mother told her that it was simply Ellis's way of coping with his grief. And so I know that unsuitable affairs are something newly widowed men often have."

Instead of being grateful for the allowances she was trying to make for him, he said explosively, "For God's sake, Delia! Sylvia isn't a White Sulphur Springs showgirl! And there is no similarity whatsoever between me and your uncle!"

It was so very much the opposite of what she had expected, that she gasped.

He rubbed the back of his neck in a sharp, convulsive movement and when he had regained control of himself, said tautly, "I'm sorry, Delia. I shouldn't have spoken like that. And I'm very, very sorry that I've been unfair to you."

"Unfair to me?" The conversation was veering so far from the course she had expected it to take, that she felt dizzy. "Unfair to me in what way, Ivor?"

"Unfair in that I married you without telling you of my commitment to Sylvia."

"Your *past* commitment," she said, her voice so strained she barely recognized it. "Surely you mean your *past* commitment, Ivor?"

He shook his head and panic bubbled in her throat. Vainly

trying to see things from his point of view, she said, "I understand what a shock our marriage must have been to Sylvia,
Ivor. And I understand that because of your friendship with
her before your relationship changed, you feel that you still
have some kind of commitment to her, but—"

"No, Delia." The expression in his eyes was one of deep
regret for the hurt he was about to cause. "Sylvia and I were
never merely friends."

She blinked, bewildered. "I don't understand."

"We were always lovers," he said and then, as if unable
to bear the pain in Delia's eyes, he turned away from her and
walked across to the window.

She didn't speak. Couldn't speak.

He lifted the curtain aside and looked out. "We've been
lovers since before my marriage to Olivia. Since before Sylvia's
marriage to Jerome." He let the curtain fall and turned toward
her again. "I would have told you when we'd been married for
a little longer, when you had gained a little sophistication and
come to understand how things are in my world."

"You married me when you were in love with someone
else?" She felt at the edge of a bottomless abyss. "You married
me without loving me?"

"It's true I had an ulterior motive when I asked you to marry
me, but that doesn't mean I don't love you, Delia. In my own
way, I do. You're a joy to look at and a joy to be with—and you
amuse me immeasurably."

She was falling now. "But I'm not your soul mate." Against
her fiery hair her face was deathly white. "Sylvia is your soul
mate. You love her more than you love me."

"I love her differently." He paused, seeking for words.
"She's my intellectual equal," he said at last. "And for twenty
years we've been bound together. It's a situation that has to be
accepted, Delia."

Her heart drummed against her breastbone. Of all the scenarios she had imagined when on her way home with Jerome, none had been as terrible as this.

"And you won't give her up?"

He shook his head. "No. I'm sorry."

She wanted to fly at him, claw his face, scream at him that he *had* to give Sylvia up; but she didn't do so. She was too numb with shock—and besides, she knew it would be of no use. In the short time they had been married she had come to realize that beneath Ivor's suave charm there was a side to him that was absolutely implacable. Tears, scenes, and demands would always fail to move him.

She realized that he was giving her a choice. She could accept her position—a newly married woman whose husband had a long-standing mistress—or she could refuse. And refusing would mean eventual divorce.

With such a choice, there was no real choice at all.

She was going to have to make the best of the hand fate had dealt her, but it wouldn't be the Delia Ivor had married who would do so, the loving, trusting, carelessly happy, naïve Delia. It would be a new Delia. A hardened Delia. A Delia well able to hold her own in the glittering, cynical, amoral world she had been plunged into.

"There are just two things I want to know," she said, as all her wonderful castles in the air tumbled to the ground. "If you have loved Sylvia since before your marriage to Olivia, and before her marriage to Jerome, why didn't you marry her?"

He took a silver cigar tube from the inside pocket of his black tailcoat and removed the cigar from it. "Olivia was the only daughter of the Duke of Rothenbury," he said, cutting the end off the cigar with the cigar cutter attached to his watch chain. "Sylvia's father, though a millionaire, was in commerce—not that many people now remember that. The distinction was one that mattered to me at the time. What is the second thing you would like to know?"

She began to shake, not knowing how it was possible to feel such pain and live. "You said you had an ulterior motive in marrying me." It was all she could do to force the words past her lips. "What was it?"

He lit his cigar and blew a plume of blue smoke upward.

"I wanted an heir," he said simply. "And I still do."

Time wavered and halted and would, she knew, never be the same again.

She remembered the time at Sans Souci when her father had said of her aunt Rose's hopes of catching Ivor, "When Conisborough marries again it will be to a woman much younger than Rose. He'll want an heir and, because of his age, he'll want one fast."

She thought of all the times he had made love to her so passionately. Had it always been only because of his need of an heir? She knew that she would never know—and that she would never know in the future, either.

The one thing she could be certain of was that he didn't love her in the way she deserved to be loved—and that her heart was broken.

FOUR

"I think I'll wear the Poiret embroidered gold silk tonight, Ellie. It's only four weeks until Christmas and it will make me feel suitably festive."

"Shibden will soon be looking suitably festive as well, my lady," Ellie said chattily as she opened the doors of Delia's vast armoire to take out the evening gown. "The head gardener always sees to it that there's an enormous fir tree in the hall and when Lady Olivia was alive, all the staff were allowed to help decorate it."

"Were they?" Delia continued opening an array of jewelry boxes. "That's interesting. I didn't know that."

"I don't suppose his lordship thought to mention it, my lady." Ellie laid the gown on the bed. "Everyone always enjoyed it very much, though."

Her meaning was clear and Delia didn't disappoint her. "If it has become a tradition it is one I shall keep," she said, trying to decide between an emerald necklace and a diamond one. "Do you know if the prime minister has arrived yet?"

"He arrived about fifteen minutes ago, my lady." Ellie helped her into the dress. "Mrs. Asquith is in her room, attended by her maid. His lordship and the prime minister are having a private conversation in the Blue Room."

Delia breathed in as Ellie fastened the gown's tiny hooks and eyes, not remotely surprised that Ellie knew the exact whereabouts of the evening's most important guests. "And Sir Cuthbert and Lady Digby?"

"Still in their room. Parkinson said that when he arrived Sir Cuthbert looked a little tired."

Parkinson was Shibden Hall's butler and, like Ellie, missed nothing.

"And most of the other guests?" Though Delia had hosted weekend house parties before at Shibden Hall, this was the first the prime minister had attended and she was anxious that everything run smoothly. The last thing she wanted was for someone to cancel.

"Yes, my lady."

"And the Damnyankee?"

Ellie grinned, knowing that though Delia often used the expression in a derogatory way, in this case she was using it with deep affection. "No. The Duchess of Marlborough has a reputation for lateness."

"Ah, well. There ain't nobody like her for niceness and so her faults can be easily overlooked." It wasn't often now that Delia's speech lapsed into a Virginian drawl, but when it did it always made Ellie laugh.

She giggled as Delia handed her the emerald necklace.

"And Sir Jerome and Lady Bazeljette?" she asked as Ellie fastened the necklace around her throat, not betraying by a flicker what it cost her to utter Lady Bazeljette's name.

"Not yet, my lady."

Delia fastened her emerald pendant earrings, knowing there was not the slightest chance of Sylvia forgoing a weekend at Shibden.

It was an issue she and Ivor had fought about. "She didn't visit Shibden when Olivia was alive," she had said furiously.

"I know, because Jerome mentioned to me that he was never invited here, and though he fudged the reason, it can only have been because Olivia put her foot down."

"And she could get away with it because she was a duke's daughter," said Ivor. "You, sweetheart, can't pull the same rank. And if she *isn't* invited here by you, it will cause just the kind of gossip you are so anxious to avoid."

No longer in awe of him, she had thrown a book at his head.

Such scenes were blessedly rare, partly because they were together far less than she had imagined. This was not because his time was spent with Sylvia but because as financial adviser to the King his workload was a heavy one.

The necessity of having to adjust with great rapidity to a life centered at court and among the royal set had given Delia little time to brood. First there had been her presentation. She had insisted Ivor make known to Sylvia her awareness that she was his mistress and that, though she realized she had no option but to be presented at court by her, she had no intention of speaking to her on the subject, then or ever.

This he had done and, from then on, whenever they met there was no trace of condescending amusement in Sylvia's violet-dark eyes. Instead, beneath a veneer of exquisite politeness, there was a frosty hauteur which Delia returned in full measure.

The presentation had been her baptism by fire, but she had survived it magnificently. After that, nothing held any terrors, not even the awesome coronation. In her crimson and ermine robe she had looked—and felt—so grand, she had doubted if anyone in Virginia would be able to recognize her. The length of the gown's train and the width of the ermine on it denoted rank and, as a viscountess, her train was one-and-a-quarter yards long, the ermine two inches wide. That Sylvia Bazeljette's train was far shorter and the ermine trim far narrower gave her a stab of satisfaction.

Three weeks after the coronation, she and Ivor had been in attendance at the investiture of Edward, Prince of Wales, at Caernarfon Castle. It had been another occasion of medieval ceremony with the seventeen-year-old golden-haired prince looking almost like a child beneath the weight of his robes and fleur-de-lis-decorated crown.

She had been so enraptured by the spectacle she had clutched Ivor's arm, saying breathlessly, "Oh, isn't it a cracking occasion, Ivor! I'm so glad I'm here!"

He had patted her hand and smiled down at her and it was almost as it had been before she had known of his infidelity. Almost, but—to her continuing distress—not quite.

She now took a last look at herself in the three-way mirror and liked what she saw. Emeralds were perfect with her flame-red hair and the gold silk was so seductive on her youthful body she couldn't imagine anyone, even Sylvia, outshining her.

There was a knock at the door and Ellie opened it to Gwen.

"Darling, nearly everyone is gathered in the drawing room and it's time for you to make an appearance," she said as she swept in, her angular frame resplendent in an evening gown of beaded gray silk, a pearl-and-diamond necklace hanging to her waist. "I've just seen Margot Asquith and she's looking very dramatic, but then she always does. She was wearing a full-length scarlet cloak when she arrived. You will remember that her Christian name is pronounced without the *t,* won't you? I only mention it because I'm sure you are nervous and Americans do have such trouble with English names. Pugh once had his name pronounced Pug by the American ambassador. I believe he quite lost control, thundering, 'Pew! *Pew!'* until someone brought him a very large brandy."

Delia chuckled. "I'm not surprised my countryman was

stumped. The difference between the spelling and pronunciation of some names is enough to give anyone a headache. Unless you heard Cholmondeley and Dalziel and Geoghegan spoken, you'd never know how to say them. And I'm not nervous, Gwen. Truly."

Gwen cocked her head to one side. "No, you're not, are you? For a girl so young you really do have the most enormous self-composure as well as the most delightful vivacity. You are becoming a great social asset to Ivor—and he knows it."

"Does he?" Delia quirked an eyebrow and then, arm in arm with her sister-in-law, she walked downstairs to meet her guests.

There were twenty at dinner. The prime minister and Mrs. Asquith. The Duke and Duchess of Girlington. Consuelo, Duchess of Marlborough. The Earl and Countess of Denby. Gwen and her husband. Sir Cuthbert and Lady Digby. Lord Curzon. Mrs. Marie Belloc Lowndes, a renowned novelist and a close friend of Margot Asquith's. Winston Churchill, first lord of the admiralty, and his wife, Clementine. Sir John Simon, solicitor-general. And Sir Jerome and Lady Bazeljette.

As Delia took her place opposite Ivor at the head of the table, he flashed her one of his rare smiles and she knew he was pleased with the way she looked and at her social confidence.

Within minutes, Sylvia began an argument. Well aware that Marie Belloc Lowndes was a committed supporter of the suffragettes and that Ivor and the majority of the other guests, particularly the prime minister, Lord Curzon, and Mr. Churchill were against the movement, Sylvia said sweetly, "I understand you took part in the last Votes for Women march dressed as Queen Boadicea. Was it not rather chilly for you, Marie?"

"I wasn't bare-breasted, Sylvia." Marie took a sip of her wine. "And if you are hoping to embarrass me, you've failed."

Mr. Asquith, whose government was refusing to give way to suffragette pressure, cleared his throat.

His wife, who was tired of having the windows at 10 Downing Street smashed, and certain the suffragettes meant to cause her husband bodily harm, intervened raspingly. "Really, Sylvia. Isn't it enough that we have to contend with suffragette nonsense in our public lives without having it made an issue at house parties as well?"

Sylvia, wearing a glittering black off-the-shoulder gown, shrugged carelessly and Delia saw her eyes meet Ivor's.

She felt a rush of anger, certain the remark had been said not in order to embarrass Marie but to lure Delia into making comments that would infuriate Ivor and distance her from the Asquiths.

She admired the suffragettes hugely and avoiding Sylvia's trap was an agony; but just when she thought she couldn't bear it for another minute, the first lord of the admiralty ignored the very broad hint that the subject should be dropped, by saying pugnaciously, "Women don't need the vote. Not when their fathers, husbands, and brothers can represent their views."

"But do they?" Viola Girlington lifted her naked shoulder expressively from a sea of indigo tulle. "Girlington doesn't represent *my* views." She looked across the table to where her husband was seated between Consuelo Marlborough and Clementine Churchill. "In fact, I'm not sure he knows them," she said, the amusement in her voice taking the sting from her words. "As for dearest Marie dressing as Queen Boadicea, the image is one I would love to sculpt."

"And I'd love for you to do so," Jerome said, "especially if the representation was bare-breasted."

There was general laughter and, as Viola was a serious artist of exceptional talent, the conversation veered away from women's suffrage and toward the arts.

Jerome caught Delia's eye and he gave her a discreet wink, indicating he well knew that she had exercised restraint only to avoid giving Sylvia satisfaction.

As the footmen cleared away the first course, she determined to join the Women's Social and Political Union as soon as she could. If Ivor didn't like it—which he wouldn't—then he could just go whistle.

Consuelo changed the subject by saying in her gentle voice, "Do you know that Lord Croomb's bride-to-be is an American?" She smiled at Delia. "We Americans are no longer going to be a minority on this side of the Atlantic."

"I understand the bride is worth millions and the groom is land-rich and cash-strapped," Sylvia said with a throaty laugh, turning toward George Curzon, who was seated on her right. "Which surely makes the arrangement more of a business merger than a marriage."

There was more laughter, but Consuelo didn't laugh and, knowing that her mother had forced her into her marriage purely for the title and that on the marriage the duke had collected millions of dollars in railroad stock from Consuelo's father, Delia didn't laugh either. She was fond of Consuelo and knew that she was desperately unhappy.

Seeing the expression in Consuelo's eyes it struck her that perhaps Sylvia wasn't quite as overwhelmingly popular as she had thought—at least not with other women.

The knowledge cheered her. She didn't want Sylvia to be well liked. She wanted her to be heartily loathed.

By the time dessert was served, the conversation had turned to politics.

"It would seem Europe is rapidly becoming two armed camps," George Curzon said, prodding at his *pêches à la Reine Alexandra*. "On the one hand is the Triple Entente of Britain, France, and Russia; on the other the Triple Alliance of Germany, Austria-Hungary, and Italy. What will happen, do you think?"

He was looking toward Herbert Asquith but it was Winston Churchill who answered. "War," he said with vigor. "And we must be prepared for it. Isn't that so, Prime Minister?"

Asquith gave a heavy sigh and Delia, who had now met him several times and become quite a favorite, realized he had been hoping for a relaxing weekend away from the pressure of his office. Not very tall, he had a rocklike build and massive head. Turning a little wearily to his first lord of the admiralty, he said, "The foreign secretary is to propose a conference be held here with Germany and Italy. That should settle things. We none of us want war, Winston, do we?"

Winston looked as though he very much wanted war, and, by the expression on his face, so did George.

As the talk continued, with the Countess of Denby saying silkily that "with foreigners increasing their armies, I'm all for a big navy," Delia experienced a moment of self-awareness.

Though not happy—happiness while Ivor continued his relationship with Sylvia was impossible—she was exhilarated. How could she not be when she was playing hostess to such distinguished, powerful, clever people? She wondered what it would be like to have nothing more stimulating than a weekend at White Sulphur Springs to look forward to, and shuddered. Much as she still missed her mother and Sans Souci, she knew she could never live there again, not when she enjoyed her life as Viscountess Conisborough so much.

With Jerome's help, she had boned up on European politics so that she not only could understand the conversations taking place at her dinner table but would also be able to take part in them. Republican to the core, she nevertheless enjoyed the theatricality of royal ceremonial, and despite finding a dinner at Buckingham Palace to be a surprisingly dull affair, the experience was one she wouldn't have wanted to miss. Neither would she have wanted to miss visiting nearby Sandringham, where she had met the Prince of Wales. He was only a year her junior and the two of them had got on like a house on fire.

It was the same with nearly all of Ivor's friends and acquaintances. Though she worked hard at being agreeable, it was their children with whom she had instant rapport. One of the Duke and Duchess of Girlington's daughters, Daphne, was, for instance, exactly her own age and breezily unconventional. The prime minister's daughter-in-law, Cynthia, was also great fun.

The only thing marring her life was Sylvia's presence at nearly every event or social function they attended. Making this marginally easier for her was Ivor's impeccable behavior whenever Sylvia was at Cadogan Square or at Shibden. At Shibden house parties, many of their guests made nighttime visits to rooms other than their own, but Ivor never did so. What he did elsewhere, of course, was very different.

One of the greatest shocks she'd had to overcome was the realization that Jerome had been speaking the absolute truth when he told her that in smart society, amorous intrigues were the norm. Sir Cuthbert, for instance, was embroiled in a passionate affair with Lady Denby, something to which both of their partners, as they engaged in banter across the dining table, seemed supremely indifferent. It was well known that the Duke of Girlington gave most of his affection not to his wife, Viola, but to Violet Vanburgh, an actress, and that his supremely beautiful wife had her choice of lovers. Even H.H. was known to prefer spending time with the daughter of Lord Sheffield rather than with Margot—though as Margot was so formidable and sharp-tongued it didn't come as too much of a surprise.

She glanced across at Winston and Clementine. They had not been married long and so far there had not been one whisper of any infidelities, nor did Delia think there ever would be. Jerome, of course, was the most blatant of adulterers. After a long affair with Princess Sermerrini, a member of the Royal House of Savoy, he was now conducting affairs with two married ladies saying that doing so was more challenging than conducting an affair with only one.

Just back from a European holiday—he had been to Berlin and Rome and Paris—he was leaning back, a brandy glass in one hand, his swarthy skin and Gypsy-dark curls setting him apart from the other men, all of whom either were elderly and white-haired or, as in the case of Ivor, George, and Winston, had mouse-fair hair worn glassily smooth.

As she watched, she saw the prime minister exchange a meaningful glance with Jerome and wondered as to their relationship, for though Jerome wasn't a member of the government he was obviously on surprisingly easy terms with Mr. Asquith.

Winston cracked a joke, and as the champagne flowed and witticisms whizzed back and forth across the table Delia knew everyone was enjoying themselves hugely. After the meal, Ivor was unconventional in that he saw no reason for ladies to leave the table while the men passed around the port. When they all had gathered in the drawing room, Gwen asked George Curzon if he would recite Tennyson's "The Revenge: A Ballad of the Fleet."

"For considering dear Winston is first lord of the admiralty, I think it would be most appropriate," she said as Ivor gave a mock groan. "Especially as our navy could very soon be facing enemy ships."

"Quite right, Gwendolyn." Curzon rose to his feet and struck a suitably grave posture. " 'At Flores in the Azores Sir Richard Grenville lay,' " he began sonorously. " 'And a pinnace, like a flutter'd bird, came flying from far away: "Spanish ships of war at sea! We have sighted fifty-three!" ' " At the last words of verse ten, "Fight on! Fight on!," the cheering nearly shook the roof.

Afterward, Consuelo insisted on Viola Girlington playing the piano and singing and then Sylvia said in a falsely sweet voice, "Your turn now, Delia. We've never heard you sing, but I'm sure your voice is exquisite."

Delia, well aware Sylvia had only made the suggestion because she assumed she was tone-deaf, hesitated just long enough to see confirmation that she had been right slide into Sylvia's eyes. In an exaggerated Southern drawl she said, "What a cracking good idea. Ah'll be only too happy to oblige."

Ivor, annoyed at the accent and knowing that after Viola any other singer was likely to sound dreadful, frowned warningly.

Delia ignored him and crossed the room to where Viola was still seated at the piano. As she whispered in Viola's ear and as he saw the change on Viola's face, his consternation grew.

"This is especially for Consuelo," she said, and launched into an exuberant, full-throated rendering of "Dixie."

Consuelo squealed protestingly. Jerome burst out laughing. When it came to the chorus everyone, even Winston, whose mother, like Consuelo, had been born on the wrong side of the Mason-Dixon Line, joined in with gusto. Everyone, that is, except Sylvia—and as all her other guests, including the prime minister, clapped and cheered, Delia no longer cared about Sylvia.

Later, long past midnight, when all their guests had gone to bed, Ivor said to her, "It was a splendid evening, Delia. It's a long time since I've seen the prime minister enjoy himself so much."

"Then why are you looking so grave?"

He stared thoughtfully at the cigar he was holding. "Because Winston has asked me to go to Germany."

"Go to Germany?" Her eyes widened. "Whatever for?"

"Because I have highly placed friends in German financial circles. One of them, Albert Ballin, is as close to the Kaiser as I am to King George. Winston wants me to have an informal conversation with him about the pace of Germany's shipbuilding program. It's just possible a man as influential as Ballin will be able to persuade the Kaiser to bring it to a halt. Otherwise, sooner or later, it will lead to war."

Delia drew in a sharp breath. When Winston had uttered the word "war" she had thought it merely typical of his desire to shock, not a serious possibility.

"When do you leave?"

"Monday morning."

She remembered the glance Jerome and the prime minister had exchanged and said hesitantly, "Do you think Jerome was doing something similar when he was in Berlin and Rome? Do you think he was speaking to people on H.H.'s behalf?"

"Jerome a diplomatic negotiator? I don't think so, Delia." He chuckled. "The only reason for Jerome to go to Berlin would be to see one of his many mistresses. The same applies to his jaunt to Rome—unless he's considering converting to Catholicism."

Still chuckling, he walked with her from the drawing room, leaving the maid to turn down the lights.

It was a moment of closeness that was repeated quite often as the cold spring of 1912 melted into a hot summer. Still there was something so coolly distant in Ivor's personality, so remote, that she doubted their relationship would have been much different even without Sylvia.

There were times when she would have liked to say as much to Jerome, but at their first meeting after she knew that Ivor's affair with Sylvia wasn't going to end, they had made a pact not to talk about their respective spouses unless absolutely necessary. Not doing so meant that the time they spent together was enjoyable. Though her other friends' extramarital affairs shocked her, Jerome's never did, probably because he never took any of them seriously. She teased him unmercifully and he teased her for her lack of lovers when nearly all her married women friends had at least one.

As the year wore on, the optimism she had gained from Ivor's impeccable behavior faded. He spent a great deal of time with Sylvia away from his home.

In September, when Sylvia was again enjoying a monthlong vacation in Nice, he took an equally long vacation in nearby Monaco. In November, when Sylvia went to Market Harborough for a month to hunt, he went, accompanied by Lord Denby and Cuthie, who were both addicted huntsmen. Ivor wasn't, and Delia knew that the only reason he was spending four weeks riding over the Leicestershire countryside in appalling weather was so he could be with Sylvia.

It was a situation she had no choice but to accept, but she didn't do so happily. Her constant hope was that when she became pregnant things would change and Sylvia would begin to play a less and less important part in his life. By the beginning of 1913, however, the longed-for baby still hadn't materialized.

"I'm starting to think I'm as barren as Olivia was," she said bleakly to Jerome as they strolled in St. James's Park. "And if I am, Ivor will divorce me."

"Has he said he will divorce you?" There was surprise in Jerome's voice. "It sounds a bit too Henry VIII for Ivor."

It was a sunny day and Delia was carrying a parasol. She twirled it thoughtfully. "No. He's never said he would divorce me if there wasn't a baby. Even though he might want to, I doubt that he would. Divorced men aren't received at court, are they? The social stigma would matter a great deal to him."

"And would put an end to his position as financial adviser to the King," Jerome said drily, "so I wouldn't worry about the possibility too much."

"But I do, because I want a baby just as much as Ivor does!" With a sudden outburst of emotion she swung to face him. "It would be too cruel to have a marriage that isn't the kind of marriage I yearn for and to have no children either! I couldn't bear it, Jerome! Truly I couldn't!"

He took hold of her free hand and squeezed it hard. "You're only twenty, Delia. You'll have babies. I'm sure of it."

There was such fierce certainty in his eyes that she was almost convinced.

Aware that she was attracting attention from passersby she said, "Sorry for that outburst," and flashed him an apologetic smile. "Do you think Jack's nanny would mind if we took him off her hands for an hour or two? We could go boating or to the zoo."

Taking his five-year-old son out on afternoon excursions was something they often did. At first, she had been reluctant to even meet Jack, terrified she wouldn't be able to look at him without being reminded of Sylvia. When she finally met him she had felt a vast wave of relief. He was raven-haired, like both his parents, but there were no other similarities. He didn't have Sylvia's violet-dark eyes. He didn't have her pre-Raphaelite perfect features.

His brown eyes had the same gold flecks as Jerome's, his hair was just as curly. Even his fun-loving, equable nature was like Jerome's. Feeling his small hand in hers always brought a lump to her throat, and the time the three of them spent together was very precious to her.

"The zoo, I think," Jerome said as they exited the park and he hailed a cab to take them to Chelsea. "Jack's having a love affair with the chimpanzees."

She laughed as he opened the cab door for her, grateful that Sylvia was so indifferent as to whom her son spent time with; grateful that the world held someone she loved being with so much—Jerome.

In the summer she made a trip home to Virginia, explaining to her parents that Ivor hadn't been able to accompany her due to his royal duties. For six weeks she spent hours riding the countryside she loved and jumping every high fence in sight. She even spent a weekend in White Sulphur Springs and was amused by Beau persistently introducing her as "ma second cousin, Viscountess Conisborough. Her husband, the viscount, is on real friendly terms with England's king, don't ya know."

In one of his regular letters to her, Jerome told her he had been ill. "Nothing to worry about," he wrote. "Just one of those childish ailments that affect adults badly. Is there much talk in Virginia about the ruckus in the Balkans?"

"Hardly any," she had written back, and, to amuse him, "which isn't surprising when you consider that most Virginians don't know where the Balkans are."

When she returned to London that autumn, it was to discover that in her absence Sylvia had acted as Ivor's hostess at Cadogan Square.

"And did you make love to her here?" Her rage and pain were so intense she felt she was going to explode. "Did you make love to her in my bed?"

"Hysteria doesn't suit you, Delia." His voice and eyes were as chilly as the North Sea. "If Gwen had been able to act as my hostess for the very important dinner I gave, then she would have done. As she was indisposed with influenza, Sylvia did so instead. You are making an undignified scene over nothing."

"Your mistress publicly acts as if my home is hers and you call it nothing?" Her face was sheet white. "Who were your guests? Were Margot and H.H. among them? Was George Curzon?"

He remained frigidly tight-lipped and she whirled away

from him, hurrying blindly from the house, intent on finding comfort in the arms of the one person who never failed her.

Four months later the political crisis had deepened to the point where war with Germany had become a very real possibility. Delia was serenely uncaring for she was happier than she had been for almost three years. She was pregnant.

Ivor was ecstatic, though not so pleased as to stay in London when Sylvia departed for one of her regular trips to Nice.

"He's gone to Monaco," she said bitterly to Jerome. "It doesn't look as if anything is going to change, does it?"

"No," he said wryly, her crushing disappointment a knife to his heart.

Six months later the many predictions of war with Germany were fulfilled.

Delia barely saw Ivor for with the outbreak of war there was a banking crisis and, as a member of the Privy Council, he was constantly in meetings. It was Jerome she missed most, though, for within days of war being declared he was off to his home county in order to volunteer with the North Somerset Mounted Infantry.

Morning sickness, coupled with Ivor's long absences, brought her social life almost to a halt. She lunched occasionally with Margot Asquith, who was a great admirer of Sir John French, the leader of the British Expeditionary Force. "With Sir John in command it will be over in six weeks," Margot said to her cheerfully the day after the Expeditionary Force sailed. "Pray God it is, Delia, for I have four stepsons of military age and two of them are married with children."

Two weeks later came the shocking news that after engaging the enemy at Mons, Sir John's army had suffered a massive defeat and was in retreat.

"So much for the war being over by Christmas," Gwen said with rare waspishness. "Thank goodness Ivor is too important to be called up."

By the end of August there was another huge defeat to come to grips with when Russian troops were routed on the eastern front in a battle at Tannenberg.

Heavily pregnant and unable to bear either the sight of the ever-growing casualty lists or the company of her anxious older friends who had sons of recruitment age, Delia left Cadogan Square for Shibden Hall.

She wrote to Jerome, who was still in Somerset.

At least it is quiet here, so quiet it is almost impossible to believe that a few miles away such terrible carnage is taking place. If only America would come and help England then perhaps the war really would be over in a few short months. How I wish you were here with me, enjoying the incredibly beautiful weather and the amazing sunsets instead of preparing to leave for heaven knows what horrors in France. I just pray that a miracle will happen and that you won't have to go.

Even as she wrote the last words she knew Jerome would not agree. Every letter showed only too plainly how much he was itching to see action.

By the end of September the prime minister had called for another 500,000 men to enlist.

"How long does Winston think it will continue?" Delia asked when Clementine telephoned, only to be told that the first lord of the admiralty's opinion was that it would go on for a very long time.

In the first week of October Ivor drove to Shibden, insisting that as Delia was now only a month or so from giving birth it was high time she returned to Cadogan Square. "You can't run the risk of going into labor here and having the local doctor attend you," he said bluntly. "You need to be within reach of your gynecologist. Apart from which," he said, looking more tired and tense than she had ever seen him, "I have news which I hope you are going to take in your stride."

Her heart almost ceased to beat as she thought of all the young men they knew who were in France. "Who has been killed?" she asked fearfully. "One of the prime minister's sons? The Denbys' elder boy?"

"No. It's not that sort of news. I'm sorry for alarming you, Delia." He poured himself a whiskey and soda. "I have to go to America. Needless to say, it's the very last thing I want to do so close to the baby's birth, but I'm going as a member of the Privy Council and I can't possibly cry off. I'm sorry."

She waited for a feeling of intense disappointment, but it didn't come. Since she had become pregnant, all lovemaking between them had ceased and he had spent far more time away from her than with her.

"It don't matter," she said, and for once he didn't criticize her slang. "I will have Gwen with me when the pains start."

"Well, I wouldn't be with you then anyway," he said. "Men only get in the way at a time like that. I would have liked to see our son within minutes of his arrival, though."

His disappointment that he wouldn't be able to do so—unless the baby was very late—was so intense she squeezed his hand comfortingly.

"Don't worry, Ivor. He'll keep."

He gave her his attractive down-slanting smile and, with an arm around her shoulders, walked her out to the car.

A week later he sailed on the *Mauretania* for New York.

The baby didn't oblige him by being late. Instead it was early.

On October 30, two days before Jerome was due to leave for France, Delia went into labor. While she was still able she made two telephone calls. One to Gwen, the other to Jerome.

Then, slightly apprehensive, she took a warm bath and waited to see what would happen next.

What happened was six hours of torture she was quite sure she would never willingly repeat.

"My goodness, what a lot of complaining over nothing," said the midwife who had assisted her gynecologist. "Lady Fitzwallender was sixteen hours in labor and not a murmur. And no, Lady Conisborough, you can't hold the baby yet. Nurse still has to bathe and dress her."

Delia watched with bone-deep joy as her crying daughter—her beautiful, magnificent, *wonderful* daughter—was bathed and dressed.

"Lady Pugh is ever so anxious to see you and to see the baby, my lady," Ellie said, taking a tissue-wrapped shawl from a nearby drawer. "Since her arrival she hasn't left the house once—and Sir Jerome Bazeljette is here as well. He came about an hour ago."

"Show Lady Pugh in, Ellie," Delia said, well aware of the furor there would be if Jerome saw the baby first. "And has Bellingham sent a telegram to his lordship?"

"Yes, my lady. Five minutes ago."

The nurse took the shawl from Ellie and swaddled the bawling baby as efficiently as if she were a parcel.

Delia held out her arms, her face radiant as the baby was placed in them. "Don't cry, little darling. Don't cry," she said gently and, as if by magic, the baby ceased and blinked up at her with hazel-green eyes.

"Shall I tell Lady Pugh she may come in now?" Ellie asked.

Delia nodded, not taking her eyes from her daughter's red, wrinkled little face.

When Gwen came in, Delia said with a smile, "It's a little girl, Gwen. Ivor will be disappointed, but I don't care. I've never been so happy in my life. Never, never, never."

Gwen leaned over her, tenderly moving the shawl a little farther from the baby's face in order to see her better. "Oh," she breathed reverently, "she's absolutely perfect! What girl's name did you and Ivor decide upon?"

"We didn't decide." There was wry humor in Delia's voice. "He only ever made plans for a boy. However, I have picked a name. She is to be Petronella. Petronella Gwendolyn. I don't think Ivor will object."

"No, Delia. I don't think he will." Gwen was so overcome that the baby was to be named after her that tears misted her eyes. "And next time, when the baby is a boy, Ivor can choose. Oh, dear. I mustn't cry over her, must I? And you must need to sleep now, Delia. Shall I tell Jerome that it is far too soon for a visit and that he must come back in a few days?"

With great effort, Delia tore her attention away from her daughter's face. "No, Gwen. Jerome is leaving for France in two days. Please ask him to come in—though I think it best he does so after you have left. Two visitors at the same time would be too tiring for me."

It was a fib, but she didn't care. She didn't want Gwen with her when Jerome saw the baby for the first time.

Gwen kissed her on the cheek and left the room. Delia turned to the midwife and nurse. "You must both be famished. If you go downstairs with Ellie, cook will make you a light meal."

"Thank you, Lady Conisborough," they said, both more than ready to eat.

Seconds after they had left, Jerome entered, resplendent in his cavalry officer's uniform.

"It's a girl, Jerome," she said huskily as he crossed to the bed and looked down at the now-sleeping baby. "I'm going to call her Petronella and she's the most wonderful thing that has ever happened to me, Jerome. Truly."

He touched the baby's cheek very gently with the back of his finger. "She's going to have your coloring, Delia," he said, his voice thick with emotion. "There is red in her hair."

She smiled up at him. "Would you like to hold her?"

He nodded, tenderly taking the sleeping baby from her arms.

When Ellie returned to the room five minutes later he was still holding her—and doing so not only with great competence but with almost fatherly care.

FIVE

On the day Jerome and his regiment left for France, not even holding Petronella eased Delia's disquiet. Unlike the vast majority of the population she hadn't been euphoric at the outbreak of war. Now, even those who had been were anxious as it became increasingly obvious that the war was going to be a long, drawn-out affair. For Delia it was much worse. With a husband a member of the Privy Council and with one friend married to the prime minister and another to the first lord of the admiralty, she knew too much of the worries felt at the very highest levels to be comforted by the remorselessly upbeat propaganda being pumped out by national newspapers.

"Please, God," she prayed throughout the day, "please God, don't let Jerome be killed. Don't let him be injured. Please, God. *Please.*"

She was soon beset by another grim anxiety for there were rumors of German submarine activity in the Atlantic.

"They won't attack civilian shipping," Gwen's husband said confidently. "Such a thing is unthinkable, Delia. Ivor will be home safe and sound within the next couple of weeks."

Despite his certainty she continued to worry, her only distraction the gossip of her visitors.

"The Queen is visiting as many as four hospitals a day,"

Gwen said, busily knitting a khaki sock as she sat at Delia's bedside. "Seeing such suffering must be a terrible ordeal for her. I remember she was once so overcome when a footman cut his finger that she nearly fainted."

"The Prince of Wales has been gazetted to the Grenadier Guards," Clementine said when she visited, delving in her bag for the khaki shirt she was making. "He must look quite odd, for he's only five foot three and the guards are all six foot and over!"

They giggled, but when Delia had tried to imagine the golden-haired prince in a guards uniform, she failed completely.

Clara Digby visited and was appalled to find Delia out of bed and seated in a chair by the window. "Goodness gracious, when doctors decree that a new mother should remain in bed for ten days after giving birth, they mean ten days. And bed means bed, not a chair!"

"I've been in bed for five days, Clara, and I'm bored to tears. What is Cuthie's latest news from the palace? Is it true the King has ordered that no more wine is to be served at mealtimes?"

Clara seated herself and said, "Yes, he's decided that alcohol is not consistent with emergency measures. How deadly dull palace dinners are to be endured without the benefit of wine, I can't think. I don't envisage Ivor enjoying boiled water sweetened with sugar—which is, apparently, what was served yesterday evening—do you? And when do you expect him home?"

Without waiting for an answer, she eased off her pale kid gloves. "He must be exceedingly impatient to see his daughter—and not, I hope, too disappointed about her sex. Cuthbert barely spoke to me for six months after Amelia was born."

She straightened the seam of her glove. "Has Sylvia been to visit? It will look very odd if she doesn't. I saw her at the Denbys' a week or so ago—your name was mentioned and the tips of her claws showed. Muriel Denby put her in her place—as, of course, did I. Why men never see that side of Sylvia is quite beyond me. Young Maurice Denby is quite besotted with her. He's Muriel's youngest and due to leave for France this week."

Delia let Clara rattle on, wondering, as she always did, just how much of a true friend Clara was. Clementine and Margot sensitively never brought Sylvia's name into the conversation. She was curious just how Sylvia had shown her claws, but she had far too much pride to ask. And Clara's remark about Ivor's reaction to a girl only increased her anxiety as to how deep his disappointment would be.

When he had received the cable informing him of the birth, his answering cable had simply read:

RELIEVED ALL IS WELL STOP HOME SOON STOP IVOR

The wording hadn't filled her with optimism.

An hour after Clara had left her, another cable arrived:

AM SAILING TODAY ON THE CARONIA STOP IVOR

When he arrived five days later she was in the frost-covered walled rear garden, cutting long sprays of yellow-berried pyracantha to fill the Chinese vases in the hall.

It was a footman who hurried out to her with the news. "His lordship has arrived, my lady. And he's gone straight to the nursery."

Thrusting the pyracantha into his arms she ran to the house, yanking off her coat as she did so.

"His lordship is in the—" Bellingham began helpfully as she raced past him.

"I know, Bellingham! I know!" Tossing her tam-o'-shanter at him, she hurtled up the stairs.

Bellingham, by now well accustomed to his mistress's easy-going familiarity, gravely carried the tam-o'-shanter toward the cloakroom.

With a fast-beating heart Delia hurried along the corridor toward the nursery. "Please don't be too disappointed, Ivor," she whispered to herself. "Please think Petronella beautiful. Please. *Please*."

She opened the nursery door.

Still wearing his traveling clothes he was standing by the crib, looking down into it with a bemused expression on his face.

She stood very still. "Do you like her?" she said, unable to voice the words drumming in her brain: *Are you going to be too disappointed to love her?*

"Like her?" He turned toward her and to her vast relief he was smiling. "Of course I like her, Delia. She's beautiful."

All her tension and fear ebbed away. Everything was going to be all right.

She crossed the room and stood beside him, taking hold of his hand and squeezing it to express her gratitude.

"Why Petronella?" he asked. "I've never heard of it before. Is it a Chandler family name?"

"No. It's a Roman family name. And I chose it just because so few people will have heard it and because I like it." She remembered how important having a son was to him and realized how magnificently he was overcoming his disappointment. "We can change it if you want to, Ivor. I don't mind."

"I don't want to change it. It suits her. Who does she look like, do you think? I don't see the faintest resemblance to myself in her—and I don't think she looks much like you, either, except for her dark-red hair."

"Imagining that babies look like family members is usually wishful thinking. Petronella just looks like herself—and I'm glad. Think how awful it would be if she had your big feet or my father's nose!"

He chuckled and she said, "Would you like to hold her?"

He shook his head. "No, I don't think I should when she's sleeping. It would only disturb her. And I have to go straight on to Downing Street. Lloyd George is waiting for my report on my meetings with the American bankers."

Lloyd George, the chancellor of the exchequer, was not a man known for patience and she didn't try to dissuade Ivor. Instead, linking her arm in his, she said as they left the room, "Where will we be spending Christmas, Ivor? Here, or at Shibden?"

"It's tradition for Christmas to be spent at Shibden, you know." He saw the expression on her face and added, "Is there a problem with that?"

"Only that Norfolk is bitterly cold at Christmas and as Petronella will still be only a few weeks old I think it would be better if she wasn't taken to Shibden until the spring."

They had reached the head of the stairs and he came to a halt, looking puzzled. "But that isn't a difficulty, Delia. She'll remain here in the care of her nurse and nurserymaids."

"And I will be over a hundred miles away. I'm sorry, Ivor, but not being with her at Christmas would make me very unhappy. I should like to stay here."

He hesitated and she knew he was thinking how odd it would look not spending Christmas at Shibden when the royal family would be spending Christmas at nearby Sandringham.

"If that is what you want," he said at last, a little reluctantly.

"Yes, it is. Thank you, Ivor."

With her arm still linked in his she walked downstairs with him, feeling more optimistic about her marriage than she had

since its first few headily careless days, her mind racing with
ideas for making Petronella's first Christmas the most splendid
Christmas the Cadogan Square house had ever known.

In the New Year, with a very satisfying nursery routine established under a new nurse—who wasn't at all disconcerted
when Delia treated her as if she were a member of the family—Delia began socializing and riding again.

Every morning at eleven o'clock she trotted into Rotten
Row, riding sidesaddle on Juno, the thoroughbred Ivor had
bought for her shortly after their marriage. Compared to riding in Norfolk, it was sedate—and certainly nothing like the
gallops she had enjoyed in Virginia.

Occasionally Sylvia would also be in the Row, her satin-
black hair worn in a bun that showed off the lovely long line
of her neck. Her hat was always tilted at a provocative angle,
the veil pressing against her face, her elegant riding habit fitting so perfectly Delia wondered if she was wearing anything
beneath it.

They would incline their heads to each other and nothing
more. When there was no one nearby to observe, they never
bothered pretending they were friends.

In February, Lord and Lady Denby's only son was killed in
his first twenty-four hours of action.

By March, the death toll of officers in the Grenadiers and
the Scots—two guards regiments packed with Ivor's friends
or the sons of his friends—was so high Delia was terrified for
Jerome's safety. But in his letters he repeatedly told her not to
worry.

*As cavalry we don't suffer in the same way that the poor
sods living twenty-four hours a day in the trenches do—
and I have the comfort of your Fortnum & Mason's food*

parcels. I made myself very popular with my fellow of-
ficers by sharing out the pâté and caviar.

In April, when he came home on leave, his description of
life at the front was very different.

"It can't be expressed in a letter," he said, his hand holding hers so tightly she thought he was going to break it. "It's
indescribable. Filth. Thigh-deep mud. The dead unburied. The
injured lying with them for hours, sometimes days, before they
can be carried to a field hospital. Constant cold. Constant pan-
demonium. And a feeling of near uselessness."

His voice was bitter, his olive-skinned face pale with fa-
tigue.

"Uselessness? But why? I don't understand."

"Cavalry might have been the army's ace in previous wars,
Delia, but they weren't on the scale of this one. How can cavalry successfully charge against machine guns and barbed wire
and six-foot-deep trenches? More and more valiant horses are
dying horrific deaths. In a charge near Ypres we lost one hundred and forty-four horses out of one hundred and fifty—and
the number of men lost is almost beyond human calculation."

She blanched.

"In the short time I have before going back to such a hell,
I want to enjoy myself—and not talk about the war." He gave
a lopsided smile. "How's Petra? As we didn't have the chance
to celebrate her birth with champagne at the time, let's toast
her now."

Delia forced herself into a cheerful mood; a mood of loving
gaiety that would enable him to forget, for a little time at least,
the horrors waiting for him when his leave was over.

"Petra?" With superhuman effort she banished the images
he had conjured up, knowing that the minute he had gone
they would resurface in endless nightmares. "No one calls her
Petra," she said, managing to giggle. "Not even Ellie."

"Well, no one will keep calling her Petronella when she's older. It's too much of a mouthful. And better Petra than Nellie!"

This time her laughter was unforced. "Just for you, Jerome— and because I would take a gun to anyone who called my lovely daughter Nellie, Petra it is." She hugged him tightly, saying, "God, but I've missed you, Jerome. I've missed you more than words can tell."

The days after Jerome's return to the front were spent in an agony of anxiety. The newspapers were full of accounts of the British spring offensive at Ypres and she knew that Jerome was in the thick of it. If Sylvia was similarly concerned she showed no sign. "There's no need to worry about Jerome," Delia overheard her saying at a house party at the Wharf, the Asquiths' country home on the upper reaches of the Thames. "He always falls on his feet."

At the beginning of May she discovered that she was pregnant again.

"Which is about the only good news I've had for many months," Ivor said. "And, once again, I'm going to be in America for part of your pregnancy, though this time in the early part."

"America? But why?"

"I'm going with a begging bowl," he said grimly. "We need American financing in order to keep armament production at its present level. I don't work only for the King nowadays, Delia. I work for the government."

She tilted her head a little to one side, her eyes reflective. "If the Atlantic is safe enough for you to cross, then it's surely safe enough for me. Petra is six months old and my parents still haven't seen her. We could sail together to New York and then you could go to Washington or wherever it is you have to go, and I could go down to Virginia. We could meet up again in New York for the trip home."

"No," he said, not even hesitating. "I'm not going to allow

you to take even the slightest risk. When the war is over, then we'll go to Virginia, Delia. And not before."

His voice was implacable. Disappointment flooded her, but she knew better than to lose her dignity in an argument she couldn't win.

A week later she lost all desire to cross the Atlantic with her precious daughter.

"There's just been a wireless announcement that a German submarine has sunk the *Lusitania,* my lady!" Ellie said, coming into Delia's bedroom with her breakfast tray. "It was on its way from New York to Liverpool carrying hundreds of civilian passengers. Mr. Bellingham says it's the worst outrage he's ever heard of. His lordship left the house in a great hurry. He'll be going to Downing Street, I expect."

Four hours later he returned home, his handsome features so grim they looked as if they had been carved in stone. "Cunard is talking in the region of over a thousand drowned." He poured a large whiskey and added the merest squirt of soda to it. "There'll be no more passenger sailings. The American financing will have to be carried out by telegraph."

He drained his glass and then said unsteadily, "The *Lusitania* was the sister ship of the *Mauretania,* Delia. What kind of world is it when a liner carrying American passengers, who are neutral and not at war, can be blown out of the sea as mercilessly as if she were an enemy warship?" He covered his eyes with his hand. "It's something I would never have believed."

Two weeks later, despite it being the beginning of the London season, they went to Shibden, taking Petra and her nurse with them. Juno, and his groom, Charlie, followed. The horse, accustomed to traveling in a horse box, was no trouble. According to the nurse, who was traveling with Petra and a nurserymaid in a separate car, Petra was.

"She's cried on and off the entire journey, my lady," the nurse said as Delia lifted Petra from her arms the instant they had all stepped from the cars in front of Shibden's porticoed entrance. "I think maybe she's beginning to teethe."

Though she knew Ivor would think it extremely undignified, Delia didn't hand Petra back to her nurse, but carried her into Shibden and up to the rooms set apart as a nursery. She had determined to take an even greater part in her daughter's day-to-day care and was setting out as she intended to carry on.

Within days, Ivor was summoned back to London for a meeting of the Privy Council. "The war is at a crisis point," he said bluntly as she walked with him to his car. "Now Lloyd George is no longer chancellor but minister of munitions, he is doing all he can, but so far it isn't enough. I hate to say this, but I think the fault lies with Herbert. He was an excellent prime minister when we were at peace, but war is a very different kettle of fish. If Lloyd George were to make a bid for the premiership he would have my support."

Delia was so shocked, she was speechless. Long after the Silver Ghost had disappeared she stood on the driveway, staring after it. Just as it was impossible to think of Buckingham Palace not being home to King George and Queen Mary, so it was impossible to think of H.H. and Margot not at 10 Downing Street.

Heavyhearted she walked back into the house just in time to take a telephone call from Gwen. "Darling," her sister-in-law said, "I'm on my way to Hunstanton to stay with the Denbys and thought I would call in at Shibden and stay overnight. It's so long since I've been able to have a really good chat with Ivor." The static on the line made Gwen's next few words unintelligible. "And so there will be two of us . . . so kind of you, darling."

The line went dead before Delia could tell Gwen that Ivor was in London and that for Gwen to go out of her way to see Ivor at Shibden was pointless.

When she rang Gwen back, it was only to be told by the butler that Gwen hadn't been at home all morning and would be in Norfolk for the next few days.

Faced with the choice of telephoning a whole host of Gwen's friends to see where she was or simply letting things stand, Delia decided to let it go.

"Lord and Lady Pugh will be staying overnight," she said to Parkinson. "Please make sure the maids have a room ready for them."

Much later in the day she put on her riding clothes and went to the stables. The horses Ivor and his guests rode looked toward her, hopeful of an afternoon ride.

"Sorry," she said, as Charlie saddled Juno. "I'm afraid I'm a one-horse woman, boys."

That Juno was there was an achievement in itself, for Ivor disapproved of her riding when pregnant.

"I'll stop in three months' time," she had said when they had argued over it, "and I won't gallop hard. I promise."

It was a compromise neither of them had been happy with but one which, as in so many other instances in their marriage, they had settled for in a spirit of give-and-take in order to keep their life together acceptably harmonious.

"And I didn't promise not to gallop," Delia said, leaning forward to pat Juno's neck as they trotted out of the stable yard. "I said I wouldn't gallop *hard*."

All through May the weather had been beautiful, and even though it was now late afternoon, it was still warm, the sky a bright blue flecked with clouds. She headed east over Shibden's parkland toward a narrow lane that led through flat country-side thick with grazing sheep. In the distance was a drainage mill, its slowly revolving sails looking, to the uneducated eye, like a windmill.

"The land is so low that without the mills it would be un-derwater," Ivor had said the first time he had brought her to

Shibden. "And don't keep using the word 'river,' Delia. In Nor-folk, the rivers and lakes are known as broads, and always be careful when riding over the humpbacked bridge that crosses it. It's treacherously steep."

As Delia carefully walked Juno over the bridge the reed-edged water beneath it was as hard in color as a stone. Sud-denly she became aware of the eerie stillness that presages a storm. She reined Juno to a halt, looking up at the sky, won-dering whether to continue to the beach, which was a mile or so away. The sky was still a vivid blue. The wispy clouds were a snowy white. Secure in the certainty that any storm was a long way off, she urged Juno into a canter, looking forward to the day when she would be able to enjoy such outings with Petra riding beside her.

When she reached the sea, the sand was deserted as far as the eye could see. She gave a deep sigh of pleasure. Here, with the waves crashing rhythmically just yards away, she was able to ride as hard as she loved without any disapproving eyes watching her.

By the time she turned Juno homeward the sky was begin-ning to smoke with the first hint of dusk. Now the sensation of a coming storm was strong. Indigo-rimmed black clouds rolled in from the sea and she knew she would be very lucky to reach Shibden before they broke.

She headed toward the bridge at a brisk canter. To her amazement she saw that a horse being ridden sidesaddle was heading toward her.

"Whoever she is, she's an idiot," Delia said to Juno. "The only place she can be goin' is the beach, and by the time she gets there she'll be soaked to the skin."

She slowed Juno down and squinted to see the figure more clearly. The only large country house within riding distance was Shibden and the only person who could possibly be riding out from Shibden—assuming, of course, that she had arrived there—was Gwen. Gwen, however, rarely rode these days and would certainly not come out with a storm about to break.

She reined Juno to a halt, sucking in her breath. The elegance of the rider, the provocative tilt of the hat, were unmistakable. When Gwen had said "and so there will be two of us," the other person she had been referring to had been Sylvia, not Pugh. And only Gwen, of everyone she knew, would so artlessly bring Sylvia on a visit to Shibden, for Delia was quite sure Gwen was the only person in London who didn't know that Sylvia was Ivor's mistress.

Having Sylvia as a guest when Jerome and sixteen or twenty other people were also there was one thing. Having her as a guest when the only other visitor was Gwen was quite another. How, in the name of all that was wonderful, was she going to survive it? Fortunately Ivor was in London and so Sylvia's hopes of being able to parade her closeness to him had been dashed. Presumably it was furious disappointment that had prompted her to take one of Ivor's horses and ride out uncaring of the storm clouds that were now rolling fast over their heads.

Delia spurred Juno into movement. If Sylvia wanted to keep riding away from Shibden, getting saturated in the process, she was welcome to do so. She, however, was going to head for home as fast as she could.

Sylvia was riding at a gallop, but whereas Delia still had a couple of hundred yards to go before the bridge, Sylvia was nearly upon it.

Delia saw her rein in far too late for safety, saw the horse skitter at the sudden steepness as lightning streaked down. The horse, now at the middle of the narrow bridge, reared and then bolted, unseating Sylvia with such force that she went flying over the low flint-stone parapet, into the water.

As thunder cracked deafeningly, Delia urged Juno into an all-out gallop, bringing him to a halt within yards of the bridge.

The rain began coming down in sheets, making visibility practically zero. Hardly able to see where the reeds ended and the water began Delia slithered from Juno's back and hurtled onto the bridge for a better vantage point.

"Sylvia!" she shouted into the darkness as the rain plastered her hair to her head. "It's me, Delia! Where are you?"

"I'm in the water!" The response was terror-laden. *"And I can't swim!"*

As another bolt of lightning streaked down, Delia saw the pale oval of Sylvia's petrified face, her hair indistinguishable from the inky blackness of the water. In the split second before thunder followed the lightning, Sylvia disappeared beneath the surface.

Delia didn't hesitate. There was no time to take off her riding habit with its heavy long skirt; no time to struggle with riding boots that always needed an extra pair of hands to successfully remove them. As the rain sluiced down she lowered herself over the edge of the parapet and then took in a deep lungful of air before letting herself fall.

Her cousin Beau had taught her to swim at White Sulphur Springs when she was thirteen and, until now, water had never frightened her. This time, though, as the water closed over her head, she was unable to kick freely with her legs: this time she was hampered by cumbersome boots and a beautifully tailored Busvine riding skirt.

As she struggled to break the surface, its weight acted like a force of gravity, pulling her down until she touched bottom. The deep mud of the broad sucked at her boots, debris swirling around her. Algae clung slimily to her face. Desperately she fought with the fastenings of her skirt. As she finally freed herself from the strap that ran through it to the hem to prevent the skirt from flying upward, her chest was bursting and her ears felt as if they were about to explode.

Then, at last, she was free of the unwieldy material. A second later she was gulping in air and a second after that, without a flicker of hesitation, she dove beneath the surface again.

It was an easy search. Though the water had seemed much deeper when she had been certain she was drowning, it was only a little over twelve feet deep. She had entered the water almost over the point where Sylvia had disappeared and she bumped into her motionless body immediately.

Seizing hold of her under her armpits, Delia kicked her way up. Sylvia offered no resistance and when they broke the surface she did not gasp for air.

With one hand under Sylvia's chin to keep her nose and mouth clear of the water, Delia swam backward.

Unlike a normal river, the broad had no firm banks to scramble up. It was edged by thick reeds and, even when she was able to stand, the ground within reach was not firm enough to lie Sylvia on in order to try to revive her.

Sobbing with exhaustion Delia fell into the squelching reeds, taking Sylvia with her. Then, as they sank ever deeper into the marsh, Delia held Sylvia around the chest as tightly as she could, alternately squeezing her with a sharp upward movement and fisting her in the middle of her back.

"Breathe!" she gasped as the thunder and lightning rolled away. "Land's sakes, Sylvia! *Breathe!*"

There was a gagging sound and a flicker of movement.

Delia summoned up all her remaining energy and squeezed Sylvia again.

Sylvia retched, spewing up water. A moment later Delia heard the sound of hoofbeats.

"We're here!" she shouted hoarsely as Sylvia continued to gag. "Here! Below you, in the reeds!"

The horses slowed to a walk to take the bridge.

"We're here!" she shouted again, certain it was a Shibden search party. "To the right of the bridge! In the reeds!"

"Holy God, it's her ladyship!" The voice was Charlie's. She

heard him vault from his horse, shouting as he did so to the other horseman, "Shine the lantern over the edge of the bridge, Dan!"

Shibden's head groom did as he was bid.

As the light fell on her Delia uttered a devout prayer of thankfulness, took her arms from around Sylvia, and staggered to her feet.

"Don't mind me," she gasped when the two men had made their way through the sodden reeds. "See to Lady Bazeljette first. She's half drowned and is in a bad way."

Then, as Charlie's arm went around her, her legs buckled and she lost consciousness.

How Charlie and Dan got her and Sylvia back to the house she didn't know and—fearful that the answer would be slumped across the horses like sacks of potatoes—never, afterward, asked.

It was enough to know that she was safe. That she hadn't lost her unborn baby. That Sylvia was alive.

"Though only just, according to the doctor, my lady," Ellie said, taking a hot-water bottle that was beginning to cool from the bed and replacing it with a towel-wrapped hot one. "He's still here and says he will be remaining with her all night."

Delia looked down at her lace-trimmed nightdress and saw she had been given a bath. She wondered how many she'd had to take to get rid of the mud and slime. Completely disoriented, she asked, "What time is it, Ellie? Is it evening or the middle of the night?"

"Neither, my lady. It's just before dawn. Both Lady Pugh and the doctor insisted you shouldn't be left on your own, and so I've been sitting with you ever since you were put to bed. You don't seem to be able to stop shivering, my lady, and you've got a very high temperature. The doctor is worried you've caught pneumonia."

Delia closed her eyes. Pneumonia. She wasn't going to give in to pneumonia. Not after all she had just survived.

When she next woke, aching in every bone, the curtains had been drawn back and Ellie, still sitting by the side of the bed, said, "Would you like a little breakfast, my lady?"

"I'd like some tea and perhaps a slice of toast." She pushed herself up against the pillows, wincing. "Has his lordship been informed of what has happened?"

"Yes, my lady. Though Lady Pugh couldn't give him exact details because neither you nor Lady Bazeljette were in condition to tell anyone. She simply said that there was a storm, that you and Lady Bazeljette were thrown from your horses, fell into the broad, and were nearly drowned. He's on his way here and is expected within the next hour."

"Is the doctor still with Lady Bazeljette?"

"I believe he's downstairs, having breakfast."

To Ellie's alarm Delia threw back the covers and eased her aching legs to the floor. "You can't get up, my lady," she said, panic-stricken. "The doctor gave strict instructions you were to remain in bed. He's forbidden all visitors, even Lady Pugh."

Delia slipped her arms into her negligee and Ellie's panic grew. "You can't mean to be leaving the room, my lady! The doctor said it was a miracle you didn't lose the baby and that you have to be very careful!"

"Stop behaving like an old mother hen, Ellie. I will be careful. All I am goin' to do is to walk fifteen yards down the corridor to see Lady Bazeljette."

"She's in the Italian bedroom, my lady—and I doubt she'll be in any condition to appreciate your visit. She was more dead than alive when Dan carried her into the house."

Delia took no offense at being spoken to as if she were a recalcitrant child. She knew that Ellie was right. Bed was the only place she should be. The problem was, though, that if she stayed in bed she wouldn't be able to speak to Sylvia before Ivor arrived and there were things that needed to be said—not least her need for Sylvia to give the same account of what had happened that Delia had decided on.

Bennett, Sylvia's maid, opened the door with the words "Her ladyship is allowed no visitors . . ." on her lips. They died the instant she saw Delia. "The doctor has given instructions that her ladyship has to have complete rest, Lady Conisborough," she said, making a valiant attempt to carry out her orders.

"I shan't tire her, Bennett. I intend to stay only ten minutes. Perhaps you would like to take advantage of my presence in order to get a cup of tea?"

It was a dismissal and Bennett knew it.

"Well . . . if you say so, your ladyship." Unhappily she allowed Delia into the room and, even more unhappily, left it.

Sylvia was lying in the center of a vast bed, propped up by a mountain of silk-covered pillows, her blue-black waist-length hair streaming loose. She looked like a beautiful ghost, her eyes darkly ringed, her skin deathly pale.

The only movement she made was a very slight turn of her head. "Ah," she said as Delia sat down in the chair beside the bed. "It's you. I knew you'd come."

"How are you?"

"Alive. Just. And for that I suppose I should say thank you."

"You don't have to. I would have done the same for anyone."

"Yes, you would, wouldn't you?" There was faintly amused mockery in her voice. "Your behavior is always admirable, isn't it? You discover you have married a man who is in love with someone else and you behave with a dignity far beyond your years—a dignity that earns you your husband's profound respect and that, in most circumstances, would have made him

end his affair. You are vivaciously unconventional—and yet no
one takes offense. Everyone is entranced by you. The Queen
is fond of you—which is saying a lot because she isn't fond
of many people, including half of her own family. The prime
minister, a man with a weakness for women young enough to
be his granddaughter, is more than a little in love with you.
Instead of being ostracized by high society, no party is complete without you. You are not as I expected—and for that I
hate you, Delia. Having saved my life makes no difference to
my feelings."

The shocking words were said in a matter-of-fact tone.

"I never imagined for one minute that it would," Delia
said, struggling to be equally impassive. "I'd like to know what
I was supposed to be, though, when becoming Ivor's wife was
such a surprise to everyone."

Sylvia lifted a perfect eyebrow. "It wasn't quite such a surprise to me, Delia. Ivor needed to remarry—and to remarry
a young woman—in order to have the son Olivia failed so
spectacularly to give him. I had no desire to see him wed the
debutante daughter of one of my friends—and English society
is such a closed circle I am on terms with almost everyone.
My last words to him before he sailed for America were that a
New York heiress would solve our problems admirably. What I
didn't expect was for him to marry a Virginian who, no matter
how well regarded her family, could in no way be termed an
heiress—and a Virginian who, instead of being disconcerted at
finding herself plunged into an alien way of life, threw herself
into it with bewitching self-confidence."

For the first time she moved, pushing herself up against the
pillows. "Having no family or contacts in England was supposed to ensure you would have no option but to be malleable
when you discovered why Ivor married you." Sylvia's voice was
withering. "Olivia was never malleable. She made life as difficult as possible for Ivor—and for me. God, what a bitch that

woman was! She made me suffer endless public humiliations. Not for one minute did she allow anyone to forget that my background wasn't as good as hers. By the time she died, Ivor could barely bring himself to speak to her."

Her eyes held Delia's with chilly frankness. "And nothing could have suited me better. I didn't want Ivor to be in love with Olivia. Even on the day he married her, he wasn't. You, however, are different."

She paused, breathing in deeply, her finely drawn nostrils whitening. "From the moment I met you at Sir Cuthbert's birthday ball I knew Ivor was more than a little in love with you. You weren't quite what he had wanted in a second wife, but you are so shatteringly beautiful and amusing, and you handle your relationship with him with the skill of a far more experienced woman."

Her eyes hardened. "But you won't win him, Delia. What happened last night, in that filthy, murderous water, makes not one iota of difference. Ivor may love you a little, but he loves me more. And that's the way I intend it to remain."

She closed her eyes, unable to continue talking. Delia rose to her feet. "There's just one thing before I go, Sylvia," she said quietly. "It's about last night."

With great effort Sylvia opened her eyes, the expression in them wary.

"Gwen told Ivor that we were together when the storm broke and that our horses threw us into the broad. Unlikely though it may be, it's a version of events I'd like to stick to. I've no desire to become known as a heroine. Especially in these circumstances."

The faintest of smiles touched Sylvia's beautifully shaped mouth.

"That's fine by me," she said weakly, closing her eyes again. "I don't want the whole world knowing I owe you my life."

As Delia opened the door, Sylvia said, "And you were very

brave, Delia. I'll give you that. We call it spunk in England. Is it something all Virginians have?"

"No, but I'm a Chandler, and all Chandlers have it."

On that note she closed the door behind her.

Half an hour later Ivor's Rolls swept up the drive. Delia's bedroom windows were open and within a second of the car coming to a halt she heard Ivor sprint across the gravel.

Thanks to Ellie, she knew exactly what Gwen had told him and since he believed both her and Sylvia to have suffered similarly, whom would Ivor rush to see first? Her, or Sylvia? He always behaved with the utmost propriety in front of servants and, as they all would know if he strode to Sylvia's room first, that alone was reason enough for him not to do so. He would also have to take into account the fact that Gwen was in the house. If he were to hurry to Sylvia's side first, even Gwen would finally realize the true nature of their relationship. Last but by no means least, Delia was pregnant—and according to the doctor, still at risk of losing the baby.

As she heard him take the stairs two at a time, she was certain he would come to her door. She couldn't see how, in all conscience, he could do anything else.

He rounded the head of the stairs and began striding swiftly along the corridor toward her room.

He reached it.

And passed it.

Seconds later, without even pausing to knock, she heard him throw open Sylvia's door.

Very slowly, Delia let out her breath. At the window, muslin curtains fluttered gently in the May breeze.

For four years she had lived in the hope of Ivor returning the love she felt for him. It was a hope often dashed, but it had never died. Only days ago, when he suggested that they spend time together at Shibden, she had felt certain that her long battle was almost won.

Now, with terrible finality, she knew she had lost. He loved her, but not enough. With Ivor, Sylvia came first, and, even pregnant, Delia came a very poor second.

But she didn't come second with everyone.

She didn't come second with Jerome.

She heard Sylvia's door open and then close. Ivor's footsteps strode down the corridor toward her, but she no longer cared about him or their marriage.

She was thinking of the letter she would write when she was next alone. The letter she would send to France. The letter she knew Jerome had given up all hope of ever receiving.

SIX

At Christmas Delia gave birth to a second daughter after a prolonged and difficult labor. This time she had no name waiting. This time, like Ivor, whose disappointment was profound, she hadn't even entertained the thought that the baby might be a girl.

"We could name her after your mother," she said hesitantly, so weak from the birth she didn't truly care what name the baby was given.

A shutter came down over Ivor's austerely handsome face at the mention of his long-dead parents.

"No," he said shortly. "I think not." He paused and then said, "What about naming her after her mother?"

"Bedelia? I don't think so. I found the name hard enough to live with until I insisted it was shortened to Delia, and two Delias would be highly confusing."

"You truly don't have any preferences?"

She shook her head, her mane of hair glowing like fire against the ivory-silk pillows.

"Then we'll call her Davina May. Davina as a mark of respect to David Lloyd George—who is certain to replace Herbert as prime minister within the year—and May after Queen Mary, who is christened May and is still known as May by everyone on intimate terms with her."

Delia closed her eyes. To name their daughter after a bull-ish, fiery-tempered Welshman was ridiculous, yet the name was both pretty and unusual and she liked the way Delia and Davina rolled off the tongue so easily when spoken together.

Eight weeks later, just as she was finally regaining her strength, news came that Jerome had been badly injured. He wrote to her from a field hospital.

I still have all my limbs, which I hope is as much of a relief to you as it is to me. Word is I'm to be transferred to a hospital in Blighty where, with luck, I'll recover fast enough to be back at the front for the final push.

"He's mad," she said, when she next had lunch with Margot. "How can he say *with luck* he'll be back at the front? And how can there be talk of a final push when things are at such a stalemate? Month after month men are gassed, mined, and mutilated with no appreciable ground taken. Things are just as bad as they were this time last year."

Margot, her face white and strained, remained silent. After-ward, when they parted, Delia regretted saying things which, though true, could have been taken as criticism of the prime minister's handling of the war.

A month later and Jerome was in a military hospital in Sussex. Wearing a sea-green bolero, a matching ankle-length skirt, and a stiff white shirtwaist, Delia took a train and taxi to see him. Though she'd had two children, rigorous corseting ensured she still had an elegant hourglass figure, and the admiring looks she received from men in uniform—and every fit man of mili-tary age was in uniform—were considerable.

It wasn't merely her deeply waving fox-red hair—topped by a saucy straw boater—that attracted attention, or the fact she was taller than most Englishwomen. It was her breezy American manner, her disarming self-confidence, and her unpretentiousness that set her apart.

When she walked into the hospital ward all eyes turned toward her.

"Whom are you visiting?" the ward sister asked, swiftly coming to greet her.

"Captain Bazeljette."

"Ah." The sister called a nurse away from settling an amputee more comfortably. "Nurse—please escort Mrs. Bazeljette to Captain Bazeljette's bedside."

Delia cleared her throat. "Lady Bazeljette is unable to visit on this occasion. I am Viscountess Conisborough—a close family friend."

Though the ward sister's eyebrows rose only the merest millimeter Delia knew that the loving greeting she had intended was out of the question.

As the nurse led her down the long ward full of injured officers she was sickeningly aware that very few of them would ever walk again without the aid of crutches or an artificial limb. With rising panic she wondered whether Jerome had lied in his letter to her. Perhaps he had not told her the extent of his injury. Perhaps he, too, had been maimed.

As the nurse came to a halt Delia steeled herself for the worst. She mustn't let horror show on her face in case he registered it as repugnance. She must be brave, as he had been for so long.

"Captain Bazeljette, you have a visitor," the nurse said sunnily, her manner completely different from that of the ward sister. "And can I ask you not to stay any longer than half an hour, Lady Conisborough? Wounded men tire easily."

With a flick of her starched skirt she was gone. With relief that made her weak at the knees, Delia saw that though Jerome's left arm, shoulder, and leg were heavily bandaged, none of the bandaging ended in a stump.

"God, but you're a wonderful sight," he said as she sat down as close to the bed as she could get.

Speech was beyond her so she took hold of his hand and pressed it against her cheek.

His hair, far longer than army regulations allowed, tumbled low over his brow and curled tightly at the nape of his neck. A livid wound knifed down through his left eyebrow.

He read her thoughts and said gently, "It could have been worse, Delia. I could have lost an eye. Of all the men in this ward I'm probably the one least grievously injured."

"I know," she said unsteadily. "And I'm grateful. But such luck can't last, Jerome. You've been at the front for almost eighteen months. The next time you could be . . . could be . . ." She couldn't finish the sentence and instead said thickly, "I want you to apply for a staff posting. You have influential friends." Her voice was urgent and pleading. "It could easily be managed. And it isn't as if you haven't done your bit. You've been mentioned in dispatches for exceptional bravery. As a staff officer you could . . ."

". . . Remain well behind lines and never be able to live with myself?" His voice was still gentle, but mulishly firm. "No, Delia. It isn't an option." He squeezed her hand. "Tell me about the new baby. Ivor didn't seriously name her after Lloyd George, did he?"

Still distraught at the prospect of his returning to the front she managed only a glimmer of a smile. "Yes, he did. Despite being so different in character, he and Lloyd George have become very close, though not so close that he has asked him to be her godfather. That position is reserved for you—and we're goin' to delay the christening until you can attend."

"Thank you." He paused and then said in a different tone of voice, "And Petra, Delia? How is Petra?"

Her smile deepened. "Very sassy. She's walkin' and talkin' and is full of mischief. I wish you could see her, Jerome. I wish I'd been able to bring her with me, but babies ain't allowed."

In spite of the pain he was in, an answering smile split his swarthy face. "And is her hair still red?"

"Yes, but not Titian, like mine. It's more a russet. And though her eyes are green, they're a hazel, not emerald. I've brought a photograph."

There was a locker by his bed and she propped the photograph against a jug of water, wondering if he would keep it there—and if he did, how he would explain it to Sylvia.

As if reading her thoughts and with his eyes on the photograph, he said, "I haven't seen Sylvia yet. She's in Scotland with the Girlingtons. Jack's been, though. My father brought him down."

He dragged his eyes away from the photograph. "He wasn't at all fazed by the bandages—not when I told him I still had an arm and a leg beneath them—and he was very admiring of the wound through my eyebrow. He said it made me look like a pirate."

Laughter fizzed in her throat. "It does. Not an evil Captain Hook. A handsome swashbuckling pirate."

"Your sort of a pirate?" An amber flame burned deep in his eyes.

"Oh, yes," she whispered. "Very much so, Jerome." And, uncaring of who might be watching, she leaned forward and kissed him long and tenderly on the mouth.

Three months later he was back in France. A month after that the Somme campaign opened. It was the biggest British army ever sent into battle and the country held its breath. Delia received regular postcards from Jerome, but the censor saw to it that they told her nothing except that, at the time of writing, he was alive. And the battle that had been meant to be so decisive simply went on and on and on, for month after month, in a seemingly endless series of partial actions. The casualty lists were catastrophic.

In September, as a second big push on the Somme began, Margot's stepson Raymond was killed leading his men.

Margot's grief was deep. "What a waste, what a waste," was all she could say, ashen-faced, when Delia went to 10 Downing Street to pay her condolences. "Raymond should have had a staff job where he could use his brains, but no one of any sensitivity will take a staff job anymore—it arouses both jealousy and the suspicion of cowardice. There's another kind of cowardice, too, Delia."

She clenched her hands. "Too many of Henry's friends are no longer loyal to him. Not Winston. Not George. Not Ivor. All the three of them ever do is praise Lloyd George—and that's tantamount to pushing Henry out of office. The consequence is that I'm losing all my friends. I had a dreadful altercation with Clemmie—she, of course, can only see things from Winston's point of view. I do hope the same kind of thing isn't going to happen with you, Delia."

Knowing such an event was likely, Delia murmured something placating and left heavyhearted, sensing that their friendship would end the day Lloyd George stepped into H.H.'s shoes.

The announcement that he was to do so came the first week in December. "Thank God," Ivor said with relief. "The war will take a new direction. Even the King—never the most optimistic of men—believes it could well be over by the spring."

It wasn't.

When Jerome came home on leave in March, he said, grim-faced, "Unless America enters the war, the fighting is going to go on until there isn't a man left standing."

He was a major now and looked a decade older than when, three years ago, he had enlisted so exuberantly. His dark hair was flecked with gray and the lines running from nose to mouth looked as if they had been carved in stone. His weariness was palpable.

"Heaven only knows what's happening on the eastern front," he said bitterly to Ivor when he dined with him at the Denbys'. "But the western front is a stalemate of cataclysmic proportions. An entire generation is being wiped out. It's kill or be killed. God knows how I'm still alive."

On the sixth of April, the day after his leave ended, America declared war. A month later Delia received a euphoric letter from her cousin Bella. It was addressed "Darling Viscountess," because Bella loved to use Delia's title—however inappropriately—at every opportunity.

> Isn't it wonderful that our American boys can now share in all the glory and the gallantry? Cousin Beau enlisted immediately and I can't tell you how handsome he looks in uniform. He's such a daredevil I just know he'll win all kinds of honors. He's as eager to go into battle as a child itching to go to a party, but we don't rightly know when American troops will be leaving for Flanders. Is Flanders in France or Belgium? One thing is certain: once Beau arrives there the men will have to look to their laurels where their girls are concerned.

Delia laid the letter down, sick at heart at Bella's foolish naïveté. More than half a million men had died on the Somme alone—and that was just the published figures. She thought of the amputees she had seen. Men in their early twenties, and even younger, who would never walk again. Men who, unable to work, would be reduced to selling matches. And to Bella the war was one of battlefields set neatly outside towns where, the fighting for the day over, gallant soldiers returned as if from the office to flirt with pretty mademoiselles.

"Don't be too hard on her," Ivor said when she voiced her despair that Bella wasn't better informed. "Three years ago that was how nearly everyone thought. All that matters is for American troopships to reach France without being blown out of the water by German submarines."

At the end of June the American troops reached France, but as the weeks passed, Delia could see no dramatic changes. If anything, things grew worse. The Germans began making zeppelin raids over London, involving civilians in a way no one had ever thought possible. One bomb fell on a school, killing a roomful of children. Another crashed into a railway station, hitting a crowded train.

Postcards from Jerome, written in pencil and with nearly every sentence blocked out by the censor, still arrived with thankful regularity. Though he had fought tooth and nail against accepting a staff job, a staff job behind lines was where he had now been assigned and Delia thanked God for it every night.

"Has Jerome said what he intends doing once the war is over?" Ivor asked on one of the rare evenings when they were dining together. "The world won't be the same place and knowing Jerome he'll adapt quickly."

"He's going to enter politics. He's already spoken to Lloyd George, who has promised to put him up as the Liberal candidate for some promising constituency."

Ivor wasn't as surprised as Delia expected. "It's something he should have done ten years ago," he said. "He's got the right manner. I suspect people will vote for him in droves."

If he lives, Delia thought fiercely but she did not put the thought into words. There was always the chance Jerome would figure out a way to return to the front.

In October, on Petra's third birthday, Delia held a party at Cadogan Square. Jack, who was now nine and at a preparatory school in Sussex, was home for half term and arrived when the party was in full swing and a conjuror was performing.

"Ooh, Jack, *Jack!*" Petra squealed, hurling herself toward him and fastening hands gooey with icing around his legs. "Come and see the man taking rabbits—live real rabbits—out of his hat. Can I have one of the rabbits to keep, Mama? Jack is going to stay, isn't he? You are going to stay, aren't you?" And letting go of his legs to grab his hands, she dragged him across the floor where a dozen children were laughing and cheering as the magician drew a live dove from his hat.

Davina, twenty-two months old, was standing as near as she could get, not clapping and cheering noisily like the other children, but simply staring at the dove in round-eyed, gray-eyed wonder.

Watching her, Delia's heart contracted with love. Where Petra was exuberantly outgoing, demanding constant attention and entertainment, Davina was quite happy with her own company as long as she had bricks or a tiny toy figure to play with. Delia bit her lip, wondering what a third child would have been like—a third child that, after Davina's difficult birth, she'd given up hope of conceiving.

Her obstetrician had told Ivor that it was unlikely she would conceive again and that, if she did, her life would be at risk. Delia feared it would mean the end of her marriage.

It hadn't.

"Divorce is simply not socially acceptable," Ivor said, when she had voiced concern. "Not for a man in my position. Two daughters are simply what I'm going to have to settle for."

He hadn't troubled to disguise his bitter disappointment

and she hadn't troubled to hide her vast relief. If he *had* wanted a divorce, it would have made it impossible for her to spend time with Jerome. It was only because she was safely married, and because her husband was viewed as Jerome's close friend, that regular contact with Jerome aroused no gossip.

As the conjuror began pulling colored-silk handkerchiefs from the back of Jack's jacket, Delia tried to think of life without Jerome. She couldn't. He had become her best friend and now that her inability to give Ivor a son had made her husband even more distant, Jerome had become the central person in her life.

A sudden uproar interrupted her thoughts. The conjuror had just drawn a live mouse from Jack's pocket. Nannies screamed and scattered, toddlers shrieked.

Aware that it was time she intervened, Delia walked swiftly across the floor, deciding that the instant the party was over she would telephone Fortnum & Mason's and order another food parcel for Jerome—one including his favorite Fuller's walnut cake.

Christmas was spent at Shibden, and over the holidays King George and Queen Mary paid one of their very rare social visits. It was a disruption Delia could well have done without, entailing, as it did, a menu submitted for approval in advance—ensuring that cook had hysterics—and a swarm of police outside the house. The Queen unbent enough to ask after Delia's charity work and the King discussed the difficulty of America's loan restrictions.

"The money can only be spent to pay for supplies bought in the United States." His Majesty was so anxious that he forgot he was discussing a political subject in front of his wife and his hostess. "We don't exact similar conditions on loans that we make to our allies. Difficult though such trips now are, I fear you are going to have to cross the Atlantic again, Conis-borough. The U.S. secretary of the treasury needs to under-stand just how critical our financial situation is. He must be told—and in no uncertain terms—that we need a more flexible arrangement."

Later, when their royal visitors had driven back to San-dringham, Delia knocked on the connecting door to Ivor's bedroom.

"Will you really have to risk crossing the Atlantic again?" she asked.

Though he had dispensed with his evening jacket he was otherwise fully dressed and she was suddenly very conscious of being clad only in her nightdress and peignoir.

"Perhaps. It will be up to Balfour."

Arthur Balfour was the British secretary of foreign affairs.

"The difficulty is," he said, talking frankly to her as he al-ways did where his work was concerned, "America now has its own vast war needs and as a consequence, the supply of credit to Britain could well begin to dry up."

"But not when we're allies! Surely now that we're allies we will receive increased lines of credit?"

"Maybe." He shot her his familiar down-slanting smile. "Perhaps it's you, not me, Balfour should be sending to Amer-ica. The secretary of the treasury's name is Mr. McAdoo."

It had been a long time since, in Ivor's company, she had giggled, but she giggled now. "It sounds like something out of a comic-strip cartoon."

His smile deepened.

Sensing his new affection and what it portended she de-cided she couldn't bear to have her emotions thrown into tur-moil again. She said swiftly, "I'm sure if you go to America your trip will be successful. Good night, Ivor." And before he could try and detain her she walked back into her own bed-room, closing the connecting door.

All through the cold months of the spring the fighting continued. On the eastern front, the Russian armies had been defeated. On the western front the French troops were so diminished they could no longer be relied upon for any operation that involved a major attack and the U.S. troops were still not being deployed. In March, when the Germans opened a massive offensive, King George was so fearful of a German victory that he rushed to France to bolster the flagging morale of the British armies.

Jerome's staff job hadn't prevented him from being injured again, though this time he was not evacuated to a military hospital in England. Instead, he spent several weeks recuperating near Boulogne and then, in June, suffering a permanent limp, he was back in the thick of it.

So as not to think, Delia kept herself so busy with charity work that she was in danger of collapsing from exhaustion. It was better, however, than reading the casualty lists in *The Times* or hearing that a soldier who had just been killed was the last surviving brother of three.

"Their poor mothers," Gwen said time after time. "To lose not one boy but all their sons. What fortitude they must need to bear such unimaginable loss."

In September it looked as if the Allies were finally winning, but just when her spirits were higher than they had been for four years, Delia learned that Beau had been killed.

The news poleaxed her. Beau had been part of her childhood; part of her youth. For weeks her thoughts were of Virginia and the carelessly happy days with her cousin.

"When the Atlantic is safe to travel again, the very first thing I'm goin' to do is visit my folks," she said to Ivor. "My parents aren't gettin' any younger and I want Petra and Davina to remember them."

The war ended in November. Throughout the country church bells rang and fireworks lit the night sky. Ivor had flags hung from every window of the Cadogan Square house. After going to the House of Commons to listen to Lloyd George read the armistice terms, he took Delia to Buckingham Palace where King George and Queen Mary stood on the balcony waving to the crowds.

Delia half expected life to return to prewar certainties. It didn't. Many of their friends who had mansions in London and stately homes in the country gave up their town houses. They still entertained, but house parties were confined to weekends.

In town, the young thronged nightclubs to listen to the new jazz. American music was played everywhere. It was a social scene Ivor disliked but Delia, whose growing friendship with the Prince of Wales had become close, often partied with him and nightclubbing was Prince Edward's favorite occupation.

"And Ivor can't very well forbid me from accepting such invitations," Delia said to Jerome in the spring of 1920 when they had escaped for an illicit picnic on the North Downs, "not when they come from the man who will be his king."

"Edward doesn't have the look of a king," Jerome said. He was lying on the grass propped on one elbow. "He looks like a fairy-tale prince—slender, blue-eyed, golden-haired—but he lacks gravitas and, in my book, gravitas is a necessary quality for a king."

Delia set down her glass of white wine, smoothed her fashionable mid-calf-length skirt over her knees and circled them with her arms. "Ivor thinks it a necessary quality too. He's hoping King George will live to be ninety."

"Which, considering how old his grandmother was when she died, he may well do." He put a chicken leg down on a serviette and lay flat, his hands beneath his head. "Did Ivor give you any idea how long he might be in Paris?"

"No. He said the peace conference was likely to go on for months. You're an MP—what's the inside gossip?"

"That it will go on for months." He shot her his wide, easy smile. "I don't think Lloyd George will want Ivor to stay in Paris, though. He needs your husband to focus on what is happening in the Middle East. If we grant Egypt independence— and we may have to—we still need to maintain control of the cotton trade, and of the canal. Without Suez, we lose our strategic link with India."

Delia's conversations with Ivor were nearly always about work—which meant they were nearly always about politics. She didn't want the same situation with Jerome. Egypt didn't interest her even a little bit, and she'd no intention of wasting one of their precious afternoons together talking about it.

She lay down beside him, her head next to his. "Let me tell you about Virginia," she said dreamily. "Let me tell you how utterly wonderful it was takin' Petra and Davina there. If only you had been with us as well everythin' would have been absolutely perfect."

He rolled over, pinning her beneath him, his eyes hot with desire. "One day," he said, lifting a stray tendril of fiery hair away from her face. "One day we'll go there together."

Her hands slid into the curly thickness of his hair. She didn't want to talk about one day, because she knew that one day was never going to come. Divorce was out of the question for Jerome because of Jack. "Maybe when he's older, Delia," he said. "But divorce while he's still at Eton would be disastrous for him." And recently Jerome had become an ambitious member of Parliament, making divorce unthinkable for a whole set of new reasons.

Delia no longer cared. Her marriage to Ivor was not one of unmitigated misery. She respected his intellect and his huge capacity for hard work. She enjoyed the prestige of being his wife. She valued the way he shared his political concerns with her and knew he held her in very deep affection. It made for a marriage far more compatible than the marriages of most of her friends.

The situation—that Sylvia was his long-term mistress and that Sylvia's husband was now her lover—was odd, but no stranger than many of the other entanglements at court and in their case the relationship was honest. Ivor not only knew about her relationship with Jerome but was deeply grateful, for it made his own affair with Sylvia far easier. The only person who disliked the arrangement was Sylvia. And Delia didn't give a rat's behind for Sylvia's feelings.

In 1921 she visited Virginia again and was there when her mother died unexpectedly from a heart attack. In 1922, taking Petra and Davina with her, she went on holiday with the Denbys to their villa at Rolle, on the shores of Lake Geneva. Jerome arranged to be in Switzerland at the same time, introducing Jack to the thrills of skiing and afterward spending a few leisurely days at Nyon, the neighboring village to Rolle.

Away from London society, Delia could relax and enjoy herself. Jack amiably coped with having eight-year-old Petra and seven-year-old Davina following him everywhere. Delia found the hours walking with Jerome along the flower-scented lake magical. Sometimes they wandered around the ruins of Nyon's Roman amphitheater. Sometimes they sailed. It was a blissful few days and when Jerome announced his intention of buying a villa at Nyon, Delia was ecstatic.

By the time 1923 dawned, Delia considered herself a very happy and fortunate woman. She had a husband whose company, on the social occasions when it was necessary for them to appear together, she found congenial. She had two healthy daughters. She had a lover who was also her best friend and who, amazingly considering his reputation, was faithful to her.

She enjoyed a privileged position in the most elite echelons of society. A member of the Prince of Wales's set, she enjoyed an easygoing friendly relationship with David. He liked American women and was the complete opposite of his staid, stuffy, dutiful father.

Life was fun and Delia never expected it to change.

When it did, things changed with such suddenness she was left gasping.

She had just arrived back in Cadogan Square after visiting the National Gallery with Cynthia Asquith.

Ivor was in the main drawing room, his back to her as he poured himself an extraordinarily large whiskey.

Without turning to face her, he said abruptly, "I'm afraid I'm to go to Cairo as an adviser to King Fuad who, with British backing, has just become king. It isn't a case of being there a few months. It's a diplomatic posting that is likely to extend for several years. Because of its nature it's essential I have my family with me. We are to leave in a month's time."

"Leave? Leave England to go to *Egypt*?"

Delia stared at his back, unable to take in the enormity of what he was telling her.

"Yes. I'm sorry, Delia."

Still not facing her, he drained the whiskey glass.

She dragged a purple cloche from her recently bobbed hair and threw it onto the nearest chair.

"It's impossible," she said flatly. "Wild horses wouldn't drag me from England to live in Egypt. There's still a revolution going on, isn't there?" The band around her heart at the thought of being separated from Jerome eased as she prepared to play her trump card. "You couldn't go," she said in a voice of sweet reason, "because you wouldn't be able to survive living so far away from Sylvia."

He turned around and she felt the world tilt beneath her

feet. His face was ashen. His eyes filled with unspeakable pain.

"Sylvia is in love with Theo, Girlington's elder son. Our affair is over, Delia. And I don't want to speak about it. I don't ever want to speak about it. As for the revolution, it ended when Egypt was granted partial independence. What the new king needs is for Britain to retain as much influence as possible—which is why I am being sent there."

"I won't go. You can't make me. Just because your life has been unexpectedly shattered—how long has her affair with the Earl of Grasmere been going on?—you can't expect me to disrupt mine."

"I'm sorry, Delia," he said for the second time. "But this isn't open to discussion. I leave for Egypt in a month's time. And you—and our children, unless you prefer to make other arrangements for them—are coming with me. Now, if you'll excuse me, I would like to be alone."

As she made no effort to leave him, he strode unsteadily past her.

Seconds later she heard the front door close.

Still she didn't move.

Egypt.

How could she possibly continue seeing Jerome if she were in Egypt? What would happen to them?

The answer came as with the roar of waves crashing on a beach.

He would be unfaithful. How could he be anything else? By his own admission he wasn't faithful by nature. Once they were separated by Europe and the Mediterranean his old habits would reassert themselves and there would be nothing, absolutely nothing, she would be able to do about it.

She never drank whiskey, had never drunk it in her life.

She crossed to the drinks cabinet.

Egypt. There would be no more Shibden Hall. There would be no more gay nights with the Prince of Wales and his friends. There would be no more country-house weekends. And above all, there would be no more Jerome.

She poured herself a whiskey as generous as the one Ivor had just drunk.

The villa Jerome had bought in Nyon would remain, by her at least, unvisited.

She drank the whiskey in three shudder-making gulps.

The way of life that meant so much to her was over—and a dreadful premonition told her she would never be so happy again.

SEVEN

Six weeks later she was standing by the rail of a P&O liner as the ship eased its way along the Egyptian coastline toward Alexandria. Ivor was in their stateroom, dictating letters to Mr. Willoughby. The new nanny she had hired shortly before sailing was a few feet away with Petra and Davina.

"When will we see the pyramids, Nanny Gunn?" Petra asked impatiently as they stared at a strangely flat countryside.

"And when will we see camels?" Davina asked, clinging to Nanny Gunn's hand.

"I'm not sure when we will see the pyramids, Petra." Miss Gunn, who came from Inverness, had a delightfully soft Scottish lilt to her voice. "And there will be camels in Alexandria, Davina."

Listening to her, Delia was sure that Kate Gunn was going to be a great success. Unlike the children's previous nanny she was young and pretty and more than capable of coping with the children.

Petra and Davina continued to chatter and as Kate Gunn answered their questions with gentle imperturbability, Delia continued to look toward land, her thoughts full of Jerome.

Was he already missing her as fiercely as she was missing him? Her kid-gloved hands gripped the rail. He had promised that he would visit Cairo often—but how long would it be before his first visit? And until he did, would he remain faithful? At the thought that he might not she felt a knife twist in her heart. It was a situation she would have to understand. How could she not, under the circumstances? The pain of it, though, would be more than she could bear.

As tears stung Delia's eyes, Davina shouted, "I can see a camel, Mama! *I can see a camel!*"

Blinking, Delia pretended to share her daughter's excitement, reflecting that she had unsuspected talents as an actress.

Even though they had two private carriages, the train from Alexandria to Cairo was unlike any she had ever traveled on. In the rear carriages people were packed in like sardines, even clinging outside on the roof. The heat was stifling; the smell overpowering.

"Why are all the men dressed in dirty nightshirts, Mama?" asked Petra. "Now we're in Egypt, Papa won't have to wear a nightshirt, will he?"

"No, of course not." Delia felt too out of sorts to explain further.

"And what about shoes?" Davina asked, noticing that the people she could see from the window didn't have anything on their feet. "Will Papa still wear shoes?"

Ivor chose this moment to rejoin them.

"Of course I will still wear shoes!" he snapped. "Miss Gunn, will you kindly keep my daughters occupied and see to it that they refrain from making such unsuitable remarks?"

"Yes, my lord," Kate Gunn said, unruffled. She withdrew two drawing books and a pack of crayons from the carpetbag she always carried. "Would you like to draw a scene?" she said to the girls. "When they are finished we'll send them to your aunt Gwen. I don't suppose she has ever seen a camel."

———

At Cairo a large reception committee greeted them. In heat that seemed to come out of the ground in waves they drove from the station: Delia, Ivor, and an Egyptian dignitary in the lead car; Kate Gunn, Petra, and Davina in the car following; Mr. Willoughby and Myers, Ivor's valet, in a third car; and the reception committee bringing up the rear.

"Your villa is in Garden City, Lord Conisborough," the Egyptian said in excellent English as their car turned onto a road in which trams, cars, horse-drawn gharries, overloaded mules, and stray sheep fought chaotically for space.

"Not Cairo?"

Delia was aware of Ivor's shoulders stiffening.

"Garden City is part of Cairo, Lord Conisborough," the dignitary said reassuringly. "The British residency and most of the ministries are situated there. It is a very elite part of the city. The grounds of your villa run down to the Nile."

Ivor's shoulders relaxed.

"We are now in Ibrahim Pasha Street," the man continued. "On your right is Shepheard's Hotel—very famous, very elegant. At the far end of the street is Abdin Palace, where tomorrow your lordship will have an audience with King Fuad. Now, however, we turn right. The building on the left is the Opera House—and very shortly we will be crossing Soliman Pasha Street, Cairo's Oxford Street."

Soliman Pasha Street, with its tiny shops and its goods all spilling out into the street, didn't look at all like Oxford Street, but Delia kept her thoughts to herself and, despite her heartache, began to look around with interest.

In front of them a camel, ridden by a small boy, was swaying with stately dignity down the center of the dusty, acacia-lined road. By the edge of the street a man with a monkey was amusing a passing group of women carrying gaily colored bundles on their heads. An overcrowded tram went past with people balancing precariously on its running board.

And then the crowds thinned until they were driving along a spacious avenue lined with sycamore trees. They turned and came to a halt in front of high wrought-iron gates. Seconds later two young boys in spotlessly white shirts opened them for the cars.

The house was long, low, and palatial and she gave a sigh of relief. Shaded verandas and balconies that reminded her a little of Sans Souci looked out over immaculately kept lawns and beyond the house was the magical sweep of the river. She could see a steamboat and dozens of smaller boats plying back and forth, each with a distinctive triangular white sail.

"Welcome to Nile House, Lord Conisborough, Lady Conisborough." An imposingly tall, very dark-skinned man wearing a royal-blue garment edged with gold braid stepped toward them and bowed deferentially. "I am Adjo. I have the honor of being Nile House's cahir."

"Cahir is a head housekeeper," the Egyptian who had accompanied them said helpfully in a low voice to Delia.

As Adjo bowed once again Delia flashed him a brilliant smile, saying, with the same easy familiarity she had always treated Bellingham and Parkinson, "Could we please have afternoon tea, Adjo? And could someone show Miss Gunn the children's rooms?"

"I want a room facing the river, Mama," Petra said urgently. "And it's so hot I want a cool white nightshirt to wear and—"

"And why were those little boys begging?" Davina interrupted.

Wishing heartily that her children understood there were occasions when they should be seen and not heard, Delia drew in a deep breath, about to silence them. She wasn't quite quick enough.

Ivor, who had transferred his attention from Adjo to the

dignitary, now whipped round, his eyes glacial. "Miss Gunn, take the children to their rooms *at once*!"

Kate Gunn's response was unflurried. "Yes, my lord," she said serenely. "Come along, Petra. Davina . . ."

Adjo clapped his hands and a young man slid quietly into the room and led Kate Gunn and Davina and Petra upstairs.

At another clap from Adjo two young men rolled in a white-naperied tea trolley. In a little dish there were slices of lemon and when Delia lifted the lid of the pot she saw that the tea was Earl Grey.

"Thank you, Adjo," she said gratefully, aware the kettle must have been boiling even before their car had turned in at the gates. "You're a treasure."

He bowed his head and she thought she saw a gleam of amusement in his eyes.

Only after she had been in Cairo for several months did she discover that Adjo, in Egyptian, meant "treasure."

The next morning Delia asked him the correct name for the garment he, and so many other Egyptians, wore.

"The word for such traditional clothing is a galabia, my lady," he said gravely. "And it is worn by all Egyptians, not just the fellahin."

"The fellahin?"

"The poor, my lady."

"And the name for the close-fitting red hats with a tassel that I saw when we drove through the city?"

"Sometimes they are called a fez, and sometimes a tarboosh—and only men wear them, my lady."

"But you don't wear one, Adjo. Is that because you are a cahir?"

Adjo folded his hands in front of him. "No, my lady. It is

because I am not a Muslim. Only Muslims wear the tarboosh and I am a Copt."

"And is a Copt a Christian?"

"The Coptic faith is one of the earliest forms of Christianity, my lady."

Delia enjoyed her conversations with Adjo and despite herself she also began to enjoy organizing her social life, and Petra and Davina's social life. Nearly every evening she and Ivor attended a formal function of one kind or another, either at the residency, the home of the British high commissioner, which was only a stone's throw from Nile House, or at Abdin Palace. Meanwhile, Petra and Davina were enjoying almost limitless freedom, for they had no school.

"The only one of excellent repute is the Mere de Dieu and the girls can't attend until they are twelve," Delia said reasonably when Ivor complained.

They were on their way to the high commissioner's birthday party. As the limousine purred its way down Garden City's main boulevard, Ivor said, "One of King Fuad's Egyptian advisers, Zubair Pasha, has suggested that Petra and Davina might like to have lessons with his daughter, Fawzia. She's nine, like Petra, and the girls could be chauffeured to his home every morning. It isn't far."

"And Davina?" Delia asked doubtfully. "She's a full year younger. Will she be able to keep up?"

"I don't know," Ivor said truthfully, "but as there seems to be no other suitable alternative we'll simply have to give it a try."

"Fawzia has an older brother," Petra said after she and Davina had finished their first week of lessons. "He's fourteen and he's very moody. I don't like him."

"Well, that doesn't matter, does it, honey?" Delia was in the middle of writing a letter to Jerome and she laid her pen down reluctantly. "He's so much older than you, that you'll never have much to do with him."

"No. I suppose not." Petra hesitated and then said wistfully, "He goes horseback riding out by the pyramids and sometimes Fawzia goes with him."

"Horseback riding?"

Petra now had her full attention for suddenly Delia knew what would lift her spirits. She would begin riding again. Not the genteel, Rotten Row riding which was the only kind she had indulged in for the last few years, but hard, fast, challenging gallops. The kind of riding she could do in the desert.

Making her daughter almost as happy as she was, Delia said, "There's a hotel out by the pyramids called the Mena House and it has stables and horses for hire. We'll go there on Saturday and I'll arrange for you to have lessons. If Fawzia's brother can ride out by the pyramids, then so can we."

Petra threw her arms around her mother then ran to tell Miss Gunn. Delia picked up her pen, eager to share her new resolution with Jerome. Riding in the desert wouldn't end the ache in her heart, but it would at least ease it.

Her life began to settle into a routine. Though there was formality at the residency and stultifying rituals at Abdin Palace, in all other aspects life in Cairo was far more relaxed than in London.

Mornings were spent either riding over hard-packed desert sand, or swimming in the Mena House pool. Later Delia would meet with friends for coffee at one of the two Groppi's tearooms, where the ice cream and the honey-drizzled pastries were to die for. Other days she would have coffee on the terrace at Shepheard's where there was a grandstand view of snake charmers, jugglers, and conjurors.

During the heat of the afternoon she rested at Nile House, the air cooled by the gently rotating mahogany paddles of a giant ceiling fan. Late afternoons were often spent at the Gezira Sporting Club, which was set on an island in the river and where there was always a wonderfully competitive sporting event taking place. Ivor played tennis there two or three times a week and they both enjoyed the polo matches.

Early evening was cocktail time. Dinner was often at the British residency—where three hundred could be seated for dinner comfortably—or at Abdin Palace, where the Oriental splendor was stupefying. If there was no formal function then she would dine with friends at Shepheard's or the Continental; sometimes, though not often, Ivor would join her. She was soon one of the diplomatic community's most successful hostesses, with everyone prizing an invitation to Nile House.

Jerome, often accompanied by Jack, visited at least three times a year. On such occasions Ivor often found a pretext for being in Alexandria. When Ivor was home, Jerome would want to sightsee farther down the Nile and as Ivor would then find he had vital business at Abdin Palace no eyebrows were raised when Delia acted as guide.

On these excursions Jack remained in Cairo, good-naturedly enduring Petra's blatant adoration.

On Ivor's annual visit to England Delia always accompanied him with Petra and Davina. For a few short weeks she was then able to renew her friendships with Clementine and Margot—and spend time with Jerome.

Their long separations never became any easier. Though none of her friends told her, she was sure there were occasionally other women in his life; women he didn't love as he loved her, but who were there nevertheless.

"For how much longer are we to remain in Cairo?" she asked Ivor despairingly at the end of 1925. "Surely the prime minister can find someone to replace you?"

"He could find someone to replace me as a financial adviser to King Fuad, but he couldn't find anyone to act as a mentor to Prince Farouk. The years I've spent earning Farouk's trust can't be thrown away, Delia. When he comes to the throne, he has to be a friend of Britain. It's the prime minister's belief that I have great influence with Farouk. That being the case, it's my patriotic duty to remain in Cairo. I'm sorry, Delia. Believe me, I wish things were different."

She turned away to hide her tears. For Ivor, Egypt was made bearable by the presence of Kate Gunn who, now that Petra and Davina were too old to need a nanny, had replaced Mr. Willoughby as his secretary. For Delia, there was no such comfort. The only thing that made life bearable was that Petra and Davina loved Egypt and had no desire to live anywhere else.

Unlike their mother, they never counted days off a calendar in the weeks leading up to a visit to London and both of them had been so appalled at the thought of going to school in England that Ivor arranged for them to attend Mere de Dieu in nearby Samalik Street.

"When they are older," Ivor said, "Petra can finish her education in England and go on to either Oxford or Cambridge."

When Petra celebrated her sixteenth birthday she showed no inclination to return to England.

"I might be academically able to go to Oxford or Cambridge, but I'm not interested enough," she said to her mother with some of Delia's Virginian bluntness.

"Jack's at Balliol," Delia said, trying to tempt her. "He thinks you'd love Oxford."

"By the time I went to St. Hilda's, Jack would no longer be at Balliol."

It was true and Delia knew that the battle was lost. When

her elder daughter dug her heels in, nothing on God's good earth would make her change her mind.

The day after Petra's adamant refusal to continue her education in England, Delia attended a garden party held at the home of one of Cairo's leading socialites, Princess Shevekiar. The princess, who had once been married to King Fuad before she had obtained a near-impossible divorce, was neither young nor beautiful, but she adored having young and beautiful people around her and was a great party-giver.

Delia was not surprised to see Fawzia's twenty-one-year-old brother, Darius, among the guests.

During the seven years she had lived in Cairo, Delia had become very fond of Fawzia, whose mother had died before the little girl was old enough to remember her. Darius—as Petra had pointed out years ago—kept himself very much to himself.

Unexpectedly he now made a beeline toward Delia. She was forced to admit that, moody or not, he was extraordinarily handsome. He always dressed in Western clothes and today he was wearing a gray-striped shirt and casual white trousers, a lock of his sleek black hair falling over his forehead.

He stood silently at Delia's side for a moment or two, surveying the other guests—nearly all British—and then said, "Are the British going to live in Egypt forever, d'you think?"

She was too startled to give him any kind of a reply and he said tightly, "They promised to leave in 1883. Did you know that? And they promised again in 1922 when they allowed us our so-called sovereignty and put Fuad on the throne. But they are still here. Are they ever going to go?"

"I don't know." It was a question no one had ever asked Delia before. She tried to imagine Cairo without the British and couldn't. "Don't the terms of the protectorate state that

Britain will leave the moment Egypt is capable of managing without her?"

"We're capable now!" His olive skin was tight over sharp cheekbones. "How would America respond if she was in the position Egypt is? You would act, wouldn't you? You would kick the British out, wouldn't you? And don't say you wouldn't, because a hundred and fifty years ago, that's exactly what you did!"

Delia looked around and was relieved to see that the British high commissioner wasn't within earshot.

"I don't think the situation was quite the same," she said. "And you have to take into consideration the help Britain has given Egypt. All the hospitals, schools—"

"The hospitals and schools have been for the English, not the Egyptians. The British have never drilled a well to bring drinking water to one of our villages. They never established medical services for Egyptians. They've never built schools or housing. They've never done *anything* to improve the living conditions of the ordinary Egyptian. They don't *care* how the vast majority of us live. They never even see the poor areas."

It was such an extraordinary outburst when half of the other guests were either high-ranking British advisers or civil servants, that Delia wondered if he was drunk.

"Westerners don't know the real Cairo," he said, his eyes narrowing. "They just see the British residency, Shepheard's, Groppi's, the Gezira Sporting Club, and the shops in Soliman Pasha Street."

From a little distance away Princess Shevekiar caught Delia's eye and waved gaily. Too near for comfort she saw Ivor in conversation with Ismail Sedki Pasha, the Egyptian prime minister.

"Seeing other parts of Cairo isn't an option, because it isn't safe," she told Darius reasonably, wondering if what he'd said was true.

"It would be safe with me. I could show you what the city is really like. Where would you like to go? The Citadel? The Mokattam Hills? The Old City?"

She could tell by the expression in his eyes that he was perfectly serious—and that he wasn't drunk. She also knew what Ivor's reaction would be if she were to tell him she was leaving the garden party in order to explore the less salubrious parts of Cairo with Zubair Pasha's handsome twenty-one-year-old son.

"The Old City," she said, deciding to merely leave Ivor a message saying she had left the garden party early and that he wasn't to worry. "How are we going to get there?"

"By tram," he said, and she could tell that he expected her to cry off going.

She *was* deeply shocked, but she only said, "That's fine, but not dressed like this. We need to stop at Nile House so that I can change into something a little less noticeable than a garden-party dress."

He nodded, seeing the sense of her suggestion. Five minutes later, after she left a message for Ivor with a footman, the two of them walked out of the garden.

"I don't suppose you've ever been on a tram before?" Darius said as they stepped from the gharry that had brought them from Nile House to the Number One tram stop at Ezbekiya Gardens.

"No." Delia was well aware that no one she knew had ever traveled on one either. "But I've always thought it looks far more exciting than traveling by car."

Within seconds of boarding she discovered that it was more than exciting. As the tram rumbled along the crowded streets it swayed like a ship in a gale. Delia also discovered that it was excruciatingly uncomfortable and that the smell of stale body odor was almost more than she could stand.

"The tram only goes to the old Roman fortress of Babylon," Darius said as with difficulty she resisted putting a handkerchief over her nose and mouth, "but since it's the very oldest part of Old Cairo, it's a good place to start."

"Babylon? That's a bit Old Testament, isn't it? Why is it called Babylon?"

"No one knows for sure. It's thought that one of the Pharaohs brought prisoners back from Babylon in Mesopotamia and that they were later given the site as a free colony. They named it after their homeland."

It was an interesting theory and one she doubted anyone else could have told her.

Once off the tram he took her into the old fort. She had expected to see only a few crumbling stones. Instead, the walls were massive in parts and the sandy space they enclosed was massive too. There were alleyways and gardens and five churches, some of them very pretty, all of them Coptic.

"Over there," Darius said, pointing across the courtyard, "is a lone synagogue that has quite a claim to distinction. The prophet Jeremiah is buried beneath it."

She was about to ask if they could take a closer look, when he said abruptly, "This isn't what I want you to see. I want you to see the people living outside the golden triangle of Garden City, Shepheard's, and Abdin Palace. I want you to see the streets of Old Cairo. They aren't far away. Just a short walk."

It was a walk from one world into another.

As they plunged into a maze of medieval alleys, the first thing that overwhelmed her was the stench. Not just cooking smells but unwashed bodies and raw sewage. The place was claustrophobic. Everyone was crowded into passageways so narrow that hardly any sunlight penetrated. Even with Darius at her side, protecting her, she was jostled in a way she had never experienced. The noise was incredible. Everyone seemed to be shouting at the top of their voices.

There were no other Westerners. Everywhere she looked she saw only turbans, red fezzes, hijabs, and all-covering veils.

Heaps of rubbish were everywhere. Tawdry shops, some little more than holes in walls, sold uncovered food. Ragged children had flies swarming around their eyes and their mouths. *She* had flies buzzing incessantly around her.

It was so hot, so fetid, that she could hardly breathe.

"People here live two or three families to a room—with no running water and no sanitation. Half the children die before they are five," he said grimly, sidestepping a pile of refuse. "How many of your friends at Shepheard's and the Gezira Sporting Club are aware of that, do you think?" His voice was taut with anger. "Our King doesn't care that Cairo's poorest live like this, and wealthy landowners like my father don't care, either."

Just when she thought she was going to faint, he said tersely, "Had enough?"

She nodded and they turned left into a crowded bazaar. "Back to the fortress," he said, making no comment on the indescribable poverty they had just witnessed.

At the far end of the bazaar they reached a street that was a little broader, a little less crowded. Heat shimmered up from the ground and she watched Darius drop some coins and a beggar grabbing at them and shouting a grateful *"Shukran! Alhamdulillah!"*

As a muezzin called the faithful to prayer, Darius said abruptly, "Do you speak any Arabic?"

"I can say 'good morning' and 'good evening' and I know that *'shukran'* means 'thank you' and that *'Alhamdulillah'* means 'thank God.' "

"That isn't much after seven years."

Not for the first time she noticed that he avoided ever addressing her as Lady Conisborough.

"Maybe not," she said, aware that their relationship had changed. "But as all the Egyptians I meet speak either English or French or both I've had no need to study Arabic. And it isn't an easy language to learn."

"Maybe not, but when you make your home in a city, it's polite to be able to speak a little of the language, don't you think?"

She nodded, wondering what Ivor's reaction was going to be when she announced she was going to learn Arabic.

"You won't be the first member of your family to learn Arabic," he said. "Davina asked Adjo for lessons a long time ago."

"She did?"

Her surprise was so obvious that he said, "She didn't want her father to know in case he put an end to them."

They reached the tram stop and Delia saw with relief that the tram going back to Ezbekiya Gardens wasn't as crowded as the one they had taken out. When they were seated on one of the dirty slatted seats, she said, "Even though my husband is a friend of your father's, you don't like him, do you?"

"You're right," he said. "I don't like him. I don't like any British, except for Davina who is, after all, half American—and Jack."

"Jack?" Delia felt as if the day's surprises would never end. "I didn't realize that when Jack visited you and he spent time together."

His eyes met hers. "That," he said drily, "is because when Jack visits Cairo, his father travels south, to Aswan. And that when he does, you go with him."

To change the subject fast, she said bluntly, "Are you more than just a nationalist, Darius? Are you one of the students at Fuad I University that my husband calls revolutionaries who ought to be imprisoned?"

"Yes," he said without hesitation. "I am one of the students your husband would like to see imprisoned. I want the British

out of my country. I want Egypt to be ruled by Egyptians—
not a king the British put on our throne, a king who is three-
quarters Albanian. As long as Fuad is on the throne Egypt will
never become independent."

She looked behind them swiftly to make sure no one was
sitting near enough to overhear him.

He smiled. "Even if people overhear me, no one who travels by tram is going to take issue with what I've said. Outside
the palace circle—a circle that includes my father—Egyptians
want Egypt for Egyptians. It's as simple as that."

The tram rattled and swayed. At every stop more and more
galabia-dressed fellahin got on board. Delia remained silent,
knowing that her own situation wasn't either plain or simple.
She couldn't tell Ivor that Darius was a revolutionary. If she
did he would refuse to allow either Petra or Davina to visit
Zubair Pasha's home again.

And she would have to admit that she sympathized with
Darius's position that the British were in a country they had
promised to leave years ago.

Even as it was, the sights she had seen that afternoon were
going to strain her relationship with Ivor, for she was certainly
going to tell him that as an adviser to King Fuad he should
advise the king on how to help his impoverished people into
the twentieth century—something he would say was none of
his business.

He would simply not understand, but Jerome would.

Jerome.

Apart from brief interludes, they had been separated for
seven years. How much longer was their separation going to
last? For how much longer could she remain the most important person in his life when he so seldom saw her and when so
many young London socialites were, she was sure, only too
willing to take her place in his heart?

Part Two

PETRA

1930–1933

EIGHT

Petra was lying flat on her back next to Jack on the grass beside the tennis court at Nile House. They had just finished a hard-fought game and were in a state of pleasant exhaustion.

"I don't think anyone else knows, apart from myself and Davina—and now you—but Darius is a very committed Egyptian nationalist," she said, shading her eyes from the sun.

"I doubt it." Jack swatted a fly away from his face. "Fawzia probably just told you he was in an attempt to impress you."

"How would her brother wanting to kick my father out of Egypt impress me? I think she was speaking the truth and I'm rather glad, as now I don't feel bad about not liking him."

"Are you sure you don't like him?" There was teasing amusement in Jack's voice. "Last year I thought you had a crush on him."

Beneath her tan Petra blushed and sat up so her back was toward him. "Last year I was fifteen and didn't know better."

"That's good. I don't like the thought of you mooning over Zubair Pasha's heir." Though there was still amusement in his voice there was also something else, something which caused her to blush even more furiously.

He rolled over to lie on his side, resting his weight on one arm, saying, "Do you think Zubair Pasha knows of Darius's political inclinations?"

"God, no! He'd skin him alive if he did." She hugged her knees. "Zubair Pasha is very pro-British. If he wasn't, my father wouldn't be such close friends with him." Her blush had safely receded and she turned toward Jack again. "As it is, Papa is almost as close to him as he is to your father."

"Which is why it's such a shame your father has meetings in Alexandria for nearly the entire length of our stay. They must both be bitterly disappointed, but it seems always that way. The last time we were here your father had to attend a meeting in Alexandria. I'm not sure, but I think my father caught up with him there for a few days. I had to stay in London for the Foreign Office exam."

"Is the Foreign Office the reason you're so interested in Darius's politics?"

He plucked a blade of grass. "No. It's just I've known Zubair Pasha's family for almost as long as you have and I've always liked Darius. I wouldn't like to see him end up in a British prison."

"Land's sakes!" The blood drained from her face. "Is that what could happen?"

It wasn't often she used any of her mother's Virginian expressions and despite the grimness of the subject, a smile twitched at the corner of his mouth.

"If he's joining the violent extremists, yes. If he's merely a member of the Wafd, which is a pukka political party calling for full independence, then possibly not."

"He may be a member of Wafd. I don't know. All I'm certain of is that his father doesn't know of his opinions."

"And does your father?"

"Do you mean did I tell him what Fawzia told me? Of course I didn't. I'm not a sneak. Besides, if my father were to suspect how anti-British Darius is, he'd probably forbid me to see Fawzia."

Jack picked up his tennis racket and rose to his feet. "How

is the lovely Fawzia? I'm surprised she didn't leave the Mere de Dieu and go to the lycée when you did. She's bright enough."

Petra stood up and brushed the grass from her tennis skirt. "She may be bright, but she's also lazy. For all her Western attitudes, life in a harem would suit Fawzia down to the ground."

He chuckled. "You're wrong, Petra. Lying about eating chocolates would make her fat—and Fawzia would die rather than lose her figure. She would also hate to wear veils when out in public. Hiding her beauty is not something Fawzia would ever do."

Crossly Petra picked up her racket and began walking back to the house. Fawzia *was* beautiful, but Petra didn't much like hearing Jack say so. She looked across at him. In his white shirt and flannels, his curly hair slicked back, he was stunningly good-looking. Over the last year, since he had left Oxford, he had become a very sharp dresser. Like his father, he stood out in any crowd. She just didn't want him doing so with Fawzia at his side.

As they neared the terrace, Davina stepped through the French doors and shouted good-naturedly, "Come on, you two. Hurry up and get changed. You're going to be late for lunch and, as Papa is away and Uncle Jerome is here, we're eating Virginian fashion. Fried chicken and lemon pie."

Petra smiled. Her mother was always in an exceptionally good mood when Jack and his father visited. Later on they were all going to the Gezira Sporting Club where Jack had been invited to play polo.

"The Prince of Wales played polo at the Gezira when he visited Cairo in 1922," Delia said chattily to Jack as lunch was served. "It was before we came here, but it's still talked about."

She was wearing a new calf-length lemon silk dress. A heavy amber necklace hung to precisely the right depth of the softly draped neckline and her fiery-red hair had been tamed into a cap of fashionably sleek waves.

"That's only because one of the other players was Seifallah Youssri Pasha," Davina said, helping herself to green beans in a mustard sauce. For her uncle Jerome's benefit, she added, "Youssri Pasha was one of the club's first Egyptian members— and he still plays a mean game of polo. If you're Egyptian you have to be royalty or an intimate friend of royalty to be a member of the Gezira. Darius is only a member because his father is such a close confidant of the King. He'll be playing this afternoon."

"Interesting," Jack said, his eyes meeting Petra's across the table.

She knew what he was thinking. Why on earth was Darius playing polo at the Gezira, when the club epitomized the foreign domination he hated?

"And talkin' of the Prince of Wales," Delia said, bringing the conversation back in the direction she had initially been trying to steer it, "everyone in Cairo was mightily disappointed that he didn't play polo when he was here last spring on his way back to London after tourin' Kenya and Uganda. He just viewed some antiquities. Even Ivor didn't get a glimpse of him. What is the London gossip, Jerome? Has he really left Freda Dudley Ward? Gwen wrote me that he has eyes for no one but Lady Furness."

Petra was intrigued to see that Jerome looked distinctly uncomfortable. "For goodness' sake, Delia," he said in fond exasperation. "Do you really expect me to discuss such a subject in front of Petra and Davina?"

"It won't shock them. You forget they live in Cairo. They're quite used to scandal."

Davina and Petra both raised their eyebrows. Scandals were never discussed in front of them. The very thought would give their father a fit, but neither girl was about to say so. Not when the conversation was so interesting.

"Well, if you must have scandal over the lunch table, yes—Gwen is doing a good job of keeping you up-to-date."

"She may be keepin' me up-to-date, but she doesn't have access to as much inside gossip as you. Do King George and Queen Mary know of David's latest infatuation?"

"Who," Davina asked, "is David? I thought you were talking about the Prince of Wales."

"He's known as David to his family and friends, honey."

"And are you one of his friends?" Davina was clearly impressed.

Petra rolled her eyes, annoyed at having her mother sidetracked.

Delia, who never minded talking about the Prince, said breezily, "I was before I left England. We are about the same age and he likes Americans. Freda Dudley Ward's mother is American and I'm guessin' Thelma Furness is half American."

"Her father was U.S. consul in Buenos Aires," Jerome said. "Her mother is Irish American and *her* mother was Chilean and reportedly a descendant of Spain's royal house of Navarre. Which is why Thelma is pronounced the Spanish way: Tel-ma."

Petra sighed. From her rare visits she knew how fascinated Virginians were with family trees. If she wasn't very careful the conversation was going to veer off onto Spanish royalty and she would be left no wiser about the Prince of Wales's current love life.

"The King and Queen, Uncle Jerome," she said, prompting him in a way she could never have if her father had been present. "Do Their Majesties know about Lady Furness?"

Jerome smiled. "The answer is that I don't think they do.

Not yet. And now that you're sixteen, Petra, I think you're old enough to drop the honorary 'uncle' title. If your mother agrees, of course."

He looked across at Delia whose eyes held his for so long, Petra actually thought she was going to object.

"Of course not," Delia's voice was filled with warmth. "So silly to use it when you are most definitely not her uncle."

"No, indeed."

Petra wasn't sure, but she thought her mother blushed. As this was patently ridiculous, she wondered if her mother had been wise to serve hot spicy chicken when the temperature was in the nineties.

"And what is the gossip about Margot?" Delia asked. "How is she coping with widowhood?"

"She spends most days at the House of Commons, in the Ladies' Gallery."

"And the Churchills?"

"I haven't seen Clemmie for a while. Winston is very hang-dog. To be honest, I quite understand his depression. Unemployment is escalating—George Curzon's son-in-law, Oswald Mosley, was recently asked to solve the problem, but the cabinet has blocked every scheme he's put forward. I suspect that by the time I get back to London he will have resigned. In Germany, unemployment is even worse. Winston actually thinks it will bring that ruffian Hitler to power."

Petra stopped listening. London gossip about the Prince of Wales was riveting. London gossip about politics wasn't. Jerome, however, was a Liberal member of Parliament and politics was one of his favorite topics of conversation.

From the other side of the table Jack gave her a wink. It was a common joke between them that when her father wasn't there, the atmosphere often bordered on the risqué.

"It's because Mama is an American," she had once said a little apologetically. "And not just an American, but a Virginian. She seems to think she can say whatever she pleases to whomsoever she pleases—and she's embarrassingly affectionate to the servants. Bellingham and Parkinson were always treated as members of the family—and she's no different with Adjo. He speaks to her as if she's an equal, not an employer, much to my father's fury."

"However free and easy she is, it works," Jack had said. "All the homes you've lived in have had the most welcoming atmosphere I've ever experienced. And there are never any staff problems. No one who's worked for your mother ever wants to leave her."

Petra was brought back to the present moment by her mother saying in a voice that brooked no argument: "I'm not surprised the Denbys are divorcing. He's an awful screw."

"Screw?" Davina said.

"Mean with money, pet. Never marry a man who is mean with his money, because he'll be mean with his affection as well." And deeming it an appropriate note on which to end lunch, Delia rose to her feet.

It was customary for everyone to retire to their rooms after the meal, to sleep until it was cooler.

Petra had far too much on her mind to rest. Staring up at her ceiling fan, she replayed the scene by the tennis court when Jack said he didn't like the idea of her mooning over Darius. Had he meant he would far prefer her to be mooning over him? And if he had, how did she feel about that?

Though everyone referred to Fawzia as being her closest friend, Jack was really her best friend and had been so for as long as she could remember. Could they ever become romantically involved? And would she even want to?

She thought of the way his hair curled at the nape of his neck, of his finely chiseled mouth and the slight cleft in his chin. She loved his perpetual good humor and the way he always made her laugh.

And then she thought of Darius.

She didn't *like* Darius, but he certainly had an effect on her. Just what the nature of that effect was, though, she couldn't decide. It certainly wasn't romantic in the way she envisioned romance. How could being intimidated be romantic? She thought of the narrow slanting eyes set above high cheekbones, of the intensity of his lean, dark face. Her mother had once said that Darius reminded her of Rudolph Valentino. There was the same panther-like grace about him, the same sense of barely controlled power.

She would much rather be with Jack than with Darius.

But it was Darius she couldn't get out of her head.

The Gezira Sporting Club had four polo grounds and Jack and Darius were to play on number one.

"Though on opposing sides," Petra heard Davina say to Jerome. "Jack will be playing on the visitors' team. They usually lose against the home teams."

"They may very well win today," Jerome said drily. "Jack is a barbarian on the polo field."

Davina giggled, but Petra didn't. She was sure that if any rider proved to be a barbarian it would be Darius and she didn't want to see Jack unhorsed.

The stands were crowded with Cairo's crème de la crème. Delia was in her element. "Don't you just wish you were goin' to play today?" she said to Jerome. "I know I do. The minute we have a women's polo team I'll be first on the field!"

Happy at having her girls at either side of her, she acknowledged a nod from the British high commissioner and then shot a dazzling smile in the direction of Zubair Pasha who, with Fawzia, was walking toward them.

"Seeing Jack and Darius on opposing teams is quite an event, isn't it?" Delia said as he and Fawzia seated themselves.

"It is indeed, Lady Conisborough." Zubair Pasha beamed broadly. "And making it even more special is that Fawzia is to present the winning trophy."

Petra leaned forward and looked at her friend who grinned, her self-satisfaction so evident she was positively purring. Petra smiled back, happy for her. No one loved being the center of attention more than Fawzia.

When the eight riders trotted onto the field Petra saw that Jack was assigned the Number Two place on his team, a position that required a keen eye and high maneuverability. Darius was Number Three on the opposing team, a position always given to the best player.

"Since you were a member of a crack cavalry regiment, you must be an excellent player also," Zubair Pasha said to Jerome.

"I carry a nine-goal handicap."

Zubair Pasha was impressed. "Then I should like to see you play. Though not for the visitors," he added with a chuckle. "With Darius."

As one of the mounted umpires prepared to start the match by bowling the ball between the two teams, all chatter ceased.

Moments later Darius made a long powerful hit, feeding the ball to his Number Two and a roar of applause went up.

From then on, play continued at terrific speed. The visitors' Number Four player made a backhanded stroke, shooting the ball away from their goal and toward his own teammates. Despite Darius riding hard against him, Jack scored a goal.

Petra rose to her feet, cheering till she was hoarse. Only when she sat down did she realize that Fawzia, too, had been on her feet.

"I think she has a crush on Jack," Davina said to Delia under the cover of applause. "Have you seen her expression? Her eyes are on him the entire time."

As one chukker followed another, with both Jack and Darius changing their exhausted ponies, Petra realized that Davina was right and that Fawzia was most certainly not rooting for her brother's team. Despite the presence of her father, she was rooting for Jack.

In the sixth and final chukker, with the home team ahead on goals, both sides played more and more aggressively.

"Land's sakes!" Delia said anxiously. "I hope Jack doesn't unseat Darius. Darius would never forgive him."

"They're both going to fall if they aren't careful," Jerome said tautly and then, barely before he'd finished speaking, Darius broke into a full gallop, bearing down on Jack who was in possession of the ball.

The crowd rose to its feet.

Jack tried to twist his pony away to avoid being hit, but was a split second too late. The impact was enormous. Both Jack and Darius were sent flying to the ground. Fawzia screamed. Umpires raced to the scene. Zubair Pasha and Jerome hurried from the stands.

"Oh God!" Delia said devoutly. "Oh *dear* God!" Her face was ashen.

As first-aiders ran to join the umpire and as the other players slid from their saddles, the air was filled with dread. Fatal polo accidents were not unknown and, as neither Jack nor Darius showed any signs of movement, everyone was gripped by the worst possible fear.

Fawzia had her hands to her mouth, but Petra remained motionless. In a moment of blinding clarity she knew that if Jack was dead, her life would have lost all meaning.

"You can't die," she whispered fiercely. "Move, Jack! For God's sake, *move!*"

He did—and she gave a sob of relief that came from the profoundest depth of her being.

An ambulance drew up and men with stretchers ran across

the field. As Jack was helped into a sitting position, Darius opened his eyes and Jerome turned toward the stands and gave a thumbs-up.

Petra watched as Jack was helped to his feet and Darius, now conscious and with what appeared to be a broken leg, was placed on one of the stretchers.

The relief in the crowd was palpable.

"Thank God," Delia was saying over and over again. "Thank *God*."

Petra was thanking God too, but she was also aware that during the entire drama her total concern had been for Jack. Darius had barely entered her thoughts.

NINE

Within weeks of the polo match Delia announced that she had arranged for Petra to spend the next two years at an international school for girls in Montreux.

"It's all arranged, honey." On this issue, if on no other, Delia was determined to brook no argument. "And before you kick up a fuss, let me tell you that it's either Montreux or a finishing school in New England."

Unaccustomed to such implacability from her usually indulgent mother, Petra was appalled.

"Don't be," Jack had written back after she had poured out her woes in a letter.

Montreux is only a little over forty miles from Dad's chalet at Nyon. We'll be able to meet up far more often than in Cairo. And think of the skiing. You'll have the time of your life.

Knowing that Jack wouldn't let her down and that he would visit his father's chalet every opportunity he could, she allowed herself to be shipped off to Montreux.

It was far more fun than she had anticipated.

Only when she found herself surrounded by a dozen girls

all her own age and from similarly privileged backgrounds did she realize just how circumscribed her life had been in Cairo. There, she'd had only Davina and Fawzia to gossip and laugh with—but Davina had barely left childhood behind her and outside of school Fawzia was allowed very little freedom. It was a situation that didn't give the three of them much racy subject matter. Within days of settling in at the Institut Mont-Fleuri she discovered that the conversation was hardly ever *not* racy.

Petra was in a class of ten split up into two dormitories. Inevitably, lights-out talks ensured that she and the other four girls became very close.

She wrote to Jack.

Suzi de Vioget is French, and manages to be sensationally attractive without being classically beautiful.

She had paused there, wondering whether to mention that Suzi had celebrated her seventeenth birthday by losing her virginity with the Mont-Fleuri ski instructor. On reflection, it was information she decided not to share. She didn't want him thinking she would do the same.

Magda von der Leyen is a member of the German aristocracy and her mother has just married for the umpteenth time. It doesn't matter what male name is mentioned, if he is over forty and has a title, at one time or another he's been Magda's stepfather.

Annabel Mowbray is English and is the great-niece of my mother's friend, Lady Denby.

Boudicca Pytchley is also English. She was conceived in Coventry and is named after Queen Boadicea. She has a terrific crush on the Prince of Wales and our dorm is

plastered with pictures of HRH launching ships, shoot-
ing big game and looking dinky in a kilt. When she es-
capes from Mont-Fleuri and comes out (we're planning
on all three of us being presented on the same day) she's
determined to capture his attention. If she becomes the
next Queen she says she'll attend the coronation bare-
breasted in tribute to her namesake.

Life at school was far from dull. Though the headmistress kept an eagle eye on the girls, they often managed to escape—as Suzi's adventure with their ski instructor proved. One of the most exclusive boys' schools in the world, Le Rosey, was at nearby Rolle and, despite all the teachers' efforts, a great deal of fraternization took place.

"Which is exactly what my mother hoped when she sent me here," Annabel said when the five of them had set off for an illicit assignation. "Every pupil at Le Rosey is either royal or rich as Croesus. Snaring one of them as a future husband would reassure my mother that my fees here had been worthwhile."

They all talked about boys nonstop, but Petra never mentioned Jack. That a family friend had a chalet at Nyon was known both to her friends and to the staff. What was also known was that her mother visited Nyon three or four times a year and that there was absolutely nothing extraordinary about Petra making occasional visits.

These visits only ever occurred when Jerome was also at Nyon. "It just isn't on, now that you're seventeen and I feel about you as I do, for the two of us to meet at the chalet when there is no one else there but the staff," Jack said when, with Suzi's seduction of the ski instructor in mind, she had suggested they do so. "Your father would regard it as a gross breach of trust and I have too much affection and respect for him to want that to happen. What we can do, though, is meet up in Montreux or Rolle."

Doing so was exciting, but was still not as steamily romantic as she yearned for their meetings to be.

When she began her second year at Mont-Fleuri Jack was posted to the British embassy in Lisbon. Every so often, when Jerome was at Nyon, he took Petra out and would let slip that as well as working hard, Jack was also socializing a lot.

"Ever since the war, Portugal seems to have become a haven for exiled royalty," Jerome said as they strolled companionably by the lake. "The daughter of the Marquis de Fontalba is featuring large in Jack's letters at the moment. If anything should come of it his mother would be enormously pleased."

She had bitten her lip and made no response. The daughter of the Marquis de Fontalba made no appearance at all in Jack's letters to her. Petra tried to take this as a sign that he wasn't seriously involved, but as the months went by she couldn't help wondering if he still felt the same way about her as she did about him.

"Do I know if Jack is on the verge of becoming engaged?" Delia repeated, surprised, when she visited Nyon shortly before Petra was due to leave the Institut. "What an odd question, honey. If he had, surely he would have written and told you. You two are close buddies, aren't you?"

"Well, of course we are. I was asking because he's going to be in London for my coming-out ball and I'm thinking of introducing him to Magda." There was no way she was going to tell her mother the real reason. If Jack did have someone else she didn't want her mother to know about her own hopes. "I think Jack is probably just Magda's type."

"Maybe he is, but Magda is still seventeen and Jack is twenty-five. It wouldn't be a good idea, Petra. Trust me."

It was a remark she took note of. If that was her mother's opinion of a seven-year age difference then it would clearly be safest not to say more.

Delia had visited Switzerland alone. "It's term time for

Davina," she had explained. "And as there has been another violent outbreak of anti-British feeling in Cairo, your father has felt it his duty to remain on the spot."

It was an explanation that Petra saw nothing odd about.

Petra had permission to stay out in the evening and Delia booked dinner at a restaurant close to the school.

Jerome had come from London to meet up with them for a few days. Aware of how hungry Delia always was for royal gossip, he said as the wine waiter filled their glasses, "George Curzon's daughter, Alexandra, has become a part of the Prince of Wales's set since she married the Prince's best friend, Fruity Metcalfe."

"I don't suppose her sister and her husband are." With great difficulty Delia resisted the temptation to reach out and touch his hand. "Gwen wrote me that Tom was so disgruntled when his unemployment bill was rejected that he left the Labour Party—and that his doing so is causing quite a furor."

"Most things Mosley does cause a furor."

He sounded amused, as he always did when in her mother's company. Looking at him, Petra realized that for a man in his late forties he was still startlingly attractive. His immaculately clipped mustache showed no hint of gray and his hair, though silvered at the temples, was still thick and curly. It meant Jack, too, would keep his looks.

"I thought the Mosley who had married a Curzon was called Oswald, not Tom?" Petra asked, distracting herself from thinking about Jack.

"He is." Delia took a sip of wine and then added, "Only he's known as 'Tom' to family and friends. And Alexandra is known as 'Baba.' "

Petra rolled her eyes. Why her mother's friends couldn't go through life with the names they had been christened with she couldn't begin to imagine. Fruity and Baba. They sounded like something out of a nursery rhyme.

She let her attention drift and it wasn't until the dessert trolley made its appearance that she again paid attention to the conversation.

". . . and so Aunt Rose, who is a friend of Wallis's aunt, has asked me to do all I can to ease Wallis and her husband's entrée into London society."

Even though Delia's aunt was now her stepmother, Delia hadn't altered the way she addressed her, a course of action Petra approved of.

"There is precious little I can do in Cairo," Delia continued. "But perhaps you could do something, Jerome?"

"I'll do my best."

Not for the first time, Petra was aware that Jack's father always did everything he could to please her mother. "I'll need to know a little about the woman," he said with his indefatigable good humor. "What is her background, do you know?"

"Some of her mother's relations live in Virginia, not too far from Sans Souci. Bessie Merryman, her aunt, visits them regularly—which is how Rose got to know her. Wallis, though, was born in Baltimore. She divorced her first husband—an American who, from Rose's account, was absolutely ghastly—and her second husband is British and a partner in a firm which buys and sells ships."

At the expression on Jerome's face, Petra stifled a giggle.

After playing for time by choosing a raspberry pavlova from the dessert trolley, he said with remarkable restraint, "Forgive me for saying so, Delia, but the Simpsons don't sound very promising material. As she is a divorcée an invitation to a royal garden party is out of the question and I can't quite see the Digbys or the Denbys taking them up—or anyone else for that matter."

"I shouldn't think Wallis would want to meet old fogies like Cuthie or Lord Denby. What I had in mind was an introduction to the more raffish elements of the Prince of Wales's set. I thought perhaps she could be introduced to Thelma Furness, a fellow American who must be about the same age . . . ?"

Delia let the sentence hang in the air, hopefully.

"I'll do my best, but bear in mind that Thelma Furness has eaten better men than me for breakfast." There was teasing humor in his voice. "Still, if that's the danger you want me to face . . ."

To Petra's amazement, her mother giggled in exactly the same way Suzi de Vioget often giggled.

It was most disconcerting.

Just as she had realized what a seriously attractive man Jack's father still was, so she realized that though her mother was thirty-nine she was still bewitchingly lovely. It was a beauty enhanced by her American vitality and wholesomeness and by the glorious color of her hair which would, Petra suspected, still be as red—by fair means or foul—when she was in her dotage.

She turned her thoughts to her immediate future. In another few weeks she would be leaving Mont-Fleuri to be presented at court. She would be sharing all the fun of being a debutante with Annabel and Boudicca and was looking forward immensely to all the razzmatazz.

"Your mother was a married woman when she was presented," her aunt Gwen said to her fondly as they waited for the third fitting of her court gown. "Under normal circumstances she would have been presented by her mother-in-law but as your grandmother was dead, Sylvia did the honors."

"I didn't know that. How odd. They never spend a lot of time together. I don't think Sylvia has visited Egypt once in all the time we've been there. I expect they'll be meeting up now Mama is in London. She's happy as a lark to be here for my coming-out season."

"And I'm as happy as a lark that she's here. She's so full of life she makes even me feel young." Her age-spotted hand patted Petra's. "Now we're going to have a rehearsal today with shoes, feathers, and fan, aren't we? I'm so glad you haven't opted for one of the fashionable high-fronted gowns. An evening dress should always be becomingly low—especially when you have a nice bosom to display. Your mother looked exquisite in her presentation gown. I came to her fittings as well. She was fresh from Virginia and rather shy and nervous. It's hard to believe that now, isn't it?"

For Petra, it wasn't hard. It was impossible.

Ever since they had arrived back in London together, Delia had socialized with fury, making contact with all her old friends and making lots of new ones, including Wallis Simpson.

"Wallis had absolutely no need of help in becoming acquainted with Thelma," Delia said, returning to Cadogan Square from a cocktail party at the Simpsons' Bryanston Square flat. "She's an old friend of Benjamin Thaw's and Bennie is married to Thelma's sister. I like her a lot—Wallis that is, not Consuelo Thaw. Consuelo is far too . . ." She paused, seeking the right word. "Too unconventional," she said at last. "Your father wouldn't approve of me spendin' time with her, and as for you, Consuelo is completely off-limits. Don't ask me why, honey. Just trust me."

She shrugged herself out of a small chinchilla shoulder cape. "Thelma is in a different category—mainly because the Prince of Wales thinks she's the bee's knees and so it's impossible for anyone to get away with snubbing her." Delia reached into her handbag for her cigarette case. "I wonder when he's going to end his unhealthy fascination for married women and start payin' attention to someone he can wed? Perhaps when you've been presented you could catch his eye. My cousin Beau would have loved the idea of my bein' mother-in-law to the future King of England."

She paused, the cigarette case in her hand, her eyes brilliant with memory.

"And are you back hobnobbing with Prince Edward?" Petra asked, before her mother could start reminiscing about her girlhood at Sans Souci.

"I'm not sure 'hobnobbing' is the right word, pet. I've known David—I can't refer to him as Edward, he hates it—far longer than most of the other people in his set and that counts for somethin'. But the King regards your father as a friend—and has done for twenty-odd years."

She lit a cigarette. "David," she said, after blowing a thin plume of smoke into the air, "is never one hundred percent comfortable with his father's friends. He's afraid the King will learn too much about his involvement with unsuitable married women."

"Then there's no chance of his coming to a cocktail party here so I can introduce him to Boo?"

"Boudicca?" Delia's eyebrows rose. "Honey, she's eighteen. No matter how crazy she may be about him, HRH would barely register her presence. He only takes an interest in women around the thirty-year mark. And talking of your friends . . . is Jack going to be in London to act as your escort at Annabel's party?"

"Yes." Her heart slammed as it always did when Jack's name was mentioned.

Delia decided against the cigarette and stubbed it out. "I've told Lady Mowbray there's nothing untoward about his being your escort. He's such an old family friend he's almost like a bro—" Her rush of words came to an abrupt end as she coughed so hard Petra thought she was going to choke.

"Do you want some water?" she asked. "You really should stop smoking, Mama. Coughing like a tramp isn't very elegant."

Delia, still coughing, shot her a glance so aggrieved that

Petra wanted to laugh, but instead she crossed the drawing room to the art-deco cocktail cabinet and hastily poured a glass of soda water.

"Here," she said to her mother. "Drink this. Now what was it you were going to say?"

Delia drank and then made an expressive gesture with her hand. "I can't remember. I think I was just about to point out that even *pre*-presentation parties are an ideal opportunity for husband-hunting and so attending one with Jack as your escort is probably not very sensible. It will give out the wrong signal. People might assume things I wouldn't want. If you are not going to try for Oxford and plan to husband-hunt instead, then you need a young man with far more wealth and position than dear Jack."

Petra was truly shocked. "That's the most snobbish thing I've ever heard you say!"

Delia looked suitably discomfited. "And probably the most unnecessary as Davina tells me you have your sights set on Darius. Now if I were *really* uppity I'd object to the idea of an Egyptian son-in-law—even though he is a Copt—but I don't, or at least not much. I just want you to meet lots of other eligible young men. Marryin' the first person you think you've fallen in love with isn't sensible. It's too easy to make a mistake and, when your father is a friend of the King, mistakes of that kind aren't easy to rectify." As if she was afraid she had said a trifle too much, she added swiftly, "And now I must hurry and have a bath. I'm having dinner at Margot's this evening and I'm tight for time."

Before Petra could speak, her mother whirled from the room.

Petra crossed to the cocktail cabinet again and mixed herself a pink gin—a vice her mother was unaware she had acquired. As her mother was so opposed to the idea of her having a romantic relationship with Jack, it was exceedingly useful that Davina had innocently suggested she was carrying a torch for Darius.

She took a sip of her cocktail. That her American, unconventional mother was, in reality, a dyed-in-the-wool snob when it came to who was or who was not eligible was a profound revelation. If her dreams were to become reality, she and Jack would need all her father's support. That they would have it she didn't doubt. For one thing, he and Jack's father were friends, and for another, when it had come to his own marriage, her father hadn't cared that her mother had neither grand family connections nor wealth.

Delia was obviously influenced by her many friends who were also bringing out daughters that season. Lady Denby, for instance, a very old chum, was cock-a-hoop that Annabel had snared a White Russian prince and was already engaged and sporting an emerald the size of an egg on her left hand.

Prince Fedya Tukhachevsky, the elder brother of one of the Le Rosey boys, was reasonably attractive and great fun. Annabel was sincerely in love with him. Petra also knew that if it hadn't been for his title, there was little chance Annabel would have accepted him. It was the prospect of becoming Princess Tukhachevsky that had rolled the dice in Fedya's favor.

If Petra had wanted, she could have made a far more prestigious conquest. Mohammad Reza was an exceptionally handsome Persian student who had never troubled to hide the fact that he had a crush on her. She had given him no encouragement, but she knew every single one of her classmates would have, for Mohammad Reza was the elder son of the Shah of Persia. His future wife would one day be an empress.

Aware of her parents' reaction if they learned she had discouraged the attentions of the future ruler of Persia, she turned her thoughts to Jack. He had promised months ago that he would be in London for her presentation. She had ringed the date in red on a calendar kept beneath her pillow.

Apart from the snippets of information his father gave her—information which was of a kind she'd rather not have had—it was hard to come by gossip about Jack's social life in Lisbon. He wrote to her mother almost as regularly as he wrote to his father, but Delia's only comment, when Petra asked about Jack's latest news, was: "It's no doubt the same news as in his letters to you, honey. Isn't it dandy how he's become such a success as a diplomat?" This wasn't information she was after.

She finished her pink gin, deep in thought.

Very occasionally Jack wrote to Kate Gunn. After Kate had replaced Mr. Willoughby as her father's secretary, Ivor had instructed the girls to address her as Miss Gunn. Davina still did so, but in answer to one of Petra's letters, her former nanny had written:

Please don't write "Dear Miss Gunn," "Dear Kate" would be much nicer and friendlier. And isn't it wonderful that your father has been able to arrange for me to move into one of the Garden City flats set aside for British government personnel? It's the first home of my own I've ever had and I'm thrilled to bits with it.

Petra decided to write to Kate, asking if she knew whether Jack was enjoying a heavy romance and confiding why such information was so important to her. It would be good to have someone to talk openly with.

She jumped to her feet, intent on writing the letter immediately, but as she crossed the hall toward the staircase she came to an abrupt halt. Bellingham was opening the front door to a visitor—and the visitor was Jack's mother.

Considering how Jerome was always popping into Cadogan Square, Sylvia's unexpected arrival should not have been disconcerting. But Petra was always disconcerted when facing

Sylvia. Brought up to address her as "Aunt," she had only ever thought of her as Lady Bazeljette. Even reminding herself that Sylvia was Jack's mother didn't help, for apart from his dark hair he looked nothing like her.

"*Nonchalante et froide,*" said Suzi de Vioget when Sylvia had been spending a few days at Nyon and they had accidentally run into her in a smart Montreux café. "Very beautiful, of course, especially for her age, but not, I think, very *sympathique.*"

Now, remembering her manners, Petra greeted the woman she hoped would one day be her mother-in-law.

"Aunt Sylvia, how nice to see you!" she said, forcing warmth into her voice as Bellingham sent a footman upstairs to inform her mother.

Sylvia tilted her head to one side, regarding her with interest. "You're looking well," she said in her cracked-ice voice. "Being back in London obviously suits you."

Willowy as a woman twenty years her junior, she was wearing a dove-gray grosgrain suit, gray suede shoes, and a small hat with spotted veiling. A silver fox fur, complete with head, was casually draped over one shoulder. Her eyes were heavily mascaraed; her flawless skin was as pale as porcelain; her lips were a glossy japonica-red and her perfume was heady and sensual. Petra found the mix of restrained elegance of the suit—it could have been tailored only by Mainbocher or Chanel—and the blatant sensuality in the way that it was worn deeply disturbing.

Good manners necessitated that she entertain Sylvia until her mother came downstairs. As she led the way into the drawing room she said, "You must be looking forward to Jack's visit to London. I expect it's an age since you've seen him."

"Jack?" Sylvia's pencil-thin, beautifully arched eyebrows rose as if she were trying to place him. "Possibly," she said at last.

Not for the first time Petra wondered what on earth her mother found to talk about when in Sylvia's company—not, she reminded herself, that her mother often was in Sylvia's company. Though Jerome had come out to Cairo often, Sylvia had never done so. "The heat wouldn't suit her," Delia had said when Petra had asked why this was.

"Davina's begun doing voluntary work in a Cairo orphanage," Petra said, drumming up the only item of interest she could think of. "It's something she's always wanted to do."

"Voluntary work?" Without removing her silver fox, Sylvia seated herself on one of the room's many sofas. "But surely she's still at school?"

"She does it at weekends."

"How extraordinary." The expression on Sylvia's exquisite face was one of bafflement. "I'm surprised your father is allowing it."

"I don't think it was easy, but Davvy can be outstandingly persistent when she wants."

There was no answer.

Just as she was wondering what would engage Sylvia's interest, she saw her eyes had turned to the cocktail cabinet.

"Would you like a drink, Aunt Sylvia?" Petra asked with a touch of her mother's breezy manner. "A martini? I've just learned how to mix them."

"Then I hope you've discovered that the secret is to mix them very dry."

Taking this to mean that the drink would be gratefully received, Petra crossed the room, glad of the diversion.

Sylvia rearranged her fur. "Is Delia going out this evening? I ask, as she isn't expecting me."

Petra was tempted to say that her mother was out every evening, but she said only: "I believe she's dining with Margot Asquith. How do you like your martini garnished, Aunt Sylvia? With an olive or a twist of lemon?"

"A twist."

The door opened and Delia entered the room, looking sensational in a halter-necked evening gown of turquoise slipper satin.

"Sylvia! How unexpected!"

"It is rather, but then so is my news."

Petra handed her the martini. Neither Sylvia nor her mother looked at her. It was as though she had become as invisible as a maid or a footman.

"Has something happened to Jerome?" Delia's voice was taut with fear. "To Jack?"

The last possibility froze Petra.

"No. Theo has just told me his father has terminal cancer. It's come as rather a shock. I hadn't anticipated his succeeding to the dukedom quite so soon. However, now that he is to do so, I have made a decision." She paused, took a sip of her drink and said, "I thought you should be the first to know, Delia, that I'm going to divorce Jerome."

Petra gasped.

"You can't mean it," Delia said, sinking onto the sofa facing Sylvia.

"But I do." Sylvia looked completely unperturbed. "Theo has wanted me to marry him for eons. Until now I've never seen it as being in my best interest. I always thought Jerome would reach a position of great distinction in the government, even become prime minister, but now the Liberals are no longer in the majority, it won't happen. That being the case, rather than face a future as the wife of an MP who will never enjoy a title any higher than that of a baronet, I prefer to seek a divorce and become a duchess."

"The divorce—" Delia came to a halt and licked her lips.

Petra wasn't surprised. Her mouth, too, was dry with shock.

"The divorce . . ." Delia said again. "Has Jerome agreed to it?"

"He doesn't know yet I want one. And in case I've given a

different impression, I shall be the one doing the divorcing and I shall be doing so on the grounds of his adultery."

"Sylvia . . . if you're intendin' to do what I think you are . . . If you're intendin' to name names . . ."

Sylvia cleared her throat and looked in Petra's direction.

Delia looked toward her, too.

"Please leave us, Petra," she said stiffly, as if she was having trouble moving her mouth. "And what Aunt Sylvia has said is private. You must not repeat it to anyone, d'you understand? Not even to Aunt Gwen."

Giddy with the enormity of what she had just heard, Petra nodded that she understood.

As she began to walk unsteadily from the room, Sylvia said, "Naming names won't be necessary, Delia. Jerome will simply book into a hotel with a blonde. The hotel register and a private detective will do the rest."

"It will ruin his reputation." Her mother sounded as though she was having difficulty breathing. "It will destroy his political career."

"Maybe so." Sylvia sounded bored. "But the alternative is for him to divorce me on the grounds of adultery, and if he did, I wouldn't admit to adultery with Theo. I'd admit to my affair with the lover who preceded him."

Petra reached the door and closed it behind her. As she leaned against it, trying to stop her legs from trembling, she heard her mother say with passionate vehemence, "You cannot, *cannot*, ruin the career of such a distinguished man by dragging his name through the divorce court!"

Petra forced herself to move toward the stairs, wondering which of her friends' husbands her mother was referring to— and wondering why Sylvia had told her mother she was seeking a divorce from Jerome, before she had even told Jerome.

She walked into her bedroom, all thought of writing to Kate forgotten.

The person she wanted to write to was Jack. And she couldn't. The divorce was news that should only be given by his mother.

As Petra thought of Jack's reaction, the breath hurt in her throat. The next few weeks, weeks she'd been looking forward to for so long, were going to be very difficult, and not just for the people most closely involved.

She hugged herself, thinking of her own difficulty. It was one that was all too clear. With his parents' marriage in disarray, Jack wouldn't be in any mood to embark on a long-overdue love affair with her. And she, God help her, didn't want to embark on one with anyone else.

TEN

Annabel's party was great fun—but Petra wasn't escorted to it by Jack. LEAVE POSTPONED his telegram read. SEE YOU IN JUNE.

It was a great disappointment, but fortunately Petra didn't have time to brood. Just as they had always planned, she, Annabel, and Boudicca were being presented at the same court. It was an evening court which made it seem more glamorous. As Ellie helped her to dress and her mother and Aunt Gwen stood by ready to help with the Prince of Wales feathers, she felt sorry for the debutantes who had been allotted an afternoon slot.

"Now remember, darling," her aunt said anxiously, "when you have been presented and before you back away from Their Majesties, *your train must be securely draped over your arm.* Otherwise you will trip over it—and why doing so is such a rarity I shall never know."

"And when Ellie has secured your headdress, do one last practice curtsey," said Delia. "A full curtsey in full fig is trickier than walkin' a tightrope blindfolded."

"Stop! Please! You're making me even more nervous than I already am. Ellie, you will make sure the feathers won't come loose, won't you? And what if they do?" she added in real panic to her mother. "Do I leave them where they fall? Do I pick them up?"

"You do nothing, honey. A gentleman-in-waiting will be only feet away from you and he'll sort out any disaster. And if there is a problem—say your train looks as if it's in danger of it tripping you up—he'll adjust it."

Her mother secured her headdress and Petra gave a sigh of immense satisfaction. Worn slightly to the left side, with the center plume of the three the highest, it made her feel like a queen.

Her gown was an absolute dream. Made of pearly-white chiffon over satin, short-sleeved and low-necked with white roses embroidered on the bodice and skirt, it looked like a cloud.

Once again she thought of Jack.

The purpose of coming-out, with the almost nonstop parties and balls that accompanied it, was to meet as many eligible men as possible and make a suitable marriage—which meant marriage to someone rich and titled.

Boudicca's dream was to attract the attention of the Prince of Wales, but Petra was certain that by the end of the season Boo would be engaged to a lesser mortal.

Annabel was already engaged, so she didn't have to bother about husband-hunting.

And as she already knew very well whom she hoped to marry, Petra had no intention of husband-hunting, either.

"Your gloves," Aunt Gwen said, handing them to her as Delia fastened the pearl necklace she had worn for her own presentation around her daughter's neck.

"There!" Delia, resplendent in a tiara and dripping with diamonds and emeralds, stepped back to look. "You are stunning, darling. Absolutely the bee's knees."

"You look beautiful too, Mama," she said truthfully. "I just wish Papa and Davvy were here to see us."

"That they aren't you can blame on nasty Egyptian politics. Your father isn't the high commissioner but you would think he was, the way the prime minister relies on him. As for Davina, she couldn't possibly have traveled to England on her own and there was no one leavin' Cairo for England who could have chaperoned her. Even if there had, being here would have been no fun for her when she's too young to be invited to any of the balls and parties."

Gwen traveled with them to Buckingham Palace. By the time they entered the Mall the stream of Rolls-Royces was seemingly endless and the road was crowded with sightseers who had come to watch the long line of cars and their occupants.

"It's like being in a zoo," Petra said as a woman carrying a toddler pressed so close to their car that the child was able to bang on the window.

"It will be like this all the time for whoever the Prince of Wales marries," her mother said, cheerily blowing a kiss in the direction of the baby.

"I think you're wrong about that," Gwen said. "The Prince always has outriders. And I have to say that I wish we had them, too. I find it unnerving hearing what the hoi polloi are saying about my gown and jewels."

As they ascended the palace's grand Carrera marble staircase, Petra saw Annabel and Boudicca ahead of her. At the top of the stairs they were shepherded into an anteroom filled with stiff gilt chairs. There were perhaps forty girls and Petra had no opportunity to speak with her friends. Under the stern eyes of the courtiers they lined up according to the importance of their father's title and all she could do was give a small, excited wave.

After what seemed to be an age she heard the national anthem.

"That means the King and Queen are entering the Throne Room," said the girl next to her. "Any minute now the head of the queue will be going in."

After handing a presentation card to a footman each girl was escorted from the anteroom. Petra watched Annabel raise her hand to her headdress to check that it was secure. Boudicca was so nervous that she dropped her card and a gentleman-in-waiting had to retrieve it for her.

At last it was her turn. At the entrance to the Throne Room a gentleman-in-waiting spread out her train. Another handed her card to the lord chamberlain.

The room seemed vast. On both sides were tiers of seats, every one occupied. In front of her, on a dais beneath a scarlet canopy, were the King and Queen. A little to the left of the King was the Prince of Wales and a little farther distant, in glittering gowns and uniforms, were minor royals and other notables.

The lord chamberlain announced her name and seconds later she was in front of King George and Queen Mary. She made a full court curtsey, her knee bending until it almost touched the floor. Then, holding the position, she made a low bow and, most difficult of all, rose without losing her balance. Her relief when her second curtsey had been successfully executed must have shown on her face, for she was quite sure she saw a rare glimmer of amusement touch the corner of the King's mouth.

Afterward, in a room on a different floor, there was champagne and small hors d'oeuvres called Windsor pies, and she was at last able to grab a few words with Annabel and Boudicca.

"I wobbled," Annabel said, not sounding too upset about it. "I wobbled so badly my mother said my feathers were bobbing as if they were still on the ostrich."

"I didn't know Prince Edward would be present!" Boudicca was starry-eyed. "I was so busy looking at him I hardly noticed the King and Queen. Didn't he look absolutely spiffing in court dress? He's more handsome than any film star. Oh, I do hope he noticed me."

"I don't think he noticed anyone," Annabel said. "I thought he looked bored to tears."

Annabel's mother sailed up to them, resplendent in a diamond stomacher that rarely left the family vault. "Who are you talking about?" she demanded, having caught only the tail end of the conversation. "If you are talking about the lord chamberlain, of course he wasn't bored. Now say goodbye to Boudicca and Petra. We have an appointment with a photographer and are already late."

Reminded that they also had similar appointments, Boudicca and Petra bade each other a hasty goodbye.

As the family Rolls sped toward the Chelsea studio of London's most prestigious society photographer, Delia said with satisfaction, "What a day! And to think that I shall be doing all this again when Davina is presented."

Petra looked at her, startled. "Are you sure Davvy wants a season?" she asked, sounding a note of caution. "She doesn't like being the center of attention and she has no friends in London."

"Which is why she needs to be presented and have a London season." Davina making suitable friends was one subject Delia was firm about. "That way she'll make lots of suitable friends, which is what the whole exercise is about. A wide social circle will help her adjust to life back in England when your father is recalled."

"Recalled?" Petra stared at her mother. "Is that going to happen? I mean, is it going to happen soon?"

They were speeding along Chelsea Embankment, the Thames shimmering on their left-hand side like black silk.

Delia made an exasperated sound. "Well, of course it must happen soon, Petra. When your father went to Egypt as a British adviser, he went believin' he would be there for four or five years, six at the most. That was ten years ago. What has kept him there is the very troublesome political situation and the fact that he has such a good relationship with King Fuad. Your father is a great help to the present high commissioner and so your father's tenure just keeps being extended. But he's sixty-two and enough is enough. He intends to be back in London by the end of the year and if he isn't, *I* shall be. I've enjoyed seeing all my old friends and I don't intend remaining in exile any longer."

There was underlying steel in her voice and Petra sank back against the upholstery, stunned.

She had always known that her father's tenure in Egypt would eventually come to an end, but until now she'd never realized what it would mean to her. For the first time, she understood just how much her life would change.

Nile House would no longer be her home. And if she couldn't return to Nile House, how could she return at all? Where would she live?

She had always planned to return to Cairo at the end of the season. Most girls were engaged by then and she hoped to become engaged to Jack. As his diplomatic posting was in Lisbon, it hadn't occurred to her that she would be spending the obligatory year or eighteen months of their engagement anywhere else but in Egypt—with frequent visits on his part to Cairo. After that, her life would be wherever he was posted and she'd seen no reason why, with a few discreet words in high places, he shouldn't be sent to Cairo.

That was the ideal scenario. And even if it didn't come to fruition, she still had never imagined regarding anywhere other than Cairo as home.

"Does Davvy know you and Papa are leaving Cairo?" she asked as the Rolls came to a halt.

"I've no idea, but though she's managed to worm her way out of going to finishing school, there's no way she's going to worm her way out of havin' a London season. It's tactless of me to say so since Papa has always thought you were the headstrong one, but I rather think it will be Davina who will turn his hair white. Beneath her sweet and gentle demeanor Davina is *very* unconventional."

As her mother swept into the studio Petra didn't know whether to be pleased her mother thought her unlikely to ever cause her father grief, or miffed. In the end she was miffed. It made her sound so dull. And to be thought of as dull in comparison to her little sister was the living end. Deciding that her mother didn't know what she was talking about Petra prepared to have a photograph taken that would, with a bit of luck, find its way into *Tatler* and perhaps even into *Vogue*.

Dear Petra,

What a hoot having your picture in Tatler! *The high commissioner's wife has just come back from London and brought a copy with her to show us. Papa says Mama is sending him a copy of the photograph so that he can frame it and have it on his desk. I expect it's the Prince of Wales feathers that make you look so regal. What on earth happens to them if you have to cross Buckingham Palace courtyard in a gale?*

I've just come back from Abdin Palace having been dragooned into acting the part of an admiring spectator while Prince Farouk displayed his falconry technique. He's thirteen but looks younger, probably because he's treated as if he's still a baby. Everything is done for him. I tried to chat to him about the orphanage I do voluntary work for—he will be the next king, after all, and you'd think he'd take an interest—but he simply said anyone not having parents was very lucky. Which has to be the most stupidly flippant remark I've ever heard. Darius said I have to remember he's only thirteen and still a child. I'm trying to, but he made me very cross (Farouk not Darius).

I'll be glad when it's August and you come back to Cairo. It will still be stiflingly hot, of course, but we can go to Mena House and swim in the pool. It's the first year I can remember when Papa hasn't moved to a rented house in Alexandria to escape the worst of the summer, but the situation is such he feels it his duty to stick things out here and so obviously I'm here with him. Things are never dull. A water buffalo trampled a fence and got into the garden yesterday. Adjo got it out again, though not without a great deal of hollering and arm-waving. It was tremendous fun. Better than a Charlie Chaplin film.

I'm thinking of asking Papa if I can train as a nurse. The problem is, where would I study? And don't say London. I can't bear the thought of living there. What I'd really like to do is to become a doctor, but I don't have your academic ability and the exams would be beyond me. It's all a bit of a problem but I'm sure it will sort itself out.

Lots of love, Davvy

As it was so obvious Davina didn't have a clue that plans were being made for her to have a London season—and, worse, that her father was certain the present year was his last in Cairo—Petra wondered how she should break the news. A letter seemed very blunt, and a phone call, directed through operator after operator, wasn't much more satisfactory.

After mulling the issue over for several days she decided to do nothing in the hope that perhaps the situation would change by the end of the summer. Her mother often spoke off the top of her head and, with a bit of luck, the remarks she had made while on the way to the photographer would prove to be no more than wishful thinking.

As Petra attended a frenetic round of dances and balls—

often barely knowing the debutante whose party it was—she enjoyed herself hugely. At every event she saw Annabel and Boudicca and they also met up nearly every day, either at Gunter's Tea Shop or at the soda fountain at Selfridges.

Petra's own coming-out ball was held during the first week of June and both Magda and Suzi came to London to attend it.

"Find me a glorious duke who owns half of England," Magda said as the five of them sunbathed in the walled garden at Cadogan Square, drinking cocktails, "and I'll be a happy girl."

"Every English duke I know is a crusty old man." Petra swirled her ice cubes around with her finger. "What you need is a young and dashing heir-presumptive."

Magda, superbly sophisticated in a black sun-top, black shorts, and white plastic-framed sunglasses, rolled from her tummy onto her back, gold hair streaming out like a fan over the grass. "As long as home is a ducal palace and the income is in six figures, I don't mind. Have I told you my mother is getting divorced again? It will be the *sixth* husband she's discarded. My grandmother says it borders on carelessness."

They all giggled. Magda's racy mother was a favorite subject of conversation.

"She was a guest at Berchtesgaden last month," Magda continued, taking off her sunglasses and closing her eyes. "I'm simply keeping my fingers crossed that she isn't setting her sights on our beloved Führer."

"*Your* beloved Führer," Petra said chidingly. "He certainly isn't *our* beloved Führer. We all think he's a horrid little man and can't understand why you Germans are getting so excited over him."

Magda opened her eyes. "He's making us feel like a nation again," she said easily. "When we lost the war, we lost our pride. Hitler is giving it back to us." She sat up, reached for the glass perched precariously near to her, and said, "A Tom Collins tastes even better, Petra, if you add strawberry schnapps to it. They sell schnapps in London, don't they? I'll try to get you a bottle."

That her father wasn't in London for her dance was a great dis-appointment to Petra, but as it was common knowledge that there had been a fresh outburst of violent anti-British feeling in Cairo, no one was too surprised that Lord Conisborough was remaining in the troubled city.

"His not being here leaves us with a sticky problem," she said to her mother while Delia was supervising the distribution of acres of fresh flowers.

"Here come the hydrangeas," Delia said as the delivery men brought in the pots of blue flowers. "I'm going to stand those in all the fireplaces."

"You're not listening to me, Mama. I said that Papa not being here presents a problem."

"Which is?" Delia didn't take her eyes off the flowers. "D'you think the carnations will look right with the lilies and roses? I'm beginning to wonder if I made the right decision when I said I would arrange them myself with a little help from Gwen. Lady Mowbray had Constance Spry do the flowers for Annabel's ball and they were absolutely cracking."

"The flowers will be fine. What will not be fine is that my father won't be here for the first dance. And I don't have a brother or even a cousin. Have you any ideas?"

She had finally caught her mother's attention. "You're right, honey. How on earth did I overlook a thing like that?" She frowned, deep in thought, and then said, "Perhaps Win-ston could stand in for Papa?"

"No," Petra said firmly. "I don't mind the fact that so many family friends are going to be guests, but I am *not* going to endure Mr. Churchill as a stand-in for Papa. For one thing, I'm far taller than he is. I'd look ridiculous."

Sheaves of scarlet late-flowering tulips were carried past them, their scent heavy and sweet.

Her mother chewed her lip. "Dear Pugh would never be able to complete a circuit of the ballroom. His gout is far too bad. Now, if only dear Cousin Beau were alive . . ."

Petra prayed for patience.

"But as he isn't," her mother continued, happily oblivious of her daughter's reaction, "we'll have to look elsewhere." She paused for a second and then said, "What about Sir John Simon? I don't think Britain has ever before had a foreign secretary who is such a wonderful dancer. His predecessor, the Marquess of Reading, was a calamity at a ball."

Petra hesitated. She quite liked Sir John Simon. He was sixty, tall, lean, patrician-faced, austerely handsome. He *looked* like her father. And that would, she knew, only make her father's absence more obvious.

"No," she said firmly. "Not Sir John Simon."

"Well, Lord Denby is out. He's been sick since March. And Cuthie Digby can barely walk anymore, let alone dance."

"The proper person to stand in for Papa," Petra decided, "is Jerome. I know he's not a relation—but then neither is anyone else you mentioned—and I can't think of anyone I'd rather have."

Instead of looking pleased that the problem was solved, her mother looked aghast.

"Why the shock?" Petra asked as the deliverymen carried the last of the flowers into the house. "Papa wouldn't mind. If you'd realized the problem earlier and spoken to him I'm sure he would have suggested Jerome. I'll ring him and ask him and

I'll tell him to think about what waltz the orchestra should play. I'd like something nice and old-fashioned. Perhaps 'Roses from the South' or 'On the Beautiful Blue Danube.' "

By the end of the afternoon, the house was *en fête*. Delicately colored carnations twined around the magnificent balusters of the grand staircase; ornate arrangements of lilies and roses graced every highly polished surface. The first-floor drawing room, its floor waxed to a high sheen, had been turned into a ballroom with small gilt chairs hired for the occasion set around the walls. A vast marquee erected in the garden was the supper room and the air inside it was heavy with the scent of the flowers decorating the damask-covered, silver-laden tables.

Before the ball there was a formal dinner party at which her mother's friends, not hers, were the guests. Among them was Margot Asquith, now in her late sixties and as caustic-tongued as ever. The former Duchess of Marlborough, now Madame Jacques Balsan, had journeyed all the way from her home on the French Riviera. Thirteen years younger than Margot, she was still sixteen years her mother's senior, and not for the first time Petra marveled at the way her mother had always welcomed her father's friends, even though they were nearly all a generation older than she was.

Petra wondered if her mother had found it tedious and if that was the reason, with her father away, that Delia had begun spending so much time with the Prince of Wales and his friends—all of whom were her age, and many of whom were American. Was her mother taking advantage of the fact that her father wasn't around? And was that why she was so careful never to refer to the Prince of Wales as "David" when in Gwen's company?

It was an interesting thought, as was the realization that so many of the people who had played a large part in her mother's life were now dead.

"No George Curzon and no Herbert Henry," her mother said sadly, making sure that all the name cards were in the right position on the dinner table. "Which is a great loss. They always made every party a special occasion."

Petra had never met either Lord Curzon or the Earl of Oxford and Asquith. Not wanting her mother to become gloomy, she said brightly, "But you are good friends with one of Lord Curzon's daughters. You see an awful lot of Baba, don't you?"

"Yes." Her mother straightened Winston Churchill's place-setting card. "And if it wasn't for Tom Mosley being such a political wild card I'd probably see far more of Cimmie, as well."

During the dinner Petra was seated between her uncle Pugh and Winston Churchill. On any other occasion she would probably have enjoyed Winston's rumbustious conversation, but she was too keyed up to appreciate it.

At ten o' clock, the dinner over, guests began to pour into the house. Magda and Suzi, who were staying with Annabel, were among the first to arrive, but there was a seemingly endless stream of other debutantes and she was staggered to realize how many of them she now counted as close friends. The point her mother had made when discussing why it was she wanted Davina to be presented was obviously a valid one. It did provide a girl with as wide a circle of suitable friends as possible. And though she wasn't interested in any of the "eligibles"—the veritable army of upper-crust young men who had been invited—it was great fun to recognize nearly all of them from previous parties and to be, for one evening at least, the absolute center of attention.

She knew she looked sensational. Her mahogany-red hair

was just as thick and naturally wavy as her mother's and she wore it fashionably short, with deep waves framing her face and a cluster of curls at the nape of her neck. Unlike many other debutantes, she'd elected not to wear virginal white. She had wanted to wear a long and slinky dress in bias-cut gold satin, with a halter neck and a plunging neckline.

Her mother had vetoed it. "Land's sakes, Petra!" she had said, appalled. "It looks like one of Thelma Furness's gowns! Wear that and you will be labeled 'fast.' "

"So what can I wear?" she had said exasperatedly, knowing full well that Magda's gown would be virtually backless and would cling to every voluptuous curve.

"Chiffon would be a good choice. Perhaps floral chiffon. Or floral chiffon and tulle."

Petra shook her head. It was Lucille, her mother's favorite dressmaker, who had come to her rescue, designing a starkly simple, foot-skimming gown in mint-green taffeta. It was arrow-straight with a wide, slashed neckline and huge puffed sleeves. It crackled as she moved and amid a sea of pale-pastel and floral gowns she stood out in just the way she had wanted. Her only ornament was a huge white rose pinned in her hair.

Her mother had looked at it with an odd expression, as if she was remembering something. Then she had given herself a little shake and said, "Unusual, honey. But it certainly works."

Catching sight of herself in one of the giant mirrors lining the walls, Petra was happy with her choice of dress.

Everything else was working, too. The orchestra her mother had hired was terrific. Gunter's had done the catering and the menu for supper included quail, lobster, chicken in aspic, and asparagus, followed with Charlotte Russe, traditional English trifle, and strawberries and cream.

Jerome did an exquisite job waltzing her around. Annabel clung to Fedya Tukhachevsky's side and Suzi hadn't sat out one dance. All her partners not only were startlingly handsome but were heirs to vast estates. Petra hadn't seen her dance with a younger son even once. It was as if she could sniff them out at a glance.

Magda's partners, on the other hand, were all distinguished older men. Winston was quite obviously utterly bewitched by her. Sir John Simon couldn't take his eyes off her golden hair and silver lamé dress. Neither, though, were bachelors. And Petra was sure that only a very distinguished, exceedingly rich bachelor was going to seriously engage Magda's attention.

Despite having met and bowled over more eligible young men than the average girl would in a lifetime, Petra knew that none of her highly agreeable partners would ever seriously engage her attention. Only Jack was capable of doing that.

And Jack was hundreds of miles away.

Wishing that he could have seen how she looked, Petra lifted a glass of champagne from the tray of a passing waiter. Jerome, an excellent dancer despite his barely noticeable limp, was performing some very nifty Argentinean footwork with Magda. It wasn't a performance any of Magda's previous partners would have been able to give. At the thought of Winston executing a tango, Petra giggled.

"Rupert Pytchley is searching for you," her mother said, looking oddly out of sorts as Jerome and Magda caught her attention. "And don't giggle when you're not in conversation with anyone. It looks as if you've had too much champagne—and you haven't, Petra, have you?"

Petra rather thought that she had, but just said, "I'm going to stand outside the room for five minutes and get a little air. Jerome doesn't seem at all put out about Aunt Sylvia wanting a divorce, does he? News that they've separated has already begun to spread. Aunt Gwen told me about it 'in confidence' an hour ago."

Her mother said nothing, but as she looked across the dance

floor to where Jerome and Magda were continuing with their cabaret-worthy performance, her generously curved mouth showed signs of strain.

As Petra walked from the ballroom she knew she shouldn't have brought up a subject that would cause her mother distress. Divorce in their social circle was not to be undertaken lightly and there was no telling what the effects of it would be on Jerome's career. It was reason enough for her usually carefree mother to look concerned.

Outside the ballroom the air was refreshingly cool. The muted strains of the tango came to an end and the orchestra began playing "Love Is the Sweetest Thing." Just then, the front doorbell rang.

From where she was standing, Petra saw Bellingham cross the marble-floored hall. Idly she wondered who the late arrival would prove to be. It was close to one o'clock and nearly time for supper. Certain it was going to be a friend of her mother's—none of her fellow debutantes would be arriving at such a late hour—she turned away to enter the ballroom again.

As she did so, she heard the sound of the door opening. And then the voice she'd been longing to hear for months.

"Good to see you again, Bellingham," Jack said cheerily. "I'm a bit late, but better late than never. I've come from Lisbon via Paris and the boat train was delayed."

Petra spun around, her heart beating so hard that for a second she had to rest her hand on the balustrade to steady herself.

As Bellingham closed the door behind him, Jack looked upward.

Their eyes met.

His face broke into a broad grin.

"Sorry I didn't make it for your presentation, but the good news is that I'm not here on leave. I'm back in England for good."

She gasped and then, as he took the stairs two at a time, she began to run down them. They met on the broad first half-landing and as he opened his arms she hurled herself into them, dizzy with joy.

His arms closed around her and she knew, even before he spoke, that things were going to be different between them.

"I've missed you," he said, and the expression in his gold-flecked eyes sent her pulse racing.

Still in the circle of his arms, she said, her voice thick with emotion, "All my life I've missed you when you're not with me—but I've never felt able to tell you so before."

"And for the last two years, there have been things I've never been able to tell you."

The throb in his voice told her she didn't have to ask what those things were.

For a long, long moment their eyes held and then, as the strains of "Love Is the Sweetest Thing" drifted down the stairs toward them, he lowered his head to hers and his mouth was hot and sweet on hers.

ELEVEN

It was the most transfiguring moment of Petra's life. She knew, deep in her bones, that what was happening between them wouldn't be a transient romance. This was love. Just as she had known ever since she was sixteen that Jack was the only man in the world for her, she now knew that he had felt the same. Her age had been the only barrier to his telling her so.

As he lifted his head she said, "I wish you'd told me you were only waiting until I was eighteen before letting me know that you loved me. Your father kept telling me how you were seeing the Marquis de Fontalba's daughter. He thought you were about to become engaged."

Amusement tugged at the corners of his mouth. "You're quite right in that I love you—though it would have been more usual for you to wait until I'd told you so. As for Beatriz . . ." He paused teasingly and, seeing the apprehension in her eyes, said gently, "Beatriz de Fontalba is an absolutely stunning girl and desperately in love with an Argentinean to whom, being neither titled nor wealthy, her father violently objects. She asked me if I would act as a cover for the two of them."

"That's all right, then," she said, her relief vast. "And now I want you to waltz me round the ballroom. Your father kindly stood in for mine at the first dance, but if you whirl me round the floor I shall remember it to my dying day."

"Best not to walk in there in such an intimate fashion," he said as, arms around each other's waist, they walked up the stairs toward the ballroom. "Not until we've put your parents wise to the situation."

She missed her footing and his arm tightened around her, steadying her.

"There's something you should know," she said. "My mother isn't going to be as happy as you might expect. And it's only fair to tell you that she rather thinks I'm interested in Darius."

He came to a halt outside the ballroom doors. "Darius?" he said, staring down at her in baffled astonishment. "Darius?"

Giggles fizzed in her throat. "I found it useful as it threw her off the scent where my feelings for you were concerned."

"But why the devil did she need to be thrown off the scent? I would have thought she'd be over the moon if we married. Our parents have always been so close. I always regarded your mother and father as family. The blunt truth is, I spent more time as a child with your mother than I did with my own."

He ran a hand distractedly through his curls. "I think you've got this all wrong, Petra. I reckon your mother was just concerned about you falling in love at such a young age. I don't think she will mind having me as a son-in-law."

Understanding flooded through her. Jack's explanation was entirely logical.

"Then we'll simply tell her that as long as we have her permission to become engaged, we're quite happy to wait until I'm twenty-one before we get married."

"I've missed something here. Was there a proposal of marriage?"

She blushed furiously, and then, as the orchestra in the ballroom began playing a popular fox-trot, he lowered his head to hers and kissed her. "Will you," he said softly, "please marry me, Petra?"

"Oh yes," she said, her face radiant. "I've *always* wanted to marry you. I just thought that you were never going to ask!"

The ballroom doors burst open and a laughing group of guests spilled out, almost knocking them off their feet.

"It's Jack Bazeljette!" a friend of his shouted. "What ho, Jack! Typical of you to get here just in time for supper!"

As the news that Jack had arrived spread Petra saw her mother turn and look in their direction. And she saw her instant reaction. It was one of such pleasure and welcome she didn't have a single remaining doubt that Jack had been right.

Certain of all the happiness the future held for her, she walked into the ballroom at his side and five minutes later was waltzing with him to the unforgettably romantic strains of a Strauss waltz.

For the remainder of her party they behaved as if nothing exceptional had happened between them. Jack danced with several of her friends. She danced with several of the eligibles. Annabel whispered to her that she thought Jack was "absolutely brill"—and wanted to know what his prospects were. Fedya Tukhachevsky asked if he was Italian. Occasionally their eyes met and her heart leaped with such violent desire she thought she would die.

As dawn broke, Jack, who was dancing with Boudicca, worked his way over to her. "How about us all scarpering off for breakfast?" he said, speaking to both of them. "Fedya has his car with him and I picked up mine en route from the station. We could be in Brighton by six thirty."

"Spiffing idea." Rupert was always up for a bit of fun. "There's nothing like an early-morning swim after too much champagne. See if you can rope Archie Somerset in. He's somewhere in the garden with Boo and Petra's French friend, doing his best to cement Anglo-French relations."

"And don't let's forget Magda," Petra said. "She'll never forgive me if we go without her."

"Don't invite her besotted dance partner!" Rupert called.

"Why not?" Petra asked. "Is there something wrong with him?"

"One hundred percent," Rupert said with deep feeling. "He's my father."

Piling into the two cars and roaring off to Brighton, while the rest of her party guests milled into the marquee for bacon and eggs, was great fun. On the outskirts of Brighton, in sight of the South Downs, they stopped at a roadside café for bacon sandwiches and mugs of steaming tea.

"I think it's time some of us changed cars." Magda, who had been squashed beside a canoodling Suzi and Archie all the way from London, looked at Jack. "How about I sit in the front with you, and Petra does a stint in the back?"

"I don't think so," Jack said pleasantly, a proprietary arm around Petra's shoulders. "It might give the impression Petra isn't my girl—and, in case there's any doubt, she's very much my girl. Just thought you'd all like to know."

Magda was unperturbed. "Then I'll travel the rest of the way in Fedya's car between Boudicca and Rupert. You'll have to crush your skirts up a bit, Boo. Why on earth did you opt for a crinoline instead of something slinky and svelte?"

"Because though slinky and svelte looks good on you and Petra, I'm too plump for it. What are we going to swim in when we get to Brighton? I can't plunge in wearing my dress."

"Take it off and go in your undies," Suzi said with French practicality as they headed back to the cars in all their evening finery, leaving a café full of bemused workmen behind them. "I shall."

Archie's roar of approval could have woken the dead.

On arriving in Brighton, the sea proved to be so cold that only Jack and Fedya stripped down to their underpants and plunged in. Archie and Rupert took off their shoes and socks and shouted encouragement as Jack and Fedya cleaved through the waves.

The girls slipped out of their evening shoes, rolled their stockings down and then, lifting their ankle-length skirts, paddled in the shallows, screaming as it seemed neither Jack nor Fedya was going to give in and turn for shore.

"It's a male-pride thing," Rupert said, shielding his eyes against the brightness of the early-morning sun on the sea.

"But I can't *see* them," Petra said, no longer enjoying herself one little bit.

"That's because of the waves. Don't worry. I can. And they've both turned. They're racing each other back. Who is your money on? Fedya or Jack?"

It was Jack who waded out of the sea first. Petra raced toward him, not caring that she was ruining the skirt of her taffeta evening gown.

Panting heavily, he came to a halt in waist-deep water and hugged her tightly against him. As she felt the reaction of his near-naked body to hers, an emotion she had never experienced before jackknifed through her. She knew, without a shadow of a doubt, that a three-year engagement was going to be an impossibility.

Though Archie and Suzi never became a serious item, and though Magda never even troubled to flirt with Rupert, the jaunt to Brighton was the first of many the nine friends enjoyed during the next season. They became a little clique that no outsider ever succeeded in joining.

In the Pytchley town house, Magda taught them all how to tango. Another day she caused controversy by casually handing round a signed photograph of Adolf Hitler. It was the only time Petra had ever seen Jack close to losing his temper. At Cadogan Square Archie improved Petra's—and everyone else's—cocktail-making skills. Whatever ball one of them went to, the others would be there also.

It was an arrangement that ensured she saw Jack almost constantly, without her mother's suspicions being aroused. They decided they would not tell her the news until the season ended.

"Though we won't be pulling the wool over her eyes for long," Jack said as he drove her home after an evening at the Savoy. "As soon as your father responds to the letter I've sent him I'll speak to her."

"As long as Papa's reply is favorable," she said, without any real fear that it wouldn't be, "then we can be engaged by the fall and married at Christmas."

It was the first week in July and the Talbot's top was down, the night air warm on her bare arms.

As Jack turned into Sloane Street, he said in amusement, "There you go again. Making all the arrangements without waiting to be asked. For all you know I may not want to marry you until you're an old lady of twenty-five."

Her head was on his shoulder and she could smell the faint tang of his lemon cologne. "By the time I'm twenty-five we'll have a house full of children," she said dreamily. "Four boys and a girl. Or would you prefer four girls and a boy?"

"I'd prefer to take things a step at a time and get engaged first." He dropped a kiss onto her hair. "Will your mother be waiting up for you?"

"No. She won't be in until the early hours. She's gone with her new friends, the Simpsons, and half a dozen others to a nightclub on Bond Street. It's a favorite haunt of Prince Edward's and Mrs. Simpson is like Boudicca, she's desperate for chance meetings with him."

That her mother's social life had become so racy amused both of them. "I sometimes think," Petra had said when telling Jack earlier about her mother dining at Quaglino's with a party that included the Prince of Wales and Thelma Furness, "that my mother tries to pull the wool over Aunt Gwen's eyes in much the same way I try and pull the wool over hers. You can bet your life that if Aunt Gwen asks who she's been dining with, she'll only mention the names of people Aunt Gwen approves, like Lady Londonderry, and conveniently omit the fact that the Prince, who Aunt Gwen does not approve of, and Thelma, who she most *definitely* doesn't approve of, were there as well."

The car turned into Cadogan Square and a few moments later slid to a halt. Because they were certain that her mother wasn't home, they risked a lingering good-night kiss.

"How soon will it be before we can expect a reply from my father?" she asked breathlessly as he reluctantly lifted his head.

"Another week. Perhaps two. With luck, he may even send a telegram."

It was a thought that hadn't occurred to her and for the next few days she left the house with the greatest reluctance, terrified a telegram would arrive while she was out.

"I think you're making a mountain out of an anthill," Magda said. Annabel was driving the little Morris Minor that had been given her for her birthday. They were speeding toward Hyde Park on a motorized treasure hunt.

"Molehill," Petra corrected automatically. Though Magda's English was nearly flawless, there were still times when she didn't get things exactly right. "And I'm not making a mountain out of a molehill. You don't know my mother. She's not always rational and if she gets an idea in her head—such as Jack not being ideal son-in-law material—then it can be the devil's own job getting her to change her mind."

"I think your mother is absolutely wonderful." Boudicca was squeezed between Magda and Suzi on the backseat. "I wish my mother was as young and as glamorous and as unconventional. And I just *love* your mother's Americanisms. You'd think after living in England for so long she would have lost all trace of her accent."

"She hasn't because she doesn't want to. It makes her stand out, and she enjoys that. Also," she added as they drove into the park, "it annoys my father. And for some reason I don't understand, she always takes a great deal of pleasure out of annoying him."

"Are you sure this statue you are taking us to is the right clue: 'a vulnerable point in Hyde Park'?" Suzi asked, changing the subject as Annabel headed in the direction of the Achilles statue. "I don't see any sign of the others heading this way."

"Yes, of course I'm sure." Annabel, still an inexperienced driver, crunched the gears. "What else can it be? And Jack and Fedya aren't driving toward it because they haven't yet worked out the answer. Now do stop distracting me, Suzi. I've already come the wrong way. I should have driven down Park Lane."

Five minutes later they had parked and walked to the foot of the giant monument. It had been erected in 1822 in honor of the Duke of Wellington and his companions and was of Achilles, nude except for a cloak thrown carelessly over one arm. Taped to the giant granite pediment was the next clue in the treasure hunt. As Petra, Annabel, and Boo pored over it, trying to decipher where they should go next, Magda and Suzi, who knew too little about London's landmarks to be helpful, surveyed the statue.

"He's wonderfully muscular," Magda murmured admiringly. "Almost Teutonic."

Suzi was less impressed. "He may be muscular," she said critically, "but for such a heroic figure his fig leaf is tragically *petit.*"

The two of them collapsed into giggles and were still laughing when Petra shouted triumphantly, "I've worked out the answer. We're being sent to the Reformers Tree Memorial. It's up near the refreshment kiosk. If we sprint we can win this treasure hunt hands down."

Later, they sprawled on the grass near the kiosk eating ice creams. Magda leaned against a convenient tree, elegant in white bell-bottomed trousers and a short-sleeved navy sweater. Annabel asked, "So who is the man you are seeing now? I know you are seeing someone. And as you so obviously don't want us to know his identity, he must be someone very interesting."

Boudicca sat up abruptly. "It isn't my father, is it? I know he made a complete donkey of himself over you at Petra's ball, but please tell me it isn't my father!"

"It isn't your father and it isn't your brother and it isn't anyone any of you are in love with. He does happen to have a wife, though. And because of that I think it best if I keep his name to myself."

"That is absolutely not playing the game!" Annabel sat up too, nearly sending her ice cream flying. "I thought it was understood that we had no secrets from each other."

Magda gave a throaty laugh. "But you don't have any secrets to keep, Annabel. I, at the moment, do."

Hoping that Magda's paramour wouldn't turn out to be one of her mother's friends, Petra shielded her eyes against the sun and said, as a group strode toward them over the grass, "Here come the others. Your fiancé is looking very miffed, Annabel. I've never known anyone who hates losing so much. Is it because he's Russian, d'you think?"

As the summer progressed, the main subject of gossip was the Prince of Wales's love life. Because her mother was now considered to be part of the raffish Prince's set, it was gossip Petra grew increasingly uncomfortable with. It was a discomfort her friends—even the sensitive Boo—remained blissfully unaware of. As far as they were concerned, having a mother who knew at first hand who was uppermost in the Prince's affections was unutterably thrilling.

"I think it's *so* naughty of him to still occasionally see Mrs. Dudley Ward when everyone knows of his liaison with Thelma Furness," Boo said, speaking of the Prince as if he were a rather mischievous little boy.

"And *extremely* naughty of him to have abandoned Thelma on Derby Day in order to escort Amelia Earhart," Magda said, tongue in cheek. "Though I rather suspect that the first woman to cross the Atlantic on a solo flight would have the advantage as an interesting companion."

"And no hope of Amelia becoming Princess of Wales," Annabel interjected. "Like all his other lady loves she's married already."

It was the kind of subject matter that could keep Petra's friends entertained for hours.

Another topic that she knew they discussed on the rare occasions she and Jack were not with them was the scandal of his parents' pending divorce.

"What makes it even worse is Sylvia's age," her mother said exasperatedly after seeing Margot Asquith who had gossiped about the Bazeljettes ad nauseam. "By the time a woman is in her fifties she should be past wanting to leave her marriage. The damage she is doing to both her reputation and Jerome's is incalculable."

Though Petra had always known that Sylvia was older than her mother, she had never realized how much. "And what of the Earl of Grasmere's reputation?" she asked, genuinely interested.

"Theo?" Her mother gave an unladylike snort. "Theo's never given a damn about reputation. He's a screwball—which is just as well, because I've come to the conclusion that Sylvia is batty as well. To be quite honest, if I'd realized she was so unconventional there's a chance we might have been friends."

Petra's eyes nearly popped out of her head. "What do you mean 'might have been friends'? I thought you were! You certainly never asked me to address anyone else I was unrelated to as 'Aunt'!"

Her mother backtracked instantly. "Is that what I said? Then it just goes to show how much Margot's visit has upset me. I hadn't seen her in a long spell and she's becoming very difficult to rub along with. Why do people get so querulous when they get older? If I do that, you have my permission to shoot me!"

Three days later, walking down Bond Street, Petra ran into Jerome.

His face creased with delight at the sight of her.

"Where are you going?" he asked affably.

"The Royal Academy. I know it's a bit late in the summer to see the Summer Exhibition, but coming-out has kept me so busy it's the first opportunity I've had."

"But you're not going by yourself, surely?"

She shook her head. "No. I'm meeting the girls in the Friends Room. Harrison dropped me off, but because I was early I thought I'd nip into Fenwick."

Harrison was her mother's chauffeur.

As he fell into step beside her Jerome said with unusual gravity, "I'm glad we've met up by accident like this, Petra. I've wanted to have a private word with you for some time."

She came to a halt, saying in alarm, "Because of my friendship with Jack?"

"Your friendship with Jack?" He looked startled. "No, of course not."

He was wearing a superbly tailored pinstriped suit, kid gloves, and a bowler hat. She wondered whether he was on his way to the House of Commons. Even dressed so traditionally, he still managed to exude an air of swashbuckling rakishness. Perhaps it was the angle at which he wore his bowler. Or the thin white scar that knifed down through his left eyebrow.

"I wanted to talk to you about my separation from Sylvia," he said as they began walking again. "There is a lot of ugly gossip flying around and it concerns me that you might . . ." This time he was the one to stop walking. "It concerns me that you might . . ."

That a man she had known since her birth—a man she was so deeply fond of and who was so effortlessly sophisticated—should be struggling so hard to say something to her, filled her with fear.

"It concerns me that after listening to some of the things that are being said, you might be disappointed in me," he said at last.

The fear ebbed. She opened her mouth to answer, but couldn't. She tried again. "Be disappointed in you? I could never be disappointed in you, Uncle Jerome. Not ever."

It was the first time in more than two years that she had called him "Uncle."

The relief in his dark eyes—eyes that were so like Jack's—was so vast it brought tears to her throat.

Impulsively she tucked her hand in the crook of his arm.

Her reward was to see his familiar, infectious smile.

"I'll walk you to the academy," he said, patting her hand with such affection she knew that when Jack told him of his plans to marry, they would receive his blessing in spades.

It was only two days later that she realized she might become crushingly, overpoweringly disappointed in Jerome.

The blinding revelation came when she accompanied Aunt

Gwen, who never liked going anywhere by herself, to a jeweler in Hatton Garden. Gwen was picking up a tiara she had left for cleaning.

It was an old-fashioned jeweler with little booths closed off by curtains, where customers could shop in complete privacy. As they waited for the salesman to bring Gwen's tiara from the vault they heard voices from a nearby booth. Voices Petra recognized.

Bewildered, she left Gwen and stepped back into the main body of the shop where she could see the adjoining booths. There was only one other occupied and the curtain was not fully closed. Magda, dressed in lavender-blue silk, a peplum emphasizing the luscious curve of her hips, was holding her wrist high, entranced by the beauty of the diamond bracelet adorning it.

"Do you like it, sweetheart?" she heard Jerome say.

"It's *wunderbar, Liebling.* Absolutely *wunderbar*!"

Jerome took hold of her hand to kiss the back of it, and as he did, his shoulder edged the curtain even farther to one side. Petra could see him clearly.

Filled with emotions she couldn't even begin to analyze she stepped back into her own booth, pulling the curtain behind her and, grateful for the length of time Gwen always took over any transaction, didn't leave the shop until Magda and Jerome were halfway down the street.

TWELVE

Petra was in a dilemma as to whether or not to tell Magda what she had seen. In the end she decided that she couldn't. If Magda put into words that she was sleeping with Jerome—and knowing Magda, Petra had no doubt at all that she was—it would be just too stomach-turning. She couldn't have felt worse if it had been her father and Magda who were having the affair.

During the next few days, one question gnawed at her. Was Jerome having a onetime fling, or was he in the habit of indulging in such liaisons? If he was, it certainly put a different light on his willingness to act the part of the guilty party in his divorce from Sylvia—and made his doing so far less of an admirable act.

The more she pondered, the more she had to have answers. And the only person she could possibly ask was her mother.

Choosing her moment wasn't easy, for the season was now so far along that her mother no longer acted as a chaperone. It was something she was deeply grateful for, but taken together with her mother's own hectic social life, the opportunities for intimate conversation were few and far between.

She caught Delia at an unconscionably early hour one Saturday morning as she was slipping into the house after having been a guest at one of the last balls of the season. Her mother, still in a negligee, was arranging a bowl of pink and white roses in the drawing room.

"What's the matter, Mama?" Petra asked, dropping her swansdown wrap from her shoulders. "Couldn't you sleep?"

"No." Her mother looked as if arranging the roses was taking all her concentration. "I seem to have gotten out of the habit."

Petra wondered how to broach the subject of the affair. Since there didn't seem to be an easy way, and as it was in her nature to be direct, she simply took a deep breath and said bluntly, "I wonder if you'd mind me asking a rather odd question about Jerome?"

Her mother ceased what she was doing and turned to face her. There were dark shadows beneath her eyes and Petra realized Delia hadn't exaggerated about her inability to sleep. "If it's about him and Sylvia, honey, I don't think it would be appropriate—"

"It isn't," she said quickly before her mother could finish her sentence, "or at least not directly."

"Well, then . . . ?" Her mother's forehead puckered into a frown.

"I just wondered if he had a bad reputation where women were concerned. It's just something I overheard."

Her mother stared at her for a long time, not really seeing her, and then said, "He used to have. Years and years ago, before you were born. Perhaps now Sylvia has left him so publicly he's just reverting to type."

"Oh, I see." It wasn't the answer she'd been hoping for, but she tried to look as if it was of no importance.

Her mother showed no desire to continue with the conversation and so Petra forced a bright smile and said, "I must go to bed and get some sleep. I've a garden party to go to this afternoon."

As she opened the door to leave, her mother said, "The

something you overheard. Did it include the name of one of your friends?"

Petra half turned, one hand on the glass doorknob. "Yes," she said. "It did."

Her mother's face was blank of all emotion. "And was the friend Magda?"

Petra nodded, and then, not wanting her mother to question her any further, closed the door behind her.

She deliberated about whether to tell Jack of his father's liaison with Magda. It was as difficult as deciding whether to tell Magda that she knew. In the end she resolved to keep the knowledge to herself. Magda would soon be returning to Berlin and the affair would no doubt fizzle out; plus, she felt Jack had enough on his plate where his parents' sexual activities were concerned. Surviving the revelation that his mother was hell-bent on divorce and marriage to a man twenty years her junior was difficult enough without also having to tackle the knowledge that his father was having an affair with a girl Jack regarded as one of his own chums.

Any doubts she may have had regarding her decision vanished completely when she met Jack at the refreshment kiosk in Hyde Park. He was jubilant, having just received a letter from her father—a letter in which Ivor said he was delighted to hear they wanted to marry.

"He's given us his blessing and, rather than sending Delia a letter, he's leaving it to me to break the news to your mother."

"Oh! Fan*tastic*!" She threw her arms around his neck, kissing him full on the mouth.

An elderly gentleman walking past them, a bulldog at his heels, cleared his throat censoriously. Neither of them paid him an iota of attention.

"When will you do it?" she asked. "Oh, please say you're

going to do it straightaway, Jack! I can't wait another minute before telling the whole world that we're in love and going to get married!"

"What are your mother's plans today? Do you know?"

With their arms around each other's waist they began walking across the park in the direction of Knightsbridge.

"She's lunching with Wallis or Baba. I can't remember."

"Baba Metcalfe?"

Petra nodded.

Jack looked bemused. "I wonder what your father is going to say when he learns that your mother is so firmly entrenched with the Prince of Wales's set? They're all at least twenty years his junior, aren't they?"

"Thirty years in the case of Baba. And they all nightclub like mad. I'm sure other debs don't run the risk of running into their mother when they go to the Embassy or the Kit Kat Club. Haven't you noticed how difficult it makes things?"

As they left the park and crossed the busy main road, she said, "I think it would be best if I made myself scarce for the next hour or so. I don't think the hopeful bride-to-be should be within earshot of the conversation you're about to have with my mother. And *please* remember to tell her we don't want a long engagement. A wedding at St. Margaret's, Christmas week, would suit perfectly."

"Followed by a honeymoon in Cairo?"

She hugged his arm tightly. "Oh, darling Jack! A honeymoon in Cairo would be *bliss*."

"I thought it would be proper to ask Ivor's permission first."

Jack smiled broadly at the woman who had been almost a surrogate mother to him ever since he was five. He drew Ivor's letter from his inner jacket pocket.

"Permission?" Delia was in the drawing room, waiting for

Harrison to bring the car around. She fumbled in her lizard-skin clutch bag for her cigarette case. "Permission for what, Jack?"

"Permission to ask for Petra's hand in marriage."

The clutch bag slid from Delia's knee to the floor. A gold compact rolled across the carpet toward his feet.

He made no move to retrieve it. Her reaction had left him rigid with shock.

"Marriage?" The blood had drained from Delia's face. "You've written to Ivor asking for Petra's hand in marriage?"

"Under the circumstances . . . his being in Egypt . . . I thought that was the proper thing for me to do." His smile had gone. All he felt was fast-escalating concern. "He was very pleased, Delia." He proffered Ivor's letter. She didn't take it.

Realizing he should have taken more notice of Petra's warning that her mother was likely to be highly irrational about their relationship, he said, "He's given us his blessing and asked that I break the news to you . . ."

He trailed off lamely, appalled by the obvious depth of her distress.

She was still holding the unopened cigarette case, her knuckles white.

"You can't marry Petra." Her voice was hoarse. "You can't, Jack. Trust me. It's impossible."

"But why?" He'd never been more baffled in his life. Delia looked like a woman who had been dealt a deathblow.

"Because . . . because . . . because you *can't*."

Against her Titian-red hair, her skin was almost translucent.

He took a deep breath. "That's obviously not the case, Delia," he said reasonably. "Once Petra is twenty-one she can marry with or without parental consent. Ivor has already given us his blessing. We can marry at any time. We wouldn't, however, wish to while you are so opposed to it. I just don't understand *why* you are so violently opposed to it. Have you heard some gossip about me? Because if you have, let me assure you it's untrue. I've never done anything dishonorable in my life."

Delia gave a barely suppressed sob. "Oh, Jack! I'm *sure* you haven't—and I've heard no gossip about you. None at all."

"Then why . . . ?"

She fumbled to take a Sobranie out of her cigarette case. He reached over and helped her.

"Thank you," she said, her hand trembling violently as he offered her a light.

She inhaled deeply and then, cupping her elbow with her free hand, her arm pressed hard against her body, she said unsteadily, "My objections have nothing to do with you personally, Jack. No woman could hope for a finer young man as a son-in-law. It's just that Petra has known you all her life. When she was a baby you often came with us when I took over from the nanny and walked her in the park. All through the years Petra was growing up, you visited regularly. I think that somehow Petra has grown up *expecting* to marry you—and that isn't the best basis for a marriage, Jack. Especially when the girl in question is only eighteen years old."

"We're in love, Delia," he said flatly. "I love her. She loves me. What better basis for marriage is there than that?"

She caught her breath. "You're not lovers already, are you?"

"No." His reply was quite unequivocal, though he was deeply shocked by the frankness of her question.

"I want you to break off your relationship. I want you to break it off until she is twenty-one. If, when she has had the opportunity to meet lots of other eligible young men, she is still of the same persuasion . . . well, we'll have another conversation about it. Until then I think it best that you don't meet. Not even as friends. Is that understood?"

He nodded, knowing that it was useless to argue with her

further. His nod wasn't one of agreement to the terms she had set. It merely signified he understood quite clearly what her terms were.

There was a light knock on the drawing-room door.

Bellingham entered. "Harrison is out front, my lady," he said, mindful of the time she was expected at the Ritz.

"Thank you, Bellingham." Still distraught, she looked around for her clutch bag.

Jack bent down and retrieved it, along with the spilled contents.

As she took them, she said, "Being in the Foreign Office will make it easy for you to arrange for another posting abroad. I think you should do so, Jack. And until then, perhaps it would be best if you spent time abroad. France, maybe? Or maybe even America."

Without kissing him goodbye as she usually did, she walked from the room, leaving him more crushingly disappointed than he had ever been in his life.

Petra was waiting for him in the gardens in the center of Cadogan Square. The instant she saw him leave the house she knew the kind of news he was bringing.

"She can't have objected!" she cried, running toward him. "She can't have! Not when Papa has given us his blessing!"

"She has," he said heavily, holding her close. "And for the craziest reason."

"That you're not yet earning enough money? That your position at the Foreign Office isn't yet one with enough status? That—"

"That I've been a part of your life for too long for you to be able to judge whether or not you are really in love with me. She wants you to meet more young men—and she wants me to go away for at least three years—after which time if you still feel the same way about me, she says the subject can be discussed again."

"Land's sakes! You're not going to take any notice of such silliness, are you?"

"No," he said, holding her even closer and kissing the top of her hair. "She's just stalling for time in the hope that one of us falls in love elsewhere. We know that isn't going to happen, so there isn't any sense in our spending three years apart."

"What *are* we going to do?"

She stepped away from him a little and looked up into his face.

"I'm going to go to Cairo and speak to your father. I can't put your mother's objections in writing. He won't understand. The only difficulty is that I don't have any leave until the end of August."

"That's only three weeks away. We can manage to see each other, without my mother knowing about it. And then Papa will make her see sense. When Papa really puts his foot down, everyone takes notice. Even King Fuad."

With a decision made she felt a tad better, but only a tad. Her mother's response was so mystifying she didn't know how to begin to understand it. What if her father decided that a three-year separation was actually quite a good idea and rescinded his permission that they could marry? How on earth would they manage to live apart for three years? What if her mother was right, and Jack fell in love elsewhere during that time? He was wildly attractive and girls were always throwing themselves at him. It might be a temptation he couldn't resist.

Her fears only heightened the almost unbearable sexual excitement she felt every time she was with him. She wanted to bind him to her irrevocably.

As the weekend drew near—a weekend she had been invited

to Boudicca's country home in Hampshire—Jack said, "Do you think you could get away with chucking Heathlands?"

"Easily. Boo wouldn't mind. Why?"

"We could have a weekend by ourselves in Brighton. It may be the last chance we have of being alone together for a long time."

She hugged his arm, knowing exactly what it was he had in mind and not having even the slightest reservation.

"Where will we stay?" she asked, her face radiant. "A hotel?"

"No. Archie has a small house on the seafront in The Lanes that his grandfather bequeathed to him. He tells me it's full of olde worlde charm and that there's a smashing little French restaurant only a few steps away."

His voice changed, becoming concerned. "If you have the slightest doubt about this, Petra, tell me. Because, if necessary, I'll do the Old Testament Jacob and Rachel thing and wait seven years for you."

She giggled throatily. "God, really? I'm very impressed, but a wedding at Christmas and a January honeymoon in Cairo is what I'm aiming for—and I don't want our plans put on the back burner for three years, let alone seven."

"Neither do I," he said grimly. "And I'm going to do everything in my power to see that they aren't."

Afterward, when she looked back at that very special weekend, she was amazed at how little shyness she had felt, of how wonderfully right everything had been. He had brought a bottle of vintage champagne and red roses, so many roses that every room in the house was scented with their fragrance.

She had bought a new nightdress in Harrods. It wasn't blatantly erotic. It was a bridal nightdress in oyster-white silk satin; the kind of nightdress she would have packed for her honeymoon.

And a honeymoon was how both of them regarded their stolen hours in Archie's little house.

The evening they arrived they dined in the candlelit French restaurant. Later, in Archie's low, oak-beamed sitting room, Jack put on a recording of Puccini's *Madama Butterfly* and the beautiful music drifted after them as he carried her up the stairs.

For the rest of her life, whenever she heard the heart-stopping strains of "Un bel dì vedremo," she was transported back to the night they became lovers, the window open to the sound of the sea.

Delia asked no questions when her daughter returned to Cadogan Square on Sunday night, saying merely, "How were the Pytchley clan? Blooming?" in a way that indicated she neither expected nor needed any real answer.

The following weekend—which was Magda and Suzi's last in England—was Annabel and Fedya's wedding day. It was a wonderfully grand and joyous occasion. Annabel's train was so long it stretched almost from the altar to the door of the Mowbray estate's fifteenth-century church.

Delia was there, of course, and so even though Jack was one of the grooms, they scrupulously avoided eye contact.

"Flirt with me," Archie said helpfully. "I've always wanted to have a redhead looking adoringly at me. Jack tells me he's setting off for Cairo next Saturday, to enlist your father's help in smoothing some rather troubled water."

"Yes." Petra wasn't sure just how much Jack had told Archie, and she didn't want any of her mother's many friends overhearing their conversation.

"Tell me about the new car you've bought, Archie," she

said, changing the subject. "Is it true you're going to start racing professionally?"

Two days later she was walking down Lower Sloane Street on her way to the hairdresser when she saw Theo Girlington walking toward her.

She ducked her head, hoping that he wouldn't recognize her and that, even if he did, he wouldn't stop.

There was no real reason why he should.

She knew him to speak to only because he was part of her parents' social circle. Since Sylvia's announcement that she was divorcing Jerome, she doubted if her mother had spoken two words to him, though as he was a duke her mother wouldn't have cut him completely.

"What ho! It's Petronella Conisborough, isn't it?" He halted in front of her. "I saw your father earlier today." He grinned at her like the Cheshire cat in *Alice in Wonderland*. "Not that I'm someone he likes to run into too often these days."

She stared at him, remembering her mother's verdict that he was a screwball.

"You can't have," she said, giving him a dismissive smile. "My father is in Cairo."

"Not Conisborough." His grin widened even further. "Your real father. Jerome Bazeljette." There was absolutely no mischief in his voice, or his smile. He simply said it as a statement of fact—a fact of which he obviously thought she was aware. He gave a jolly laugh. "In a rum kind of way we're almost family. Not that I imagine Jack will ever call me 'stepfather.' Can't blame him. I'm only ten years his senior, after all. Give my regards to your mother, Petronella. Goodbye and toodle-oo."

He sauntered off down the street, happily oblivious of the effect his words had had on her.

She stared after him in a daze. Jerome, her father? She wanted to laugh the idea off as too ridiculous for words, but she couldn't.

She remembered her aunt Gwen telling her of how Jerome had been at Cadogan Square the day she was born; how he had held her almost immediately after her birth. She remembered how he had always been there for her; of how, fond though he was of Davina, he had always singled her out. She remembered the interest he had taken in her education and that the Institut Mont-Fleuri had been so conveniently near to his villa at Nyon.

She remembered how, when she was sixteen, he had suggested that, if her mother had no objections, she put an end to calling him "uncle." After a long, tension-filled pause, her mother had said, "Of course not. So silly to use it when you are most definitely not her uncle" and, when Jerome had responded drily, "No, indeed," that her mother had blushed furiously.

She remembered how aghast her mother had been when she had suggested that Jerome should stand in for the traditional father-and-daughter waltz.

Other memories, too, fell into place like the pieces of a jigsaw puzzle. Jerome's constant presence in her mother's life; the way that though she'd been brought up to believe Jerome was her father's friend, her father always had important business elsewhere whenever Jerome visited. The way her mother had made so many lone visits when Petra had been at school in Montreux, always staying with Jerome at Nyon when she had done so. She recalled how her mother's joie de vivre had vanished overnight when Jerome began paying attention to Magda. Most of all, there was her mother's horror when Jack told her they wanted to marry.

Last, but by no means least, she thought of the two nights she and Jack had spent together in Archie's cottage.

She couldn't breathe. Couldn't move. She had to know the

truth. And only two people could tell her. Her mother and Jerome.

She stared around, looking for a telephone booth. There wasn't one in sight and she began walking numbly toward the one in Sloane Square.

Once there she fumbled clumsily in her bag for money. Twice she dropped her sixpenny piece. By the time she fumbled it into the slot she was so terrified of what she was possibly about to hear she thought she would faint.

"Chelsea 3546," Jerome's dearly familiar voice said. "Bazeljette speaking."

She pressed button A. The coin fell into the box.

"It's Petra," she said. "I have to ask you . . . I have to know . . . Are you and my mother lovers?"

There was a stunned silence at the other end of the line and then Jerome said in a voice almost as unsteady as hers, "Petra, my dear. This isn't a conversation we should be having over the telephone. You are obviously very distressed. Where are you? I'll come and meet you—"

"I don't want to meet you, I just want to know the truth." Tears coursed down her face. "Are you and my mother lovers? Have you been lovers for years?"

There was a long silence and she knew he was trying to think of the right words. "Petra, sweetheart," he said at last. "The answer is yes. You are old enough now to understand and I suppose someone who should have known better has told you. I love your mother dearly. I've loved her from the very first moment I met her and—"

With a cry of anguish she dropped the receiver and pushed blindly against the telephone-booth door.

Jerome's voice calling her name followed her as the receiver dangled in midair. She hadn't asked her next question, "Are you my father?," because there was someone else she wanted to hear answer the question. And that someone was her mother.

Tears still raining down her face, she walked the short distance from Sloane Square to Cadogan Square.

Her mother was in the drawing room, seated at her pretty
Chippendale writing desk. She was wearing a pale-mauve
voile dress and her favorite item of jewelry, a three-string pearl
necklace.

As Petra entered the room her mother turned to greet her
but the instant she saw Petra's face her smile vanished.

"What on earth has happened, honey?" she said, jumping
to her feet.

"I ran into Theo Girlington in Lower Sloane Street." Petra
put her hands up, to forestall her mother from hugging her.
"He told me he'd just seen my father."

Delia stopped, her face whitening. "Unless Theo was hot-
foot from Cairo he has bats in the belfry."

"He wasn't referring to Ivor, Mama." Petra's voice sounded
to her as if it were coming from a million miles away. "He was
referring to Jerome."

Her mother tried to speak but couldn't.

"I spoke to Jerome, Mama. He told me that you and he
are . . . that for years you and he have been . . ." She tried to
say the word "lovers" but she could not utter it. "Is he my father?" she managed at last, her voice breaking. "Is what Theo
Girlington said true?"

Her mother's lips were now as white as her face. She looked
as if she were in the seventh circle of hell, impaled on the past,
paralyzed by the present, and unable to conceive of the future.
"I don't know," she said at last. "It's a possibility, Petra. There
was one instance, in the early spring of 1914, when I went to
Jerome for comfort just after I had returned from a trip to
America. It was an isolated instance. Our affair didn't truly
start until much later, after Davina was born. I'm so sorry,
Petra. I never dreamt that there would be such complications."
She made a helpless motion with her hands. "That Jerome may

be your father is something Jerome and I have never talked about . . . never openly acknowledged . . . and he may not be, Petra. Under the circumstances, though, I couldn't allow you and Jack to become engaged. Not when there was even the faintest possibility that Jack was your half—"

"Don't say it!" Petra clapped her hands over her ears, *"Don't say it!"*

She struggled to breathe, numb with pain. She had lost not only Jack but her mother, too, for things could never be the same between them, just as things would never be the same between her and Jack.

"I'm going back to Cairo," she said, fighting to keep hysteria out of her voice. "And I don't want Jack to ever know about this. Do you understand?"

"I understand, Petra dear, but you have to listen to me. You have to let me explain the circumstances—"

"No." Petra's voice was hoarse. "I don't have to listen to another word about you and Jerome. Not now. Not ever." And turning her back on her mother she ran from the room.

She didn't stop running until she was once again in Sloane Street, and when she did, she had three thoughts clear in her mind. First, she couldn't possibly see Jack again, for it would be an agony she would never survive. Second, because Jack would follow her to Cairo, she would stay not at Nile House but with Kate. And third, she had two letters to write: one to Jack, breaking off their relationship; and one to her father telling him she had turned down Jack's proposal for private reasons, and informing him that she was returning to Cairo but would be staying with Kate and on no account wanted Jack told.

On the far side of the street was a travel agent. Hardly able to believe that the world was still turning exactly as it had been doing when she had seen Lord Girlington striding toward her half an hour earlier, she crossed the street.

Minutes later, in a voice she could barely recognize, she booked a Channel crossing and a train first to Paris, then Marseille, and passage on a ship sailing to Alexandria. Unable to face returning home, she walked into Hyde Park and sat on a bench beside the Serpentine and sobbed until she could sob no longer.

Part Three

DAVINA

1934–1939

THIRTEEN

Davina boarded a tram that was packed to capacity and squeezed onto a seat next to a heavily veiled Muslim woman. The tram was traveling from the Mokattam Hills down into the city center, and because she was the only non-Egyptian on board, she immediately became the object of disapproving scrutiny.

She ignored it. She had just spent the morning—as she did every morning—working as a volunteer at an Anglican orphanage tucked away in the tumble of streets at the foot of the Citadel. It was early afternoon and Cairo's March sun was uncomfortably hot. She wiped her forehead and tried to ignore the hen trapped in a wooden cage on her neighbor's knee. When it became a little cooler, she was going to the Gezira Sporting Club with Fawzia to watch Darius play in the club's annual tennis tournament. Petra was also going, though not with them; she would be with her new group of friends.

The hen squawked and its owner slammed a silencing hand down on the top of the cage. Davina averted her eyes and continued to think about her sister.

Ever since Petra had returned to Cairo the previous summer, the closeness that they had always enjoyed had become marred by a strain that Davina couldn't understand. Petra rarely chatted to her in the old carefree manner and never about anything that mattered, such as why she was living with Kate Gunn and avoiding Jack, who had arrived in the city a few days after her.

All she had ever said on that subject was, "We were about to become engaged and then I decided it would be a mistake. That's all there is to it, Davvy. Now if you don't mind, I'd rather not talk about it."

And she hadn't. Ever.

Jack had been totally bewildered by her action.

"I'm sorry, old chap," her father had said. "She doesn't want to see you. I have to respect her wishes. I can't tell you her whereabouts."

"But why is she behaving like this?" Jack had demanded. "She must have given a reason! One minute everything was all right—the next she bolted. The letter she left me explained nothing except that she'd had second thoughts about marrying and was ending our relationship."

"Where relationships are concerned," her father had said, with an edge to his voice Davina had never heard before, "women often do the most inexplicable things."

The tram was now trundling toward Abdin Palace. She wondered whether her father, who had been meeting with King Fuad earlier in the day, was still at the palace, spending time with Prince Farouk.

"You are the very best kind of Englishman," the King had once said to Ivor. "And I want my son to grow up emulating all that is best in the English character."

If any good had come out of Petra's return to Cairo, it was that she had become more aware of what a remarkable man their father was.

"I don't believe he's ever wanted to be in Egypt any more than Delia has," she had once said. "He's here simply because he feels it his duty to help Egypt find her way into the twentieth century."

That Petra now nearly always referred to their mother by her Christian name was one of her newfound oddities. Another had been her decision to learn shorthand and typing.

"Because I'm not going back to London—and if I'm going to remain in Cairo I have to fill up my time with something other than parties," she told Davina. "Kate taught herself shorthand and typing and she's going to help me. Until I become proficient enough to find a job as someone's secretary, Sir Percy is letting me act as a general dogsbody at the residency."

And that was what she was still doing. Her social life was now spent exclusively with the other girls who worked at the residency and Davina rarely saw her.

As the tram rattled toward the Ezbekiya Gardens stop Davina rose to her feet and forged a way to the door. Not only did she now see very little of her sister, she saw even less of her mother. Although Delia had returned to Cairo at the end of last year's season, she had stayed for only a couple of months. At the end of October she had gone back to London where the Bazeljettes were in the middle of their divorce, had come only briefly for Christmas in Cairo, and had then returned again to London.

"She enjoys a different life in London," Petra said when Davina had asked why their mother was now spending so much time in England. "Instead of mixing with Papa's friends—such as Sir John Simon, the Digbys, and Margot Asquith—she's become friends with the Prince of Wales. She and the Prince have always been chummy. There are only a few months' difference between them in age and though some of his friends are a good bit younger than she is—Baba Metcalfe, for instance, is only thirty and Delia is forty-one this year—it doesn't seem to make any difference. She's unconventional enough to fit in very well."

There had been such an odd inflection in her voice when she had uttered the last sentence that Davina was totally bewildered. It was almost as if Petra didn't like their mother much anymore.

Putting on her wide-brimmed sun hat, Davina began walking toward Shepheard's Hotel. Besides being the most popular meeting place in British Cairo, it also boasted the finest English bookshop in the city. The owner had called that morning saying a book she had ordered had arrived.

Once it was tucked under her arm, she didn't linger. The distance between Shepheard's and Garden City wasn't far, but in the hot, noisy city it took long enough on foot—and unlike anyone else she knew, Davina far preferred to walk everywhere. It was her way of keeping in touch with what she always thought of as the *real* Cairo. And to Davina, the real Cairo was Egyptian, not British. As she made her way down Ibrahim Pasha Street, toward its junction with Fouad el-Auwal, she pondered the difficulty of living between a world of grinding poverty and a world of luxury and privilege.

The only other person she knew who had a foot firmly in two such very different ways of life was Darius. Darius's loyalty was to the most extreme wing of Wafd, the political party that wanted to negotiate the British out of Egypt. In private he expressed nothing but contempt for King Fuad. "He's a mere puppet of your government," he often said. "And the reason your father spends so much time with the Prince is to ensure that when he inherits the throne, he, too, will dance to Britain's tune."

She'd long been aware that her father's unofficial role in Cairo was to tutor and mentor Farouk. She wasn't happy about it, but she didn't think it was going to matter too much if, under her father's influence, the fourteen-year-old Prince grew up as pro-British as his father. She was quite sure that by the time he was king, Wafd would have peaceably freed Egypt from British rule.

Her thoughts were diverted by a rumpus in front of her. In the midst of a sea of cars, motorbikes, and gharries, a bullock had come to a sudden and very determined halt. Half a dozen men were pushing on its haunches. As a gang of barefoot boys whooped their way through the traffic to join the fun she began walking faster, well aware that if she didn't get a move on she wasn't going to be ready when Zubair Pasha's chauffeur brought Fawzia to Nile House so they could go to the club together.

There was a surprise waiting for her when she walked into the marble-floored hallway. "Your mother has just arrived!" Adjo announced, a smile nearly splitting his face. "How long for, Missy Davina, I do not know. She's out in the garden. I think you are going to need to explain about the donkey."

Davina had rescued the donkey a few weeks ago when, after being furiously whipped, it had collapsed in the street. She'd paid its owner and, not knowing what else she could do with the starved animal, she had hired another donkey cart and had paid the driver to take his cargo to Nile House.

Fortunately her father had been out when the cart and its pathetic load had rattled through the gates. By the time he had returned, the donkey was installed on the long sloping rear garden beneath the shade of the jacaranda trees, water and alfalfa grass within easy reach.

By now, six weeks later, its ribs were not nearly so visible, but Davina hadn't the slightest intention of exposing it again to life on the Cairo streets. What she could do for the countless other donkeys suffering similarly she didn't yet know, but she knew that she was going to do something.

As she burst out of the house and into the garden she saw that her mother, still in her traveling clothes, was regarding the donkey as fixedly as the donkey was regarding her.

"Mama!" Davina shouted, running across the velvet-smooth lawn. "How smashing! Why didn't you let anyone know you were coming?" Breathlessly she hurtled into her mother's arms.

Laughing with pleasure her mother hugged her tightly. "I assume you're responsible for this animal's presence in the middle of my garden. He can't possibly stay here, Davina. Nile House isn't a zoo."

"No, it's a home. And a home is a sanctuary. And that is what this donkey—and others like it—need."

Her mother who had often expressed horror at the condition of the city's donkeys, looked at the animal.

The donkey looked at her mother.

It was a battle Davina knew was already won.

"There's someone I must put you in touch with," her mother said thoughtfully, stroking the donkey's muzzle. "Her name is Dorothy Brooke. She came to Cairo a few years ago when her husband, an army general, was posted here. Finding that former cavalry horses were living out their lives on the streets as exhausted, emaciated beasts of burden came as a pretty nasty shock to her. She's organized a committee to raise funds to buy those in the last stages of collapse so that they can die peacefully. And yes, before you ask, I've already sent her a hefty donation. The thing is, Davina, if she feels so passionately about the cruel treatment of old cavalry horses, she'll be equally impassioned about the condition of the city's donkeys."

Delia tucked her daughter's arm in her own. "Donkeys, however, are not what I came back to Cairo to talk to you about."

Davina felt her heart sink. "If it's about my having a London season I simply don't want one."

"I know you don't, darling." Her mother began walking down the garden, toward the broad glittering river. "And though you slid out of going to finishing school last year, you're not going to slide out of having a season this year." She raised her free hand to silence all protest. "I'm sorry, honey, but it's absolutely essential. You don't know anyone of your age in London society—and you can't go through life that way. By the end of your season you will have made enough friends to see you through the rest of your life."

"I have friends already. I have Fawzia and Darius and the people I work with at the orphanage—"

"Those are Cairo friends—and quite honestly they are not all suitable, but we'll talk about that later. What I want to talk to you about now is making sure you always have plenty of invites to weekend house parties and balls and having a coterie to go with to point-to-points and to Ascot and Cowes—"

"But I'm *never* going to want to go to house parties and balls and race meetings! I'm just not like that! I don't see the sense in spending three months in London attending dances that I don't want to go to. And I certainly don't want to suffer the silly rigmarole of curtseying to the King with feathers stuck in my hair. Petra may have enjoyed it, but I won't."

"It isn't a silly rigmarole, Davina. It's ceremonial. There's a difference."

"Well, if there is, I honestly don't see it."

They came to a halt, staring out across the river, Davina mutinous, Delia resolved. From across the water there came the sound of lions roaring in the zoo on Gezira Island.

Her mother finally said pleasantly, but with underlying steel in her voice, "When I leave Cairo in four weeks' time, you will be coming with me. And now, if I am to bathe and change before going to this evening's tennis tournament, I have to hurry. Adjo tells me you are going with Fawzia."

"Yes." Davina nodded, knowing that though she had won the battle over the donkey, she had lost the one that counted. When her mother made up her mind to something there was no moving her. However much she hated the thought of it, Davina was going to have to endure a season in London doing all the things she most loathed. The only good thing about it was that she still had four weeks in which to get in touch with Mrs. Dorothy Brooke.

"But you're so *lucky*!" Fawzia said as they drove across the Kasr el-Nil Bridge onto Gezira Island. "I'd give anything in the world to be presented to King George and Queen Mary at Buckingham Palace! Think of all the parties! Think of all the rich, handsome young men you will meet!"

"I am thinking of them and I'm fairly certain that they will bore me to tears."

Fawzia, wearing a knife-straight scarlet silk dress with a heavy gold belt cinching her waist, shook her head disbelievingly. "You can't mean it, Davina. *No one* could mean it. Not if they were in their right mind."

"Then perhaps I'm not in my right mind," Davina said equably, knowing that Fawzia was never going to think the way she did no matter how many years they were friends. "Why don't you ask your father if you can come to London with me? It would make it a bit more bearable for me and it's about time you saw British high society in action."

Fawzia gasped, overcome at such a dizzying prospect. "Oh, Davina! That would be marvelous! I'd so love to see London. And Jack is there now, isn't he?" Her face fell as another thought struck her. "But will my father agree to it? I'd have to be chaperoned. He never lets me go anywhere without being chaperoned. I know how you hate turning up at the club in a chauffeured car, but it's the kind of thing my father insists on. And don't take offense, but he doesn't think much of your mother's chaperoning skills—that you are allowed to wander around Cairo on your own shocks him to the core—and so he might very well not let me go."

"Then we'll just have to assure your father that it won't be my mother, but my aunt, Lady Pugh, my father's elder sister, who will take care of you."

Hope flooded Fawzia's delicately boned face. Her father's admiration for Lord Conisborough was boundless and would extend to his blood relations. He was almost certain to approve of Lady Pugh as a chaperone.

"Oh goodness! This is going to be so wonderful!" she said ecstatically as the limousine entered the club's immaculately kept grounds. "Your mother is a friend of the Prince of Wales, isn't she? And that means I'll probably meet him. He's very attracted to dark-haired women. I've seen photographs of Mrs. Dudley Ward and Lady Furness. I'm far more beautiful than either of them and—oh, Davina!—wouldn't it be utterly heaven if I was to become the Princess of Wales!"

Remembering what Petra had let slip about the Prince's preference for sexually experienced married women, Davina thought this highly unlikely but was too kind to say so. As far as she was concerned, Prince Edward could do far worse than fall for Fawzia—and she rather liked the idea of the future Queen of England being Egyptian.

As they walked to their seats in the crowded stands they drew a lot of attention. Fawzia always turned heads and Davina didn't realize that her fair hair, slim figure, and the simplicity of the apple-green and white polka-dot dress were drawing their own share of admiring glances.

She waved to Petra, who was seated with her friends a few rows behind them. Her mother and father had seats in the front row with Zubair Pasha. On the opposite side of the court Davina could see the willowy figure of Kate Gunn.

There was a ripple of female excitement as Darius came onto the court and Davina could understand why.

He glanced up at the stands and she knew he was looking to see if she was there. She didn't wave, knowing how much he would hate it if she did so. Instead she gave him a discreet thumbs-up sign. He gave her a barely discernible nod and then turned all his attention to the game.

Even though his opponent, the reigning champion, played like a demon, it proved to be a one-sided game. In a nearly faultless display Darius won 6–1, 6–3, 6–2.

Still breathing heavily, he accepted the trophy from the deputy high commissioner with an elation Davina knew had nothing to do with the match. For an Egyptian to beat a British opponent so spectacularly in a club that permitted very few Egyptian members was his own private way of thumbing his nose at people like her father.

As he held the trophy aloft he was surrounded by people congratulating him and she didn't even attempt to join in the crush. She would see him later, when they would be on their own.

That night she couldn't sleep. As she lay in the darkness, the windows of her room above the terrace open, she heard her parents' voices drifting toward her. "I think Ramsay MacDonald is a skunk," her mother was saying of the prime minister. "Insisting you remain here for another two years until Farouk is sixteen is simply not fair. Surely that is a task for Sir Miles Lampson?"

"Sir Miles replaced Percy Loraine as high commissioner because he has a more military cast of mind. But a military education isn't what Farouk needs. Which is where I come in."

There was a long silence and then her mother said, "And just why did our government think a military man was needed here, Ivor?"

"The violent nationalist groups splintering off from Wafd are growing in such strength it's a necessity, Delia."

"I hadn't realized things had got quite so bad."

"The young educated Egyptians who are behind most of

the street violence are becoming dangerous. Containing the movement isn't easy and we can be thankful for the fact the King is still resolutely pro-British. If he weren't, it would be a very different matter."

"Which is why it's necessary for you to continue to influence Prince Farouk?"

"Yes, Delia. I'm sorry. I know how much you hate being here."

"Oh, it's not so bad now that I'm dividing my time between Cairo and London. Things there aren't exactly a bowl of cherries." Her mother's voice sounded depressed. "Jerome is still carrying on his affair with Petra's German friend, who is in London far more often than she is in Berlin."

Her father sighed and then said, "There will be problems for Kate when I'm released from my posting here. Tongues wagging in Cairo are one thing. London is quite a different kettle of fish." He gave a mirthless laugh. "We haven't exactly made life easy for ourselves, have we, Delia?"

"No, Ivor." Delia's voice was full of an emotion Davina couldn't place. "I think it's safe to say that we haven't."

Not understanding the last part of the conversation Davina dozed off, troubled by the thought of the violent nationalist groups—and the possibility that Darius had become a member of one of them.

FOURTEEN

Nothing made the journey to London pleasurable for Davina, not even going with her mother to visit her favorite fashion designer, Madeleine Vionnet. All Davina wanted was to be back in Cairo, especially now that she had made contact with Mrs. Brooke and was helping with the street animals.

"Another few months and we'll have a hospital where our poor war horses will be able to meet a merciful end," Mrs. Brooke had said fiercely. "At the moment the horses we are able to buy are only in temporary stabling, but we have made a start, Lady Davina. And when we have taken care of every old exhausted ex-cavalry horse working in heat they were never bred for, then the next step will be ensuring there are ample water troughs and shade shelters in Cairo's streets."

It was work Davina passionately wanted to be involved in and no number of beautiful evening gowns—gowns that even she knew made her breathtakingly lovely—could compensate for the fact that she wasn't in Cairo.

Out of respect for her mother she suffered the ritual of coming-out with as good a grace as possible. Some events, such as attending the opening of the Royal Academy Summer Exhibition and a Covent Garden opera, she enjoyed hugely. The vast majority of events, though—the never-ending round of parties at which she always met the same people time and time again—bored her to tears. The only ameliorating factor was watching Fawzia's delight. Her exotic looks made her the center of attention at every ball they attended, much to the displeasure of Davina's fellow debutantes.

"She hasn't been presented and so she shouldn't be invited to everything as if she has," was the general complaint.

Davina felt sorry for the grumblers. All of them were keen to snare a highly eligible suitor and it couldn't be easy for them knowing that Fawzia was receiving proposals of marriage nearly every week. She didn't, however, let her sympathy for them alter her insistence that anyone who invited her also had to invite Fawzia.

"She's been presented to her own monarch, King Fuad, and that is all that matters," she would say airily, not knowing whether it was all right or not, nor caring.

Just when she thought she could not endure another week of partying, her mother said, "You're going to the Dartington House ball tonight, Davina, aren't you?"

"If you say so." It wasn't in her nature to show exasperation, but sometimes she just couldn't help it. "Why?"

"Because I'm having a rather special small dinner party this evening. Prince Edward is going to be guest of honor and I thought, before you and Fawzia left, that the two of you might join us for cocktails."

"Smashing. I haven't met him since I was a little girl and you took me with you to Sandringham. As for Fawzia . . . she's been champing at the bit to be introduced to him socially. Who are your other guests?"

"The Metcalfes. Lord Denby. And Wallis Simpson."

Davina didn't take the interest in her mother's social life that Petra did, but even she could see there was something a little odd about the guest list. "What about Mr. Simpson?"

"Ernest has business affairs to attend to," her mother said, looking uncomfortable.

Davina frowned. Surely her mother wasn't setting up a dinner party to facilitate an affair between her friend and Lord Denby? Wallis Simpson was, she knew, only a year or two younger than her mother and, according to her mother, Lord Denby was elderly and more than a little doddery. "I'm sorry. I don't quite understand—"

"And neither do I, honey," her mother said drily. "All I know is that Wallis is just back from a trip to the States and David . . . Prince Edward . . . has asked me to arrange tonight's party—and to invite Wallis."

Davina stared at her. "You mean he wants to meet Wallis?"

"No, darling. Thanks to Wallis's friendship with Thelma Furness, the Simpsons and David are already on easy terms. They've been his guests at Fort Belvedere several times. I think tonight's dinner is to be a welcome-home party for her."

"Oh! I see," Davina said, not sure that she saw at all. She shrugged her shoulders. Her mother's friends and her mother's social life were, after all, nothing to do with her. She was more worried about how she was going to survive the rest of the season.

Surprisingly, it was a dapper-looking Prince Edward who provided the answer.

"Toynbee Hall," he said helpfully when she had told him how she spent her time when in Cairo. "It's in the East End—Commercial Street, Whitechapel—and it's the most radical center for social reform there is." The Prince had the most unexpected accent, plummy vowels embellished with a dash of pseudo-Cockney and, at times, a pseudo-American drawl. "I know about the place," he continued, "because a friend of mine took me on an incognito visit. It's a settlement house, the idea being that those giving aid to the poor should also live among the poor. It's a good idea, don't you think? If I were you I'd trot along there. I'm sure you could be useful."

Davina was so astonished that the Prince of Wales was giving her such advice, she had to try hard not to let her jaw drop. Her mother couldn't very well forbid her to volunteer at Toynbee Hall when it was the Prince's suggestion. He had solved her problem and she gave him a grateful smile.

Relaxed, he smiled back, his eyes twinkling. Even wearing low-heeled shoes she was the taller, and though she could well understand why women all over the world considered him a pinup to rival any Hollywood star, she didn't find herself attracted to him. He was too slightly built and, despite the premature pouches beneath his eyes, too boyish looking. She liked him, though. It would have been impossible for her not to like him when he had visited a place such as Toynbee Hall out of genuine interest.

The Metcalfes and Wallis hadn't yet arrived and though Fawzia was doing all she could to make an impression on him and though Prince Edward was putting her at her ease chatting about a trip he had made to Egypt, Davina could tell, by the way he kept looking toward the door, that his thoughts were elsewhere.

Bellingham entered the room to discreetly announce that the Pughs' car had arrived. Though it was the custom not to leave a room until the Prince did, he accepted their apologies with easy, almost American informality.

Fawzia spend the rest of the night talking about him: his interest in Egypt, his handsome looks.

Gwen, who had a low opinion of Prince Edward's dalliances with married women such as Freda Dudley Ward and Thelma Furness, endured Fawzia's rhapsodies with gritted teeth. Davina barely heard them. Even though she had yet to visit Toynbee Hall, she had already made up her mind to volunteer. Doing so would mean no more daytime socializing. To say that her mother would not be pleased was putting it mildly.

Fawzia too was going to be upset if it meant her own socializing was curtailed.

Davina bit her lip. She decided that even if she missed the
daytime events it didn't mean Fawzia couldn't attend them—
especially as Gwen would be chaperoning her.

A few days later, telling Gwen and Fawzia that she wanted a
little time to herself, she journeyed by bus and tube to a part
of London she doubted any member of her family had ever
visited. It was like another country.

Walking up Whitechapel's Commercial Street she was reminded of Cairo. The difference between the elegant streets
and palatial villas where she lived and the squalid streets beyond it was the same. Even though she was wearing a very
modest candy-striped dress, she stuck out like a sore thumb—
and knew it.

The majority of those bustling past her looked to be Jewish and spoke a language she didn't recognize. The small dark
shops sold fruit and vegetables she didn't recognize, but the
smell was familiar. It was the smell of unwashed bodies, the
smell of cheap fried food. The smell of poverty.

None of it came as a surprise to her. What did come as a
shock was Toynbee Hall. She had expected a smoke-scarred
building in keeping with the neighborhood. Instead, screened
from the street by a block of dingy warehouses, it was fronted
by an Elizabethan gatehouse with an oriel window.

Intrigued, she stepped through the arched entrance and
found a large Tudor-style, redbrick building, its walls covered in ivy. Set around a narrow quadrangle, the house had
steep gables, tall chimney stacks, and mullioned windows with
lovely leaded panes.

Encouraged she hitched her shoulder bag a little higher and
walked toward the open door.

A few moments later she was standing in what she took to be the reception area, talking to a middle-aged woman in twinset and pearls who eyed her doubtfully. "Volunteer work? Have you ever done any voluntary work in a critically deprived area? It's very hands-on here in Whitechapel. It isn't just making cups of tea and handing out biscuits. And you do seem a little young, if you don't mind my saying so."

Davina's eyes held hers steadily. "I'm nearly nineteen and I've got lots of experience working in extremely deprived areas."

A troop of children clattered past.

"Have you, indeed?" the woman said when the children had disappeared from view. "And just where was this?"

A pleasant-looking bespectacled man of about thirty, wearing good tweeds and carrying a doctor's bag, hurried out of a nearby room and scooped up a file from the reception desk.

Knowing that the woman was expecting her to say something foolish, such as "the less fashionable part of Piccadilly," Davina said pleasantly, "Cairo. The Old City. And no matter how horrific Whitechapel's slums, they can't be worse than the slums of Fustat or Khan el-Khalili."

"Cairo?" The young man turned toward her, his face alight with interest. "Now that must have been educational, don't you think, Miss Scolby?" There was the soft burr of the Scottish Highlands in his voice and more than a hint of Celtic red in his hair. "What kind of volunteer work did you do there, Miss . . . ?"

Davina made a split-second decision not to say "Lady Davina Conisborough." "Conisborough. Davina Conisborough. And I helped out in an Anglican orphanage."

"Then you're good with children?"

Miss Scolby, who had been startled when Davina mentioned Cairo, pursed her lips, clearly not too pleased at having the interview taken out of her hands.

"Yes," Davina said to him, untroubled by the woman's ruffled feathers.

"Then if you've got the rest of this afternoon free, come with me. My wife usually gives me a hand, but she's visiting her parents in Scotland and won't be back for two more weeks. Do you have any nursing experience?"

She shook her head.

"It doesn't matter. I'm off to a local school to do a general medical inspection. The children are from five to eight years and some of them need a little reassuring. You look as if you might be quite good at that."

"I am." Davina was too much her mother's daughter to have any truck with false modesty.

He shot her a friendly grin. "Then let's go." And tucking the file under his arm he led the way out of the building, saying, "I'd better introduce myself. My name is Fergus Sinclair. Aileen and I are fairly new to Toynbee. Would you like me to tell you about the work we're doing?"

"No, Davina," said her mother when Davina came home. "No, no, and no. Occupying your time with a little charity work in Cairo is one thing. Acting as an unpaid nursing assistant in the East End of London is quite another. Heaven only knows what you may have picked up from those children. Some of them probably had head lice."

"They all did—and sores and rashes. And nearly all of them were malnourished."

"Malnourished?" She had caught her mother's attention.

"Malnourished," she said again firmly. "Men in the East End have been unemployed for so long that all their wives put on the table is bread and dripping and tea laced with condensed milk. Because the children are underfed, they're vulnerable to

disease. Dr. Sinclair and his wife are carrying out an inocula-
tion program. That is where I come in. East End children aren't
used to seeing doctors—and they're certainly not used to the
sight of a hypodermic needle. I'm to be what Dr. Sinclair terms
'a reassuring presence'—and I'm also to make myself useful to
Mrs. Sinclair, who is a state registered nurse."

They were in her mother's bedroom and Delia was seated
at her dressing table. She drummed scarlet-painted fingernails
on its art-deco surface.

"It's not that I *mind* you doin' charitable work," she said at
last. "I'm glad you have a well-developed social conscience and
that you care about people less fortunate than yourself. This
summer, though, when you're halfway through your season,
just ain't the right time."

It wasn't often that her mother said "ain't" anymore. Davina knew that the lapse revealed just how upset she was.

Taking a deep breath she set about trying to make her
mother feel better. "It won't make much difference to my
season," she said, sitting beside her on the vanity bench and
sliding an arm around Delia's waist. "If you let me help Dr.
Sinclair during the day, I promise you I'll attend every evening
event."

"And as most evening events don't finish until the early
hours of the morning, when will you catch up on your sleep?"

"I'll manage." She kissed her mother on the cheek, knowing that she had, for once, got her own way. "And to show you
how much I love you, I'll put in an appearance at your cocktail
party this evening. Where's Fawzia? If our evening is going to
start a little earlier than usual she'll need to know."

"Jack has taken her to an exhibition at the Tate."

"Unchaperoned?" This time it was Davina's turn to raise
her eyebrows.

Her mother reached for her scent. "Yes. It won't harm for

once. They make a very attractive couple and if Jack should propose to her—and I don't see why he shouldn't considering how many other proposals of marriage she's received—then I think Zubair Pasha would give them his blessing."

It was on the tip of Davina's tongue to remind her mother that Jack was quite possibly still in love with Petra. She didn't do so. On the few occasions when she'd spoken of Jack and Petra, her mother had speedily changed the subject. A cloud of Jean Patou's Joy enveloped them and Delia rose to her feet.

If her mother wanted to do a little matchmaking she was, after all, quite entitled to do so—and Petra's heart wouldn't be hurt, for she'd made it quite clear that she no longer loved Jack. Which, as far as Davina was concerned, was a shame, for Jack would have made the best brother-in-law she could imagine.

The first person she saw when she went down for cocktails was the dark-eyed, dark-haired Baba Metcalfe. Baba was the daughter of the late Lord Curzon, a man who had been a close friend of her father's. Over the years, Davina had met her quite often. Her husband, though, came as quite a shock.

She had imagined Fruity Metcalfe as being a mild-mannered kind of chap. The powerfully built man who removed his arm from around Baba's waist to shake hands with Davina exuded power. As dark-haired as Baba, and abnormally pale-skinned, he had a fierce, almost overpowering intensity about him.

"We haven't met before, though I've known your mother for years," he said, holding her hand in a strong grip far longer than was necessary. "She tells me you prefer the exoticism of Egypt to bread-and-water life in London."

His piercing black eyes moved over her face, focusing on her mouth in a way that was so blatantly sexual, she flushed scarlet.

His lips parted in a smile—and she knew it was with satisfaction at the effect he was having.

"I prefer Egypt because I think of it as home," she said, forcing herself to look away from his hypnotic gaze.

Baba was no longer anywhere near. Across the room Fawzia was standing close to Jack. He was deep in conversation with Argentina's ambassador to Britain and Fawzia was looking at him with an expression on her face that indicated Delia could have been right in thinking a proposal from Jack was one Fawzia might well accept.

"Have you ever traveled to Germany?" Baba's husband asked, his sexual magnetism coming at her in waves. "I think you would like it. Under Hitler it's becoming very youth-conscious. Something it would do Britain good to emulate."

She was just about to say that she had never been to Germany and to excuse herself and escape from him when Jerome walked into the room, his slight limp a little more noticeable than usual. On seeing them, he strolled toward them.

"Hello, Davina," he said, giving her an affectionate smile. "I haven't seen much of you while you've been in London. Perhaps it's something we can remedy. As for you, Tom, I thought you were still in Italy paying homage to Mussolini."

"And I thought you were in Germany, with Brunhilde."

Jerome gave a slight shrug of his shoulders. "If you're referring to Magda, I did go to Berlin to spend time with her earlier this year. I won't be going again. Unlike you, I'm not an admirer of Hitler and I don't like what's happening in Germany and—as Magda does—I won't be seeing her again. And now, if you'll excuse me, Tom, I'm going to steer Davina into a quiet corner in order to catch up on some family gossip."

With his hand beneath her arm he propelled her as far away from Fruity as, in the confines of the drawing room, it was possible to get.

"Thank you for that, Uncle Jerome," she said, her nerves still jangling. "He made me very hot and bothered. I was well out of my depth."

"I'm not surprised. Tom is a seducer on a massive scale. I suggest you steer well clear of him. Now, what are you going to have to drink? Do you do cocktails—it looks as though Delia's mixing some rather lethal gin fizzes—or d'you stick to champagne?"

"I stick to champagne. And why do so many people refer to Tom as Fruity? It's doesn't suit him. It's too comic a nickname for someone who looks like a demon king."

"The answer is, that they don't," he said, amused. "The only Fruity, is Fruity Metcalfe."

"Then who have I just been talking to?" she asked, looking back to where the demon king had been joined again by Baba.

"Sir Oswald Mosley. Tom is his nickname. Far from being Baba's husband, he's her brother-in-law. His wife, Cimmie, died a couple of months ago."

Her mother, looking sensational in a dress of lime-green chiffon that fitted close to her slim figure yet floated as if in a breeze, was carrying two gin fizzes in Baba and Tom's direction. As she handed them the drinks, Davina saw Tom Mosley slide his free hand once again around his sister-in-law's waist.

If Jerome also saw what looked to Davina to be a shocking intimacy, he made no comment on it.

"Tell me how you are enjoying your first season," he said with the kind of avuncular interest in her activities he'd always shown. "In the general way of things your mother would have kept me in touch about it, but I haven't seen a lot of her lately." There was deep regret in his voice and his gold-flecked eyes were no longer on her but on her mother, who was again mixing cocktails with great expertise. "It's something I intend to rectify."

———

Two weeks later Aileen Sinclair returned from Scotland. She was tall, with a square-jawed, high-cheek-boned face and a mass of dark hair. Like Fergus, the clothes she wore were good quality, but had seen better days. Her mauve-flecked tweed skirt was faded; her pink twinset had suffered far too many trips to the laundry; and her sandals were inelegantly flat and serviceable.

"We're going to make a wonderful team, Davina," she said with a wide, friendly smile and Davina knew instantly that she had at last found a friend who, unlike Fawzia, shared her passion for helping others.

"Fergus thinks you should be taught how to give inoculations and so I have a couple of oranges with me for you to practice on. Have you always wanted to learn a little nursing?"

"Yes—though when I was very young I wanted to be a doctor. And then I realized that I wasn't clever enough."

"Then be a nurse. You could do your training at Guy's Hospital. For now, though, let's have you practicing puncturing these oranges."

And with another wide smile her new friend passed her an orange and a syringe.

FIFTEEN

For the next two weeks Davina enjoyed every hour of every day. Before anyone else was awake she left the house and traveled to Whitechapel on public transport. While Fawzia, with Gwen—and sometimes Jack—attended de rigueur events such as the Wimbledon tennis championship, Davina accompanied Fergus and Aileen on their tireless rounds.

At first she had thought that was what Toynbee Hall was all about.

"Heavens, no," Fergus said with a chuckle when she put her assumption into words. "Toynbee has a far broader aim. It's a social workshop on a grand scale, Davina."

They had taken a break from treating the seemingly endless stream of lice-ridden children. Fergus wrapped his hands around a mug of tea. "One of our prime aims is education. There are year-round day classes for the unemployed—all free, of course. There are also weekly debates—often with leading political figures as speakers. Those days the hall is packed to overflowing."

He put his mug down, took his glasses off, and pinched the bridge of his nose. "One of our central tenets is that education should be a two-way street. How can politicians, for instance, fight poverty and unemployment if they never see these conditions face-to-face? By living for a few weeks at Toynbee they do so. Men with the experience of Toynbee behind them are men who can truly make a difference."

He gave a wry grimace. "I just wish more of this country's useless aristocracy would follow their example instead of spending their time drinking cocktails and going to balls so lavish the cost of even one would provide an adequate meal for the half of Whitechapel. How they can live as they do, in their vast houses and estates, while most British people have neither running water nor heating is beyond my ken."

At the stricken look on her face he gave an apologetic grin. "Sorry. I didn't mean to go off on a rant. It's just something I feel very passionate about. I think we'd better start work again or we'll be here till midnight and Aileen won't want that. Usher in our next snotty-nosed patient, will you?"

Afterward she knew she should have told him about her privileged background, but she hadn't known how to bring up the subject again. There was something else, too.

Whitechapel was an area of Jewish immigrants. The language she'd heard on the streets the first time she had walked from Aldgate East station to Toynbee Hall was Yiddish. Synagogues stood at nearly every corner. And vicious attacks on Jews, by members of Sir Oswald Mosley's new and growing British Union of Fascists, were a daily occurrence.

"And it will only grow worse," Aileen had said to her gravely. "Like Hitler, his Fascist rhetoric appeals to bullies and thugs, especially when they can parade around in Blackshirt uniforms and give stiff-armed, Nazi-type salutes."

Whenever Davina thought of Sir Oswald Mosley she cringed. If Fergus and Aileen were to discover that Mosley frequently dropped in for cocktails at her home, they wouldn't want anything further to do with her.

———

"Have you given any more thought about applying to Guy's for nursing training?" Aileen asked her one day when they were taking a lunch break. "Fergus would have to manage without you, but we'll still be able to see quite a bit of each other. Things aren't as draconian for student nurses as they used to be. You are now occasionally allowed out of the hospital grounds."

They were sitting in Toynbee Hall's quadrangle. Beside them was a tub of brilliant orange nasturtiums and a bee was darting into the heart of first one flower and then another.

Davina took a deep breath and said, "I am going to apply, but not at Guy's."

"Not at Guy's?" Aileen stared at her, dumbfounded. "But Guy's is the most famous teaching hospital in the world! You can't possibly consider applying anywhere else. Especially not when you're a Londoner!"

"I'm not really, Aileen. Though I was born here, it isn't my home. I'm only here for the summer because . . . because it's the season and my mother insisted on it."

Aileen blinked. Fergus simply said, "Your mother insisted on you being in London during the season? You're not making sense, Davina. What do you mean?"

"Season with a capital S, Fergus. It's a class thing," she added unhappily. "Presentation at court and . . . and all that."

Aileen's jaw dropped. "You mean you're a debutante? You're one of those young women whose photograph appears in *Tatler*?"

Davina nodded and waited for a chill to descend.

Neither Aileen or Fergus seemed upset.

"But how on *earth*," Aileen asked, "do you manage when you're working for such long hours every day? Don't debutantes have to go to lots of parties and to Henley and Ascot and places like that?"

With thankful incredulity Davina realized that instead of being appalled, Aileen was intrigued.

"Yes. But because I'm working here my mother has let me off the Henley and Ascot stuff. I still have to go to other coming-out balls, though. It would be awfully bad manners not to."

"Dear heaven! How much sleep are you getting?"

"Not much."

Their eyes held and then simultaneously they burst into laughter.

Later, when they were packing up their medical equipment, Fergus said to her, "Just out of curiosity, Davina. Who is your father? He must be fairly well-heeled."

Secure that her background wasn't going to affect the friendship she enjoyed with the Sinclairs, she said, "Viscount Conisborough. He's a British adviser to King Fuad. That's why I can't apply to Guy's. I'm going to have to do my training in Cairo."

The Sinclairs stared at her as if she'd said she was going to have to do it on the moon. Dazed, Fergus put his stethoscope into his doctor's bag and fastened it shut.

"Ye gods," he said. "And does your father know the kind of work you've been doing this last few weeks?"

Always truthful, Davina hesitated. Since she'd begun working at Toynbee Hall and going to parties at night, she hadn't had a minute free for letter writing. "I'm not sure. I'm certain my mother will have told him. He won't object," she added as she saw the expression on Fergus's face. "I've always done lots of voluntary work."

"I've heard of Conisborough." They were ready to leave the cramped little room that had served as their clinic. "He's a financier, isn't he?"

Davina was taken aback. "Yes," she said, alarmed. "But he's just as much committed to a life of service as you and Aileen are. It's a different kind of service, of course. Yours is to people and my father's is to his country. He serves the British government in Egypt—and does so often under very difficult circumstances—because his work is in the best interests of Britain."

Fergus nodded, though he didn't look convinced.

"And is your mother Lady Conisborough who is the famous American high-society hostess?" he asked, finally picking up his doctor's bag and leading the way to the door.

"Well, she is American," Davina said as they stepped out into a narrow cobbled street, "and she does have a lot of friends. I hadn't realized she was famous."

With the air of a man trying to get to the bottom of things, Fergus said patiently, "Davina, is your mother the Lady Conisborough who is friends with Sir John Simon, the foreign secretary? And with Winston Churchill, who used to be chancellor of the exchequer and is the only person in the government who realizes what a risk to our peace Hitler is? The Lady Conisborough who is known to be a longtime friend of the Prince of Wales?"

"Yes," Davina said doubtful of the reaction this was going to meet with. "How do you know so much about my mother?"

"The whole of the country knows about your mother. Hannen Swaffer, at the *Daily Sketch,* writes about her every chance he gets. Nothing on earth would induce me to read *Tatler,* but you can bet your life that her photograph is in it nearly every month. She's acknowledged as being one of the country's greatest beauties. Didn't you know?"

"No," she said, feeling a little foolish, "I didn't. And if my mother does, she wouldn't take it seriously. She's too busy being interested in other things to care about her looks."

One of the things her mother was very interested in was Aileen Sinclair's plan to open a free clinic for women.

"Tell me more about it, Davina," she said, sitting in bed with a breakfast tray across her lap. "Is it to be a general-health clinic?"

"No." Davina seated herself on the edge of the bed. "It's to be a clinic to help the women who have nine or ten children, and can't afford to feed them, from having any more."

Her mother had been in the process of pouring herself a cup of coffee, and now spilled it over the embroidered tray cloth.

"Land's sakes, Davina! You're a single young woman of eighteen! You can't be fitting women with diaphragms! Your father would have ten fits!"

Davina giggled. "I wouldn't be doing anything like that. I'm not qualified. And besides, by the time the clinic is up and running the season will be over and I will be back in Cairo."

Her mother looked relieved. "What is the clinic going to be called, honey? Because if it's called a contraceptive clinic, or a family planning clinic, a lot of men won't let their wives be seen entering it."

Glad that her mother was so unshockable, Davina mopped up the spilled coffee with a napkin and said, "Aileen intends calling it simply the Free Clinic because apparently men do kick up a fuss when their wives are given the power to have only the children they want. It's a fuss I don't understand when they are living in such dreadful poverty that half the babies die when they are only a few weeks old. Parts of Whitechapel are just as bad as parts of Cairo."

Her mother said nothing, but looked grim. Davina didn't know if it was because her mother disapproved of the fact that her daughter was familiar with such parts of Cairo, or because she was thinking of the women who, living in tenements with no running water and no sanitation apart from a lavatory that had to be shared with thirty or so families, gave birth in unutterably squalid conditions.

"I'd like to meet the Sinclairs, Davina," Delia said thoughtfully. "They sound as if they could do with financial help to get their free clinic idea off the ground. Why don't you bring them to Cadogan Square this evening? Early. I'm dining with Margot at eight."

Davina had great reservations about asking Fergus and Aileen to Cadogan Square. She couldn't imagine either of them feeling comfortable when they were greeted by a butler and waited on by maids and footmen. But if her mother was going to sink some money into Aileen's free clinic, Davina knew she would have to invite them.

"My mother would like to meet you both," she said when she met them in the dreary little room that was to serve as their clinic for the day.

Fergus quirked an eyebrow and for a dreadful moment Davina thought he was going to decline the invitation. Then Aileen said, "Well, that's only natural when you're spending each and every day with us. If I was your mother, I would want to meet us as well!"

The three of them traveled by tube from Whitechapel to Kensington and then walked from Sloane Street to Cadogan Square.

As they approached the splendid porticoed entrance Fergus made a sound in his throat that, for a Scot, could mean anything and which Davina suspected was disapproval at the private wealth the house signified.

Bellingham opened the door and Davina was acutely aware that though she'd always taken a butler for granted, Fergus and Aileen most certainly did not.

"Fergus and Aileen, let me introduce you," she said, trying to put things on as casual a footing as possible. "Bellingham has been the butler here since before I was born. Bellingham, Dr. Fergus Sinclair and Mrs. Sinclair."

"How do you do. Sir. Madam." Bellingham inclined his head and at that moment the doorbell rang again and this time a footman opened the door.

To Davina's delight it was Jerome.

"Davina, my dear," he said, and immediately gave her a hug and a kiss on the cheek. "What a pleasure to find you here—and what a rarity. I understand you've more or less exchanged Kensington for Whitechapel?"

Happy for the opportunity to introduce Fergus and Aileen to the person she loved more than anyone else in the world, apart from her real family, she proceeded to make introductions. "Sir Jerome is an MP, an old family friend," she said to Fergus and then, to Jerome, "Fergus and Aileen are resident volunteers at Toynbee Hall. It's an—"

"I know exactly what Toynbee Hall is, thank you, Davina. I'm speaking there on the Liberal Party's stance on trade unionism next week."

Jerome, resplendent in a beautifully tailored dinner jacket, shook hands with Aileen and Fergus. "You get to the debates, do you, Dr. Sinclair? It would be nice to see you there next Wednesday." And with easy familiarity he steered Aileen and Fergus toward the drawing room's double doors.

Davina could hear the sound of laughter and the clink of glasses. As the realization dawned that her mother was throwing one of her early cocktail parties Davina's horror knew no bounds. All she could think of was that the three of them needed to leave immediately.

"Uncle Jerome!" she called after him. "Please stop!"

It was too late. The footman threw open the double doors and Jerome squired Fergus and Aileen into the drawing room as easily as if he'd known them for years.

Several eyebrows rose, not so much at the leather elbow patches on Fergus's jacket as at Davina's cotton day dress. Where Fergus was concerned, nearly every one of her mother's friends dressed similarly when at their country estates, shabby good-quality tweeds being de rigueur, and it was easy for everyone to make the assumption that Fergus had driven straight up from the country.

The way she and Aileen were dressed was, however, a different matter. Her pink-and-white candy-striped dress and Aileen's Sunday-best floral were grossly inappropriate.

Her mother, wearing a midnight-blue, seductively cut lamé dress, her hair fashionably upswept, gave a cry of delight and headed straight toward them.

Any discomfort the Sinclairs might have felt vanished within seconds. They were charmed by Delia's American informality and her warm welcome.

"I've so much I would like to talk to you both about," she had said immediately. "I've been wondering if Toynbee Hall organizes holidays for disadvantaged children? My husband's family home, Shibden Hall, is in Norfolk, within sight of the sea. We've had tenants in it for most of the years we have been in Egypt, but their tenancy came to an end some months ago. That being the case, it occurred to me it would make a cracking good holiday home for deprived children. What d'you think, Dr. Sinclair?"

Fergus was bowled over as most men were on first meeting her mother. He said, "A feasible idea, Lady Conisborough? I think it's an absolutely grand idea!"

"Then let's talk about it more over a drink." And tucking a hand through both Fergus's arm and Aileen's, Delia led them away from Davina and across the room, introducing them to various people as she did so.

Davina said apprehensively to Jerome, "There's no chance

of Sir Oswald Mosley dropping by, is there? If there is, I have to get Aileen and Fergus out of here PDQ."

"Not a hope. Delia went to one of his public meetings with Baba and said it was like a Nuremberg rally. Banners, martial music, and black-shirted thugs giving short shrift to any hecklers. Mosley started raving about the Jews. Delia told him later that as a large number of her friends were Jewish he might find it more comfortable not to visit Cadogan Square again. And he hasn't."

He shrugged his shoulders unhappily. "I wish everyone had the same reaction, but they don't. Sylvia and her husband have become hard-line converts. It makes it hard on Jack. The last thing his career needs is for him to be linked politically with the British Union of Fascists."

Vastly relieved that Sir Oswald Mosley wouldn't be making an appearance, Davina looked around the room.

Petra's friend, the former Annabel Mowbray, was standing near one of the windows with her husband, but Davina did not recognize the vast majority of the other people in the room. "Who is the plain, neat-looking woman sitting on the sofa chatting with Lady Portarlington?" she asked.

The corners of Jerome's eyes crinkled. "That's your mother's bosom chum, Wallis Simpson. Have we to go over and have a word? I like her. She's full of wisecracking vitality."

As they crossed the room toward Wallis, Winnie Portarlington rose to her feet, blew a kiss in Jerome's direction, then walked languidly over to join Annabel.

"There's no need for introductions, Jerome," Wallis said in an attractively rasping voice when they reached her. She turned to Davina, "I've guessed who you are." She flashed a lightning-quick smile. "And I can tell from the way you are dressed that you didn't expect to walk into a cocktail party, but your dress is exactly the kind I like: unfussy, yet pretty."

Davina was certain Wallis was sincere for she was wearing a dress unadorned by sequins, bugles, or beads. It was of black crepe de chine and it was tailored to within an inch of its life, its only adornment a square-cut emerald pin. Her hands were large and, perhaps in order not to bring attention to them, her nails were unpolished. Her dark hair, parted in the center and taken back in crimped waves over her ears, was so sleek she might have been Chinese. She didn't look at all as Davina had imagined.

Wallis patted the space on the sofa vacated by Winnie Portarlington. "Sit down and tell me all about yourself," she said in the tone of a headmistress speaking to a prefect, and then, to Jerome: "Delia may be a divine hostess, but not, apparently, where her daughter is concerned. Davina is still without a drink. Would you get her a cocktail, Jerome, please?"

Jerome looked startled. Her mother could be breathtakingly direct, but for sheer bossiness Wallis beat her hands down.

"I'm afraid I don't drink cocktails, Mrs. Simpson," she said affably.

"Of course you do. Everybody does—and your mother makes swell cocktails. She should. I taught her." Again came the lightning-quick grin that took the sting out of her words. She looked across to Fergus and Aileen who were talking to a beautiful woman Davina didn't at first recognize. Then she realized it was the film actress Merle Oberon.

Wallis took a sip of her highball and said musingly, "Your friend's husband reminds me of the Prince of Wales, Davina. He has the same quiet manner and charm."

It was said with an air of such proprietary knowledge of the Prince that Davina, remembering the gossip her mother had passed on with regard to Wallis's relationship with Prince Edward, could think of nothing to say in response. She was saved by Wallis saying, "Even in a cotton dress your friend looks spectacularly lovely. Tell me all about her and her husband. Who are they? Where are they from?"

And as Jerome handed her a very welcome gin fizz, Davina proceeded to tell Wallis all about the pioneering work Fergus and Aileen were doing in London's East End.

SIXTEEN

The next day, before the three of them left Toynbee Hall for the school where they were scheduled to do inoculations, Fergus said, "Your mother is an exceptional person, Davina." He shifted his heavy doctor's bag from one hand to the other as they walked across the cobbled quadrangle. "Offering Shibden Hall as a holiday home is such a generous gesture, I don't know how Toynbee will ever be able to thank her."

"She doesn't need thanks," Davina said, happy that the Sinclairs' introduction to her mother had turned out so well. "She just doesn't like the thought of Shibden standing empty."

Aileen linked arms with her. "And she was *riveted* by the idea of a clinic giving free advice to women on contraception. She said she'd never seen a diaphragm and would I show her one."

Davina's eyes nearly popped out of her head.

"Great God, Aileen!" Fergus said, when he was able to speak. "You didn't do so at her cocktail party, did you?"

"No, silly." She giggled. "They aren't something I carry around in my handbag."

As they crossed a busy road to enter a narrow street of tenement buildings, Aileen hugged Davina's arm. "The financial help your mother has promised the clinic is going to make all the difference to how soon it can be opened. I never imagined a viscountess being a Socialist, Davina, but your mother is one. Through and through."

It was, Davina knew, the highest accolade Aileen Sinclair could give.

A day or two later she mentioned Darius, prompted when Aileen commented, "I expect your mother is hoping that you'll meet a nice young man and fall in love during the season."

They were seated at opposite sides of a table, writing up Fergus's barely decipherable medical notes.

Davina put her pen down. "That's the general idea, but I think by now my mother knows it isn't going to happen."

Aileen finished the sentence she was writing and then looked up at her. "Why not?" she asked, curious.

"My mother doesn't know why not—apart from the fact that I never want to live anywhere but Cairo which is certainly not where any of the young men I meet live. But the real reason is that the only person I can ever imagine falling in love with is the son of one of my father's friends."

She had never put her feelings for Darius into words and now she flushed a bright pink.

"But surely that's perfect? What could be better? I can understand your father may well view having spent money on a London season for you as having been a waste of time, but think how pleased he and his friend will be."

Davina shook her head. "No. Darius is Egyptian and he hates the fact that Britain controls Egypt. Nearly all the wealth from the country's cotton crop goes into British pockets, and what doesn't goes into the pockets of a handful of Egyptian landowners. None of it filters down to the peasants who work the land. My father doesn't realize yet just how fiercely anti-British Darius is but when he does, Darius will be the last person in the world he would want me to marry."

"And how does Darius feel? Is he prepared to take on your father?"

Davina's flush turned a fiery red. "We're just friends at the moment, Aileen. We've been friends ever since I was a little girl. And that's how Darius still thinks of me," she added miserably, "as if I'm a little girl."

"Then when you return to Cairo, you'll just have to convince him that you're not. And it may be that he's been holding off changing the nature of the relationship between the two of you because he knows that if he did so, your father would disapprove of it."

It was a view Davina hadn't thought of before and it cheered her. Well aware of how much she was going to miss Aileen when she returned to Cairo, she gave her friend a grateful smile and picked up her pen again.

An hour later she was watching Fergus stitch the scalp of a young boy who had been hit over the head with a glass bottle by a member of the British Union of Fascists.

It was the kind of incident that was happening daily. As Fergus sent the boy on his way, suitably stitched and bandaged, he said heavily, "This is the result of Mosley emulating Hitler and Mussolini. Fascists always need a scapegoat and, like Hitler, Mosley has chosen the Jews. His anti-Semitism is a political strategy and if we don't want to go down the ugly road Germany is going down, we are going to have to fight it tooth and nail."

He took off his horn-rimmed glasses. "The irony is," he said, polishing them with a handkerchief, "that if Mosley had stayed in the Labour Party he could have been a force for good; some of his economic ideas with regard to the ending of unemployment were brilliant."

He put his glasses back on and she didn't tell him that she had met Sir Oswald Mosley in her own home. She was just deeply grateful that such an occasion wouldn't arise again.

The next morning it was Fergus who was being treated for injuries received in a street disturbance. "But what *hap-*

pened?" Aileen asked him, white-faced as she dealt with the cuts and welts he had received.

"Mosley's thugs had set on a couple of Jewish youths. I couldn't stand by and do nothing, Aileen."

"But did you have to get involved in the fighting?" Her hands trembled as she squeezed out the bloodied sponge.

"Yes," he said levelly, "I did. And I'm going to become even more physically involved. There's a British Union rally to be held at Olympia tomorrow evening and there will be a large number of protestors there. I shall join them and give out hundreds of pamphlets. I'm not going to remain passive in the face of this kind of racial intimidation, Aileen."

Later, when Davina and Aileen were alone, Aileen said, still pale-faced, "I'm going to go with Fergus tomorrow evening, Davina. If we want to show Sir Oswald Mosley that we don't want a totalitarian state with him as its leader, then we have to oppose him every opportunity there is. Fergus says that if there are enough protestors, Mosley could well begin to lose his credibility."

Not for even one minute did Davina consider not going with her.

What she hadn't realized was just how hard it would be to get into the exhibition hall. Traffic on the main road was at a standstill as a crowd of several thousand pushed and jostled, struggling to get near to the several entrance doors. Mounted police were out in force as were massed groups of Blackshirts. Though she and the Sinclairs weren't carrying a placard, scores of other demonstrators were and the Blackshirts descended on them, knocking them to the ground and kicking and punching as they wrested away the signs.

To Davina's disbelief police offered no protection. They simply dragged off the bloodied demonstrators.

"At this rate no hecklers are going to get into the meeting!" Fergus shouted, trying to shield her and Aileen as they pushed and shoved their way forward.

By some miracle they reached an entrance door.

By an even greater miracle they jostled their way through it.

"How many people d'you think are here?" Aileen shouted over the din as she looked around the packed-to-capacity auditorium.

"Thirteen or fourteen thousand," he shouted back to her. "Possibly more."

Everywhere Davina looked there was a sea of flags. The familiar red, white, and blue of Union Jacks, black-and-yellow Fascist flags, and swaying banners carrying the names of all the various London districts of the BUF.

Seating immediately front of the platform had obviously been reserved for family and friends, many of whom, to her horror, she recognized. In sharp contrast to the vast majority of those present, who were clearly working class, those in privileged seats were in evening dress. Baba Metcalfe was clearly visible, as was her sister, Irene. There was no sign of Fruity, but clearly visible was the person she still, out of habit, thought of as Aunt Sylvia.

"There's Neil Francis Hawkins," Fergus said suddenly, looking down at the platform. "He's Mosley's second-in-command. And there's John Beckett, a former Labour MP."

A band, made up entirely of Blackshirts, began to play a patriotic march and she dragged her eyes away from Baba and Sylvia, scanning the main body of the hall.

"There's a shocking number of women present," Fergus said. "It isn't something I would have expected."

Aileen agreed with him and Davina could hardly say Mosley's sexual magnetism was such that she wasn't at all surprised at the number of women tensely waiting for him to make his appearance.

The time when he was scheduled to speak came and went. Blackshirts lined the central aisle from the main entrance to the large platform. As they waited for him to stride down the aisle, tension mounted. Mosley's followers launched into a deafening rendering of the BUF anthem. Though Davina couldn't catch all the words she recognized the emotively rousing tune as the Nazi "Horst-Wessel-Lied."

Hearing it in England made the hair at the back of her neck stand on end. Then great arc lamps were switched on, trumpets blasted a fanfare, and Sir Oswald Mosley entered the hall.

Seeing the man she had met in the drawing room of her home swaggering down the huge auditorium to deafening roars of "Hail Mosley!," as if he were a latter-day Messiah, was a surreal experience. He held his arm high in the Fascist salute. A squad of black-uniformed stewards preceded him and he was followed by his personal bodyguards.

The scene was pure Grand Guignol. In black boots, black shirt and breeches, he leaped onto the platform to a storm of cheering.

When at last the noise dropped enough for him to be heard, he thumped the lectern with his fist. "Thousands of our fellow countrymen," he thundered, "have come tonight to hear our case and thousands more have already rallied and joined the Fascist ranks!"

Most of the audience began stamping their feet.

"This movement, represented here tonight, is something new in the political life of our country."

Fergus leaped to his feet. *"And we don't need it!"* he shouted at the top of his lungs.

If Mosley heard, he showed no sign. "It is our intention to challenge the power of the Jews in Britain!"

Other protestors were on their feet now.

Blackshirts began running down the aisle in their general direction. As they did, Mosley finally acknowledged the hecklers.

"Ignore the interruptions!" he roared. "They don't worry me and they needn't worry you!"

The cheers were deafening.

As the Blackshirts reached the protestors nearest to them, instead of escorting them outside the building, they pitched into them with raised arms and fists. Men fell. Blood flew. Chairs were overturned.

Mosley stabbed the air with his fist. "These protests are futile, for what is being represented here goes further than any other movement this land has ever known! This meeting symbolizes how far the Blackshirts have come in the first twenty months of existence. In that time fascism in Great Britain has advanced more rapidly than in any other country in the world."

Fighting had broken out all over the hall. Davina saw a chair leg being wielded. A boot flew through the air, and then a shoe.

Mosley was prowling the platform as he spoke, his aura of sexual power palpable. "And it is not because our people had adopted our views under the lash of economic necessity, as in other lands," he continued. "They joined because they desired a new order in our land, a creed which elevates the nation above the individual."

Davina could bear no more. "Fascism equals Hitler, equals Mussolini!" she shouted as a fellow woman protestor was grabbed by two Blackshirts and hustled up the nearest aisle toward an exit, her arms twisted behind her.

It took minutes for the chaos to settle down. When it did Aileen shouted urgently, "Where is Fergus, Davina? Where has he gone?"

Davina looked around her, searching for a sight of him. There wasn't any.

"I don't know. But we can't leave our seats to look for him, Aileen. We might never make contact with each other again if we do."

Her stomach muscles taut with anxiety she heard Mosley thunder, "Masses of our people have shown in no uncertain way that they are weary of the present order; weary of political parties and of the present parliamentary government—"

Suddenly, a hundred feet above him a voice with an unmistakable Scottish inflection shouted, *"Down with fascism!"*

Davina's eyes flew upward.

Beside her, Aileen screamed.

Fergus was balanced precariously on an iron girder, and as thousands of people drew in a concerted breath he began raining pamphlets down.

Mosley didn't even pause in his tirade but he had lost everyone's attention.

Arc lamps swung away from the platform and illuminated Fergus. Within minutes half a dozen Blackshirts had reached the girder.

People directly beneath the girder scrambled out of the way.

Aileen, her eyes wide with horror, had both hands pressed to her mouth. Davina was praying harder than she ever had in her life.

"The soldiers who fought in the Great War are weary of the privileged Conservatives," Mosley continued as if nothing untoward was taking place. "Our people are weary of the inertia of socialism. The Labour Party is nothing but a Salvation Army, taking to its heels on the Day of Judgment."

As the Blackshirts reached Fergus, he swung himself up onto an even higher girder and from there onto a platform that disappeared into the shadows of the roof. Within seconds he, too, was out of sight, his pursuers hard on his heels.

"What is wanted is a new creed," Mosley declared with passion. "We are fighting for nothing less than a revolution!"

From somewhere came the sound of shattering glass.

Someone had fallen—and from a great height.

Aileen and Davina didn't hesitate. They began pushing and stumbling past everyone seated between them and the nearest aisle, intent only on reaching Fergus.

Once in the aisle Aileen, with Davina behind her, began to sprint. A fight had broken out ahead of them. A missile intended for one of the Blackshirts hit Davina at the side of her head. She felt blood pour down her face and though she tried to stay on her feet, the world spiraled into darkness. With Aileen's screams ringing in her ears, she buckled at the knees, falling senseless amid a forest of booted feet.

SEVENTEEN

When she regained consciousness, Davina knew she was in a hospital bed. The ward was dark and she realized it was night.

"Fergus Sinclair?" she said weakly to the nurse who came to check on her. "Did he fall? Is he hurt?"

"Quite a lot of people were hurt last night," the nurse said briskly. "And I don't know anything about the men who were brought in. You've had a very nasty knock to the head and you need to rest and not worry. We'll make inquiries about your friend in the morning."

Though she tried to stay awake, she fell almost immediately into an exhausted sleep.

In the morning she opened her eyes to find her mother sitting next to her bed. "Fergus?" she said again, before even wondering how Delia knew what had happened. "He was a hundred feet above the auditorium and then Aileen and I couldn't see him. We only heard a huge crash. Is he all right?" Her gray eyes were dark with worry. "Is he here in the hospital? Is Aileen with him?"

"He's in men's surgical and yes, Aileen is with him." Her mother's lovely face was tense and drawn. "He wasn't over the hall when he fell. He's hurt badly, though, and at the moment Aileen is the only visitor allowed."

"Was Aileen hurt as well?" she asked, feeling as if her heart was being squeezed within her chest. If Fergus was badly hurt, what would happen to Aileen's plans for a clinic?

"Aileen received some cuts and bruises in the melee, but otherwise she's all right."

Davina gave a prayer of thanks. "Are you going to take me home now?"

"Home?" Her mother's eyebrows rose. "You may think you just have a sore head, honey, but it's a *very* sore head. Can't you feel how tightly it's bandaged? There's no way you're goin' to be comin' home for another two or three days."

Davina didn't protest. Men's surgical was probably only a short walk down a hospital corridor. As soon as she was able, she was going to find him.

It was the next day before she was able to walk without becoming dizzy. On the pretext of having a bath, she left the ward and, in her nightdress and dressing gown, made her way to men's surgical.

Before she reached the ward itself a nurse hurried up to her.

"I'm afraid this is a men's ward, miss. You've got terribly lost. Would you like me to get someone to escort you back?"

Davina was about to shake her head but then, remembering her still massive headache, said, "No. And I'm not lost. A friend of mine, Dr. Fergus Sinclair, is a patient on this ward. I know he isn't allowed any visitors other than his wife, but I'd like to know how he is doing and I was hoping to have a word with Mrs. Sinclair."

The nurse eyed her doubtfully. "Dr. Sinclair is still very poorly, but if you'd like to take a seat in the waiting room, I'll tell Mrs. Sinclair where you are."

"Thank you." There was nothing Davina wanted more than to be able to sit down. The effort it had taken to walk the short distance from her bed had left her feeling not only dizzy but profoundly sick.

The waiting room was blessedly empty and she sat down

gingerly on a slippery-looking leather chair and took deep breaths in order to fight off her nausea.

As the sick feeling receded, Aileen opened the waiting-room door. Her face was ashen with anxiety and there were blue circles beneath her eyes.

Davina started to rise to her feet, but Aileen forestalled her.

"Don't get up, Davina," she said, her voice breaking. Then, as if her legs would hold her upright no longer, she collapsed on the chair next to Davina's and took a tight hold of her hand. "Fergus has broken his back," she said starkly. "It's going to be months and months—perhaps a year—before he'll be able to walk again. They are going to do the bone grafts here and then as soon as he can be moved by ambulance they are going to transfer him to a hospital near our home in Caithness. He'll be in traction to allow the bones to align properly as they heal."

Davina closed her eyes for a moment, trying to take it all in. Fergus wasn't going to be paralyzed. That was the main thing. It would, though, end his work in Whitechapel. And it would mean the shelving of Aileen's plans for the free clinic.

As if reading her thoughts, Aileen said, "When Fergus is recovered—and no matter how long that process takes—we'll come back to Toynbee Hall, Davina. And there will be a free clinic for the women of Whitechapel. It is just going to have to wait a year, that is all."

Davina squeezed her hand, knowing that no matter when it was, her mother would still be a staunch financial supporter.

Aileen said quietly, "I have some other news, Davina, and this time it's good." Despite her exhaustion, she smiled. "I'm pregnant. Fergus doesn't know yet. I was going to tell him on our wedding anniversary at the end of the month, but now I'm going to tell him just as soon as he's well enough to appreciate the news."

———

"Aileen is having a baby? But that's wonderful, honey." Delia's face lit up. "It will give both of them something to look forward to during Fergus's recovery."

Davina had told Delia when they were back home in the garden, having afternoon tea with Wallis Simpson.

"Is Aileen the friend you introduced me to at the cocktail party?" Wallis asked. "The young woman married to the doctor?"

Davina nodded.

Her mother waved a hand in the direction of a cane chair, indicating that Davina should join them, saying as she did so, "Dr. Sinclair had a ghastly accident and broke his back. He's going to be able to walk again, but it will be a long time before he does so. Now do tell me about Fort Belvedere. Are you meeting with lots of objections?"

"Not from the Prince. He's given me a free hand." Wallis, bandbox smart in a navy dress edged in white, flashed Delia a broad smile. "And I just love fixing furniture and choosing decor. Lady Mendl is giving me a hand. We spent the whole of last week pulling up carpets and taking down curtains. There isn't one room that looks as it did in Freda Dudley Ward's time."

"Or Thelma Furness's?" Delia asked naughtily.

Wallis's smile broadened. "Or Thelma's. That gal really did have appalling taste, Delia. Her bedroom at the Fort was done in the most frightful shade of pink and the bedposts were decorated with Prince of Wales feathers!"

As her mother and Wallis shook with laughter, Davina, who wasn't remotely interested in how the Prince of Wales's home was decorated, ignored the vacant chair.

"I won't join you, if you don't mind," she said to her mother. "I haven't seen Fawzia for ages and I want to be with her."

"Then you'd better go fast, Davina. She has a river cruise with Jack this afternoon. He'll be here at any moment."

"Is Aunt Gwen going with them?"

"I don't think so." Her mother avoided looking her in the eye. "I don't think Gwen likes water."

Davina pursed her lips disapprovingly, well aware of what Zubair Pasha would think of such an arrangement, knowing he had been right where Delia's chaperoning skills were concerned.

For the next few weeks Davina visited the hospital daily. Whenever she could, she persuaded Aileen to leave the hospital for a short walk or to a café for elevenses or lunch.

"Fergus is going to be transferred to Inverness soon," Aileen said as they sat having tea and sticky buns around the corner from the hospital. "I can't wait for him to be somewhere his parents can visit him, but I shall miss you, Davina."

"I shall miss you, too," Davina said sincerely. "It will mean I will see more of Fawzia—I have a guilty conscience where she is concerned—but we don't have much in common anymore. All she can think about is being the exotic center of attention at parties and balls. When you and Fergus go to Scotland I'm not going to stay in London. Even though the season isn't quite over, I'm going to return to Cairo. My mother will be disappointed but I don't think she'll raise any objections. She knows she has lost the battle to turn me into a debutante."

It turned out her mother was more than disappointed; she was seriously cross.

"It just isn't fair to Fawzia," Delia said. "She is having a great time and yanking her back to Cairo before the season is finished is cruel."

"She doesn't have to come back with me. She can stay in London with you and the two of you can travel out to Cairo together in a few weeks. I can go to Cairo alone."

Her mother was about to leave the house for dinner at

Quaglino's and, taking a leaf out of Wallis's book, was dressed with stunning severity in a narrow, backless sheath of black crepe. The skirt skimmed high-heeled black suede shoes and her fiery red hair blazed like a flame.

She picked up her slim evening bag and said, "No, Davina. You can't. You're only eighteen."

Davina shook her head in disbelief. "Of course I can. You were married when you were my age. And before that you used to ride for miles in the Blue Ridge Mountains unaccompanied. All I shall be doing is catching a couple of trains and a boat. I have Chandler blood, remember? I'm quite capable of doing things without a chaperone."

"Sweetheart, I've been at Fort Belvedere all afternoon watching the Prince of Wales fetching and carrying for Wallis as if he were a slave and she was the Queen of Sheba. Where that relationship is going heaven only knows and I'm beginning to have great concerns about it. What I don't need is to be worried about you, as well."

She turned to pick up her chinchilla stole, revealing a flawlessly creamy back.

"You don't need to be concerned about me." Davina's voice was one of sweet reason. "All you have to do is give me a kiss, send me on my way, and tell me that you'll see me in Cairo in a month's time."

"Land's sakes, you really are the most exasperating child! All right, go back to Cairo by yourself—and don't blame me if you fall into the hands of white slavers!"

"I won't," Davina said, loving her mother so much that it hurt, "but white slavers aren't very likely. Daddy has already agreed to my plans and has bought me the tickets and I don't think white slavers travel first class."

————

Four days later, when her train from Alexandria steamed into Cairo's chaotic station, Darius was waiting to greet her.

"How did you know what train I would be on?" she asked, tingling with pleasure as he took her small suitcase from her hand.

"Petra told me. We don't usually socialize, but she kindly made an exception since she can't be here. She's at Abdin Palace with your ambassador. He's having a meeting with King Fuad. I don't think your sister is Lampson's official secretary yet, but she might as well be. Why the nifty head bandage? Did you fall?"

"Yes, but only after I was hit with a flying object."

He stared at her, but said nothing. She didn't mind. She wasn't ready to launch into an explanation of what had happened at Olympia.

Since she obviously didn't want to talk about it, he asked, "What are you going to do now you're home?"

"I'm going to spend as much time as possible in Bayram el-Tonsi Street," she said, checking that the horse pulling the gharry they had chosen showed no sign of ill-treatment.

"That's where the Old War Horse Memorial Hospital is, right?"

She nodded. "And I'm going to approach the Anglo-American Hospital and see if they'll take me as a student nurse."

He helped her into the gharry, saying to the driver, "Garden City, *minfadlak*."

He was wearing dark glasses and a white linen suit that looked as if it had been tailored in London. A group of heavily veiled young women stopped and stared at them.

Davina didn't blame them. Where looks were concerned, Darius was film-star class.

As they moved out into a tumultuous stream of cars, buses,

bicycles, and donkey carts, she leaned back against the leather seat. In a little while she would tell Darius all about Toynbee Hall and the Sinclairs and Sir Oswald Mosley. For now, though, she just wanted to relish her happiness. The heat was overpowering, but she didn't care. Heat meant that she was in Cairo, and Cairo meant that she was home.

EIGHTEEN

"And so it was hideous, Petra. The most hideous thing you can possibly imagine." Petra and Davina were seated in cane chairs on the lushly watered lawn of Nile House. Nearby, the donkey Davina had rescued munched happily on alfalfa. Davina gazed unseeingly at him. "All Aileen and I heard was glass shattering and then as we struggled to get to Fergus I was hit on the head and went down like a ton of bricks."

Petra adjusted her large-brimmed sun hat, so that her face was in a little more shade. "From the sound of it you were lucky not to have had your skull fractured."

"And Fergus was lucky he wasn't killed."

Their drinks were on a small table positioned between them. Petra reached for her Tom Collins. "How were things in London when you left?" she asked, stirring the ice cubes around with a straw. "Did you see much of Jack while you were there?"

Her voice, as always when she spoke of Jack, was queerly abrupt and her eyes didn't meet Davina's. Instead she looked with studied intensity across the Nile toward the hazy outline of the pyramids.

"I didn't, though I would have liked to. All my time was spent in Whitechapel. I did see Uncle Jerome a few times. Since meeting Fergus he's become even more involved with Toynbee

Hall. He's helping to set up a council of East End citizens to take whatever action is necessary to try to put an end to the present street violence. The Archbishop of Canterbury is the council's president."

A shutter came down over Petra's face at the mention of Jerome's name. Thinking that it was because Petra was tired of hearing about London's East End, Davina said, "What is the situation here, at the palace? Why was Sir Miles Lampson meeting with the King?"

"Oh, the usual." Petra stopped stirring the ice cubes. She popped a maraschino cherry into her mouth and Davina noticed that it was the exact same color as her lipstick. "Street violence here never completely comes to an end, Davvy. The King took away parliament's full constitutional rights ages ago—it now operates only in an advisory capacity—and the Wafd is agitating to have full constitutional power restored."

"And Farouk? Is he as exasperating as ever?"

Petra pulled white-framed sunglasses down her nose and looked at her over the top of them. "Farouk," she said, "has the attention span of a gnat."

Davina giggled.

Looking at the donkey gently rambling across the lawn, Petra took a sip of her drink and then said, "What about Fawzia? We haven't talked about her. Is she enjoying the season? According to Delia's letters she's received lots of proposals."

"Shoals of them. Not, though, from the person she might have accepted."

"And who was that?" There was amusement in Petra's voice. "The heir to a dukedom?"

"No." Davina hesitated and then, aware that Petra had declared ages ago that she no longer had the slightest interest in Jack, said, "The person she spent most time with was Jack."

To Davina's horror, Petra turned white.

Terrified she had miscalculated, Davina said anxiously, "It doesn't matter to you, does it, Petra? I mean, it was you who did the chucking."

"Most definitely. Of course it doesn't matter to me." Petra shot her a brittle smile, but there was no longer any amusement in her voice. "If you don't mind I'm going to find some shade, Davvy. The sun is giving me a headache. It's good to have you back, though. I did tell you that, didn't I?"

As she watched Petra walk back to the house Davina was touched at how much Petra had obviously missed her. Though Darius hadn't said so when he had met her at the station, she was hoping he, also, had missed her very much.

"D'you fancy a ride out beyond the pyramids?" Darius said, standing with one foot on the wide shallow steps fronting Nile House.

He was dressed in jodhpurs and boots, his white shirt open at the throat. Behind him, parked in the graveled driveway, was a low-slung cream sports car. Wryly Davina noted that it wasn't British, but a German Mercedes-Benz.

"I thought it would give us a chance to catch up," he added, making no attempt to come into the house.

"Give me five minutes," she said, her smile radiant, "and I'll be right with you."

She didn't suggest that he should come inside to wait. For the last couple of years Darius had chosen never to enter Nile House, regarding it as part of the enemy camp.

Ten minutes later, in a caramel-colored silk shirt, jodhpurs, and riding boots, her shoulder-length hair braided into a fat pigtail, she ran down the steps and across to the car.

"Why a German car?" she asked as she slid onto the cream leather seat beside him. "Is it another one of your too-subtle-for-most-people-to-understand anti-British statements?"

"Yes, it's an anti-British statement." He put the car into gear. "But what do you mean about people not understanding?"

His face was unsmiling, but then it nearly always was.

She knew him too well to mind.

"Well, it's like your never coming into the house," she said as he drove toward the Kasr el-Nil Bridge. "*I* know why you don't, but I doubt if anyone else has even noticed. You can't expect them to, not when you still go to the Gezira Sporting Club and other British hangouts, like the Turf Club and Shepheard's."

"I go to those places because I am Egyptian and most Egyptians cannot."

"But who knows that is why you do it? No one knows apart from yourself—and me," she added, aware that she was the only person to whom he ever revealed his feelings.

He swerved to avoid a group of black-garbed women carrying large baskets on their heads.

"People are going to know soon enough." The handsome planes of his face were nearly as harsh as his voice. "I've had enough of Wafd's hope for change through political negotiation. The only way Egypt is going to free itself of the British is by taking far more extreme measures."

The car swooped up onto the bridge and a breeze from the river cooled her face.

She looked across at him. His jaw was clenched so tightly a nerve was pulsing.

Stifling her growing anxiety, she said, "Your father is one of King Fuad's key ministers. If you came out as a revolutionary he would disown you. He'd have no choice."

"And d'you think I'd care?" A lock of hair fell over his forehead as he swung his head toward her. "D'you know how long it is since Britain promised to get out of Egypt? It was in 1883—*1883!* And you're still here!"

"I won't be for much longer if you don't keep your eyes on

the road. Mind the bullock cart, Darius. You're going to clip its load."

Driving with only one hand, he swerved past it.

"And it isn't only the British who have to go," he said, speeding off the bridge and onto the straight dusty road leading to Giza. "Fuad and Abd al-Fattah Yahya Pasha have to go, too."

Abd al-Fattah Yahya Pasha was the prime minister and, having been appointed to office only recently, was not a man Davina knew much about.

"He's a Whitehall puppet." Darius almost spat out the words. "He and the King both dance to a British tune. And our new high commissioner, Sir Percy Loraine, is a man who reminds me very strongly of your father."

Davina remained silent. She'd briefly met Sir Miles Lampson, the new high commissioner, when he had visited Nile House. She thought Darius's opinion rather astute. "Lampson's going to be far more heavy-handed on student demonstrators," her father had said after Sir Miles had left.

It wasn't a snippet of gossip she felt inclined to share with Darius. Neither did she think it wise to ask him what he intended doing for polo ponies and sports cars if his father did disown him.

The road was flanked on either side by fields of alfalfa and maize. They made a brilliant checkerboard of green and gold, interspersed occasionally by narrow irrigation ditches. As she looked out at them, her arm resting on the top of the car's low-slung door, Davina sympathized with his anger and impatience over Britain's refusal to give Egypt unconditional independence, and worried where his anger and frustration might lead him.

If he supported terrorism his father would disown him. Her own father—if he were to find out—would ensure that Darius was arrested. His career in one of the city's most prestigious law firms would be at an end. Yet he was right about Britain's intention.

"The Foreign Office doesn't think the time is right for Egyptian independence," her father had said when she had questioned him. "Egypt is incapable of governing herself without British help."

If that was what her father thought, she knew there was no chance at all of the government thinking differently.

"Not one British minister would take the slightest interest in Egypt if it weren't for the Suez Canal," Darius said, breaking in on her thoughts. "Sometimes I wish the bloody thing had never been built!"

He swerved through the gates of the Mena House Hotel where the stables were within easy walking distance. Once he was out of the car, his mood changed.

"D'you fancy riding to the Step Pyramid?" he asked. "On the off-chance of you saying yes I've brought fruit and water with me."

The Step Pyramid of Djoser, at Saqqara, was ten miles south of Giza and was where he had taken her on their first ride together.

"As long as there's no chance of a dust storm," she said equably.

"No chance at all. It's the wrong time of year."

As they walked into the stables, he said, "You haven't talked about London. What did you do there?"

"I met two of the nicest people in the world. People I will be friends with for the rest of my life."

And while they rode into the vast expanse of shimmering desert she told him all about Toynbee Hall, the Sinclairs, and Sir Oswald Mosley's rally.

———

For the next year she spent most of her time at the newly opened Old War Horse Memorial Hospital in Bayram el-Tonsi Street. And when she wasn't at the hospital with another volunteer, she was out on the streets, buying broken-down horses in order that they could spend their last days being lovingly cared for.

"The cruelty isn't always maliciously intended," one of the senior workers said to her. "You have to remember that an ex-cavalry horse needs far more food than a donkey or a mule and that their owners are so poor they aren't even able to feed their children. Another thing to take into account is that the owners often don't realize that animals feel pain."

She did her best to educate all her friends.

"Never use a gharry when the horse looks half dead," she said fiercely. "Never ask a gharry driver to hurry, no matter how late you may be. The horse will only get whipped. Never ever tip anyone who wears out his horse and *never* travel more than four to a cab. The weight is just too much for the horse."

Before long even her mother's acquaintances were paying attention to the condition of the gharry horses and Davina remembered Fergus telling her that to effect social change, education was essential.

Just before Christmas she was accepted as a nurse in training at the Anglo-American Hospital. "I start after Easter," she said to her mother. "Do please try and look a little happier about it."

Her irritation more pretend than real, Delia said, "I'd be more pleased if you were engaged to marry one of the eligible young men you met in London. Twice your father has gone to the expense of a London season, only to have Petra a glorified secretary and you about to empty bedpans all day."

"All that matters is that we're happy. Or at least *I'm* happy," she said, not at all sure that Petra was.

Her mother made a sound that could have meant anything and continued with the letter she was writing to Wallis Simpson.

At the end of January her mother announced she was returning to London for three months, King George died peacefully at Sandringham, and a spate of anti-British demonstrations rocked Cairo.

"There was a battle between students and police in Ezbekiya Gardens," her father said. "Twenty youths have been arrested. All university students."

An hour or so later Adjo asked Davina if he could have a word with her.

"I was there when the trouble started, Missy Davina," he said, keeping his voice low. "One of the leaders of the demonstration was Zubair Pasha's son."

"Darius?"

He nodded, and something small and tight turned over in her stomach.

"You could have made a mistake, Adjo. There were a lot of people and it must have been chaotic . . ."

Adjo shook his shiny head. "It was Darius, Missy Davina. I have known him since he was a small child. I could not have made a mistake."

"Well I think it best that no one else is told, Adjo. It would cause great distress to Zubair Pasha. Darius could be arrested. He might even go to jail. And the students were just expressing what many Egyptians feel."

Adjo's face was grave. "People could have been hurt. The police could have started shooting."

"But they didn't." Her mouth was dry. "I'll speak to Darius. I'm sure it won't happen again."

Three days later Darius told her that it would most certainly happen again; that demonstrating was his democratic right.

"If he was in love with me," she had written to Aileen, "there's a chance he would listen when I say that being a member of Wafd is one thing and inciting acts of violence is quite another. But since I am not his girlfriend, I don't have that kind of influence."

"Dear Davina," Aileen had written back. "Who is his girlfriend? From everything you've told me, there must be one. He doesn't sound the sort of man to live like a monk."

Davina had written back, hardly able to believe the pain it cost her. "He dates lots of girls and they are nearly always members of what Cairo calls the 'fishing fleet.' Debs who come out from England in the hope of snaring a wealthy husband. They are glamorous and sophisticated and I'm not. And as I've no desire to date anyone else, it looks as if I'm on the way to becoming an old maid."

Davina was also in constant touch with her mother, whose main topic, now that David was King, was his love affair with Wallis.

"Things are moving ahead fast," her mother wrote at the end of February. "Gossip is now rife within the palace circle. The King now never holds a party without Wallis acting as his hostess. She's such a straight-forward kind of gal she doesn't realize the animosity this is causing at court. And if David realizes, he obviously doesn't care. As far as he is concerned, Wallis is his sun, moon, and stars."

"I cannot understand your mother sharing such tittle-tattle," her father said when Davina told him her mother's news. "She seems to forget you're still only nineteen."

"Lots of girls are married at nineteen."

It was late evening and she had come into his study to say good night.

"Well, I'm glad you're not. I like having you and Petra around."

"That's not the impression Mummy gives. She seems to think that not ending our season with an engagement was a crushing disappointment."

He chuckled. "No, she doesn't. She just wants to keep abreast with her London friends. And of course she likes to have her daughters close by."

"It's you she wants living back in London, Papa. She thought you would be home last year and yet here you are, still in Cairo."

"Yes . . . and the odd thing is, after years of hoping to be recalled to London, I no longer want to leave Egypt. So many of my best friends in London are dead—George Curzon, Herbert Asquith, Cuthbert Digby. And your mother has a whole new circle all her own age. I can't see me fitting into the King's playboy set, can you?"

She slid her arm around his shoulders and dropped a kiss on the top of his head. His hair had receded at the temples, but it was still the same pale-gold color as her own.

"No," she said with a giggle, "but not all your closest friends are dead. Uncle Jerome is very much alive and kicking."

"Jerome?" He looked startled, as if the thought of Jerome being in London hadn't occurred to him. After a pause, he said, "Jerome is actually far more your mother's friend than mine, Davina. He's a good bit younger than me, you know." He frowned. "I feel sorry for him. If he hadn't taken the blame for his divorce he would be in the cabinet. Instead he's languishing on the back benches."

Since becoming a duchess, Sylvia's name had never been

mentioned at Nile House. Remembering seeing her at Olympia, Davina was grateful for her father's silence.

The doorbell rang and moments later Adjo announced Kate Gunn.

"Ah, yes." Ivor rose to his feet. "I was expecting her."

To Davina, he said, "I have a report that needs typing up pretty urgently and Kate will make short work of it."

She nodded, well aware of how reliant on Kate he had become. Nearly everywhere he went, Kate went with him.

"If Delia doesn't mind, I don't see why you should," Petra said dismissively when she had voiced her concern. "And our mother is very, very fond of Kate. She's become family."

It was true. She had been part of their lives since they were small.

All the same, Davina couldn't help but wonder if Kate was one of the reasons her father wanted to stay in Cairo.

A week later Davina received another letter from Aileen. She was sitting on a bench in the Citadel, near the Muhammad Ali Mosque. To the right of her the Citadel's ramparts fell away with dizzying steepness, affording a view she loved more than any other.

Cairo in all its turbulent, noisy density lay spread out before her. Amid the jumble of narrow streets and bazaars she could see the roof of the orphanage where she had done so much volunteer work and, farther away, the roofs of the Coptic churches of Babylon. Everywhere else there was a sea of domes and minarets spreading down to the broad glitter of the Nile. Though the heat haze was heavy she could see Garden City, the Kasr el-Nil Bridge, and Gezira Island. Most wonderful of all was the sight of Giza's three pyramids in the far distance. The most substantial, enduring monuments of all time, they looked ethereally insubstantial in the heat haze, almost as if they were floating in the air.

She rested her eyes on them for a few moments and then withdrew the envelope from her pocket.

Dearest Davina,

    Prepare yourself for a big surprise! The Free Clinic is finally up and running in Whitechapel! It's been a long haul and we wouldn't have achieved it without the financial support of your mother and her friends. Having it as a goal has helped Fergus's recovery enormously. He still limps, but that he is walking at all is a miracle we are deeply grateful for. I've enclosed a photograph of baby Andrew—though I shouldn't refer to him as a baby now that he is a toddler and running about all over the place. He's an absolute delight—the light of my life.

Deeply happy for her friend, Davina rested the letter on her knee, wishing that Cairo was closer to Britain and that she could give Andrew Fergus a hug and a kiss; wondering if the day would ever come when she, too, would have a son.

NINETEEN

At Easter Davina began nursing training.

Her way of life and Petra's couldn't have been more different. When she came home from the hospital, Petra's social life was just beginning. Swimming parties at the Mena House Hotel were followed by picnics in the shadow of the Saqqara pyramid. There were tea dances at Shepheard's and evening dances at the Continental. She never missed a polo match at the Gezira Sporting Club and played tennis there several times week.

The tidbits of gossip she brought home were often political. In early summer Petra said with unusual seriousness, "You must end your friendship with Darius, Davvy. He's joined an anti-British group that are little more than terrorists. Even Fawzia has given up on him."

"I know."

"How?" They were sharing a quick breakfast together. "You hardly ever see Fawzia these days. You're always either at the hospital or at Bayram el-Tonsi Street."

"Jack mentioned it in his last letter to me." She poured herself a glass of mango juice. "And Darius told me that he's no longer speaking to his father."

Petra picked up a slice of toast. "How," she asked with a different expression in her voice, "does Jack know?"

"Because Fawzia writes to him all the time."

"Oh!" Petra said frowning, and then, ignoring her toast, she hastily pushed her chair away from the table. "I must get off. I'm going to be late. Bye, Davvy."

Petra began mentioning the name of Sholto Monck, a diplomat recently stationed in Cairo.

"He's Anglo-Irish. Very dishy. I rather like him, Davvy," she said, looking happier than Davina had seen her in a long time.

In August, they were married in London, at St. Margaret's.

Davina, Fawzia, and Sholto's younger sister were bridesmaids.

Though the Conisboroughs were short on close relatives, her father had done his best to see that their side of the church was impressively represented with an army of distinguished friends.

Walking down the aisle, Davina recognized the aged figure of Lady Asquith, swathed in her perpetual black; Winston Churchill and Clementine; Sir John Simon; and—to her surprise—Wallis Simpson.

With difficulty she tore her eyes away from Wallis's beautifully dressed figure. From being a woman whom only a few royal insiders had known about, Wallis had become a woman the whole of high society now gossiped about.

"Which wouldn't be the case if King George were alive," her mother had said. "Now that David is king, he keeps Wallis in the public eye every chance he gets. Insisting she act as hostess for an official function was sheer stupidity. Poor Wallis's nerves are in shreds. She doesn't particularly want to divorce Ernest, but that is what the King is pushing her to do. And when *that* becomes public knowledge the jig really will be up!"

Aware that nearly as many eyes were on Wallis as on Petra, Davina continued walking to the strains of Mendelssohn. She passed Aunt Gwen, Pugh, and her mother in the front row and wondered if Delia was already crying.

Her father and Petra were now at the foot of the altar. With Sholto on her right, his best man next to him, Petra took her hand from Ivor's arm and handed Davina her bouquet.

And then Sholto and Petra stepped up to the altar.

Remaining in the nave with Fawzia, Davina focused on the man who, in another few minutes, would be her brother-in-law.

He wasn't the brother-in-law she had wanted and seeing Jerome in a pew set aside for family had only made Jack's absence more obvious.

"Of course I've invited him," Petra had said tartly when Davina had inquired whether Jack would be at the wedding. "But he can't come. He has another commitment."

Davina hadn't pushed it, but she'd been quite sure that if Jack *had* been invited, it had only been with the knowledge that he wouldn't attend.

"Dearly beloved," the bishop intoned, "we are gathered together here in the sight of God, and in the face of this company, to join together this man and this woman in holy matrimony . . ."

From the back, Sholto looked unnervingly like her father, being tall—at least six foot three—and slender. Their coloring, too, was similar. Like her father, his hair was fair, though not fair enough to be truly blond—and like her father's hair, Sholto's was glassily sleek and smooth. His eyes, though, were not gray. They were a quite startling blue. He had a wide, mobile mouth and the kind of charm that so often goes with being Irish.

It had won her parents over instantly, but for some reason it hadn't won Davina over. There was something about him just a little too glib. Petra, though, was happy and so, for her sister's sake, she was determined to get along with him.

". . . which is an honorable estate," the bishop continued, "instituted of God, signifying unto us the mystical union that is betwixt Christ and His Church . . ."

She looked across at Fawzia. Over the last few months Fawzia, always obedient, had begun to show that beneath her delicate beauty there was a streak of steel.

"I shan't be returning to Cairo after Petra's wedding," she had said when they had gone for the last fitting of their brides-maid dresses. "Your mother has said I can stay on at Cadogan Square for as long as I want. My father is livid, but I'm twenty-two. I've pleased him for long enough and now I'm going to please myself."

Though Fawzia hadn't mentioned Jack's name, Davina was certain he was the reason she wanted to remain in London. Davina wondered what would happen if Jack were to propose. As an Egyptian Copt, Zubair Pasha would want only an Egyptian as a son-in-law. She suspected Fawzia would be quite uncaring of his wishes. Like Darius, she would do as she wanted.

"Into this holy estate," continued the bishop, "these two persons present come now to be joined. If any man can show just cause why they may not lawfully be joined together, let him now speak, or else hereafter forever hold his peace."

In the silence that followed she noticed that Petra had tensed, as if she was expecting Jack to interrupt, but nothing happened.

The bishop concluded, joining Petra's and Sholto's right hands together, saying, "Those whom God hath joined together let no man put asunder."

It was over. Petra was Mrs. Sholto Monck.

A month later Delia wrote Davina to say that the King's affair was becoming public knowledge.

*Wallis has begun divorce proceedings and David—
though I must stop referring to him as David now that
he is King Edward—has chartered Lady Yule's yacht, the
Nahlin, for a Mediterranean cruise. They won't be on
their own, of course, a whole coterie of friends are going
with them—but I don't see how such a jaunt can be kept
out of the newspapers.*

Thanks to self-imposed censorship by newspaper mag-
nates loyal to the King it *was* kept out of the newspapers—but
only out of British newspapers. American newspapers had a
field day.

The passion of Delia's feelings showed in the flamboyance
of her handwriting.

*The American press are being absolute skunks. Instead
of playing down the situation, they are printing head-
lines such as* WILL WALLIS BE QUEEN? *She is terrified that
her relationship with the King is endangering his position. I don't think she ever grasped how taboo divorce
is in royal circles and how impossible it would be for the
King to marry a woman who will have been divorced not
once but twice. She's written two letters trying to break
things off—both of which he has ignored. What more the
poor gal can do I really don't know. He's totally depen-
dent on her and is insistent that he is going to marry her
no matter what the cost.*

In October, Davina learned Wallis had been granted a decree nisi. Delia was distraught.

*Which means that in six months' time she will be free to
marry. What will happen then is anyone's guess. Most*

of the people who professed to be Wallis's friends have distanced themselves from her, fearing the King may lose his throne. Though how brother Bertie could step into his shoes I can't imagine. He doesn't have an ounce of David's charisma and the poor lamb can't utter two words without stuttering.

When, in December, the King abdicated and Prince Albert became king, announcing he would be known as King George VI, the Conisboroughs were not surprised.

Egypt too had a new king, the sixteen-year-old Farouk.

"Not that I think things will change much," Darius said darkly when, fifteen months later, they attended Farouk's investiture. "Even with the new treaty granting Egypt independence the British still have control of the canal and British troops remain on Egyptian soil."

The ceremony took place in the Hall of Deputies. The Queen Mother and other dignitaries sat facing the Egyptian king. Behind them were members of the court circle. Davina could see Zubair Pasha's stout figure and scores of senior officials and European dignitaries—including her parents and Sir Miles and Lady Lampson.

By rights Darius should have been seated with his father, but he made his way across to Davina, forcing the people next to her to squeeze uncomfortably closer.

"He's young," Davina whispered as the gold crown that Tutankhamen had worn 3,300 years earlier was placed on Farouk's head. "He's going to feel as you do, Darius."

"Good," he said, bending his head so close to hers that his lips brushed her ear. "It's time Egypt changed, Davina—and it's time our relationship did as well."

She gasped as the imam placed the crown on Farouk's head, proclaiming, "In Allah's name! Farouk, King of Egypt!"

"When we get out of here," Darius said, his eyes on hers, "let's drive to Giza and ride into the desert."

Even though there was a celebratory ball that night at the palace, she didn't hesitate for a second.

"Yes," she said, her heart hammering.

They left Garden City with champagne and a picnic of pita, hummus, and figs.

Getting out of Cairo wasn't easy. Thousands of people had flooded the city for the coronation. The streets were jam-packed with flag-waving fellahin. Farouk's picture was everywhere. The Kasr el-Nil Bridge, usually choked with donkey carts and gharries, was filled with limousines and Cadillacs as guests began inching their way toward the Abdin Palace.

By the time Darius's Mercedes-Benz swooped into Giza it was dusk.

They parked at the Mena House Hotel, its gardens and balconies thronged with partygoers, and made straight for the stables.

Saqqara and the Step Pyramid—and Davina knew they would be riding to nowhere else—was an hour's ride south and by the time the distinctive shape of the pyramid loomed before them their horses were wet with sweat.

Darius reined in and speedily dismounted. Seconds later his hands were hot on her waist as he helped her down and pulled her hard against him.

"Why now?" she asked, her mouth a millimeter from his, a pulse beating wildly in her throat.

"Because it's time," he said. One hand moved to the ribbon that held her hair back and pulled it free, sending her ivory-pale hair tumbling to her shoulders.

As the blood surged through her body, his mouth came swiftly down on hers.

It was a long, sweet kiss. When he finally raised his head

he said, "Until now, you've been too young for this kind of relationship."

"I'm twenty-one," she said, so filled with desire she could barely stand. "You could have kissed me years ago."

"No, I couldn't," he said with a rare smile. "When you were seventeen you were still wearing headbands and socks. Compared to other girls you've always been young for your age. It's probably why your mother didn't mind waiting for your debutante season until you were nearly nineteen."

"I didn't go earlier because I didn't want to."

Though it was hard to believe at such a moment, she knew they were on the point of having an argument.

Realizing it, he said gently, "Let's put a blanket on the sand and unpack the food and I'll explain just why our being in love would have been so difficult for you to handle a year or so ago—and will still be difficult for both of us to handle now."

He took the blanket roll from off his horse and laid it beneath a date palm. Then he set out the bowls of hummus and figs.

As he began pouring Heidsieck she sat on the blanket, her legs curled beneath her.

"I chose my political course a long time ago, Davina," he said, champagne fizzing over the top of the glass as he handed it to her. "Your family has only tolerated our friendship because of my father. A full-blown love affair will be viewed very differently."

"A love affair," she said, her voice even more unsteady, "is what I want."

At the blaze of passion in his eyes a tremor ran through her.

"Apart from your father's opposition—and make no mistake, Davina, his opposition is going to be fierce—my nationalist friends will object as well."

"And a British girlfriend will destroy your credibility with them?"

He shook his head. "Not necessarily. Dating members of

the 'fishing fleet' is considered a joke—at least it is among those who are Coptic. But a British wife wouldn't be."

His eyes held hers intently.

She knew he was waiting for a sign that she understood that nothing was going to be easy for them. There would be no early engagement celebrated by their families and the Egyptian and British communities.

The moonlight fell across his handsome face, highlighting its harsh planes. She was aware, as never before, of the passionate intensity that was so much a part of his personality. Of the sense of danger he carried with him.

She put her champagne glass down. "I love you," she said. "I don't care what problems we face, Darius, just as long as we face them together."

She saw the overwhelming relief in his eyes and realized with amazement that he hadn't been certain of her response. He reached out for her with powerful yet careful hands. Knowing that she was as central to his life as he was to hers, she had never been so happy in her life.

"And so we're a couple now, not just friends," she told her father.

It was early evening and the two of them were in his study. He had just come back from a meeting with Nahas Pasha, the new prime minister.

"*Excuse me?*" Ivor slapped a document onto his desk and wheeled around to face her. "Are you trying to tell me that you and one of the biggest political troublemakers Cairo has are unofficially engaged?"

She had never seen him look so angry. Others, she knew, were often intimidated by him, but neither she nor Petra had ever feared him. He had never been overly affectionate, but he had always been approachable.

"I don't know when we can marry, but we are romantically

involved. I thought it best for me to tell you so, before anyone else did."

She had never seen her ice-cool father splutter, but he spluttered now. "Romantically involved? What, in the name of all that is holy is that supposed to mean? Is his family aware of this 'romantic involvement'? Can I expect Zubair Pasha to mention it when next we meet? It has to end, Davina. It has to end *now*. D'you understand? Darius is a dangerous young man. His politics are dangerous and the ways he pursues them are dangerous."

"You don't know that," she said, trying to sound reasonable. "Most of the gossip about Darius is rumor. If there were hard facts, he'd be in a British prison."

"The only reason he's not is because his father is so strongly pro-British! And as Britain needs every friend she can get in Farouk's court, Zubair Pasha is not a man we would wish to offend by imprisoning his son!"

He paced to the window.

"No more of this nonsense, Davina," he said. "I always felt it was a bad move allowing you to continue your friendship with Darius. His politics have already caused his father great distress. Even Fawzia has very little to do with him."

"Maybe so," she said quietly, "but I will continue to see him, Daddy."

He looked ashen. "Then you had better make arrangements to live elsewhere, Davina. That is my final word on the subject."

"You're asking me to leave Nile House?"

"Only in order to bring you to your senses."

"Under the circumstances I think you could be more understanding."

"What circumstances?" He breathed in hard, his nostrils white.

"Kate Gunn," she said. And left the room.

———

"I have left the house," she said the next day to Petra. "I've moved into the Nurses' Home. It will probably be quite jolly."

Petra stared at her gentle-natured young sister. "Are you telling me," she said disbelievingly, "that you and Darius are now lovers and that you told Ivor so?"

"I didn't tell him that we were lovers," Davina conceded. "The expression I used was 'romantically involved.' "

"And Kate?" Petra asked, quirking a finely penciled eyebrow. "How long have you known about that little secret?"

They were on the terrace at Shepheard's, the position of their table giving a view of the hotel's Moorish Hall, a favorite meeting place for men.

"I don't know," Davina said slowly, looking at several of their father's friends, deep in conversation, drinks to hand. "It didn't come as a sudden revelation. I just gradually realized the part she played in Daddy's life. I think Mummy knows about it, don't you?"

"Oh, most definitely," Petra said with the hardness that was so often in her voice when she spoke of their mother. "And as she doesn't appear to mind, there's absolutely no reason why we should."

She leaned back in her chair, her mahogany-red hair gleaming in the sunlight. "Where Ivor and Kate are concerned there will never be a whisper of gossip—they are both too careful. You, however, are in a different position, Davvy. When news of you and Darius breaks, Cairo society will regard you as an addition to the fishing fleet."

"They can regard me however they like," Davina said with her quiet composure. "I really don't care. All that matters to me is what my real friends think of me. And as they are not interested in my personal life, their opinion won't change."

———

Gossip among the British community about Davina was eclipsed by talk of war in Europe. There suddenly were a far greater number of Germans in the city than there had been only months earlier. Farouk was rumored to admire them.

"Which could be a bit tricky if Britain declares war on Germany," Sholto said languidly to Davina. "The recent Anglo-Egyptian Treaty is pretty specific. If Britain declares war on a hostile nation, that declaration includes Egypt—but if Farouk doesn't want to keep to the treaty, it will be hard to make him."

As Christmas approached and Delia came out for her usual long stay, she brought news which she seemed oddly reluctant to tell Petra.

"But why?" Davina asked her, perplexed. "It's four years since Petra ended her love affair with Jack. She's been married to Sholto for more than a year. Why will she be distressed to learn Jack is to marry Fawzia? And why are they going to get married in a London registry office, and not in Cairo?"

"I don't know why a registry office, darling, except that Fawzia is a Copt and Jack isn't. And I don't know why London, either, except that while Zubair Pasha likes Jack—and has enormous respect for Jerome—it probably isn't *quite* the marriage he would have wanted for his daughter. He probably hoped that she would catch Farouk's eye and become Queen of Egypt. Instead of which Farouk is marrying Safinaz Zulfikar in January—though according to your father she won't be known as Queen Safinaz but as Queen Farida. Farouk has the same quirk about names beginning with *F* as his father. He believes it's lucky. Which means that if Fawzia had remained in Cairo, she might have been in with a chance."

"She's too old. She's twenty-three. Farouk is still a month short of his eighteenth birthday and Safinaz is just fifteen."

"Sixteen," her mother corrected.

"Fifteen," Davina repeated. "The official announcement that she is sixteen is only a sop to the British."

Her mother's presence in Cairo ensured that her father stiffly requested that Davina be at Nile House for Christmas. Knowing that he hated their estrangement as much as she did, she did as he asked. He did not invite Darius, but that hadn't mattered because he wouldn't have accepted.

At a Christmas Eve party at the American legation, Davina watched as her mother told Petra about Jack's impending wedding.

Petra, wearing a halter-necked backless gown of emerald-green lamé, her thick mane of hair coiled into a sleek chignon, had been laughing at something someone had said. She looked sophisticated and *soignée*—and as if she was trying far too hard to enjoy herself.

It was not a new impression.

As their mother approached, radiant in a mauve gown shimmering with crystal beads, Davina had a sense of deep foreboding. Perhaps her mother was right to be apprehensive. Perhaps there was far more to Petra's breakup with Jack than Davina had realized.

Delia touched Petra's elbow in order to gain her attention. Petra turned and flashed their mother a wide smile. As her mother spoke, Petra's smile vanished.

The blood drained from her face.

The glass of champagne in her hand fell, spraying her gown and splintering into shards on the floor.

Sholto, who had been at the far side of the room chatting

with a young diplomat from the Argentine legation, excused himself and began making his way to her.

Davina crossed the room toward her and as she did so, Petra turned on her heel and ran out.

It was an exit that Davina knew would be the talk of Cairo for weeks to come.

It was quite obvious that her mother was also well aware of this. She was saying loudly, "Poor gal. News of the death of a dear friend in London. I'm afraid I chose a bad moment to break the news."

Sholto, deceived, said merely, "Then she probably wants to be alone for a while," and made his way unhurriedly back to the Argentinean diplomat.

Her mother said softly, "Please don't go after Petra, Davina. Sholto is right. She'll want to be by herself for a while."

Because Davina always trusted her mother's judgment she did as Delia asked, but it was hard—and it was even harder realizing that her mother knew something about Jack and Petra's breakup that she didn't.

Next morning, straight after breakfast, she left Nile House for Petra's villa.

Petra was sitting on the terrace, an untouched breakfast on a cane table before her. She was still in her dressing gown, her hair unbrushed.

"Don't ask, Davvy," she said wearily before Davina even spoke to her. "It was a bad time of the month. The news was unexpected and I reacted to it badly. The coffee is still hot. Why don't you have a cup and tell me what you are wearing to Farouk's wedding?"

As Petra so obviously didn't want to confide in her, Davina reluctantly went along with the abrupt change of subject; but she hated knowing there were secrets between them and desperately hoped that Petra would eventually open her heart to her.

She didn't do so.

Petra never spoke about her reaction to the news of Jack's wedding, but that summer, when Jack and Fawzia came to visit Fawzia's family, she acted as if she was happy for the two of them. Jack seemed completely at ease. The only person who behaved with slight reservation was Sholto.

"And that's probably because he's jealous," her father said when Davina mentioned it. "Jack's been moved into MI6. With war on the horizon, I rather think Sholto fancies himself as an intelligence officer and doesn't like the fact that Jack has pipped him to it."

Her father's prediction that war was imminent proved correct. On September 3, 1939, Prime Minister Chamberlain announced in the House of Commons that, as from noon that day, Britain was at war with Germany.

"And Egypt?" Ivor said grimly. "Who will Egypt support? Germany? Or us?"

Part Four

DARIUS

1940–1941

TWENTY

Darius preferred the Groppi's nearer to the Opera House. He liked its garden better than the more famous one on Soliman Pasha Square. It was small and intimate and much less crowded. Here, white jasmine and purple bougainvillea climbed the trellised walls and provided a feeling of secluded intimacy. He was early for his meeting, but he didn't mind. He had a lot to ponder and couldn't think of a better way of doing it than over thick Turkish coffee and pastries drizzled with rose water and honey.

The Egyptian government was outwardly complying with the Anglo-Egyptian Treaty of Friendship and Alliance. Martial law had been established. Known Nazis in the city—and there were a lot—had been interned in the Italian School in Alexandria. The railways and aerodromes had been put at Britain's disposal. To all intents and purposes Egypt was supporting Britain, but the government had not declared war on Germany. And it would not, Darius thought grimly.

He wondered if Sir Miles Lampson, no longer a high commissioner but, since the signing of the Anglo-Egyptian Treaty, an ambassador, was taken in by the dutiful actions of Ali Maher, the prime minister. Darius doubted it. Lampson was too smart. And Germany was well aware that Egypt would give no real help to a country it wished so heartily to be rid of.

He ordered another coffee and wondered what would happen to the mighty British Empire when she lost the war. She would no longer be an imperial power—and that would end the British presence in Egypt. It was reason enough for not wanting to see Britain emerge victorious. Someone else who didn't want to see Britain emerge victorious was a Romanian he had become friendly with. Constantin Antonescu was a diplomat at the Romanian legation, and it was Constantin he had arranged to meet.

At a nearby table an elderly businessman in a tarboosh and Savile Row suit was sharing what Darius judged to be a few stolen moments with a beautiful girl young enough to be his granddaughter. At a farther table two Egyptian matriarchs were making great inroads into cream-filled cakes piled high on a glass cake stand. No one was paying any attention to him.

He looked at his watch, not because Constantin was late—he wasn't—but to envisage where Davina would be and what she would be doing. It was nearly five o'clock and as it was a Wednesday, he knew she would be at the Old War Horse Memorial Hospital, putting her skills as a nurse to veterinary use.

A shadow fell across the table. "I see we have the garden more or less to ourselves," Constantin said as the two matriarchs heaved themselves to their feet, leaving an empty cake stand behind them. He glanced over toward the businessman and his companion, adding, "I think we had better wait until we are completely alone before I tell you my plans. If they are successful, Germany will win the war."

That evening he and Davina went to the Continental Hotel for dinner. Opposite Ezbekiya Gardens, the Continental boasted a rooftop restaurant with a small dance floor that they were particularly fond of.

As they walked through the crowded public rooms they

passed the entrance to the bar and spotted Sholto at the center
of a noisy group of people. He shot Davina a quick glance to
see if she had noticed him. Seeing the way she was avoiding eye
contact, he guessed that she had.

"You don't like him, do you?" Darius said matter-of-factly
as they took the caged lift to the restaurant.

"No. Not much. He's not making Petra very happy."

"Because of his drinking?" he asked when they were seated.
"Or because of his gambling?"

"I don't think she *likes* the fact that he spends more time
propping up the bar here or at Shepheard's than he does with
her, but his drinking is something Petra would take in her
stride if everything else was all right."

Davina didn't say anything about the gambling, but there
was a frown on her face and Darius knew she was deciding
whether to divulge something Petra would rather he didn't
know.

At last, toying with her champagne glass, she said, "Sholto's
background isn't all he's claimed. His having lied about it has
shaken her trust in him."

"And in this background was there another woman?"

"No. Sex doesn't come into it at all."

She looked across to the small band. They were playing
Cole Porter's "Night and Day" but no one was dancing. It was
too early.

Darius didn't say anything, just looked at her.

Her fair hair was held away from her face with ivory combs
and fell satin-smooth to her shoulders. Her evening dress was
the same shimmering color as her eyes. Her fingernails were
painted silver and instead of her mouth being a fashionable
crimson red, her lipstick was a pale rosy pink. He thought she
looked like an ancient Egyptian moon goddess and it was a
look that aroused him far more than Petra's obvious glamour,
or the hard sophistication of the fishing fleet.

Still looking toward the band, she said, "Sholto lied to Petra—and to everyone else—about being Anglo-Irish. He's simply Irish."

"And there's a difference?"

"There is where class is concerned. The Anglo-Irish are the landed elite."

"And so an Anglo-Irish son-in-law would have been acceptable to your father while a merely Irish one wouldn't have been?"

She nodded.

"Then it's quite obvious why he practiced a little deceit."

"But not why he lied to Petra." Davina took a sip of champagne and finally looked away from the dance band and toward him. "It's also a question of money. Sholto always gave the impression that he had family money and that he would inherit considerably more, but in reality there isn't any family to speak of and there isn't any money, though he behaves as if there were. Petra's terrified of what will happen when his bluff is called."

"Your father will shore him up," Darius said, rising to his feet and leading her out onto the still-empty dance floor. "And I'm not surprised Petra is terrified. At the thought of breaking such news to your father, I'd be terrified too."

After that conversation Darius found himself watching Sholto Monck more closely. And on Constantin's advice, he began to play down his fierce anti-Britishness.

"You have social access to people very few Egyptians have," said Constantin. "It is something that could be very useful to your fellow nationalists. Think of it, Darius. In the home of a man such as Lord Conisborough you will be at the heart of the British government in Cairo!"

Darius had seen the sense of the advice. Within a few months he had managed to once again be on social terms with Davina's father. Constantin's belief that Nile House was virtually the center of British government in Cairo had, though, proved optimistic.

Although for many years Lord Conisborough had enjoyed the confidence of King Fuad, primarily as his adviser, his position had become defunct when Farouk became king. The sheer length of time he had known Farouk—which was for most of Farouk's boyhood—ensured that he was still welcome at Abdin Palace, but the days when Farouk could be influenced by a man who had been his father's friend were long gone. Darius knew this from his own father, whose role at the palace had also come to an end.

"The problem is that the King is too young for his position," his father had said on one of the rare occasions when they had spoken on almost friendly terms. "He thinks more about his cars than he does about politics. Getting him to take the present situation seriously is almost impossible."

Now in his late sixties, Ivor Conisborough had not been recalled to London and no longer held any high official position. He had not, though, chosen to return to England.

"He's been in Cairo for so long that he can't bear the thought of acclimatizing himself to London," Davina had explained. "Most of his friends there are dead and when the prime minister let him know that there would be no wartime post for him he decided against returning. At least here, in Cairo, his long experience in Egyptian affairs makes him very useful to Sir Miles Lampson."

Darius also knew that Davina's father would not have found it as easy to continue his relationship with Kate Gunn in London as it was for him to do so in Cairo.

His visits to Nile House usually took place only when he

knew Ivor Conisborough was elsewhere and even then he always parked his distinctive Mercedes discreetly, a little way from the house.

On one such visit Davina was upstairs getting ready for an evening at the Gezira Sporting Club and he was enjoying a large gin and tonic in the drawing room. The spacious room faced the lawns and though the French windows were open, he didn't hear Ivor's Rolls sweep up the front drive. The first he knew Ivor was home was his unmistakable cut-glass voice as he strolled around to the terrace.

Darius sighed in irritation, knowing exactly how unwelcome his presence was going to be. He sat down on the sofa and, one knee carelessly over the other, pretended to enjoy his drink.

Instead of entering the house, Ivor and his companion sat down in fantail chairs on the terrace.

"It's a shame you are on such a tight schedule," Ivor said. "Petra and Davina would have loved to spend a little time with you."

"I'll do my best to lunch with them at least once," replied his companion and Darius tensed in shock.

The voice was Jerome Bazeljette's.

"So your brief is to assess Cairo's civilian wartime readiness, is it?" Ivor continued. "Trust Chamberlain to be fussing about something unimportant."

Jerome laughed in agreement and then said, "Important or not, I was glad of the opportunity to see you. We have a problem, you and I, and it needs to be dealt with."

He heard Ivor give a long, heavy sigh, as if well aware of what the problem was.

"You cannot allow Delia to remain on her own in London. The city is certain to be bombed," Jerome said bluntly. "Either you must return to London or, while there is still time, Delia must join you here. Winston is first lord of the admiralty again. There'd be no problem about her leaving England."

"And is the problem that she doesn't want to come?"

Darius could sense Bazeljette's annoyance when Ivor did not even mention the possibility of returning to London.

"Of course she doesn't want to come! Good God, Ivor! If she comes we'll be separated for as long as this show lasts—and unlike the optimists in the cabinet, I think it's going to go on a devil of a long time. I want to be separated from Delia as little as she wants to be separated from me. But I want her to be safe—and Cairo isn't likely to be bombed."

"It could fall into enemy hands. Ethiopia is part of the Italian empire. Italians are also to the west of us in Libya. There's bound to be a buildup of German troops in both countries."

"Italy isn't as yet at war with us—and even if she were, any fighting would be hundreds of miles away, in the desert. Any real danger to Cairo and there would be a mass evacuation of British women and children to Palestine."

Darius's head reeled: not at the speculation as to Cairo's safety as opposed to London's, but at the way the two men were talking about Delia Conisborough.

Ever since their trip together to Old Cairo Darius had maintained a definite friendship with Davina's mother. It wasn't something he had discussed with Davina, but he knew she was aware not only that he liked her mother but that Delia was more than a little simpatico where Egyptian nationalism was concerned.

Now he wondered how long Delia had been Sir Jerome Bazeljette's mistress. And how long had Ivor Conisborough known? Did Petra and Davina know? Did Jack know of his father's affair?

He hadn't seen Jack in years, but they had once been very good friends.

"I need your help in persuading her to leave London," Jerome was saying. "She takes great notice of your opinion and if you emphasized that she was *needed* here, it would probably do the trick."

There was a short silence and then Ivor said gravely, "Yes. You're right, Jerome. London is no place for Delia if the Germans start bombing. She must come here. Leave it with me. I'll make sure she does so."

Darius heard Jerome give a sigh of relief and knew it was time for him to make an exit.

As quietly as possible he eased himself off the sofa and then, as he heard Ivor say, "I think you'd better have a snifter before you hare off to the embassy, Jerome," he walked quietly from the room.

Just as he reached the stairs Davina came down them. He put a finger to his lips.

"Your father is on the terrace with a guest," he mouthed, purposely not telling her who the guest was. "Let's leave quietly and PDQ."

She nodded and, slipping her hand into his, allowed him to hurry her toward the front door.

A month later, two weeks after Jerome had returned to London, Delia arrived in Cairo. But she did not arrive alone.

"Good gracious! Fawzia is with her!" Davina exclaimed to Darius as the train from Alexandria steamed into the station and she saw the two figures leaning from an open window.

Lord Conisborough, Petra, and Sholto were also there to welcome them. Darius was so curious to see the way Ivor Conisborough greeted his wife that he barely noticed his own sister.

"Sorry you had to slum it on a troop train, sweetheart," he heard Ivor say as Delia kissed him on the cheek while scores of soldiers streamed past them. "Under the circumstances I expect your journey was ghastly."

He couldn't hear Delia's response as Fawzia flung herself into his arms with a quite unexpected display of sisterly affection. He responded in kind, wondering if marriage had made Fawzia forget that they rarely had time for each other.

As he released his hold of her he saw the expression on Petra's face. It changed swiftly to one of delighted welcome when Fawzia turned toward her, but he knew that Petra was more appalled than pleased by his sister's return as Mrs. Jack Bazeljette.

"Isn't this grand?" Delia said as, hemmed in by Tommies, they made their way down the platform. "So nice to know you are doing well in your new law practice, Darius," she said, referring to his growing professional reputation and flashing him her wide, beguiling smile.

"And what news of friends in London?" Ivor asked, returning her attention to himself. "How is Margot Asquith? When Jerome was here he said she now went out very rarely."

"That's true, but I don't think she minds. Marie Belloc Lowndes keeps her company. They have been friends forever and have similar worries."

"Which are?" Ivor asked as his Rolls came into view.

"Family abroad. Margot's daughter is in Romania. Her husband was the Romanian ambassador in Paris until war broke out, and when he was recalled to Bucharest she went with him. Margot is terrified that she won't live long enough to see her again. As for Marie—all her family are in France."

As the chauffeur opened the door Ivor said smoothly, "Fawzia is coming with us, and Petra and Sholto are following. Davina and Darius have an engagement."

It wasn't true, but when Davina opened her mouth to protest, Darius squeezed her arm. That he had been tolerated in the family party to greet her mother was improvement enough.

If Lord Conisborough didn't want him intruding any further on the reunion that was okay with him. There would be other occasions when he would visit Nile House and possibly pick up other useful nuggets of information.

A few days later when he and Davina had tea with Petra at the Gezira Sporting Club, Petra brought Davina up-to-date with their mother's London gossip. "Delia thinks Winston Churchill will soon be stepping into Chamberlain's shoes," she said, adding with a wry laugh, "Hitler will have to look to his laurels if he does. And Ivor's old friend, Sir John Simon, will probably be out. Winston thinks he is indecisive."

"What about Uncle Jerome?" Davina asked as Darius continued to affect disinterest by watching the cricket match taking place nearby.

"Jerome?" A studiedly careless note entered Petra's voice. "Jerome still doesn't have a ministry of his own, but Chamberlain has kept him very busy ever since war was declared and, as his relations with Winston have always been good, no doubt if he becomes PM, Winston will keep him equally busy."

Later he shared the news with Constantin, who said enviously, "You probably know more about what goes on behind the scenes in the British government than anyone else in Cairo, Darius."

Having Fawzia back in Cairo was something of a mixed blessing.

"I don't trust this apparent abandonment of fierce anti-British feeling," she said when he visited the family home—a home he hadn't lived in for years—to see her.

"I haven't abandoned it. I've just stopped giving noisy and futile expression to it."

She was lying in a hammock slung from the lowest branch of the cedar tree. Her orange sundress revealed a great deal of flawless olive skin and her fingernails and toenails were painted a searing scarlet.

"Father doesn't approve, either," she said, sensing his disapproval, "but I'm a married woman now and I'm no longer answerable to him."

"And where is Jack?" Darius asked. "Still in London?"

He was lying sprawled on the grass, a drink in his hand.

She laughed. "Would you believe me if I told you I don't know? London isn't Cairo. No one talks about where people are posted—that is, if they know. Most of the time they don't. It's the kind of security consciousness Cairo could use. I've heard rumors that the city is awash with spies. You aren't one of them, Darius, are you?"

The look he gave her was withering. "Hardly. What do I know of troop movements and troop numbers? What I am curious about is you. Why did you opt to come back to Cairo with Delia? I thought you were enjoying yourself in London."

"I was when I first went. But that was when I was single. Once I married the fun faded because my going to parties without Jack wasn't the done thing—and though Jack's posting was London, he was always being sent abroad."

She sat up, swinging long legs over the side of the hammock, her scarlet-painted toes touching the grass.

"And Jack is not as wealthy as I thought. I couldn't shop the way I had in Cairo—"

"When Father paid."

"—and we didn't live in a grand house as I had imagined we would," she said, ignoring his interruption. "We lived in a small flat in Knightsbridge that would fit twenty times over into this villa."

"And court social life?" he prompted.

She pulled a face. "Court social life doesn't exist in England. King George and Queen Elizabeth are the most boring married couple you could ever hope to meet and, anyway, Jack scarcely knows them. It will be different here. With a king as young as Farouk, the palace circle is bound to be glamorous."

"It may be," he said drily. "I wouldn't know. I haven't been inside Abdin Palace since I was in my teens. As far as I'm concerned, Farouk is as useless and corrupt as his father and his grandfather, but as he's only three generations out of Albania, what can you expect?"

Fawzia wasn't interested in King Farouk's heredity and didn't answer him. Instead, she said, "I've heard rumors that he's already unfaithful to Queen Farida. I wonder how generous he would be to a mistress? Do you think he would shower her with jewels?"

It was said carelessly, but Darius's eyes narrowed.

He knew discontent when he saw it. And he knew his sister.

"Stay away from Farouk," he said bluntly. "He would be far more trouble than you can handle."

TWENTY-ONE

Throughout February and March Allied troops continued to pour into the city. Everywhere one looked there were men in uniform: Englishmen, New Zealanders, South Africans, and Indians began to arrive. Cairo seemed to be drowning in khaki and Darius, like so many of his countrymen, gritted his teeth, appeared indifferent—and hated it.

"There are so many suede boots and swagger sticks in Shepheard's that it's nearly impossible to get a drink these days," he said exasperatedly.

They were on his houseboat, the *Egyptian Queen*. Moored at the north end of Gezira Island it had been his home ever since he had moved out of his father's house.

Davina was lying in the crook of his arm, naked apart from a cream-colored silk slip. He was wearing a galabia made of expensive black cloth lavishly edged with gold braid. When on the houseboat, he always wore a galabia. Western clothes were for when he was making a public statement to the British and other Europeans.

As Davina slid her arm across his chest and he hugged her even closer, he thought about the British.

If they had been a thorn in the flesh before they had declared war on Germany, they were more so now. Though Egypt itself was not at war, the city had become a military base. The

Semiramis Hotel on the banks of the Nile had been turned into the military headquarters for British troops in Egypt and was known simply as BTE. A large block of luxury flats in Garden City had been commandeered as the General Headquarters Middle East and cordoned off with great rolls of barbed wire. Open-air cinemas had sprung up everywhere to entertain the troops. The brothels in the squalid El-Birkeh district were busy day and night and the British Tommy was noisily—and often drunkenly—making his presence felt.

Hating that presence, Darius avidly gleaned every bit of gossip he could to relay back to the Romanian legation. He wasn't sure where his nuggets went, but he was fairly sure he was helping the German war effort.

"And if Germany wins the war, it will be the best possible result for Egypt," he had said unthinkingly to Davina.

She was so horrified that it had nearly ended their relationship.

"I want an independent Egypt as much as you do," she said vehemently, "but helping Germany isn't the way to achieve it. Have you any *idea* of what the world would be like if Hitler won the war? It might end British presence, but they would just be replaced by Germans. Instead of British soldiers at Suez, there would be German soldiers. German propaganda telling Egyptians they'll give Egypt independence are blatant untruths. It isn't in Nazi Germany's nature to give any country its freedom."

It was a valid point, and Darius knew it. Constantin's network of informers—barmen, waiters, shoeshine boys, and prostitutes—were organized to help Berlin. Darius had once thought that was in Egypt's best interest. Now he wasn't so sure.

Davina stirred beside him. "Is it five o'clock yet, darling?" she murmured, her eyes still closed. "I should go."

She was temporarily assigned to a clinic in the north of the city and at that time of the day the roads—and especially the Bulaq Bridge—were choked with traffic.

"No," he said gently. "We have another hour."

He lowered his head and kissed her. Her lips were like the petals of a flower and he felt himself tremble. That he cared for her so deeply always amazed him. He didn't care for anyone else deeply—not even Fawzia. As for his parents—he'd been fond of his mother and intensely sorry when, sixteen years ago, she had died. For his pro-British father he had only contempt.

At the touch of his mouth Davina's eyes opened. They were an unusual gray with the merest hint of blue. Many years ago, he'd heard her father liken the color to English bluebells just before they opened. Darius had never seen English bluebells, but he'd always remembered the description.

Everything about her entranced him. Unlike Fawzia and her Egyptian girlfriends, Davina's beauty wasn't obvious and was never used as a bargaining chip to get what she wanted. And not only was she different from the Egyptian girls he knew, she was also different from the other English girls. She never strove to look glamorous. He couldn't even begin to imagine Petra without Hollywood-style glossy red lips and long lacquered nails.

Davina seldom wore makeup and when she did it was little more than a touch of powder on her flawless skin and a muted pink lipstick. She never dressed provocatively. Though he was not Muslim, he disliked the clothes the fishing-fleet girls wore. Davina's dress was always understated. Today when she had arrived at the houseboat she had been wearing her nurse's uniform, but if it hadn't been a working day he knew she would have been wearing a simple cotton dress, her only jewelry her wristwatch.

As time ran out he watched her dress, his hands behind his head.

"I can get a taxi back to the clinic if you don't want to face the early-evening traffic," she said as he made no effort to reach for his shirt or trousers.

"Then how would I know you'd got back safely?" he said, swinging his legs from the bed.

She laughed, bending down to ease her feet into wedge-heeled sandals, her pale-blond hair falling forward like skeins of silk. "I walk Cairo from end to end unescorted and well you know it."

He knew it, and he didn't like it, not when the city was choked with Tommies. He didn't say so, though. Davina had made Cairo her own over the years. Her work at the Old War Horse Memorial Hospital, which she still continued despite her full-time nursing work, often took her into parts of the city even he would be loath to enter.

He tucked his white silk shirt into lizard-skin-belted trousers, picked up his jacket, and, his arm around her shoulder, walked her across the houseboat's gangplank to where his car was parked, pondering yet again how Egypt could rid itself of the British.

In April, as the Nazis occupied Denmark and Norway, it looked as if Germany was winning the war. A month later they had invaded France, Belgium, Luxembourg, and the Netherlands. In June Italy declared itself to be at war with the Allies.

A few days later Constantin said, "The head of the Italian legation has been asked to leave, though whether King Farouk's Italian friends will be interned remains to be seen. Personally, I think the King will protect them."

Darius agreed. Ever since King Fuad's day, a large number of the palace servants had been Italian. Farouk had grown up with them and trusted them. If he insisted on their staying it would be a source of great irritation to the British.

To Darius's great delight, Farouk did insist, and to his even greater delight, did so by taking advantage of the British ambassador's Achilles heel. Sir Miles Lampson's wife was Italian, and the whole of Cairo was soon laughing at the King's riposte to the embassy's demand that the palace Italians be interned. "When Lampson gets rid of his Italian," Farouk was reported as saying, "I'll get rid of mine."

Two weeks later, France fell.

"It's unbelievable," Petra said when she joined Darius and Davina for drinks at Shepheard's. "Nazi flags flying the full length of the Champs-Élysées! Swastikas on the Eiffel Tower and the Arc de Triomphe!"

They were sitting around one of the small tables in the Moorish Hall. Petra was wearing a gold lamé cocktail dress with a slashed neckline that left one golden-skinned shoulder completely exposed and Darius was aware that their table was the focus of much male attention. Sholto was supposed to join them before he and Petra continued on to a party at the Spanish legation, but there was no sign of him and Darius noticed that when Petra's hand wasn't holding her champagne glass, it was constantly fiddling with her wedding ring.

"Mummy's hardly spoken to anyone since she heard." Davina's voice was bleak. "The only ray of light she can see is that Winston is now prime minister. It's something she says should have happened months ago."

It was the kind of insight into British military morale that always intrigued Darius.

"Poor Delia," Petra said without too much real sympathy. "One minute she was over the moon at Winston becoming PM, the next she was devastated when he interned that creep Sir Oswald Mosley."

Darius's interest was caught. "Why was she devastated? Mosley is a Fascist, isn't he?"

"He is now, but he used to be a quite respectable MP and he was on very friendly terms with Delia. His late wife was the daughter of Lord Curzon, an old family friend. My mother doesn't believe he would be disloyal—he was decorated for bravery in the Great War." Her eyes flicked to Davina. "What do you think, Davvy? You've met him. I haven't."

Davina thought of the effect the demon king had had on the thousands of people at Olympia. "I think he might do anything," she said quietly. "I think Winston was probably right to put him out of harm's way."

Every table around them was crowded and people constantly traversed the hall on their way to the Long Bar.

A member of the diplomatic corps spotted them and strolled across.

"If you are waiting for your husband, Mrs. Monck," he said genially, "you may be waiting for some time. I've just left him at the Muhammad Ali Club and he's deep in a hand of chemin de fer. The King is gambling at an adjoining table and it's doubtful which of them is playing for the higher stakes. I'll say this for your old man—when it comes to cards he has nerves of steel!"

With good-natured laughter he left them, heading a little drunkenly in the direction of the terrace.

With a strained smile Petra rose to her feet. "No use my hanging around here if Sholto isn't going to show," she said, her voice studiedly casual. "I think I'll give Kate a ring and see if she'd like to party with the Spaniards this evening."

Darius smiled as if he thought there was nothing odd about her husband failing to meet her, wondering about her carefree friendship with Kate Gunn when he knew that she was well aware of Kate's relationship with their father.

Whether either Davina or Petra was aware of their mother's relationship with Jerome Bazeljette was something he'd never attempted to discover. Petra, though, was far more worldly than Davina and it was just possible that she knew and was protecting Davina by not telling her.

In August the Italians attacked British Somaliland from Ethiopia. With the war now very firmly taking place much nearer to them, tensions in Cairo increased. They increased even further when Italian troops crossed the border from Libya and established a base in the Egyptian desert.

Talk as to the number of German troops with the Italians was rife, but rumor wasn't hard-core information about British tank numbers and battle plans, and it was these Constantin was hungry to get his hands on.

"And I will," Constantin said optimistically as he sat across from Darius at one of the city's most popular nightclubs. "I'm in contact with a big fish now, Darius. A truly big fish."

"Someone in the British military?"

"No, the diplomatic corps."

For once Darius was staggered. Keeping his voice low, he said, "And how much German gold did that take?"

"I don't know. I didn't do the bribing. He's someone who has been on the Nazi payroll for years and he contacted me. Whatever his payoff, I assume the money is on par with what was paid the prime minister."

Rumors that the prime minister was being bribed with German gold were rampant. The only thing that surprised Darius was that the Germans thought a bribe necessary, for though the King abided by the Anglo-Egyptian Treaty and went through the motions of being pro-British, the widespread belief that Berlin would support Egyptian independence after a German victory ensured that the reality was far different.

Every Egyptian he knew was certain that Egypt would be better off if the Axis forces in the desert chased the British army into the sea.

The difficulty, of course, was in knowing just how many British forces were in the desert. The general consensus was that the British were heavily outnumbered.

Unable to see Davina, who was working a night shift, Darius left Constantin ogling his belly dancer and strolled down Soliman Pasha Street to a more elite nightclub.

Within minutes of his arrival, the King made an entrance. Slickly suited and wearing dark glasses, he was accompanied by a couple of people Darius didn't recognize and half a dozen muscular bodyguards.

As a boy Darius had often accompanied his father to Abdin Palace and despite their difference in age the two boys had played together in the palace gardens.

Now, to his surprise, Farouk recognized him and flurried his entourage by not seating himself at the table permanently reserved for him, but by walking across to Darius.

"Good evening," he said affably as Darius rose. "It is a long time since we have had the pleasure of seeing you."

"Yes, sir. Several years."

Farouk had been a handsome little boy and his good looks were still in evidence, though there was a chubbiness about his face that was beginning to blur them.

"Then let us make up for it," he said, seating himself and leaving his companions standing a few feet away in awkward confusion.

Having no other option, Darius sat down again. Champagne speedily arrived. "You are a great friend of Lord Conisborough, I believe," the King said.

Aware that this wasn't how Ivor would describe their relationship, he said evasively, "I've known Lord Conisborough's family for nearly twenty years, sir."

"Yes. Quite so. And his daughters? We see Mrs. Monck at many events in Cairo. Like her American mother, she is a great beauty, is she not?"

"Yes, sir." Darius wondered where this extraordinary conversation was leading. "Mrs. Monck is indeed very beautiful."

He took a drink of champagne. Farouk—a Muslim—ignored his.

"We think Mrs. Monck looks like Rita Hayworth. We would like to see more of her," Farouk said blandly. "Perhaps she would like to see the art treasures of the palace? Maybe you would like to invite her to do so?"

Darius nearly choked on his champagne, but recovered speedily and said with equal blandness, "I'm sure Mrs. Monck and her husband would be delighted by such an invitation."

Farouk smiled and waved a finger in lazy admonishment. "We find that English gentlemen are not as interested in art as English ladies. It has been nice renewing our acquaintance. But no childish games next time we meet at Abdin. Only art and Mrs. Monck." He rose to his feet and the singer on the stage came to a deferential halt as the King crossed to the table reserved for him.

A few minutes later Darius exited the club, a pulse pounding furiously at the corner of his jaw. Behind him, the club's entertainer resumed singing. Out on the pavement he sucked in a great breath of air, unable to get over the fact that his twenty-year-old king had asked him to pimp for him.

Farouk's unfaithfulness was legendary. There was widespread talk that many a court official was reluctant to attend court functions with his wife in case she attracted Farouk's attention. If she did, there was little the man could do about it. If the husband didn't comply with the King's command, his career would end. Darius, though he had little time for Farouk, had hoped the rumor was untrue.

Now he knew that it wasn't.

He lit a cigarette and began walking in the direction of the river. That Farouk would have the gall to approach one of Lord Conisborough's daughters was so outrageous he was still dazed by it. There were European women in the city who would be flattered at the thought of intimacy with a king, but Petra certainly wasn't one of them.

When he thought of her reaction—if she were to know of it—the corners of his mouth twitched. Then, as he strolled past a couple of red-capped military policemen, he burst out laughing. The idea of Petra frolicking naked with Farouk among Abdin Palace's artworks was so surreal he almost wished he could share it.

That he couldn't went without saying.

But when he failed to escort Petra to Abdin, Farouk would take great umbrage. And when a king took umbrage, anything could happen.

TWENTY-TWO

A few days later, at the office, Darius had an unexpected visitor.

"Lady Conisborough would like five minutes of your time," his secretary said. "Shall I tell her you'll see her?"

"Of course I'll see her," he said, hiding his astonishment. "Have tea sent in. Earl Grey."

He swept his papers into the top drawer of his desk and rose to his feet, wondering why on earth Delia wanted to see him. Even Davina never visited him at his chambers.

"So you really *are* a lawyer," Delia said teasingly as she strode into the room, trimly dressed in a St. John Ambulance Brigade uniform.

The tailored black jacket and pencil-straight skirt emphasized her slim figure and her black peaked hat made her Titian-red hair seem more fiery than ever. The hat sported a jaunty striped cockade that he suspected was an honorary symbol of rank. It suited her outgoing personality, and not for the first time he found it remarkable that a woman in her mid- to late forties could still be so breathtakingly dazzling.

"I always thought your legal practice was a scam," she continued as she sat down, "and that you simply claimed to be an advocate so people wouldn't accuse you of being a playboy."

He laughed and she said, "I've come to see if you can supply me with names for the Red Cross ball I'm helping to organize in order to raise money for the war effort. Lady Lampson and I have contacted everyone we know in the British community and your father has kindly shared with us his entire address book. But your social circle is a much younger one and I wondered if I could ask the same favor of you? I have four hundred tickets to sell and so I need all the help I can get."

Keeping amusement out of his voice with difficulty, he said, "I can give you the names of some of my polo-playing friends, Delia, but the tally won't come anything close to four hundred."

"Never mind." She took off the gloves she was wearing. "Every little bit helps."

His secretary brought in the tea tray.

Delia checked the contents of the china teapot and then poured.

Watching her, he wondered what had been missing in the Conisboroughs' marriage that had resulted in her long-standing affair with Sir Jerome.

Probably Ivor had been unfaithful first and she had chosen Jerome to comfort her. The odd thing was her relationship with her husband seemed perfectly compatible. Conisborough had remained friends with Bazeljette. And certainly Delia—who Darius was sure must be aware of her husband's affair—accepted Kate. They were often seen together at polo matches and race meetings.

He wondered if Jack was aware of the nature of his father's relationship with Delia. Since Jack had married Fawzia, Darius had found it difficult to come to terms with the fact that they were now brothers-in-law. When they had been boys and Jack had spent long periods of time at Nile House, the two of them had been friends, though it had always been a fiercely competitive friendship—as when they had both damned near killed themselves at the Gezira Sporting Club polo match.

It had been a long time since the two had met; not since

Jack and Fawzia had visited Cairo as newlyweds. Now, with Jack's move into military intelligence, their relationship was even more strained.

Before he could ponder the problems of Jack being posted to Cairo, Delia said, "Something else I'm tryin' to do, Darius, is to think of ways of entertainin' the troops when they are on leave. They need something to take their minds off the fighting. At the moment most of them simply flock to the El-Birkeh district and then end up in the VD clinics. Alternatives are needed. D'you have any ideas?"

He couldn't think of another woman of her age and class who would so unself-consciously mention prostitution and venereal disease.

Aware of how much he liked her, he said, "You could try tea parties and concert parties or historical trips to the city's mosques, but I doubt such activities will tempt soldiers away from the brothels—especially when women are in such short supply in the city."

"But what about proper clubs? Somewhere they could get something resemblin' British food—eggs and chips and home-made cake, for instance?"

"If the club in question also had hot showers, baths, and a barber, you just might be successful. And if the British weren't so class conscious, there wouldn't be a need for such clubs. If privates and NCOs could go to Shepheard's, the Continental, the Gezira Sporting Club, the Turf Club, or any of the other decent places in Cairo that are out of bounds to anyone other than officers, the problem wouldn't exist."

It was a provocative thing to say, but he was gambling on her agreeing, for she was, after all, an American. And he was damn sure American soldiers wouldn't put up with such segregation.

His hunch proved correct.

She made a despairing gesture. "I quite agree with you,

Darius. But strict segregation between officers and noncoms has always been the way in the British army. That's why it is important that there are other places the British Tommy can go."

Darius pushed his half-drunk cup of tea to one side. "I'm not going to be able to come up with any ideas unless I get some coffee and decent pastry. How about we go to Groppi's?"

"That's a grand suggestion," she said. "I like Groppi's. They make the best sugared almonds in Cairo."

And with the suppleness of a woman twenty years her junior, she rose to her feet and slipped her hand companionably in the crook of his arm.

"I understand you squired my mother to Groppi's," Davina said teasingly as they met up at the Gezira Sporting Club to watch a polo match.

"I'm not quite sure who was squiring whom." Darius shielded his eyes from the sun as the ponies trotted onto the field. "It was my idea that we go there, but only after she'd taken me by surprise at work. She wanted a list of names to invite to a Red Cross charity ball. She also asked me for alternative ways to keep the troops out of the El-Birkeh district and the VD clinics."

"Dear Lord! What did the two of you come up with? Or would it be better for me not to know?"

"No. Her idea was for a well-run club providing everything the Hilmiya Camp doesn't."

The British had established the existing camp a tram ride out of the city at Heliopolis. It was common knowledge that apart from its sea of tents it boasted no facilities other than a bar and an inadequate football pitch.

The umpire tossed the ball between the opposing teams and the action exploded in a great clacking of mallets. Darius was caught up in the furious excitement of the match and all conversation between them ceased.

During the intermission they walked onto the field with other spectators and began the ritual of stamping the divots back in.

"Petra is very happy at the moment," Davina said, searching out another clump of grass that had been unearthed by the ponies and toeing it back into the ground. "She's just heard that one of her closest friends, Boudicca Pytchley, is coming to Cairo as an ambulance driver. Another of her old friends, Archie Somerset, is already in Cairo. She ran into him at a party at the Scarabée Club."

"Is he a regular soldier?"

"No. Special ops."

There was a whole clutch of such outfits operating deep in the desert, reconnoitering and raiding behind German and Italian lines.

He was still thinking about the special operation units when Davina said, "Mother's had an awful dustup with Sir Miles. She thinks he should be taking a stronger position about the army directive that wives and children of military personnel are to be evacuated and that only wives with official war work are to be allowed to stay."

They were nearing the stands and a welcome breeze sent the skirt of her ice-blue silk dress fluttering against her legs.

"And what was Sir Miles's response?" Darius asked, wishing he could have seen such a head-on confrontation.

"Oh, he agreed with her that the action was unnecessarily alarmist, but said it was something he could do nothing about. Not being a military family it doesn't affect us and, as Petra is a secretary at the embassy and I'm a nurse, it wouldn't affect us even if we were. It's causing a lot of distress, though, and many wives are applying for clerical jobs in order to stay."

Not feeling the remotest sympathy for the Englishwomen

desperate to stay on in a country that wasn't theirs he slipped his arm around Davina and said, "Let's miss the second half of the match. We can go to the houseboat."

As they continued walking she leaned against him. "Yes," she said, loving the feel of his body close to hers and the fact that he wanted to make love to her so urgently.

They walked past the stands and, avoiding the Lido terrace that was always full of people they knew, they left the club grounds.

Zamalek was only a short walk and as they strolled along the riverbank, her arm now comfortably around his waist, she said, "I think Fawzia must be becoming very friendly with Queen Farida. We went to Cicurel's department store yesterday to look at the new picture hats and while we were there a police officer came up to us and said Fawzia's presence was wanted at the palace. Then he whisked her out of the store and into a limousine. It was pretty rude of him."

Darius stopped short. High above his head a kite circled slowly. "Did the policeman say specifically that it was the Queen who wanted her company?" he asked, a nerve beginning to throb in his jaw.

"No, but who else could have wanted her at the palace? If it had been the King she wouldn't have gone. Not unaccompanied. And I've heard your father say that Farida gets terribly lonely."

"Yes," he said, his voice carefully devoid of expression. "I expect you're right."

The kite, spying prey, dived.

Davina, always on the side of the victim, winced.

As they started walking again, she said, "I imagine your father would like it if Fawzia and Queen Farida became friends, because I think Fawzia is also lonely. I see little of her and she and Petra are prickly with each other these days. The best solution would be if Jack were posted to Cairo. It can't be easy being separated from your husband. She must miss him very much."

He didn't say anything. He thought of how discontented Fawzia already was in her marriage—and of how shocked Davina would be to know the reason.

He remembered Fawzia wondering how generous Farouk might be to a mistress. And he was pondering the oddity of there being no comeback from the palace over his failure to deliver Petra there in order that she could, in Farouk's words, "see the art treasures of the palace" with him. Was it because Farouk's interest had shifted elsewhere? To Fawzia?

The next day Darius drove through streets choked with military vehicles to his family home in Garden City.

The house faced a tree-lined boulevard and he swerved to a halt outside a wide, high gateway. It was too early for Fawzia to be out, but not, he hoped, so early that his father would still be there. He wasn't in the mood for filial courtesies.

As he slammed the low-slung door of the Mercedes behind him a black Nubian, sitting cross-legged in front of the heavy cedarwood door of the gateway, leaped to his feet. It was his sole task to open and close the door to visitors and though he had been there ever since Darius was a child, Darius still had no idea of his name.

Striding past him into the huge rose-filled courtyard, his only thought was whether or not his sister was behaving like a whore.

His father's majordomo hurried to greet him.

Told that Fawzia was having breakfast on the garden terrace, he strode through the high-ceilinged, lavishly furnished rooms toward it.

When she saw him, she almost dropped her coffee cup.

"Darius! What on earth . . . ? Nothing is the matter, is

it?" She put the cup down unsteadily onto the beautifully laid breakfast table. "There hasn't been an accident?"

"There hasn't been an accident, but there certainly is a problem."

She went rigid and he knew instantly that she understood what he was referring to.

"Davina told me about your visit to the palace. She assumed it was a summons from Queen Farida, but I don't think it was. And I don't think it was the first such visit."

Abruptly she pushed her chair from the table and sprang to her feet, her negligee swirling around her ankles. "What I do and whom I see is my own business!"

"Not if it means you've become one of Farouk's whores!"

"I'm not a whore!" Her eyes blazed fire. "I'm the mistress of my King!"

He'd never hit her, not even when they were children, but he slapped her face so hard that she staggered. A second later she slapped him back with all the strength she had.

The urge to seize hold of her and give her the kind of beating she would never forget was almost too much for him.

Well aware of the danger she stood in, and heedless of it, she didn't back away from him. Instead, she moved closer.

"Keep out of my affairs," she spat, fire in her eyes, "and I'll keep out of yours."

"And just what the hell do you mean by that?"

"I mean that I know all about your friendship with Constantin Antonescu—and if you tell our father about me, I'll tell Davina just how close your links are to Britain's enemies."

"At least my loyalties are to my country!" Rage streamed through him in a dizzying tide. "Where are your loyalties? What do you think Jack's reaction would be if he knew?"

"His reaction would be about as disastrous as Davina's if I told her what you are up to."

"And you think you know what that is, do you?"

"Oh, yes," she shot back at him. "I know."

At the certainty in her voice, he said, "Then you won't be surprised if I ask you to keep me informed of any interesting conversations you overhear at Abdin. If you have to whore, it may as well be for something more valuable than the jewels you're no doubt receiving."

"That's quite a lot to ask, considering my husband is a British intelligence officer."

Sometimes her effrontery was so shameless that he almost admired it.

"You should have thought of your husband before you got into bed with Farouk," he snapped as she seated herself once again at the breakfast table.

She crossed her legs. "King Farouk," she corrected with insolent composure. "His Majesty, King Farouk, by the grace of God, King of Egypt and of Sudan, Sovereign of Nubia, of Kordofan, and of Darfur. One of the richest men in the world and a man who is going to divorce Farida and make me his queen."

"Sweet heaven," he said devoutly. "I do believe you think it's possible."

"It's more than possible. It's already in the cards." Her voice was amused. "Like you, I play for very high stakes—and I can't wait for the day when you have to comply with royal etiquette and walk away from me backward."

"That day, Fawzia," he said through clenched teeth, "will never come!"

He strode away from her, slamming the French doors so hard behind him that the glass in the frames splintered and shattered, falling at his heels in great ugly shards.

TWENTY-THREE

"I don't care how many other parties there are this Christmas, the one at Nile House is going to be the biggest and the best," Delia said as she sipped a gin sling on Shepheard's terrace. "We have so much to celebrate. General Wavell has chased the Italians all the way back across the Western Desert and there are no enemy troops now on Egyptian soil. It's a cause for great celebration, don't y'think?"

Her vivacity was always contagious and, keeping his thoughts to himself, Darius said mildly, "It's rumored Hitler is sending General Rommel to Libya."

It was early evening and the terrace was crowded with military personnel. Darius had seen Delia quite by accident—she had been sitting with a friend, waiting for Ivor. When her husband failed to appear on time, the friend, having an engagement of her own, was happy to leave Delia in Darius's company. "It's a rumor I've heard as well," said Delia, "but not one we should be chattering about here."

"Why not? I'm pretty sure every soldier in the city is aware of it."

"Maybe so," she said equably, "but it doesn't do to take risks. According to General Wavell, the city is chock-full of German informers."

Below the terrace, in the crowded street, a black chauffeured

Rolls-Royce came to a halt. Recognizing it, Delia reached for her white muslin gloves and began pulling them on. She was wearing a broad-brimmed picture hat in pewter-blue, a color he had never seen her wear before. It suited her, but then he had seldom seen her in anything that didn't. The brim of the hat, decorated by a single white rose, dipped low over her eyes, shading them from the sun.

Half a dozen commissionaires hurried down the hotel steps to escort her husband up to them. Dressed impeccably in a dark-gray suit and a silver, gray-spotted bow tie, he cut through them like a knife through butter.

"I'm sorry I'm late, Delia," he said when he reached their table. "There is opposition to Lampson's attempts to expel the Hungarian and Romanian legations. Ah! Darius. How unexpected. Still, I'm glad that you've been able to keep my wife company."

Darius, who fiercely wanted more information, knew it would be fatal to make a direct inquiry. Ivor Conisborough was far too shrewd not to find such interest suspicious. It was equally obvious that as far as Ivor was concerned Darius was now de trop and should take his leave.

A week later, when he was making Turkish coffee for Constantin aboard the *Egyptian Queen,* Constantin said, "There's someone I want you to meet. Have you heard of a group of Egyptian army officers who go by the name the Free Officers Movement?"

Darius added sugar to coffee grounds and water in a small copper pot. "No," he said, stirring the grounds until they sank to the bottom of the pot and the sugar dissolved. "Who are they?"

As he put the pot on the stove to boil Constantin came and stood in the galley's doorway. "It's good you haven't heard of

them. It means their security is watertight. The Free Officers
Movement is a subversive organization within the army that is
waiting for the right moment to rise up and trigger a revolution. I've arranged for you to meet with one of the leaders. His
name is Anwar Sadat."

His first meeting with Sadat took place just after Delia's Christmas party. By the time Darius arrived at Nile House the long
curving drive was thick with parked cars, as were the nearby
streets. Adjo opened the door, resplendent in a royal-blue galabia lavishly embroidered in gold. One glance over Adjo's shoulder was enough to tell him that everyone who was anyone had
arrived before him.

Sir Miles and Lady Lampson were clearly in evidence, as
were the heads of all the foreign legations, except for Romania and Hungary, and the room was crowded with bemedaled
high-ranking military men and their bejeweled wives.

Prince Muhammad Ali, Farouk's extremely pro-British
uncle, was there, dapper in a velvet dinner jacket. Only his
tarboosh and ostentatious cabochon ruby ring singled him out
as an Egyptian.

Princess Shevekiar was holding court in a far corner of the
room. Avoiding her as well as his father—who was deep in
conversation with a broad-shouldered American Darius had
never seen before—he sought out Davina.

Her face lit up at the sight of him and he felt, as he always
did when she looked at him in such a way, as if he had been
punched in the chest and all the breath had been knocked out
of him.

"Darling, isn't this wonderful?" she said, sliding her hand
into his. "Have you seen the Christmas tree? It's fake, of course,
but it's even bigger than the one at the embassy. We only finished decorating it seconds before the first guests arrived."

Her pale gold hair waved softly to shoulders that were naked. It wasn't often she wore a strapless evening gown—strapless evening gowns were far more Petra's style than hers—but the rose-pink shot-taffeta gown looked magical on her.

"I want us to introduce ourselves to Petra's friend, Boudicca Pytchley," she said, leading the way to where a fair, plump young woman with beautiful hands was talking with Kate Gunn. "She's with the Motorized Transport Corps and has only just arrived. All the new ambulance drivers in her medical unit are women which has caused quite a flap at Hilmiya Camp."

". . . thirty thousand Eyeties taken prisoner is rather a good Christmas present, what?" Darius heard a staff officer saying to Sholto as they squeezed past him. "And with Sidi Barrani back in our hands it looks as if it's going to be victory all the way."

Sidi Barrani was one of the villages on the Egyptian side of the border with Libya. The Italians had hoped to make it a base for further operations. Darius would have liked to have listened a little longer, but Davina was saying, "And this is Boo. She's been Petra's friend for years and years and years."

The first thing Boo Pytchley said was, "If Kate and Darius don't mind, I need to have a quiet word with you, Davina. Jack's father asked me to pass on some Toynbee Hall news."

Her eyes had become very troubled, her voice grave, but Davina and Kate didn't sense her change in mood.

"Oh, good." Davina put her hand in his again. "News from Uncle Jerome is always welcome."

From the room beyond there came the sound of a jazz band launching into "Jingle Bells" and Kate Gunn clapped her hands in delight. "Jazzed-up Christmas songs! How typical of Delia."

All around them chatter and laughter competed with the efforts of a brilliant saxophonist.

"Boo has been telling us how absolutely ghastly life is in

London," Kate said, raising her voice in order to be heard. "The Christmas food rations are measly. Sugar has been reduced to only four ounces and tea to two ounces. I can't imagine how people are managing. It makes me feel very guilty when food is so plentiful here. I bought a whole armful of oranges this morning. Boo says Londoners have forgotten what an orange looks like."

Not wanting to continue with the conversation, he looked across the room to where Ivor was chuckling with Lady Wavell and wondered how Ivor could possibly prefer Kate's company to Delia's.

On cue Delia descended, arms outstretched, a radiant welcome on her face. "Where have the two of you been? I thought you were never goin' to arrive. Isn't the band grand? They've begun to play every Thursday night at the Continental and the minute I heard them I just knew I had to have them."

She was wearing turquoise chiffon and there were diamonds at her neck and her wrists and threaded in her upswept hair.

Kate, at least a decade younger, looked colorless in comparison. Her mauve silk evening gown had a narrow fluted skirt embroidered with tiny purple flowers. It was a pretty dress and should have flattered her peaches-and-cream complexion, but it merely made her look a little faded.

Delia slipped a hand affectionately through her arm and said, "It's been so good, Kate, getting really up-to-the-minute gossip from London. Jerome took Boudicca out to lunch only days before she and all the other girls in the medical unit set sail and said to tell us that Shibden Hall is packed to the rafters with refugees. Toynbee Hall have re-homed an entire East End orphanage there. And now," she added, looking around at them, fizzing with vitality, "y'all understand if I shanghai my daughter for a few minutes. Bruno was an early supporter of the Old War Horse Memorial Hospital and as he's so rarely in Cairo, he's eager for an update on what is happening there."

Davina squeezed Darius's hand and allowed herself to be whirled off in her mother's wake.

"Bruno?" he asked, raising an eyebrow questioningly.

"Bruno Lautens," Kate said as he watched Delia making a beeline for the man his father had been talking to a little earlier. "He's an American archaeologist based near the Sudanese border. Before the war he was an experienced desert traveler."

"Golly." Boo Pytchley was impressed. "Where did that little nugget of information come from?"

"Lord Conisborough." As she said his name a faint flush of color touched Kate Gunn's cheeks. She took another sip of her champagne. "He thinks Mr. Lautens will be very useful to some of the people in special ops."

That social talk was often so careless never ceased to amaze Darius. Any hope of further indiscretions on Kate's part was, however, dashed, as Petra approached and kissed Kate, and then Boo, on the cheek.

"So glad you two have made friends," she said, paying Darius not the slightest attention. "And Archie has just arrived," she said to Boo. "If only Rupert was here as well it would be just like old times."

"Rupert's my brother," Boo explained. "He's in the RAF."

"Darius wouldn't know about the RAF—or any other branch of the British military." Petra's voice was blatantly caustic. "He's not even in the Egyptian army. But then Egypt isn't officially at war with Germany—something it's always best to bear in mind, Boo."

The inference was so obvious that he knew she'd had far too much to drink.

"Oh golly." Startled and bewildered Boo looked around for a way out of the suddenly sticky situation and, seeing Archie, she said, "Excuse me for a moment, Petra. I'm just going to catch up on old times."

The minute she'd left, Darius said in a low voice, "Let's talk in the garden. Delia wouldn't thank either of us if we had a shouting match in here."

For a second he thought she was going to refuse to leave the room with him, but then she gave a careless shrug. Her nearly backless gown was of silver lamé and clung sensuously to her every curve.

If Sholto Monck saw her leave the room with him, he gave no sign of it. It was an indifference no Egyptian husband would display.

The garden was lit with fairy lights and there were almost as many couples outside as there were in. He strode onto the darkened lawn and then across the lawn toward the Nile. Only when they had reached the foot of the garden did he turn to face her.

"Just what the *hell*," he said through gritted teeth, "was that little scene about in front of your friend? You might just as well have said I'm not to be trusted!"

"Are you? I don't know. I'm not even sure if you know."

The silver of her dress shimmered in the moonlight as she folded her arms tightly across her chest.

"I've never much liked you, Darius. You come with too many complications. And I don't like your affair with Davvy."

"My affair with Davina hasn't anything to do with you."

"She's my sister. It has everything to do with me." For the first time he noticed that she was barefoot. "What is going to come of it? Are you going to marry her?"

It was a question he asked himself almost every single day, and because he couldn't answer it Petra pushed her glorious hair away from her face and said explosively, "Yet you won't give her up so that she can find someone who not only loves her but will also marry her!" Her voice shook with passion. "The last thing Davvy needs in her life is you, Darius. You've always been trouble. And you're trouble now on a monumental scale."

Yanking up her tight fish-tail skirt she whirled away from him and stormed back to the lights and the music.

He stared grimly at the black-silk surface of the river and didn't walk back to the house until he'd smoked his cigarette down to a stub.

Back inside a fishing-fleet girl was singing "A Nightingale Sang in Berkeley Square" and nearly everyone was dancing. There was no sign of Davina, and taking a glass of champagne from a passing tray he went in search of her.

He found her in the den. She was laughing at something Bruno Lautens was saying. Archie Somerset was running a finger across the many books on the bookshelves, a paper party hat on his head. A girl who had arrived at the party with one of Archie's friends had her arm hooked proprietarily over Lautens's shoulder.

Davina's eyes lit up at the sight of him. "We're taking a breather. Bruno's got some very funny stories. The fellahin south of Aswan believe Hitler is a Muslim!"

He gave a polite smile, not at all liking the admiring expression in Lautens's eyes when he looked at Davina.

He was just about to suggest that they return to the crush when Boudicca Pytchley pushed past him into the room.

"Oh goodness, what a party! Your mother has just promised she'll sing 'Dixie.' Look, I must have a few words with you, Davina, and it's as quiet here as anywhere." She drew in a deep breath. "Jack's father asked me to tell you that a doctor and his wife you used to know . . . Dr. and Mrs. Sinclair . . . were killed in a car accident. It was dreadful. They were both killed outright and there's a child . . . a boy . . ."

That Boo obviously didn't realize just how close Davina and the Sinclairs had been only added to the hideousness of the moment.

Davina gave a low cry, and as her legs gave way Bruno caught her and lowered her into the nearest chair.

"Where . . . ?" she croaked, her face chalk white. "How . . . ?"

"A place called Dunbeath, in Sutherland. I hadn't realized the Sinclairs were such close friends, Davina." Boo's voice was full of remorse.

"I think Davina needs a little time to get over the shock," Darius said brusquely.

Davina said, as if he hadn't spoken: "How, Boo?"

"It happened at night on a coast road, and from what Sir Jerome said, the road was steep and there was a sharp bend. The crash was head-on. The driver of the other car was drunk."

Davina shuddered so violently, Darius thought she was going to collapse completely.

"Fetch her a brandy," he said abruptly to Bruno. "And a shawl, or a blanket of some kind."

No one had ever had the nerve—or been so foolish—as to speak to Bruno in such a way before, but at the sight of Davina's ashen face Bruno merely said, "Sure. Will do."

"Their little boy . . ." Davina's teeth were chattering. "Andrew. Was Andrew hurt?"

"He wasn't with them. I don't know why, but Sir Jerome thought there were no relatives on either side of the family to take care of him. Muriel Scolby went to the funeral and when she realized the situation she brought Andrew back down to London with her. With the family solicitor's permission, he's now living at Shibden Hall."

"Can he be adopted?"

The question was so unexpected that Boo blinked.

"Well, yes," she said, "I suppose so. Though he may be a

little old now. He's nearly six and I know older orphans don't seem to have much of a chance."

"This one will." The light in her eyes was almost as fierce as the tone of her voice.

Bruno came back with a brandy and a tartan rug. Darius pressed the glass of brandy into Davina's hand and laid the blanket around her shoulders.

"When this bloody war is over," she said unsteadily, "I shall adopt him, Darius. It's the least I can do for Aileen and Fergus."

Beads of sweat broke out on his forehead. He might survive having an English wife, but what about having a Scottish stepson?

It would be impossible, but he couldn't tell Davina so when the Pytchley girl, Bruno Lautens, and Archie Somerset were clustered so anxiously around her. Instead he said heavily, "I think we should leave Davina alone for a little while."

"Yes, of course, old chap." The speaker was Archie and as Archie duly opened the door the incongruous sound of Delia singing "Dixie" filled the room.

TWENTY-FOUR

Later that night, back on the *Egyptian Queen,* Darius sat on the deck, a cigarette in one hand, a glass of arrak in the other. Talking Davina out of adopting the Sinclair child wasn't an option; for one thing, he knew he wouldn't be able to do so, for another, he fully sympathized with her intention. The Sinclairs had been her close friends. If their child was left with no family, Davina wouldn't be the person he loved if she hadn't responded as she had.

By the time Sadat arrived for their meeting the sun was beginning to rise.

"You're a lawyer," Sadat said when he had seated himself in a chair on the deck. "And a skilled lawyer will have a vital role when we take control of Egypt. We'll want men whose loyalty and commitment are proven. A minister of justice who has been with us from the beginning."

Darius would have taken such remarks from anyone else as empty daydreaming, but Constantin had told him enough about Sadat for him to know that Sadat was a hard-nosed realist.

"There's a new breed of officers in the Egyptian army now," Constantin had said. "And they are ready to stage an uprising when the moment is right. Their real leader is an officer named Gamal Nasser. Sadat is his deputy."

Constantin hadn't told Darius that Sadat was only in his early twenties. He had been expecting someone far older, but his shock didn't last.

"It isn't only the British we need to expel," Sadat said bluntly. "We have to overthrow the monarchy. As long as there is a king, Egypt will remain poor and backward. All our country's wealth from cotton, from the canal, goes into the pockets of a handful of self-indulgent and corrupt men. The King has to go. The great landowners have to go. Parliament, as it exists, must be stripped of power and a new congress reelected."

The future Sadat painted—where the old feudal estates were broken up, where the wealth from cotton was used to build a modern state—was beyond anything Darius had ever dared to hope.

By the time Sadat had left the houseboat, Darius had decided on his future. Along with Sadat, Nasser, and the idealistic young officers they had gathered around them, he was going to be instrumental in the rebirth of Egypt. He would ensure that she was never again subordinated to another nation.

"And that includes Germany," Sadat had said, stuffing tobacco into a pipe. "I know that at the moment it looks as if the tide of the war is turning against her, but it won't be so for long. Hitler will send in German troops under Rommel. It is imperative we have direct contact with him when he arrives. We can't stage an uprising that will help him take Cairo without a guarantee that when the war is over, Egypt will be independent."

"What kind of contact?" he had asked. "Wireless?"

"Only to arrange the meeting," Sadat had said, lighting his pipe. "Our intention is to fly one of our officers across the desert for a personal meeting. It's risky, of course. When the British realize he's heading for enemy lines they'll try and shoot him down. Unless the Germans offer cover, the RAF will blast him from the sky before he can land. Constantin is already in touch with Berlin and they will tell him the wavelength needed for their headquarters in Libya. When the time is right, we'll be able to make contact."

Darius lit another cigarette and poured himself some more arrak. Golden light was now streaking the sky and gilding the surface of the Nile. In a few more hours Davina would arrive.

He wondered how much he could safely tell her.

And he wondered if it was fair to tell her anything at all.

"I didn't break the news to my mother of Aileen and Fergus's death until breakfast," Davina said sitting down wearily on one of the lounge chairs. "I just couldn't bring myself to do it last night when she was having such a wonderful time."

"And this morning?"

She winced. "It was terrible. She admired both of them so much and had grown very fond of them, particularly Aileen."

Her eyes were red-rimmed, her face etched with grief.

Seeing her pain was a knife to Darius's heart.

"Would you like a coffee?" he asked, wishing there was some way he could comfort her.

She nodded. "Yes, please. But not Turkish."

He went down the companionway to the galley. Though he hadn't been to bed he had changed out of the Western clothes he had worn to Delia's party, and into a galabia. It was black trimmed with narrow silver braid and he was quite sure that he had never looked—or felt—more Egyptian.

When he returned to the sundeck, he said, "I've met the most remarkable young man, Davina. His name is Anwar Sadat and he's an Egyptian army officer."

He described Sadat's vision of an Egypt without foreign domination and without a self-indulgent monarchy and a corrupt Egyptian elite. He told Davina that Sadat envisioned a place for him in the new republican government. He knew he should tell her how difficult their future would be, but he couldn't bring himself to do so. At least not while she was so distressed over her friends' death.

Always able to read each other's minds, she did it for him.

"I doubt if the Free Officers envision a future minister of justice who is married to an Englishwoman." Her voice was filled with despair. "And my adopting Andrew only complicates matters further, doesn't it?"

He wanted to say that no, it didn't. But because they had always been truthful with each other, he couldn't.

She put the tips of her fingers to her forehead as if trying to ease a pain that was too much to bear. "Perhaps we should end things now, Darius. Perhaps it would be easiest—"

He seized hold of her arms and pulled her roughly to her feet. "No," he said fiercely, knowing it was something he couldn't, yet, survive. "Nothing has to be done now. It will be years before the Free Officers' dream comes to fruition. And it could be a long time before you are able to adopt Andrew. Who knows how long this bally war is going to continue? Who knows who is going to win it and what the circumstances will be? For now, we go on as we've always done. Together."

She sagged against him with relief.

His arms closed around her and as he hugged her to him, he knew he was only forestalling the day when she would leave his life forever.

A month later a Romanian diplomat was expelled from his legation on suspicion of spying. The legation, however, was not closed down.

"Can't be, old boy," Archie Somerset said in his infuriating English public-school accent. "You have to remember that Egypt's not at war with Romania—or anyone else for that matter. Much as Ambassador Lampson would like to close the

Hungarian and Romanian legations, he can't. Getting rid of a spy was the most Lampson could do. It must make him crazy with rage."

Archie was the kind of jovial Englishman that most annoyed Darius. Always jolly, always joking, he would disappear from Cairo for weeks on end and then turn up again with pale marks around his eyes left by sand goggles and no explanation of his absence other than that he had been "in the blue"—British slang for the Western Desert.

When he was in Cairo, Archie was everywhere. No matter what the party, Archie was a guest. And Darius regularly ran across him in places British soldiers normally never visited. One day Archie said, "How about a party on your houseboat, Darius? That's what houseboats are for, aren't they? A bit of music, a lot of dancing. Have you got a radiogram? I've got plenty of records you can borrow."

Darius replied stone-faced that he never held parties, but he increasingly wondered if Archie was Constantin's British contact.

British euphoria over the collapse of the Italian advance changed to an atmosphere of tension in February when General Rommel landed in Libya with two crack panzer divisions.

Even before the month was out the Afrika Korps launched into an engagement with British troops at El Agheila, the point in Libya where, a couple of months earlier, the British had defeated the Italians. There was no running German troops to a standstill, and the prospect of Rommel striding into Shepheard's and commandeering the best suite suddenly seemed a very real possibility.

Sadat, using Constantin's wireless transmitter, contacted Rommel's headquarters in Libya from the *Egyptian Queen,* but to his great consternation, there was no reply.

———

In March, as more successful attacks were launched by the Germans, Britain's foreign secretary, Anthony Eden, flew into Cairo in order to give a firsthand report to Churchill. He was accompanied by the chief of the imperial general staff, Sir John Greer Dill, and Sir Jerome Bazeljette.

Though nearly every moment of the three men's time was spent in discussions with the military hierarchy, Jerome did manage to squeeze in an appearance at a party thrown for him by Delia.

Darius and his father were among the many guests.

Their hostess was radiant. Wryly Darius wondered if he was the only person—apart from her husband and Jerome— who was aware of the reason for Delia's glowing happiness.

"Sylvia and Girlington are at Skooby for the duration," he overheard Jerome say to Lady Tucker, the wife of an army general.

He hadn't a clue who was being talked about.

Aware he was eavesdropping, Davina glided past him and whispered helpfully, "Sylvia is the former Lady Bazeljette. Girlington is her husband, the Duke of Girlington. Skooby is one of their many homes, a castle in the north of England."

His lips twitched in amusement which quickly vanished when Fawzia entered the room on their father's arm.

She looked ravishing, as always. Her blue-black hair was coiled in an elaborate chignon. Her cocktail dress was ruby-red brocade and she was wearing magnificent diamonds at her ears and throat. He regarded them cobra-eyed, certain that whatever she may have said to their father, they were not a present from her husband.

He remembered Sadat's passionate promise that when the Free Officers Movement liberated Egypt, Farouk and all he stood for would have to go. Darius looked at the waterfall of diamonds hanging from his sister's ears and felt that day couldn't come soon enough.

"Did you forget that Sir Jerome is my father-in-law?" Fawzia said when their father had moved off to speak to Ivor. "Unfortunately he has no more news of Jack than I have. The last we heard he was in Palestine."

Darius said nothing. Palestine was too close to Egypt for comfort. Now that Sadat was attempting to contact Rommel from a wireless transmitter onboard the *Egyptian Queen,* the last thing Darius needed was a British intelligence officer turning up in Cairo—especially when that intelligence officer was both a brother-in-law and a friend.

Behind them Delia, who had become temporarily detached from Jerome's arm, was saying cheerily to Lady Tucker, "It's so dandy getting reliable news of the Duke and Duchess. When I heard the Duke had been given the governorship of the Bahamas my heart sank. It's so far from Europe I couldn't imagine either of them feelin' it was anything but a form of exile, but apparently the Duke is doing a cracking job and Wallis, who is just as sweet as she can be, has thrown herself into Red Cross work."

Lady Tucker's face was a picture. He had long ago realized that no one in the British community had a good word to say about the woman for whom King Edward VIII had renounced his throne, but Delia never left anyone in doubt as to where she stood on the issue of Wallis Simpson. Wallis was her friend and, as she said often, "a grand gal."

Lady Tucker stiffly changed the subject to Delia's highly successful club for noncommissioned troops and Darius watched Davina as she threaded her way through the guests. Her pale-blue cocktail dress was simply cut, her shoulder-length fair hair held away from her face by a mother-of-pearl comb. Though she was twenty-five, she looked barely twenty and he was strongly reminded of an illustration he had seen of Alice in the children's storybook *Alice in Wonderland*.

Jerome immediately gave her a bear hug. Petra, he noted, was keeping her distance, though he also noted that her eyes followed Jerome wherever he went. Hard as he tried to read her expression, he couldn't. All he could assume was that she was aware of the nature of Jerome's relationship with her mother and wanted as little to do with him as possible.

The conversation between Jerome and Davina had become earnest. He heard the words "Shibden Hall" and "Andrew," and tension churned his guts. He turned away, not wanting to be reminded of the devastation that would take place in his life on the day Davina adopted Andrew.

Leaving the party early, he arrived back at the *Egyptian Queen* not long after midnight to find Constantin seated on one of the deck's loungers.

"What's the matter?" he asked abruptly, not in the mood for a late-night chat. "I thought I'd told you I'd be at the Conisborough party this evening."

"Did you? I'd forgotten. Still, if you're not in the mood for a drink I'll wander off." He waited for Darius to dissuade him and then, as Darius remained silent, he heaved himself to his feet. "*Noapte buna,*" he said, wishing him good night in Romanian.

" 'Night," Darius said, knowing he'd been inhospitably churlish.

By April Rommel was advancing on Egypt at such a pace that the British, fearful that the Egyptian army units stationed near the frontier would surrender, replaced them with Allied troops.

"And our generals acquiesced!" Anwar said explosively to

Darius. "If only Rommel had contacted us, agreeing to meet with one of our officers and sign the treaty, it would have been the perfect time to stage an uprising. As it is, there is still no word from Rommel. Why, Darius? Why?"

By May the war in the desert was being conducted on such a vast scale that the streets of Cairo were clogged with dispatch riders and trucks packed with equipment and men. The talk in the Long Bar at Shepheard's was that the Germans could be expected to arrive at the pyramids within the week.

Tobruk, a coastal town of great strategic value because of its deep harbor, had been encircled by Rommel. Darius didn't expect talk of anything else, but was wrong. The news Davina brought superseded even that of Tobruk, at least in the British community.

"My parents are divorcing," she said, white-faced, as she stepped aboard the houseboat.

"Sit down," he said. "I'll make coffee."

Only when the coffee was made did he allow her to begin talking again.

"My father is going to marry Kate," she said dazedly. "And the incredible thing is, my mother doesn't mind. She says that as Kate is thirty-nine and is desperate to have a baby, it's best they marry now before it's too late for her to have one."

Davina passed a hand across her eyes. "I feel so odd, Darius. Knowing Kate was having an affair with my father was one thing. But I never dreamed my father would divorce my mother so that he and Kate could marry. He and my mother have always been so close. He tells her absolutely everything. And that is how my mother says it will stay. She says that they will always be each other's best friend."

She took a sip of her coffee and added, "My mother seems *relieved* by the divorce. She says it is something that couldn't have happened when my father was an adviser to King Fuad. A divorce then would have meant his immediate recall to London and the end of his career. Now, even if their social life suffers, I don't think either of them cares. And it probably *won't* because the war has changed everything. People think differently now."

"Where will Kate and your father marry?" he asked, bemused.

"I don't know. In the Church of England, people who have been divorced can't have a church wedding. My mother is hoping—as it matters to Kate so much—that after a civil marriage ceremony they will be able to have a blessing on their marriage in the English cathedral."

"If that's what your mother is hoping for, then I daresay it will be what your mother gets," he said, aware that Davina was soon going to have to face the even more profound shock of learning her mother was in love with Sir Jerome Bazeljette.

"Who is going to be the one to move out of Nile House?" he asked, wondering how the three protagonists were going to survive the deluge of gossip.

"My father. He's already moved into a house here, on Gezira Island, close to the sporting club."

She looked exhausted and he said abruptly, "Let's go to Fleurent for lunch. You can tell me about Petra's reaction to the news over a glass of wine."

According to Davina, Petra hadn't revealed even a glimpse of what she was feeling. Instead she had affected great indifference. It wasn't a reaction shared by anyone else in the British community. Wherever he went, Darius heard about the Conisborough divorce and Lord Conisborough's intended remarriage. For any another couple it would have been social death. The Conisboroughs, however, rode out the storm with admirable élan, thanks mainly to Delia, who behaved as if nothing very extraordinary was happening. She continued to give the best parties in Cairo at Nile House.

In order not to prejudice the proceedings, neither Ivor nor Kate was present at any of the parties, but even the most blinkered of Cairenes realized that if Delia could have had them there, she would have.

"Of course, she's *American*," Darius often overheard in Shepheard's or Groppi's, but it was always said with admiration.

"She's sassy," he once heard Lady Lampson say, using an American expression often used by Delia.

It had amused him. He'd wondered if Lady Lampson also regularly told her husband that the jig was up.

As the first shock waves died, conversation reverted to the continuing siege of Tobruk. The garrison there consisted of the Australian Ninth Division, under General Morshead, and British troops who had withdrawn there before the start of the siege.

"They make a total of twenty-five thousand men," a brigadier said in Shepheard's Long Bar.

It was the kind of careless talk Constantin would have been euphoric to overhear.

Two days later the Free Officers received a coded message from Rommel. He was agreeable to meeting with one of them and would give consideration to the treaty. To guarantee the safety of the plane flying the officer over German lines, he requested the date and time of his flight.

Sadat called Darius, saying, "I'll be at the houseboat tonight at midnight, to transmit."

Darius had a party to go to that evening—in Cairo there

were always parties to go to. He and Davina had been invited by Momo Marriott, wife of Brigadier Sir John Marriott. Momo had transformed the basement of her house into a lavish private nightclub and was nearly as popular a hostess as Delia.

Even though it would mean leaving the party early Darius didn't consider not going. All the usual crowd would be there, which would include Bruno Lautens. Darius knew that Lautens was smitten with Davina and that there was nothing he would like more than to be able to spend time with her when Darius wasn't around.

The moment they stepped into Chez Marie, the name Momo had given her nightclub, they were swallowed up in a glittering throng, for Momo went out of her way to play hostess to many European royals who had sought sanctuary in Egypt when their countries had been overrun by the Germans.

King Zog of Albania was dancing with his wife, Queen Geraldine. King Victor Emmanuel of Italy was also dancing, though not with his wife. Prince Wahid al-Din, Princess Shevekiar's son, was standing by the bar talking with Petra. Jacquetta, Lady Lampson, was laughing at something Sholto Monck was saying. Winston Churchill's son, Randolph, who was in Cairo as a press officer, was flirting with Momo.

There were a score of glamorous fishing-fleet girls; an entire contingent of British officers on leave from the front; a rowdy bunch of New Zealanders, also on leave, and an even rowdier bunch of Australians. The singer Momo had purloined from the Scarabée Club was singing Johnny Mercer's "Jeepers Creepers" and Archie Somerset was doing an energetic quickstep with Boo Pytchley.

"Squeeze through the crush and get a couple of glasses of champagne!" Davina shouted to him over the music. "I'll wait for you here!"

He launched himself into the fray and as he did so Princess

Shevekiar accidentally bumped into him. She was elderly and he immediately steadied her.

"Thank you so much," she said regally, not seeming to recognize him. Then, looking in the direction where he had left Davina, she said, "Lady Russell Pasha has just pointed out to me what a wonderful match Bruno Lautens would be for Davina Conisborough. He's a widower with a seven-year-old son, did you know that? His little boy would make a perfect stepbrother for the child Davina is going to adopt."

Darius swung around. Several couples now separated him from Davina, but she was no longer standing alone. Lautens was with her. Seeing them together it was as if he had been transported in time to the future; a future where the war was over and he was part of the government of an independent Egypt. A future where Andrew Sinclair was Davina's son. A future where she and Lautens were married and Darius, as Egypt's minister of justice, was doomed to seeing them together at every social occasion he attended.

As passionately as he loved his country, he knew in a moment of blinding revelation that high office would never compensate for losing Davina. She was as essential to him as breathing. So what if her father was English? And what if her adopted child was Scottish? It was something the Free Officers Movement would simply have to accept.

And if they didn't?

If they didn't, he would still have Davina and as long as he still had Davina then his life would be worth living.

As the singer began singing "All the Things You Are," he understood for the first time why King Edward VIII had renounced his throne rather than give up Mrs. Simpson.

Darius weaved a way through the dancers to Davina. He saw Lautens turn toward him and ignored him.

Davina smiled. It was the smile that had entranced him

when she had been little more than a child. It was the smile that would entrance him as long as he lived.

He took her hands and held them tightly in his. He knew that if Petra asked him now if he intended marrying Davina, the answer would be "of course." Any alternative to the two of them being together was totally unthinkable.

Part Five

JACK

1941

TWENTY-FIVE

Jack's satisfaction when his commanding officer told him he was to be transferred to Cairo was so deep it was all he could do to keep from punching the air.

"You'll still be part of Security Intelligence Middle East, but you'll liaise with Cairo's Special Investigation Branch."

The officer shuffled papers into a file.

"All the usual rules apply. You can wear civvies or the uniform of any other rank below your own as the situation necessitates. And the situation, I may tell you, is grim. Someone in Cairo is passing classified information to the enemy. Your task is to hunt him out before Rommel is on the terrace at Shepheard's ordering a beer."

The officer leaned forward, resting his elbows on his desk and steepling his fingers.

"I see from your file that your wife is Egyptian and is living in Cairo." He frowned slightly. "It's a situation that could prove good cover for intelligence work, but I think I'd keep it under my hat. And there are no married quarters. Army wives, apart from those of brigadiers and generals, have been evacuated. Not many went willingly and so you can see the bad feeling that would arise if you were to move in with your wife."

Jack nodded. The minute he'd heard of his transfer his thoughts had flown to Fawzia and the difficulties his work would cause them. Not being able to live together would ease those difficulties immeasurably.

He flew from Jerusalem to Cairo crammed uncomfortably in a Wellington bomber, realizing to his shame that his thoughts were centered not on Fawzia but on Petra.

The last time he had seen her was when he visited Cairo after his marriage. She'd spent as little time as possible in his company, and when she'd been in his company she hadn't wanted to talk to him. She hadn't even seemed to be the same woman. She had been so tense, so buttoned-up that it was as if she were going to explode at any moment. Only one thing had been clear. If she had ever been in love with him, she no longer was. Their affair was over. And to make sure he had got the message she had married that long shallow streak of facile charm, Sholto Monck.

Monck, he knew, was still in Cairo and because of his position at the embassy, he was someone Jack was going to have to rub along with. It wasn't something he looked forward to.

As the Wellington set down at an airstrip near Hilmiya Camp he put aside all thoughts of Petra, allowing the pleasure of returning to Cairo to flood through him. Without doubt, Cairo remained his favorite city in all the world.

Stepping onto the tarmac and breathing in the familiar hot, spicy air, he suddenly relaxed. After eighteen months he was about to be reunited with his wife, and though his marriage had always been far shakier than he had ever admitted, it was a union he was determined to make work.

He knew from several sources—Davina's letters, Delia's letters, his father's trips to Cairo—that Darius had suspended his anti-British activity. That he had was certainly going to make things easier where their friendship was concerned.

A young lieutenant saluted courteously, took his briefcase, and led him across to a waiting staff car.

"It's a filthy city, Major Bazeljette," the lieutenant said, assuming it was his first time there. He slid behind the wheel. "The bloody wogs are a nightmare. You can't trust them as far as you can throw them."

Jack took a packet of Camels out of his pocket. "My wife is Egyptian," he said, lighting up.

The jeep almost slewed off the road. "I'm sorry, Major!" The lieutenant spluttered apologies. "I didn't know . . . Didn't think . . . Oh, Christ!"

Jack didn't tell him not to worry. He let him suffer. The news that his wife was Egyptian would, he knew, now spread throughout the British military community. This was directly opposite to the advice he had been given, but he didn't care. It would save him from hearing the word "wog" every few minutes and that, for his temper's sake, was of prime importance.

Hilmiya Camp was six miles from the center of Cairo and, as it was an approach to the city he had never made before, he settled back to enjoy the ride. The narrow road was so congested with army traffic that there were times when he thought it would have been quicker to walk.

Quicker, but far more exhausting. It was July and the heat was so intense that he could feel the sweat trickling down between his shoulder blades. By the time the Citadel and the gleaming white alabaster walls of the Muhammad Ali Mosque came into view, he was gasping for an ice-cold beer.

As they entered the city he saw that the cafés were thronged with troops who all had the same idea. There were British, Australian, Free French, South African, and Indian uniforms. Always a crowded city, Cairo was now bursting at the seams.

Almost submerged under the endless sea of khaki he spotted the familiar sights. Sherbet-sellers wove their way through the crowds. Beggars stood on every corner. Old men in dirty galabias pushed hand barrows piled high with fruit and vegetables through the traffic, dusty leather slippers slapping against their bare heels. Overloaded donkeys fought with cars for road space and survival.

At Ezbekiya Gardens the ancient bandstand was untouched. At the corner of Opera Square and Kasr el-Nil Street, Cicurel's department store still boasted a window display of hats so fashionable they could have done the Champs-Élysées proud.

The long wailing notes of the muezzins calling the faithful to prayer sounded as they motored down Kasr el-Nil Street and then, minutes later, he caught his first glimpse of the Nile.

His driver swerved left out of Kasr el-Nil onto the road that flanked the river bank, heading straight for the British army headquarters.

GHQ was situated in a modern block of flats called Grey Pillars at the southern end of Garden City, not far from his father-in-law's family home and close to Nile House. Knowing that a reunion with Fawzia was going to have to wait until he had checked in with his commanding officer, he fought down his impatience and wondered if his CO in Jerusalem had got it right when he had said that Jack's prime task was to hunt down one specific spy.

Brigadier Haigh, the director of military intelligence, left him in no doubt about it.

"The bugger's got to be caught, Major, and so far we've no lead on him. We just know that the German military learns everything we're going to do before we do it. The information could be coming from anywhere. The former prime minister, Ali Maher Pasha, is still a force politically and is so pro-German he'd inform the Germans of our plans at the drop of a hat. The King is no different. Ambassador Lampson has a terrible time getting His Majesty to toe the line."

That the brigadier regarded Lampson's relationship to the

King as that of a schoolmaster to a fractious pupil would have been comic if it didn't mean good relations with the palace were well-nigh impossible.

Hoping to aid his superior officer's understanding without finding himself on the first plane back to Palestine, Jack said mildly, "Since Egypt has never declared war with Germany, Farouk is always going to be fractious. It can't be much fun for him having his cities full of foreign troops."

"The bugger's lucky to have us here!" the brigadier snapped. "If it wasn't for us, the Italians would have swarmed into Cairo a year ago and sent him packing. You're here, Major Bazeljette, because you have knowledge of the city and studied Arabic at Oxford. Being a Gyppo-lover isn't a requirement—and it won't make you many friends."

Wisely keeping further thoughts to himself, Jack saluted and made a judicious exit.

The next two hours were spent in familiarizing himself with his office and staff. Grey Pillars was a massive rabbit warren. Scores of what had once been separate flats had had their walls ripped out and partitioning put up to make offices out of every available inch of space. Narrow corridors linking what had been one flat with another were thronged with harassed army personnel.

Jack's own corner was furnished with a desk, a chair, a filing cabinet, a telephone, and much to his great relief, a window.

"I'm Doris, your typist, sir," said a pleasant-faced young woman in army uniform. She put a huge sheaf of files on the desk. "I'm also the typist for six other officers, so if you want me you have to shout quite loud. Would you like a cup of tea? Some of these files haven't been dusted off for months. You'll probably find them thirsty work."

It wasn't the way he'd been addressed by WACs in Jerusalem, but he preferred a free and easy working atmosphere to a stiff and formal one. "A cup of tea would do the job, Doris. I was told my staff included a Captain Reynolds and a Corporal Slade. Is either of them about?"

"Captain Reynolds has been transferred to another unit, sir. We're expecting a replacement, but he hasn't shown up as yet. Corporal Slade is hunting down a staff car for you to use. Nothing in Cairo is as organized as you might be used to. I believe Corporal Slade is also checking out your quarters. Or rather, finding you quarters. Sleeping space is more precious than gold. As you are intelligence you'll probably find yourself sharing a flat with a couple of other officers. The barracks are packed to overflowing."

An hour later, after meeting with his radio-room staff, he left Grey Pillars to make the short walk to Fawzia's family home.

It had been eighteen months since he had last seen her, and when they had parted it had been after a furious, blistering row about money. Fawzia simply could not understand why they didn't live the same lifestyle Delia or his mother and Theo Girlington lived.

"But your father is a baronet and your mother is a duchess!" she said. "So why are we living in a flat that would fit into my family home six times over?"

That the flat was palatial by London standards made no difference to her. It wasn't the equivalent of a mansion in Cadogan Square—and a mansion in Cadogan Square was what she had expected.

Jewelry had been an issue, too. His wedding present to her had been a diamond-and-emerald brooch that had been his paternal grandmother's. The family tiara that in normal circumstances would have been given to her was in the possession of his mother, and despite the fabulous jewelry collection that had come her way when she married Theo, she had shown not the slightest desire to relinquish either it or any other items of family jewels. To compensate, his father's wedding gift to Fawzia had been a splendid tiara from Aspreys.

Fawzia's false expectations were not ones he could make good. His Foreign Office salary and the private income left to him by his grandmother ensured he was relatively well off, but even looking to the future, he had no expectations of being rich on the scale Fawzia aspired to.

That she'd had so little idea as to the realities of being Mrs. Jack Bazeljette, he blamed on himself. In Cairo she had been brought up in a luxuriously cocooned world. Though she had been friends with Petra and Davina she had never, apart from the lessons they had shared as schoolgirls, lived as they lived. By the time she was fifteen Davina had volunteered at the orphanage and was traveling unaccompanied on public transport. Fawzia, he knew for a certainty, had never been on a Cairo tram in her life.

In London as Delia's guest, she had been equally cocooned. Delia had been far stricter about where Fawzia could and couldn't go than she had ever been with her own daughters.

When Jack reached the heavy cedarwood door he addressed the Nubian guarding it in Arabic. Seconds later he stepped into the familiar shade of the courtyard.

Two safragis ran to meet him dressed in blindingly white galabias sashed in crimson. Hard on their heels was Zubair Pasha, a welcoming smile on his heavily lined face.

"So you are finally back in Cairo, Jack!" he said exuberantly, clapping his son-in-law on his shoulders in a gesture of affection. "Fawzia said you would move heaven and earth in order to get posted here. I will have the guest bedroom made ready immediately. And where is your kit?"

"No kit, I am afraid." Jack's answering smile was rueful. "Orders are not to draw attention to the fact that I have a wife in the city. The evacuation of the army wives is apparently a very sensitive issue."

Zubair nodded. After a lifetime at Abdin, first with King Fuad and then with Farouk, he knew the nuances of pussy-footing around sensitive or potentially sensitive situations.

"You must have a drink," he said as a safragi appeared at their side with rose-scented water on a silver tray. "And I must tell you that Fawzia is not at home. She spends a lot of time at Nile House, with Davina."

Grateful that Zubair Pasha showed no intention of delaying him, Jack drank the sickly sweet water and minutes later was making his way down the elegant winding roads of Garden City.

Adjo greeted him with deep affection.

Delia was in the drawing room arranging yellow lilies and, when he walked in on her unannounced, she dropped the flower she was holding and with a cry of delight ran toward him, a smile of blazing pleasure on her face.

"Jack! How grand!" she gasped as he hugged her tight. "We'd no idea you were coming! Does Fawzia know? And if she did, how could the little minx have kept it to herself?"

"No one knew," he said, filled with the huge sense of well-being Delia always imparted to those she loved. "I didn't know till two days ago. Is she here?"

"Here?" Delia stepped away from him. In her late forties, her beauty was more full-blown than it had once been, but he knew that she would never lose it. She was wearing a straight-skirted white linen dress, the waist cinched by a wide, cornflower-blue belt. "No, she isn't here," she said, looking a little startled. "Apart from running into her at parties I haven't seen Fawzia for weeks. If she isn't at the palace, she'll be at home."

"She isn't at home," he said easily, not letting his faint sense of disquiet show. "Why should she be at the palace?"

Delia tucked her hand comfortably into the crook of his arm. "She's always at the palace. Farouk neglects his little queen quite disgracefully and Farida relies on friends such as Fawzia for company—sometimes too much so. Davina says that more than once when she and Fawzia have been out a royal car has drawn up, a servant has announced that Fawzia's presence is required at the palace, and Fawzia's been borne off whether she really wanted to go or not."

A pergola had been built over the terrace since he had last been at Nile House and as they stood beneath the shade of the vines growing over it, he said, "Zubair Pasha didn't mention her palace visits. He said she spent most of her time with Davina."

"Well, she probably would if she could," Delia responded drily, "but Davina is always busy. Every nurse in Cairo is working eighteen hours out of twenty-four—and then some. And Zubair Pasha isn't well versed in what's going on at Abdin. Pride will prevent him telling you, but he's been out of favor with the King for some time now—probably because he's too pro-British for the King's comfort."

As they began walking down the terrace steps onto the lawn, she said, "Now what else d'you need bringing up-to-date on? There's the divorce, of course. Ivor is going to make an honest woman out of Kate at last and hopefully father a son and heir. Needless to say, everything is extremely amicable—though I think Cairo society rather wishes it weren't. Back in England, Shibden Hall is full with evacuees and orphans—including a little boy I think will soon be a member of the family."

The news that she and Ivor were divorcing wasn't a total surprise. The little boy, however, was a complete mystery.

"The orphan," he prompted, seeing with amusement that the lawn by the river had been turned into a field for aged donkeys.

"Davina's friends, Aileen and Fergus Sinclair, were killed in a road accident in Scotland. Miriam Scolby, the receptionist at Toynbee, notified your father. She went to the funeral and realized there was no family to take care of the Sinclairs' six-year-old son. For the moment Andrew is at Shibden, where your father visits him as regularly as he is able. The long-term plan is for Davina to adopt him."

They reached the stone embankment and Delia said, "As for Shibden, when the war is over, it will remain a children's home. Ivor has no use for it—he and Kate intend to remain in Cairo—and though I shall return to London when the Allies have put paid to Hitler, I won't have much use for it either. The days of keeping a house Shibden's size are long gone."

She turned to face him, the light breeze from the river blowing hair that was still a defiant Titian-red. "The same goes for Sans Souci, of course. But I have every intention of spending long periods of time there when the world regains its sanity." Her smile lit up her face. "And when I do go back to Sans Souci," she said in a sudden burst of confidence, "I shall do somethin' I've wanted to do for twenty-eight years, Jack. I shall take your father with me."

It was, he knew, the broadest hint possible that when her divorce was finalized, she and his father were going to spend the rest of their lives together.

Finally Jack asked the question that had been on his mind since he landed in Egypt. "How is Petra, Delia?"

TWENTY-SIX

"Petra," Delia said, looking toward the house, "is fine. You will stay for a late lunch, won't you? We can catch up on all the other gossip. Boo Pytchley is in Cairo, and so is Archie Somerset. I don't think Petra has had news of Rupert and all we know of Annabel and Fedya is that Fedya is in the RAF. It's impossible to get news of Suzi. What life is like in occupied Paris is hard to imagine, but at least Suzi isn't Jewish. I say my prayers every night for the French who are. As for Magda . . ."

She tucked her hand once more in the crook of his arm and they began walking back to the house. "As for Magda, I sincerely hope she no longer thinks Hitler is the Savior of Germany. In the days when she admired him much of English high society shared her opinion. In 1936, when Ribbentrop was the German ambassador to London, he was accepted nearly everywhere. I met him twice when we were both guests at the same dinner party. Sholto, I believe, knew him quite well. As for poor Wallis . . ."

She lifted her shoulders in a gesture of despair. "According to your father there's a rumor that she and Ribbentrop were lovers. It's the usual bunk. Wallis would never have put her relationship with David at risk in such a way. Why people are such skunks about her is beyond me."

It was a familiar refrain and Jack's thoughts turned to Petra again. Delia's brief comment about her had been infuriatingly unsatisfactory. He was fairly sure he knew why she'd changed the subject so quickly. She didn't want him upsetting Petra's marriage, or his own to Fawzia.

And she was quite right about the dangers. British social life in Cairo had always revolved around a handful of venues: the Gezira Sporting Club, the Turf Club, Shepheard's, the Continental, Groppi's, and a few others. That he would meet Petra continually went without saying. For him, seeing her could easily destroy his own shaky union.

Resolved to make his marriage work, he stepped into the shady coolness of the dining room and began paying attention again to Delia's conversation.

"Your father don't get to ride half as much as he would like these days," she said as they took their places at the beautifully laid table. "In Virginia he'll be able to ride to his heart's content."

With amusement he saw that Adjo had taken it for granted that he would be staying for lunch and that the table was laid for two.

"When I was a girl," she said, her green eyes growing dreamy with memory, "I had the most wonderful horse; his name was Sultan. Saying goodbye to him was one of the hardest things I've ever had to do."

A young safragi, who Jack suspected was probably one of Adjo's great-nephews, poured the wine and then left them to enjoy their meal.

"Was that when you married Ivor?" he asked, dipping a piece of warm pita bread into a dish of hummus.

"Yes," she said, unusually thoughtful. She took a black olive from a blue-and-white glazed bowl, bit into it, and then said, "He wasn't in love with me when we married, although he was deeply attracted and had a genuine affection for me—an affection that has lasted, I'm glad to say."

It was something he had long suspected, but hearing her speaking so frankly was a shock. He said carefully, knowing he was on dangerous ground, "But if he didn't love you, why did he marry you?"

She put some fava-bean salad onto her plate and added a stuffed sweet pepper. "He was a widower who had no heir. I was young and he thought I would be able to provide him with a son. As it was, after Petra and Davina there were no more children. Considering his disappointment, he took it mighty well."

"If Ivor didn't love you," Jack said, "who did he love?"

Her eyebrows rose slightly, as if it was a question she was surprised he had to ask. "Why, your mother, of course," she said.

Her eyes held his with perfect candor.

"Your mother was the love of Ivor's life when he was a young man. He was in love with her when he married Olivia, and he was in love with her when he married me—and she remained his love long after she ended their affair and married Theo Girlington."

There was no bitterness or resentment in her voice and he realized that all resentment and hurt were long over.

"Kate, who is so utterly different in every way from your mother, brought happiness back into his life." Her affection for Kate was clear. "I've always been grateful to her. With luck she'll be able to give him the son he has waited so long for."

Jack didn't have to ask where Delia's own happiness lay, but there was one question he had to pose while she was in such a starkly honest mood.

"Why," he said, as she took a sip of her wine, "did you object so strongly to my marrying Petra?"

The instant the words left his mouth it was as if all the air in the room had been sucked out. The tension was palpable.

Delia hesitated and just as she was finally about to answer, the door of the dining room opened and Fawzia walked in. Her black hair was looped into a knot on the top of her head. Her skin gleamed pale gold. She was wearing a vivid emerald brocade dress more suitable for a cocktail party than the early afternoon, and she looked like a princess straight out of the *Arabian Nights*.

"Daddy told me you were here!" she said a trifle breathlessly. "Isn't this wonderful? To be together again like this?"

He rose from the table, agonizingly aware that the moment between Delia and himself had been lost.

He kissed Fawzia with as much passion as Delia's presence allowed, noticing that her perfume was as unsuitable for an afternoon as her dress. It was heavy, exotic, and very, very sexy.

"How long are you here for?" she asked, her arms still around his neck. "Your father was in Cairo with Mr. Eden a few months ago, but only for three days. Then they flew off to Ankara. Is that what you will be doing, Jack?"

"No," he chuckled, amused at her naïveté. "I will most likely be here for the duration of the war. We can't live together, though. Did your father tell you? We're going to have to behave like illicit lovers."

She laughed. "But that will be fun! Will you be in an apartment, or the barracks?"

"An apartment. I'll be sharing it with a couple of other officers."

She gave a small pout, but one that indicated she was going to accept the living arrangements. He was deeply grateful. Not many wives would have been so understanding, and it indicated that Fawzia had done a lot of growing up during their eighteen-month separation.

"Adjo is bringing some champagne," Delia said, as they

joined her at the table, their arms around each other's waist. "So if you two happy people can bear to stay for just another few minutes, we'll drink it in celebration. D'you have a staff car yet, Jack? If not, you can borrow mine. The best place for a little privacy is still the Mena House Hotel."

Thirty minutes later, in Delia's open coupe they were on the road leading to Giza.

A mile out of Cairo Fawzia's hair suddenly tumbled free of its pins and cascaded past her shoulders, long and heavy.

He took his eyes from the road to shoot her a swift, amused glance. "You must have put your hair up in an awful hurry."

"Pins can never be trusted," she said, blushing slightly.

When they finally reached Mena House there wasn't a free room, but Fawzia's father's name carried a lot of weight.

A room was found for them—and not just any room. It looked south to a glorious view of the pyramids.

"It's a good job we can't see the Sphinx," she said as he tipped the bellboy and closed the door. "It's covered in sandbags—presumably in case the Germans attempt to bomb it."

He wasn't interested in the Sphinx.

He was only interested in taking her to bed.

Considering Fawzia's protected upbringing and her strict schooling at the Mere de Dieu, her abandonment in bed had always both surprised Jack and given him great pleasure. Now, within seconds, he knew that during the long months of their separation she had changed.

She was no longer delightfully abandoned in bed.

She was lasciviously wanton—and skillfully so.

Certain of what her new expertise signified, he pulled away for a moment, but his body wouldn't allow him to stop. It was like being on a roller coaster with no way of abandoning the ride until it came to a cataclysmic end.

As he finally collapsed on the tangled sheets, exhausted and covered with sweat, he knew that she hadn't been faithful to him. That she'd had—and possibly still had—a lover. A lover who, if the sexual tricks she had revealed were anything to go by, was Egyptian, not English.

He slid from the bed, picked up his khaki shorts and put them on. Then he scooped up his shirt and took out a packet of Camels and a lighter.

Fawzia didn't move. She was lying on her back making small purring sounds, her eyes closed.

He remembered her first words to him: "How long are you here for?" He had thought she was desperately anxious for him to stay. But it had been just the reverse. She had been hoping to hear that in forty-eight hours or so he would be on his way back to Palestine. And her easy acceptance of the fact that they were not allowed to live together hadn't been a sign of understanding. It had been relief. Her dress, the exotic scent she was wearing, the way her hair had been so precariously pinned, this all made sense now. When she'd heard the news of his arrival she had come to him straight from her lover's bed.

He walked to the window and stood looking out toward the pyramids, his guts twisting deep in his belly.

He'd known, when he'd been transferred from Jerusalem to Cairo, that he was going to face emotional difficulties, but not this. Fawzia's affair had come straight out of left field.

He had to decide what to do. One thing was obvious: he had to be fair.

They had been apart for eighteen months—and it was wartime. Old values, old standards, had been overturned. She hadn't known they were about to be reunited. If she had, she would, no doubt, have ended the relationship with her lover immediately.

He wondered how many people knew about it. Someone had told her of his arrival and he didn't think it was her father. Though he knew that Zubair Pasha would have far preferred an Egyptian son-in-law, he couldn't imagine him condoning Fawzia's adultery. The person who had known where to find Fawzia and who had told her of his arrival was more likely to have been a house safragi in Fawzia's confidence, or, even more likely, her personal maid.

Delia obviously did not know that Fawzia was being unfaithful to him. It was one secret that Delia would never, in a million years, have been a silent party to.

It didn't mean, though, that other people weren't aware of the other man in Fawzia's life.

Behind him he heard Fawzia stir.

He turned around. As she pushed herself up against the pillows, her silk-black hair grazing her breasts, he said tersely, "Your lover, Fawzia. Who is he?"

Her face immediately became impassive, her expression shuttered. It was a look with which he was familiar. When necessary, Egyptians were more skilled at hiding their thoughts than any people he had ever met.

"I don't know what you mean," she said pettishly. "I don't have a lover."

There was a large brass ashtray on a nearby table and he ground out his cigarette. "Don't make this any harder than it needs to be, Fawzia. I'm not a fool. I know you have a lover. I need to know his name."

He saw something flicker in her eyes and read what it was immediately. She thought someone had told him. That he had been told even before he had left Jerusalem.

Angrily she swung her legs from the bed and stood up. "If you know that I am having an affair, then you also know who I am having it with." She snatched a lace-trimmed black bra from a chair.

"I don't, as it happens." He watched her as she reached for a pair of silk camiknickers. Though she wasn't tall, her body was magnificently proportioned: her breasts full, her waist so narrow it was literally a handspan, her legs slim and exquisite.

Knowing Fawzia's body would never again have the power to move him, he said, "I do know that your father believes you've been spending time with Davina when, according to Delia, Davina is working all the time. Delia believes you've been spending time with Queen Farida, but I very much doubt that you've been anywhere near the palace. So where have you been?"

From the far side of the bed she glared at him with the venom of someone who has been tricked and who, if she'd realized how little he knew, would have kept her mouth very firmly shut.

"You're the intelligence officer!" she hurled at him. "You find out! I'm not going to tell you!"

The desire to shake her till her teeth rattled was almost more than he could control. He said through clenched teeth, "I'll find out all right. And when I do I'll make sure he never attempts to make contact with you again!"

"And how are you going to do that?" she spat, stepping into her brocade dress.

"I'll let him know that if he does, I'll kill him."

It wasn't an idle threat. He'd never been in a fight yet when he hadn't truly thrashed his opponent.

As she slipped her feet into her high-heeled sandals, she said with amusement, "You'll deck my lover? A lover I have no intention of giving up? And in public?"

His eyes held hers. "Yes," he said white-lipped. "That's a pretty accurate description of what I'll do, Fawzia."

She began laughing.

He reached for his shirt and pulled it on over his head. "I'm going back to GHQ," he said. "You'll have to get yourself a taxi. As you've no intention of breaking off with whoever it is you're sharing a bed with, we won't be having another re-union. It's over, Fawzia."

Controlling her laughter with difficulty, she said, "And will you still punch him on the jaw when you find out his identity?"

"Oh, yes," he said grimly, yanking the door open. "That's a pleasure I've no intention of forgoing."

She laughed again and he slammed the door, knowing, as he strode away, that his unwise marriage was over.

As Delia's bright-yellow sports car was brought from the car park, he resolved to tell Zubair Pasha at the first opportunity. He wouldn't tell him why. He would simply say that he and Fawzia had always been incompatible and that it was a mutual decision. What Fawzia chose to say was up to her.

He punched the motor into life. He had decided to tell Delia as well. He knew she would believe that his ongoing feelings for Petra had played a major part in the breakup and that she would be deeply perturbed, but it couldn't be helped. Enough secrets had been kept from her in the past, without him adding another.

It was five o'clock by the time he got back to Grey Pillars, and with the heat of the afternoon over, the place was a hive of activity again.

"I've left another sheaf of files on your desk," Doris said efficiently as he entered his office. "Captain Reynolds's replacement hasn't arrived yet. Corporal Slade has found you a comfy billet with two other officers in a flat on Sharia el-Walda. He says it's pretty shabby, but the location is hard to beat. It's so near to the embassy, you can see into its garden."

"Thank you, Doris—and now a mug of tea if you can rustle one up." He flopped into a battered swivel chair, putting his feet up on the desk and reaching for the files. "Two sugars, please."

And then, with the paddles of a ceiling fan rotating creakily above his head, he settled down to do his reading. Two hours later he knew the names of all the informers on the British payroll—and the names of many anti-British informers.

"Though who the anti-British informers pass their information on to, we're not sure," said Slade, a young Cockney, when he handed Jack a key to the Sharia el-Walda flat. "The Romanians are always suspect. One of their number has already been expelled. Peter, the barman in the Long Bar at Shepheard's, is also a favorite bet but, to be honest, sir, there's not much to back up the suspicion. The only thing anyone's sure of is that the enemy is getting military information and that it's coming from an A-one source. Which has to mean from someone within GHQ or the embassy."

Having already come to that conclusion, Jack merely nodded and went on with his reading. Rommel had apparently earned himself the nickname of "Desert Fox" and Jack wryly noted that the nickname was even used in official communiqués.

On the military front the Australians, with some British help, were still holding out at Tobruk. Rommel had the port city encircled and major British offensives were being undertaken to relieve it.

None, so far, had been successful. Despite the huge number of tanks and troops, Rommel's use of 88-mm antiaircraft guns ensured that every British offensive ended in a murderous defeat. The enormous guns were dug deep into the sand with their snouts disguised by sand-colored tents. Even with field glasses it was impossible to distinguish them from the dunes.

Rommel's trick was to send light tanks on a fake attack. When the British tanks engaged in battle, the panzers would withdraw and the enormous flaks would open fire. The result was carnage of epic proportions.

It made for grim reading and Jack was glad when Doris

waltzed in on him again. "Captain Reynolds's replacement has arrived, sir. Shall I send him in?"

"Pronto, Doris, please."

He swung his legs off the desk and as he did, Archie walked into the room.

Jack's eyes widened and as the realization dawned that it was Archie who would be his second-in-command, all the misery, anger, and tension of the afternoon vanished.

He rounded the desk in a flash. "Archie, you old sonofagun!" he said, giving him a great bear hug. "I thought you were with special ops."

"Ah, well. You know what thought did, old mate," Archie said, a wide grin splitting his homely face. "It thought wrong."

"Let's go for a beer." Jack snatched his peaked cap from the corner of his desk. "You and I have a spy to catch."

Three days later Jack was in the Khan el-Khalili bazaar. A reliable informer, a barber, had told him of a conversation he had overheard. "The father is a grocer and the son is in the Egyptian army," he had said. "The son wants money to pay his mess bills and his father won't give him any unless he lands a British army contract for vegetables. His exact words were, 'You'd do better to get that contract instead of involving yourself with crazy army plots that are bound to fail.' "

The term "crazy army plots" was one that couldn't possibly be ignored and Jack thought he could see a way of getting hard inside information about them.

The Khan el-Khalili was a mammoth maze of twisting alleys so crowded with narrow stalls that it was only possible for two people to pass each other by coming into jostling, physical contact. The bazaar sold far more than fruit and vegetables. Egyptians hawked perfumes, rugs, spices, silver, alabaster—

and jewelry so fine that it was the one place in Old Cairo where Europeans could always be found.

Jack pushed his way through the noisy crowds. A few yards in front of him Petra suddenly stepped out of a dark shop doorway, her arms full of silks.

He came to such a sharp, abrupt halt that the Arab walking immediately behind him tripped hard over his heels.

"*Maalesh,*" he said as the Arab struggled to regain his balance. "Sorry."

Petra, too, had come to a halt. With the shopkeeper standing beside her, she was examining the silks in sunlight coming from a gap in the long tin roof above their heads.

It was the first time he had seen her since his arrival in the city. Her glorious mahogany-red hair fell in a turbulent riot of deep waves to her shoulders, pushed away from her face on one side with a tortoiseshell comb. Tall and slender, she was wearing a white linen suit with scarlet sandals. Her legs were suntanned and bare of stockings.

He felt as if his heart had ceased to beat.

She was completely occupied with what she was doing, frowning in concentration as she fingered first one roll of silk and then another.

He saw, as if for the first time, the long thick sweep of her eyelashes, the faint hollows under her beautifully sculpted cheekbones, the rich, generous curve of her mouth.

In that moment he knew that his love for her, and his need of her, would never fade.

And she no longer loved him. For years he'd been trying to hammer that information into his head and still there was a part of him that refused to believe it. He'd tried to move on; he'd tried to find happiness with Fawzia. But his marriage had ended with the hideous scene at Mena House.

In bitter despair he stood and drank in the sight of the

woman he'd loved for as long as he could remember. Suddenly she raised her head from the rolls of silk and their eyes met.

One of the rolls of silk slipped from her hands and the shop-keeper darted forward to catch hold of it.

Jack forced himself into movement. Striving to look relaxed and at ease he strolled up to her.

"Hello," he said as she clutched a roll of crimson cloth to her chest. "I wondered when we'd run into each other. Did your mother tell you I was back in the city?"

"Yes." The word came out clipped as if someone had just punched her. "It was bound to happen, wasn't it?" she said, her voice now as falsely bright as if she was talking to a casual acquaintance. "You know Cairo so well and you speak Arabic. Not many intelligence officers in Cairo do. Ivor says it's a wonder you weren't sent here a year ago."

"I wish I had been. Can I take that roll of silk from you before it follows the other one?"

Without waiting for her response he lifted the silk from her arms. As his hands touched hers, she trembled.

"Could we go for a drink together, Petra?" A pulse was throbbing at the corner of his jaw in exactly the same way a pulse always throbbed at the corner of his father's jaw when he was under intense stress. "The terrace at Shepheard's, or perhaps coffee at Groppi's?"

"I . . . no." She looked around wildly for a way of escape. "It isn't possible, Jack. I have an appointment—"

"Sholto," he said, determined to keep her talking for at least a few moments longer. "How is he? He's someone else I haven't run into yet."

"Sholto?" Her face took on an expression not so different from Fawzia's when he had asked her to name her lover. "Sholto's fine, thank you. And now I'm sorry, Jack, but I really do have to go."

Shattering all the stallholder's hopes of a hefty sale, she turned and plunged into the sea of humanity streaming down the narrow alleyway.

Jack didn't follow because he knew she didn't want him to.

Within seconds, as the crowds pressed around her, all he could see between a bobbing mass of white turbans and black veils was her Rita Hayworth mane of hair. He wasn't sure, but as she disappeared from view he thought that her shoulders were shaking—almost as if she was crying.

TWENTY-SEVEN

"I wasn't sure the powers that be were going to agree to the grocery contract," Archie said a few days later as they reviewed the successful outcome of what they referred to as their "grocer and son" operation.

"They had to." There was wry amusement in Jack's voice. "It was the only way of getting the son to give any information. Once the British army contract for vegetables was in place I had him exactly where I wanted him. It was a case of talk or lose the contract—and by bluffing that I knew more than I did about his 'crazy army plots,' I scared the living daylights out of him. The poor devil thought he was going to be charged with treason if he didn't cooperate."

Archie lit a cigarette. "So we now know there's a group of Egyptian army officers itching to rise in revolt and we have the name of one of the ringleaders. Captain Anwar Sadat," he said with great satisfaction. "I'm not surprised the brigadier is pleased."

It was late evening and they were in Jack's office. Doris had long gone, as had the great majority of people who worked at GHQ. Jack was in his favorite position—slouched comfortably in his swivel chair, his feet on the table.

"It doesn't bring us any nearer to finding our spy, though," he said, frowning. "The information the German military is getting isn't the kind a captain in the Egyptian army would be privy to. We need to be looking closer to home. I'm interested in every high-ranking officer at GHQ who has an Egyptian girlfriend. That's the way I see the information being obtained, Archie. Via pillow talk."

"And Sadat?" Archie asked. He was perched on the corner of the desk, one leg swinging. "What is our next move where he's concerned?"

"Our informant will continue to give us information—he's too deeply compromised not to. And Sadat will be followed. I've assigned that task to Slade. If Sadat is in contact in any way with the chap we're after, we'll get him." He glanced down at his watch. "It's past midnight, Archie. What say we trawl the nightclubs and check every officer we see with an Egyptian girlfriend? Where shall we start? The Kit-Kat or the Sphinx?"

"There's a small club off Kasr el-Nil Street, near the Turf Club, that would be better. The belly dancer there is great."

"Let's give it a try, then." Jack lifted his feet from the desk and reached for his Sam Browne belt and holster. He was quite sure that his theory about a British officer with an Egyptian girlfriend was the right one. He couldn't imagine a British officer knowingly passing secrets to a German spy, but Cairo was a city where, given the number of troops that were in it, women were in chronically short supply. If a man found an Egyptian girlfriend she could be passing secrets either for the money or as a true Egyptian patriot. The way he saw it, when her boyfriend was asleep the girl would copy information from the papers in his briefcase and then pass that information to a German informant, who would then transmit the information to the German military.

Before Jack had left Jerusalem he'd assumed that tracking down such an officer would be relatively straightforward. There couldn't, he had thought, be that many officers at GHQ with access not only to top secret documents but to top secret documents they had the clearance to take out of the building in a briefcase. Such an officer had to be extremely high-ranking, which would automatically cut down the list of suspects.

But then he had seen the number of high-ranking officers crammed into Grey Pillars and had known that even if his theory was right, tracking down the officer responsible was not going to be easy.

The club off Kasr el-Nil Street was exceedingly small and the minute he stepped through its beaded curtains he doubted many officers would be found there.

"Welcome to club King Cheops, Major," a waiter said, swiftly taking in the crowns on Jack's shoulder straps. "Would you like champagne? Company? We have very nice girls at King Cheops. Very good dancers."

"We'd like a table and two Stellas," Jack said pleasantly. "No girls. Not tonight."

As they were led across to a table in front of the stage Archie said, "Not tonight? I thought you were a happily married man and that Fawzia was in Cairo?"

"Fawzia is in Cairo," Jack said as he sat down, "but our marriage is over. And I don't want any sympathy, because I don't need it. Now, how long d'you think we're going to have to wait until your belly dancer comes onstage?"

They sat through a dreadful acrobatic act and an even more dreadful snake-charming act and then, with a roll of drums, the tension in the little club mounted and the noisy clientele at the other tables became even noisier.

"Zahra's good. Really good," Archie said in happy anticipation, raising his voice so as to be heard. "I reckon her father must own the club, because I can't see any other reason for her not being in demand at the Sphinx or the Kit-Kat."

When Zahra glided barefoot onto the tiny podium dressed in a gold-sequined halter top and a chiffon hip skirt, bracelets on her arms and ankles, and tiny cymbals on her fingers, Jack could see that she was exceptionally beautiful in exactly the same way as Fawzia. Her kohl-rimmed eyes were doe-shaped and slanted, her eyebrows perfectly symmetrical arches, her waist-length hair a gleaming blue-black curtain.

Over the years he had seen many belly dancers, but as the familiar sinuous music began and Zahra's hips swiveled slowly and sensuously, Jack thought that perhaps Archie was right. Zahra was far too good a dancer for such a tiny club.

Beside him, Archie had hunched forward, mesmerized. Under other circumstances Jack was pretty sure he would have been similarly mesmerized, but he had too much on his mind. Earlier that afternoon, when Brigadier Haigh had congratulated him on infiltrating the subversive officers within the Egyptian army, he had also given him a grim warning: "Now that Claude Auchinleck has replaced General Wavell as C in C, it's going to be all systems go to relieve Tobruk. With a big push like this in the offing it's vital no information is passed on to the Germans. Their spy in Cairo has to be found, Jack."

It was, Jack reflected, a task easier said than done.

The music had now become frenetic. Her spine arched and her head thrown back, Zahra's hips were gyrating faster and faster.

It was then that he saw Darius.

He was seated with another man at a corner table. As their eyes met Jack knew Darius had been observing him for some time. Later he was to wonder whether Darius had intended to make his presence known.

For now he merely said to Archie, "I've just seen an old friend. It might be a good idea if you wandered down to the Kit-Kat. This place is far too seedy for the officer we are looking for."

"Will do," Archie said as Zahra exited the stage to a storm of applause.

Jack was already halfway to Darius's table. Seeing his approach, the thin-faced man with Darius rose to his feet and walked speedily off to the bar.

Darius also stood. "I'd heard you were in town," he said as they slapped each other on the back in an old-friends' gesture. "Are you just passing through or here for the duration?"

It was reminiscent of the way Fawzia had greeted him and he said wryly, "As far as I know, I'm here for the duration. How are things? The only person I've caught up with so far is Delia."

"What about Fawzia? Surely you've seen her?"

"I have, but she's been seeing someone else and has no intention of giving him up. I'll be filing for a divorce at some point."

Darius said with an odd smile, "And do you intend naming the boyfriend as corespondent?"

"I will. And if you know his identity I'd appreciate you telling me who he is."

Darius remained infuriatingly silent.

"Come on, Darius," he said impatiently. "Don't try and score points. I haven't the time for it. I may not look as if I'm working, but I am. I've another half-dozen clubs to visit before I hit the sack."

"So you've come to the King Cheops to find a German spy?" He topped up his drink. "Rumor has it the city is crawling with them. You'll probably have a cell full before morning."

"I doubt it, but I would appreciate the name of Fawzia's friend. I'm assuming he's an Egyptian and that you know his name."

"You assume right on both counts, but I'm not sure you're going to cite him as a corespondent."

Suddenly Zahra, who had changed into a scarlet cocktail dress, approached the table and sat down. "Where has Constantin gone to, Darius. Do you know?" she asked.

"The bar, I think. Let me introduce my brother-in-law to

you. Zahra, Jack Bazeljette. Jack, Zahra. Her boyfriend is a friend of mine."

Jack nodded, then turned back to Darius. "The name," Jack said, barely able to keep his patience in check, "and then I'll be on my way."

"Farouk." There was naked disgust in Darius's voice. "His Majesty, King of Egypt and of Sudan, Sovereign of Nubia, of Kordofan, and of Darfur. And if you attempt to lay a finger on him his aides will have your head. If you cite him as co-respondent in your divorce action your government will have you cashiered."

Jack knew instantly that Darius was telling the truth. Everything now made sense. Fawzia's amusement when he had said he intended to give her lover the hiding of his life; the cavalier way royal aides had whisked her off to the palace. The Queen had never been the object of her visits there. It had always been the King. And because it was the King there wasn't a damn thing he could do about it.

One word of accusation and he would be whisked out of Egypt before he could bat an eyelid. Not only that, any word of accusation would be utterly pointless, for Farouk would merely deny everything.

In furious frustration he slammed his fist down on the table. The bottle fell.

Champagne soaked the lamp. The lights fizzed and the club plunged into chaotic darkness. It was, Jack often reflected later, a fitting end to his reunion with Darius.

A week later and Jack had the lead he'd been praying for. His unit had picked up an unidentified transmitter in the Gezira/Zamalek area. "We've picked it up a few times now," his signals officer said. "It's broadcasting in code. Must be our guy, don't you think?"

"It's some bastard up to no good. How long is he on-air?"

"Not long, sir. Too short a time for us to be able to pin-point his exact position. We'll just have to hope he soon gets a bit chattier."

Later that afternoon Jack drove out to Gezira Island deep in thought. Until now he had been working on the assumption that top secret information was being transmitted by a German. It had been the only scenario that had made sense, but Gezira Island was one of the most elegant and expensive areas of Cairo, making it the very last place for a Nazi to hide.

Dominating the southern end of the island was the sporting club and it was inconceivable that anyone could be transmitting from there. Also on the southern end of the island were a hospital and a delightful area of tree-lined avenues boasting palatial houses, their residents mainly British officials connected with the embassy. It was where Petra and Sholto lived. It was where every British diplomat lived if they didn't have a residence in Garden City.

Jack took the road that rounded the island's southern tip. On his left-hand side was the Nile, glittering myriad shades of green under the hot rays of the afternoon sun. On his right were the little-visited Khedive Ismail gardens, where meandering gravel pathways were flanked by acacias and shaded by flowering jacarandas.

As he motored up the west side of the island he came to the bridge leading to Giza and the pyramids. Known as the English Bridge, it marked the beginning of a whole line of houseboats. He slowed to a standstill and lit a cigarette. A houseboat would make a good hideaway—but not for a German. In a place such as Gezira's houseboat community, everyone would know one another. A stranger would stand out, particularly a stranger with an accent.

Determining to have every houseboat searched Jack stubbed out his cigarette and put the jeep into gear again.

Within minutes he was driving along the western boundary of the sporting club. Beyond were the botanical gardens and with the botanical gardens behind him he was in the residential district of Zamalek. Here, several palatial houses faced the Nile, though this time, from the names on their high, carved gateways, it was clear that the owners were rich Egyptians and not British.

He stopped and smoked another cigarette. Had he been barking up the wrong tree? Was it a royal aide he should be seeking? But would a royal aide have access to British military plans?

Jack drove the quiet streets and then headed in the direction of the Bulaq Bridge. Here and there were a few more houseboats and the area they were in was far more deserted than the area of houseboat mooring adjacent to the English Bridge. Resolving that in the morning he would also have those searched and their owners questioned, he continued down the east side of the island until, once again, he was at the Kasr el-Nil Bridge.

Driving past the two bronze lions that guarded the entrance to the bridge he reflected that if his signals officer was correct, the German transmitter was in the area he had just circled. Though the homes of rich and influential Egyptians couldn't be checked without far more evidence than he presently had, the houseboats could be searched and his gut feeling was that such a search would be successful.

That evening he met with Brigadier Haigh and the commander of the Egyptian police force. Later he had dinner with Davina. It always amused him that she still looked like an English schoolgirl. Her pale blond hair was held away from her face by a dark-blue velvet headband and she was wearing a gray pleated skirt and pastel-blue twinset, her jewelry a single string of pearls.

"It's so absolutely wonderful to have you in Cairo, Jack,"

she said when they had ordered from the kind of menu people in rationed Britain could only fantasize about. "We've hoped you would be posted here. I haven't seen Fawzia since you arrived—Queen Farida monopolizes all her time—but she must be over the moon to see you."

He'd ordered a bottle of Chablis Premier Cru and as the waiter filled their glasses he said, "I thought your mother might have brought you up-to-date where Fawzia and I are concerned."

She shook her head. "Things are so manic at the hospital that apart from phone calls I haven't spoken to my mother for an age."

Jack waited till the waiter had left and then said, "Fawzia and I will be getting divorced, Davina. Our marriage never had very deep roots. We both had expectations of each other that neither of us could fulfill and she's now into a love affair that's far too important to her for her to consider ending it."

"But she can't be!" Davina looked shocked. "Fawzia loves parties of course—and there are lots of parties in Cairo. But if she had met anyone, word would have spread. Cairo thrives on gossip. Besides, I don't know when she would have found time for an affair. She's nearly always at the palace, visiting Queen Farida."

He shot her a wry smile. "You're right about her being always at the palace, but it's not the Queen she's with when she's there. It's the King."

Davina gasped. "You can't mean it! King Farouk's got an awful reputation—but King Farouk and *Fawzia*?"

"Why not?" he said reasonably. "She's exceptionally beautiful. She's Egyptian and from a good family. Zubair Pasha is a member of the Senate and he's served as a minister in one cabinet or another for more than thirty years. Farouk will have seen Fawzia at the palace several times when she visited with her father. When she returned to Cairo from London she must have come to his attention almost immediately. And from Fawzia's point of view there's a lot at stake. Farouk is one of the richest men in the world, and, knowing Fawzia, I'm pretty sure she already has a fabulous collection of jewels safely squirreled away. If he's led her to believe he may divorce Farida and marry her, Fawzia might become Queen of Egypt."

"But she'll be a divorced woman! And she is a Copt! The King will never marry her!"

"He isn't a British king, Davina. He can't be forced to abdicate like King Edward. I must admit he is unlikely to marry her, but Farouk's never given a damn about convention."

"And what if he doesn't marry her? What will happen to her then?"

"Then he'll provide for her."

Despite the hard certainty in his voice she said, not understanding, "But how can you be so sure? No one can make Farouk do what he doesn't want to. Not his prime minister. Not Sir Miles Lampson. No one."

Suddenly his face hardened. It was the expression of a man who could be very tough. And who intended to be very tough indeed.

"Farouk will provide for her—and provide for her lavishly—because I'm going to make him," he said grimly. "Fawzia and I have too much shared history for me to see her being treated shabbily. I may not be able to cite the King in my divorce action, but I can still put the fear of God into him. And I'm going to, Davina. Trust me."

She looked so unhappy that he abruptly changed the subject.

"Tell me about the little boy you are going to adopt. What is his name? Angus? Alfred?"

"Andrew," she said, the sparkle back in her eyes. "At the moment he's at Shibden Hall and your father is checking on him. I think Andrew is going to love it in Cairo. I know when

I was a child I would have adored spending time onboard the *Egyptian Queen*."

"The *Egyptian Queen*?"

"Darius's houseboat at Zamalek."

The trio had been playing slow waltzes in order that as many couples as possible could squeeze onto the dance floor. Now they began playing something more up-tempo.

Jack couldn't have cared less what they were playing. In his mind's eye he was seeing again the handful of houseboats moored in the quiet area north of the Bulaq Bridge. In a matter of hours members of the Egyptian police force would enter every one. If there was anything remotely suspicious on the *Egyptian Queen* it would be found.

And he passionately hoped that the *Egyptian Queen* would be as clean as a whistle.

TWENTY-EIGHT

Jack's tension the next morning, as he oversaw the large search operation he had put in place, was enormous. When many hours later it was concluded, crushing disappointment and overwhelming relief swamped him in equal waves.

His disappointment was because despite every houseboat having been rigorously searched, no radio transmitter was found. His relief was that Darius was as in the clear as every other houseboat owner.

"How many bearings indicated the transmission you picked up was sourced on Gezira?" he demanded of his signals officer. "Could your triangulation have been wrong?"

"No, sir. I've got three different bearings on it. It's so accurate that next time sonny boy starts transmitting our monitoring unit stands a chance of being able to jam his messages."

Jack drummed his knuckles on his desk. Jamming the messages was all very well, but the German listening station would tell the radio operator transmitting that he was being jammed and then there would be no more transmissions—and no hope of catching the spy supplying the information. All that would happen was that when transmissions began again, they would do so from a different locale. Alexandria, possibly. Or the desert. Rommel would continue to get vital British military information and any chance of the tables being turned on him would be lost.

It was that chance of turning the tables that was so vitally important. If they could capture the radio operator in the act of transmitting—if they could get hold of his codebook—then they could broadcast false information to Rommel, which might mean the difference between winning or losing the war in the Western Desert.

"With stakes like those to play for, we've got to allow the transmissions to continue," Brigadier Haigh said, relaying Downing Street's take on the problem. "Once we jam them, he'll know we're onto him and go to ground. But we can't allow them to continue for long. And we've got to lay our hands on that codebook. With that in our possession we can scupper Rommel once and for all."

Back in his office Jack studied the file that was the only tangible result of the massive search operation. It listed the name of every houseboat, the name of every owner, and if the occupier was different from the owner, the name of every occupier and any relevant details.

Opposite the name *Egyptian Queen,* the name of the owner was given as Darius Zubair and his occupation was listed as lawyer. The officer in charge of searching the *Egyptian Queen* and questioning Darius had made a note to the effect that Darius had been extremely cooperative.

Deep in thought, Jack closed the file. He was still deep in thought when Archie walked in on him.

"So what's our next step?" Archie asked glumly. "Do we just check on the private life of every officer with clearance to take top secret information out of the building?"

Keeping the information that Darius was one of the houseboat owners to himself, Jack said briskly, "We'll keep as many people as we can spare doing that, but I think we should be looking at the embassy staff as well. Gezira is the place where most of them live. I know tradition has it that no British diplomat can be suspected of treason, but there's a first time for everything. What's that you have in your hand? Another file resulting from the search operation?"

"No. Sadat has left Cairo for Manqabad in Upper Egypt. It's his official army posting, so no surprise there."

"None at all. If he is on friendly terms with our spy and our spy's radio operator he won't be maintaining contact with them in Manqabad, so we can forget about Sadat for the moment. But the minute he returns, I want to know."

Jack ran a hand through his hair. "I'm going to ask Haigh for clearance to speak with Sir Miles Lampson. Someone is going to have to tell our ambassador that his diplomatic staff will be coming under surveillance. Wish me luck, Archie. Lampson stands six foot six, weighs in at eighteen stone, and is going to be one very angry man."

Lampson was so angry that Jack thought he was going to explode.

"A member of my staff a spy?" he thundered.

"It's a possibility, sir. Transmissions are being made to Rommel from Gezira and—"

"*A member of my diplomatic staff a spy?*"

"—we need to know just what kind of military information embassy staff are privy to—"

"*A MEMBER OF MY DIPLOMATIC STAFF A SPY?*"

"—and then check everyone with access to vital information," Jack continued manfully as the ambassador's face went from an indignant red to choleric purple.

It took a full half hour for Sir Miles to gain control of his temper. When he did, Jack got the information he was after.

"Embassy staff at attaché level are allowed to see every-thing, Major Bazeljette. The authority for them to do so comes from the highest possible source."

"And that includes military information?"

"Of course. And if you think for one moment that a member of my staff is leaking such information to the enemy, then you are stark raving mad. You should be looking for a German, not an Englishman. And if not a German, you should be investigating officers in the Egyptian army. In fact they are the most likely source."

Jack didn't bother to point out that the British scrupulously kept the Egyptian army ignorant of high-level military information. He didn't need to get into an argument with Sir Miles. Embassy attachés had access and that was all that he needed to know.

As he left the embassy he reflected that as Farouk couldn't possibly be as intimidating as Sir Miles had been, it was high time he had his confrontation with him.

"Where to, Major?" Corporal Slade asked him as he slid into the passenger seat of his staff car. "Back to GHQ?"

"No, Slade. The next stop is the palace."

"The palace, sir?" Corporal Slade looked at him as if he'd said the moon.

"Yes, Slade. The palace. Now get a move on, will you? I want to see the King before he starts on one of his gargantuan lunches."

"The King, sir?"

Slade was now looking at him as if he was suffering from heatstroke and that a hospital would be a more appropriate next stop.

"Either you start driving, Slade, or I drive myself. Now get this damn jeep into gear!"

It wasn't far from the embassy to Abdin but, as always in

Cairo, a short distance could take a long time. Today it was tanks that were causing a major traffic jam as they rolled in the direction of the Kasr el-Nil Bridge.

As Slade drove past a small alleyway off Sultan Hussein Street, Jack saw Sholto Monck's distinctive Chrysler parked at the entrance to it and then he saw Sholto going into a small café—and he was with Constantin. Zahra's boyfriend.

There was no reason at all why one of Darius's friends shouldn't also be friends with Sholto. Sholto was, after all, Davina's brother-in-law. All the same, it seemed a surprising friendship and as Slade battled on through the traffic toward the palace, Jack wondered just how long it had been going on.

Once they reached Abdin they were forced to an ignominious halt.

Jack showed his SIB warrant card that gave him carte blanche to go anywhere he wanted, but it cut no ice with the palace guards.

He telephoned Haigh for help. "I've spoken with Sir Miles and now I need to speak with the King," he said tersely through the usual static. "Get Sir Miles to sort it out for me, would you?"

Two hours passed. Jack spent the time sitting in his jeep at Abdin's gates with Corporal Slade.

"Do you mind me asking what we're doing here, sir?" the young Londoner ventured as the day's heat grew ever more intense and beads of sweat rolled down his face.

"I have an issue with King Farouk, Slade," Jack said, wondering whether that was, perhaps, the understatement of the year.

Just when he thought he wasn't going to be able to stand the heat for another minute, one of the guards walked toward him.

"The first chamberlain will see you," the guard said as the giant gates opened. "His Majesty does not give audiences to

British army officers. His Majesty only speaks with generals and the British ambassador."

Jack nodded, as if accepting the situation, but as Slade drove into the palace grounds he was determined that Farouk *would* see him, no matter how many courtiers he had to argue his way past.

Leaving an unhappy Corporal Slade sitting in the jeep, Jack was shown into an ornate anteroom where he was offered tea.

Tea always prefaced any dealings with Egyptians—even the buying of a carpet demanded the ritual—and Jack knew better than to attempt to hurry things along.

After nearly an hour an aide appeared.

"The first chamberlain will see you now, Major Bazeljette. If you will please follow me?"

Jack followed him. It was his first time in Abdin and he found the beauty of the rooms stunning. The main public chamber, the Byzantine Hall, was as long as a rugby pitch with high gilded ceilings, exquisite mosaics, and an awesome number of massive chandeliers. They walked through several more rooms before reaching the room where the first chamberlain was waiting. He was wearing a tarboosh, but his suit could have been tailored in Savile Row.

"I understand from your ambassador that you have business to conduct with me," he said, making no attempt at small talk. "Is it, perhaps, to do with the safety of His Majesty?"

"No. His Majesty's safety is very adequately taken care of, I believe. And my business is not with yourself but with His Majesty. I trust the ambassador made that quite clear?"

The first chamberlain breathed in so hard his nostrils turned white. "His Majesty is not at the beck and call of British majors! Nor is he at the beck and call of the British ambassador! If you would please state your business and—"

At the far side of the room a door was ajar. Jack sensed that the King was behind it—and listening.

Not allowing the first chamberlain to finish his sentence, Jack said, speaking in a voice that would carry clearly, "Perhaps His Majesty is unaware that Bazeljette is an uncommon name in England and that there is no other Major Bazeljette in Cairo. If he could be informed that my wife is the daughter of Zubair Pasha, and that my reason for seeing him is bound up with a delicate family matter, perhaps then he will see me. If not, of course, I am only too happy to lay the matter before you, or anyone else who—"

The door slammed open.

The first chamberlain flinched.

The King glared at him.

"I'll speak with Major Bazeljette alone," he said with an imperious gesture of dismissal, a huge cabochon emerald weighing down his little finger.

As the first chamberlain fled, Jack regarded his wife's lover with interest. Though his huge appetite ensured he was already beginning to look a little portly, the King was a good-looking young man—the emphasis being very much on the adjective "young." Sovereign for five years, he was still only twenty-one. Jack had heard it rumored that Sir Miles Lampson often referred to King Farouk as "the boy" and could well understand why. This boy, however, had the kind of absolute power British kings had lost three hundred years ago.

"Many thanks for granting me this audience, Your Majesty," Jack said, giving the bow protocol demanded, when what he yearned to do was land a very solid fist on the royal jaw.

The King, dressed in an exquisitely tailored suit and wearing a tarboosh, inclined his head.

And waited in stony silence for Jack to continue.

Jack had thought very carefully about how to gain his objective without ruining Fawzia's life. Any suggestion that he intended making the affair a public scandal would result in Farouk instantly ending it. And since Jack did not want to take his wife back, such an outcome would, for Fawzia, be disastrous. What Jack wanted, despite his anger toward her, was protection for her when the affair ended on its own accord.

He cleared his throat. "It has come to my attention, Your Majesty, that a very eminent member of the court circle is having an affair with my wife, the only daughter of Zubair Pasha. Zubair Pasha has, I believe, held many cabinet posts in Your Majesty's government."

Farouk continued to regard him in silence, but his eyes had taken on a distinctly nervous look.

Jack said pleasantly, "I will not cause embarrassment to Your Majesty by citing a member of your court circle in a divorce action. Nor will the divorce reflect in any way on my wife's reputation. Gallantry demands that she be seen as the innocent party."

"Quite so," Farouk said, now with relief in his eyes. "English gallantry. A very commendable quality."

Jack nodded. "Indeed it is, Your Majesty. Which brings me to the crux of what I wish to speak with Your Majesty about."

Farouk put a pudgy hand into his jacket pocket and began running worry beads through his fingers.

"I feel it would be gallant, on the part of my wife's lover, to make provision for her in the event of his leaving her. Such a provision would enable her to leave the relationship with dignity. It is the kind of magnanimous gesture an English gentleman would make," he said, knowing damn well that if it was, it was a pretty rare one, but seeing no reason why Farouk shouldn't be led up the garden path as far as he could take him. "A chivalric, knightly gesture."

"Ah, yes." Farouk was beginning to look happier. "Quite so. When Prince, I had an English tutor. I am familiar with historical instances of English chivalry."

"Then I think you will agree, Your Majesty, that the time to make the promise of such provision is not when an affair ends, when emotions are painfully raw, but that a written promise of such provision should be made by the gentleman in question now—and lodged with Zubair Pasha's lawyer who will, if the time should come when it is necessary to do so, expedite everything without the gentleman in question having to be further involved in any way."

The worry beads continued to rattle and click.

Jack waited.

"And what sort of . . . provision . . . do you think this particular gentleman should make, Major Bazeljette?"

"Not knowing the extent of the gentleman in question's wealth, I think perhaps Your Majesty would be the best judge of that. Perhaps Your Majesty could indicate the kind of provision you deem gallant?"

Farouk pursed small rosebud lips and then drew a gold-backed notebook and gold pen from one of his inner pockets. He scrawled down a figure, looked at it, and then wrote something else down.

He gave the notebook to Jack.

With great difficulty Jack remained nonchalant. "That would be very satisfactory, Your Majesty," he said, continuing the charade. "And now perhaps I could wait while you confer with the gentleman in question and a legally binding document is drawn up? I shall then deposit the document with Zubair Pasha's lawyer. Fawzia will know nothing whatsoever about her lover's chivalric action until the day comes when it is requisite for her to do so. And perhaps," he added in a moment of devilment he couldn't resist, "perhaps that day will never come? Perhaps her lover will marry her?"

Farouk's dark eyes gleamed. "Perhaps he will, Major Bazeljette," he said, holding out his hand. "And though I know that such an event would surprise you, it would not surprise me. And now, if you would like to return to the anteroom, an aide will bring the document to you very shortly."

With that Farouk exited the room fast, on feet that were very nimble for such a plump young man.

As he realized that he had achieved his objective, Jack let out a deep sigh of relief. Not only had the King made ample financial provision for Fawzia, he had also stipulated that the deeds of a palatial Saint-Tropez villa would be made over to her. It was, Jack thought, with sneaking admiration for Farouk's farsightedness, a very good way of ensuring that if and when the affair came to an end, Fawzia would very conveniently be living several hundreds of miles away.

And if the affair didn't come to an end? As he left the palace, the document guaranteeing Fawzia's future in his breast pocket, he couldn't help reflecting that Fawzia would make a quite spectacular Queen of Egypt.

The next morning, as he set about prizing from the embassy a list of the names of the staff along with their biographical details, Brigadier Haigh put his head around the door. "Just thought you'd like to know your father is about to land at Heliopolis airfield," he said in a manner far more genial than usual. "He's here to chinwag with Auchinleck and give Churchill a firsthand account of our situation. I keep forgetting what a bigwig your father is. If you want to join the reception committee, you may."

Knowing that his father would probably have no time to spend with him except at the airstrip, Jack was out of Grey Pillars within minutes.

"Where are we going, sir?" Corporal Slade asked as he put the jeep into gear.

"Heliopolis airport, to meet a plane."

"Anyone important, sir? It's not the prime minister, is it? Or the foreign secretary?"

"No, Slade," he said as Slade slewed the jeep out into Sharia Qasr el-Aini, "it's someone far more important than that."

Completely mystified, Slade shot him a quick glance, narrowly missing a camel plodding down the center of the road.

Jack grinned. "I'm going to meet the prime minister's envoy, Sir Jerome Bazeljette."

"Blimey." Slade was impressed. "Fancy you having the same name as a nob like that. I bet he won't half be surprised when he finds you have the same moniker. I don't think he's more important than the prime minister, though, Major. If you don't mind me saying so, that is."

Jack chuckled, in high good spirits. "I don't mind you saying so, Slade. But in my books he is. Now how about we try to avoid this flock of sheep and take a shortcut through El-Ahmer?"

They reached the airstrip just as the plane landed. As Jack vaulted from the jeep, he saw that Ivor was there to welcome his father on behalf of the ambassador and a brigadier was there to welcome him on behalf of Sir Claude Auchinleck. There were a couple of minor aides also standing on the runway and as Jack strode to join them, and Ivor gave him a nod of greeting, the door of the plane opened.

His father had never looked like a conventional Englishman. Though his hair was now silvered at the temples, Sir Winston Churchill's fifty-seven-year-old envoy was still so dark-haired and swarthy that he looked almost Egyptian. And the scar through his left eyebrow made him appear not only raffish but as if he would be an ugly customer in a fight—a fight that he wouldn't need much excuse to begin.

Instead of immediately descending the steps that had been run up to the door Jerome paused, turning around to speak to someone behind him. A second later a sandy-haired little boy stepped uncertainly out of the plane's shadowed interior to stand beside him.

"Dear God," he heard Ivor say disbelievingly, "he's brought the Sinclair orphan with him. Now how the devil did he get permission to do that?"

As the brigadier's eyes nearly popped out of his head, Jerome walked down the steps, his hand reassuringly on Andrew's shoulders.

"On behalf of Sir Miles, welcome to Cairo, Sir Jerome," Ivor said, mindful of official protocol.

Jerome shook his old friend's hand hard. "It's good to be here, Conisborough. As you see I have a young companion with me. I shall be dropping him off at Nile House before continuing with my schedule. Will Davina be there, do you know?"

"It's not likely, Jerome," Ivor said, forgetting about the formalities and the presence of the brigadier and the aides. "She works, breathes, and sleeps at the hospital, but I'll have a message sent to her—and to her matron. I think I can guarantee she'll be at Nile House by the time you and Andrew arrive."

Jerome gave a nod of thanks and turned his attention to the brigadier. "I believe I'm to meet with General Auchinleck at 1300 hours. Is that correct?"

"Yes, sir. At general headquarters, sir."

It was just after ten o'clock and Jack noted that his father looked deeply pleased at the pocket of time he had been given.

"As for you, Major Bazeljette," his father said, smiling as he greeted him last of all. "Who dropped word to you of my arrival?"

"Brigadier Haigh, sir," Jack said with a grin, as mindful as Ivor had been that this was a formal occasion.

"Then I'm sure Brigadier Haigh will be happy for you to accompany Andrew and me to Nile House," Jerome said, adding in a low voice as he turned away from the reception committee, "The ride into Cairo might be the only time we get to talk to each other, Jack."

Hoping that the male secretary who had accompanied his father would be traveling in a separate car, he strode across to where Slade was waiting for him.

"You're to return to GHQ on your own, Slade."

"Yes, Major." Slade was bewildered. "And how will you be traveling back to Cairo, sir?"

"I'll be traveling with my father, Slade," he said, and as Slade's jaw dropped, Jack walked back to where Jerome and Andrew were seated in the rear of a black limousine.

"Andrew, I'd like to introduce you to my son, Jack," Jerome said as the big car swung away from the airstrip. "Jack wasn't much older than you now are when he first came out to Cairo and stayed at Nile House. You'll find living there very different from Shibden Hall, but you'll soon get acclimatized."

Andrew gave both of them a shy smile. "I already like the sun, sir. It doesn't shine much in Norfolk."

Jerome said, gently putting the boy at ease, "Jack and I have quite a lot of talking to do, Andrew, and only a little while in which to do it. It would be best if you tried not to listen and concentrated on looking out for camels and a glimpse of the pyramids. Anything you hear I'd like you to keep to yourself. Okay?"

"Okay, sir," Andrew said solemnly. "I'm a Cub Scout. I know all about keeping secrets." And he turned his back to the two of them and began looking intently out of the window.

"I'm here for forty-eight hours, Jack." Jerome gave Jack's hand a fatherly pat. "It's the usual thing. Winston wants me to talk with Auchinleck and Sir Miles Lampson and get the feel of the mood out here. Needless to say, I'm going to squeeze in as much time with Delia as I can. Incidentally, my secretary is going straight on to general headquarters and Ivor isn't following us to Nile House. He doesn't want his divorce from Delia to be scuppered by the accusation of collusion. Now, what is the situation with your brief?"

Jack's response was unhesitating. "It's grim. My monitoring group have targeted a coded transmission being sent from Gezira Island. So far they haven't been able to pinpoint its exact location. The bugger transmitting doesn't stay on the air long enough. I reckon he's only a radio operator, but if we could trace him we'd then be able to lay hands on our spy. It has to be someone with access to military secrets, and I've scrupulously checked every bloody brigadier and colonel at GHQ with authority to take top secret information out of the building. None of them has an Egyptian girlfriend or buddy who could be passing them on."

As the limousine neared Cairo's poverty-stricken outskirts Jack paused for a second, and then said, "I've also learned that embassy staff at attaché level have authorization to see whatever military information they deem necessary, so they are my next line of inquiry. Getting information on names and backgrounds isn't easy because the embassy doesn't want to cooperate. I've got a gut instinct about the leak coming from the embassy. When you get back to London, I'd greatly appreciate it if you would send me the kind of information I'm after."

"Will do. Your brief allows you to go anywhere and interrogate anyone, doesn't it?"

Jack nodded.

"Then don't be afraid of tackling the embassy. If Tobruk falls, Cairo will be Rommel's next stop. And the domino effect won't stop there. If he takes Cairo, he'll have control of Suez and once that happens, we'll lose our route to India, Singapore, and Australia, and access to the Arabian oilfields."

Jerome didn't add that then the war would be over, with the Allies defeated and the Axis powers victorious, because he didn't need to.

The prospect of losing the war was so horrendous that they

were silent for a minute. Then, as the limousine became clogged in the chaotic traffic of Kasr el-Nil Street, Jerome turned the conversation to family matters. "How is Fawzia, Jack? I should have asked you earlier. Was your arrival in Cairo a surprise for her?"

"It was. And not a pleasant one. We've agreed to divorce."

Jerome's eyebrows rose but to Jack's relief he made no comment. Jack realized that his news hadn't come as a surprise—though he was pretty sure that when he mentioned Farouk's name, Jerome would be shocked.

As the limousine cruised through the wide leafy streets of Garden City Jerome said, "I've asked whether the Royal Horse Artillery could organize an ad hoc polo match while I'm here—and if so, you and Darius could play."

"Brilliant. I've barely seen Darius since I've been here and far too little of Davina."

His father was, he knew, about to ask after Petra, but they were already at the house. Andrew was saying, round-eyed, "Is this where I'm to live? Right next to the river?"

Jack could see Davina's little Morris parked on the far side of the drive and as Jerome said, "It is, indeed, Andrew. And at the rear of the house there are donkeys," Davina hurtled out of the house.

The chauffeur opened the door for Jerome while Davina ran around to Andrew's side of the car. "Welcome to Nile House, Andrew," she said with a beaming smile. "I'm Davina, and please don't look so startled. Nile House isn't a hospital. I'm only in nurse's uniform because I've come straight from work in order to welcome you."

"That's all right," Andrew said comfortably as he stepped out of the car. "I didn't think it was a hospital," he added as she held out her hand and he slipped his hand into it, "because hospitals don't have gardens and donkeys, do they?"

"Jerome! Jerome!" Delia came out of the house as if her feet were winged, a blazing smile of joy on her face.

With a shout of exultation Jerome strode toward her and as she threw herself into his arms he swung her off the ground as if she were a young girl.

It was extraordinary behavior for a middle-aged statesman and Jack was grateful there was no one there to witness it but himself, Davina, Andrew—and a rather startled chauffeur.

"You must have a drink," Davina said to Andrew, as Delia, her feet once more in touch with the ground, led the way into Nile House. "A welcome drink is traditional and Adjo will be impatient to meet you. When I arrived in Cairo, Adjo was my very first Egyptian friend and I'm sure he'll soon be yours."

In the relative coolness of the vast drawing room Jack took off his peaked cap and accepted from a safragi one of the rose-water drinks he found so sickly sweet. Jerome and Delia still had their arms around each other's waist and he looked across to Davina to see how she was taking this blatant statement of the open way the two of them now intended conducting their relationship.

She showed no sign of being startled and he realized that, like him, she had probably known for a decade what the lay of the land was between his father and her mother.

"I'm just going to show Andrew to his room," she said as Andrew manfully downed his drink, "and then, as matron has given me the rest of the afternoon off, I'm going to spend it showing him around Cairo."

"I'm seeing General Auchinleck at one o'clock," Jack heard his father say to Delia. "Then I'm meeting with Sir Miles Lampson. Tomorrow I shall be going into the desert to have a look at our forward positions. Winston wants a firsthand account. I'm hoping a polo match is going to be arranged, but whether I'll be able to get to it is doubtful. Other than that, this next hour is all the time we're going to have together."

Aware that their conversation was becoming increasingly personal, Jack moved away. When Davina and Andrew rejoined him the boy said happily, "I can see the pyramids from my bedroom window. And Davina is going to take me on a sailboat on the river. Adjo says the sailboats are called feluccas."

"I shall be staying here for a little longer," Jerome said to Jack, putting his arm around Jack's shoulders. "You can take the limousine if you need it—just as long as you send it back."

"I don't need it, Dad. If I don't see you at the polo match, have a safe flight back to London."

Aware that it was highly possible they wouldn't see each other for a long time they hugged and then, following in Davina and Andrew's wake, Jack walked out of the room and out of the house.

Davina and Andrew were already piling into her open-topped little Morris and she asked him if he wanted a lift.

He shook his head. "I'm going back to Grey Pillars. Getting in and out of that car would be more trouble than it's worth."

It was then he realized he'd left his cap behind.

With a sigh of irritation he turned back toward the house.

As he walked from the entrance hall into the drawing room there was no sign of his father and Delia.

He picked up his cap and as he left the room, he heard the sound of laughter from the floor above him and seconds later the slam of a bedroom door.

He looked at his watch. It was eleven forty-five. As he walked into the fierce sunlight he grinned, knowing very well why his father had been so pleased to have an hour free before he had to leave for his meeting with General Auchinleck.

The polo match took place on the day his father was scheduled to leave. As it was such an impromptu match the only spectators were family and friends. Neither Jack nor Darius cared. For the first time they found themselves playing on the same team and as their ponies twisted and turned it was as if the years had rolled back to the days before the war, when they were just competitive friends.

Jack was playing in Number Three position and as he fed the ball to Darius, he gave a whoop of triumph. Despite the attacking Royal Horse Artillery he knew Darius was going to score.

Riding like a barbarian, his friend defeated all the opposing team's efforts to block him and thwacked the ball straight between the posts. Elatedly Jack stood up in his stirrups, his polo shirt soaking wet, unable to remember when he had last enjoyed himself so much.

Lunch was a family picnic in a quiet corner of the sporting club's flower-filled grounds. To Jack's disappointment, Darius had an urgent meeting and so wasn't able to be with them. Sholto, who hadn't been at the polo match, wasn't with them either.

"So far, I've never seen Petra and Sholto together," Jack said to Davina as they sat a little distance from where Petra was spreading a white tablecloth on the grass and Delia was unpacking the picnic food prepared by the club's chef. "When I asked Delia how Petra and Sholto were, she simply said 'fine' and changed the subject. When I asked Petra how Sholto was, she also changed the subject. From which I gather that things are far from fine."

"You're probably right, but I truthfully don't know, Jack. Petra never speaks about her marriage."

As Delia lifted silver cutlery from a hamper, Andrew said chattily, "When we had picnics in Caithness, my mother always used to sing the Happy Song."

"The Happy Song?" Delia had begun slicing a large quiche. "Now what song would that be?"

"It's always the same one. It's any song you sing when you are really happy. We always chose 'The Bonnie Banks of Loch Lomond.' Don't you have a Happy Song?"

"I don't think we do, Andrew." There was regret in Delia's voice as she slid a slice of quiche onto a plate.

"Oh, yes, we have," said Davina. "It's 'Dixie.' You've been singing it at every family occasion since I can remember."

"That's true, Delia," Jerome said, a gleam in his gold-flecked eyes. "Though I remember an occasion, on the day we first met, when Ivor specifically forbade you from ever singing it again."

"Ah, well." Delia's voice was full of mischief. "That was when dear Ivor thought he'd married a very different girl from the one he actually had. How about I sing it now? Would you like that, Andrew?"

Andrew nodded and Delia handed the plate of quiche to Jerome and then launched into the song that reminded her of Sans Souci and her long exhilarating rides in the rolling countryside of her birth.

Jack looked across at Petra. All afternoon she had done her best to put as much space between them as possible. She had hardly spoken to anyone else, either. More often than not, when he had looked across at her, she had been looking toward his father, an expression in her eyes that he couldn't for the life of him fathom.

As Delia came to the last verse, they all joined in the chorus. Afterward Petra said, her voice strained, "I'm going for a walk. I won't be long, Jerome. I'll be back to say goodbye before you leave."

It was a reminder that the car that was to take Jerome to the airport was already waiting. In less than an hour he would be speeding to Heliopolis.

Jack watched her walk away. He knew she was bitterly unhappy. Everyone knew she was bitterly unhappy. But she wouldn't talk to him; she wouldn't let him close to her in any way at all.

He stood up and walked quickly after her.

She was heading in the direction of the clubhouse and he caught up with her at the lavender-lined path.

Seizing her arm, he swung her around to face him. "Talk to me," he said urgently. "We may not be lovers, but we can at least be friends! Don't keep yourself so isolated. I love you. I've always loved you. I want to help you. Tell me what's wrong."

"I can't!" In the strong sunlight he saw that there were deep circles under her eyes, and her skin was so pale it was almost translucent. "There's so much wrong, Jack! It isn't just you and me—it's other things. Things I can't speak about; not until I'm sure."

"What kind of things?" There was a different urgency in his voice, for her green eyes were frantic with an expression he'd seen all too often in interrogations. She was frightened—and he had to know why.

"Later, Jack. I just need a little more time." Her face was bloodless. "Please give my apologies to Jerome. I can't go back and say goodbye. Not now."

She tried to turn away from him, but he held her fast, his heart pounding. "You have to tell me what it is you're so scared of, Petra," he said fiercely. "I'll slay every dragon in the world for you, but I have to know where danger lies. I love you. You can trust me with your life!"

"I know that, Jack! Please don't ever think I don't know that!"

A group of people were coming down the pathway and she twisted so suddenly that this time she escaped his grasp. He tried to catch hold of her again, but a woman between them stumbled and fell in front of him. By the time he had disentangled himself from her, Petra was yards away, running toward the car park.

He was about to sprint after her when a club official hurried up to him. "There's an urgent phone call for you from general headquarters, Major Bazeljette."

Uttering a curse he seldom used, Jack gave Petra one last look and headed for the clubhouse.

The caller was Archie.

"Sorry to disturb you, Jack," he said apologetically, "but thought you should know that Sadat's in Cairo again. The minute our informer at the station rang in I set Slade on his tail and he has just contacted me to say that Sadat has boarded a houseboat on Gezira."

Jack felt as if a ton weight had just slammed into his chest.

"South of the island?" he said, praying to God it was one of the houseboats near to the English Bridge.

"No." Archie was happily oblivious of Jack's concern. "At the Zamalek end. The name of the houseboat is the *Egyptian Queen*."

TWENTY-NINE

Jack fought the temptation to head straight to Zamalek. No law was being broken and Sadat was being tailed only because he was known to be a member of a subversive group. It wasn't a crime for which he could be jailed. Action could be taken against the Free Officers only if they began an open rebellion. If Sadat became aware that he was being tailed—and he would become aware of it if a British intelligence officer showed up on the houseboat—keeping close tabs on him would become impossible. All Jack could do was step up the surveillance on him—and instigate surveillance on Darius.

It was the very last thing in the world that he wanted to do.

Back at GHQ he hesitated, but he knew he had no option. That Sadat had made contact with the owner of the *Egyptian Queen* was now a matter of record—as was the owner's name.

Jack knew he had to confront Darius about the meeting with Sadat. Darius may have successfully fooled people into believing that his days as a fierce nationalist were over, but Jack knew differently. The war had just caused Darius to go undercover.

He wrote a terse report for Brigadier Haigh. Rang Petra's home number and received no reply. Rang Nile House only to be told that Lady Conisborough had not returned from the airfield. Then, just as Jack was about to send his report to the brigadier, the brigadier sent for him.

With Sadat's file tucked under his arm he made his way along the warren-like corridors to Haigh's office.

The director of military intelligence was not alone.

He had a friend of the Conisboroughs, Bruno Lautens, with him.

As an experienced intelligence officer Jack was well trained in maintaining an impassive expression, although it took some doing now.

"Sit down, Jack." Since the reminder that Jack's father was a close intimate of the prime minister, Brigadier Haigh's attitude toward him had become increasingly matey. "Circumstances require that the three of us have a very private talk."

"Circumstances?" Not looking toward Bruno, Jack put the file down on Haigh's desk.

The brigadier looked at the name and tapped it with his forefinger. "Yes, Jack," he said meaningfully. "*These* circumstances."

Bruno was seated to one side of the desk; Jack took the other chair facing the brigadier.

"The latest update in this file," said Brigadier Haigh, "will detail Captain Anwar Sadat's unexpectedly speedy return to Cairo and his visit to your brother-in-law's houseboat. I know all this, Jack, because we're not the only ones interested in Captain Sadat, nor are we the only people keeping him under surveillance. The Americans have a strong interest in him too. I know that you are on social terms with Mr. Lautens, but what he has not been able to disclose, until now, is that he is a high-ranking American intelligence officer."

Jack looked at Bruno. "And archaeology?" he asked. "Was that just a front?"

Bruno's grin was as affable as always. "No. I'm a pukka archaeologist. It was when I was on a dig down near the Sudan border that I was recruited by Washington." He looked toward Brigadier Haigh. "Do you want me to put Major Bazeljette in the picture, or would you prefer to do so, Brigadier?"

Haigh pursed his lips and then said, "I shall, if you don't mind. America's take on the Free Officers Movement, Jack, is that when this war is won, America and Britain are going to need their members to build a modern Egyptian state that Britain and America can work with. We all know that the monarchy's days are numbered. Farouk is as corrupt as they come and certainly not the man to help Egypt into the twentieth century. There's a feeling that Gamal Nasser, who is head of the Free Officers, probably is."

"And does this . . . scenario . . . assume an Egypt completely free of a British presence?" Jack asked, looking from the brigadier to Bruno.

"America doesn't like imperialism," Bruno said pleasantly.

"And we have to be realistic," Brigadier Haigh said heavily. "I don't have a second's doubt that we're going to win this war, but when we do, the world will be a different place. The Americans may well be right that in postwar Egypt there will be no place for Britain. And, on the chance that Nasser and Sadat will be the men we then have to deal with, my orders are to keep a tight watch on them and on their friends, but not so tight that we won't be able to come to an accommodation with them, should the occasion arise."

"And is Darius Zubair counted as one of those friends?"

Bruno leaned forward, his big hands clasped. "Not only a friend, but according to our intelligence reports, a leading member of Nasser's future government. And that it *is* Nasser and his friends who one day form it is vital if the danger of the Muslim Brotherhood taking control of Egypt is to be avoided."

"That wouldn't be something any of us would want to contemplate," Haigh said with feeling. "The long and the short of it, Jack, is that you keep your brother-in-law and Sadat under surveillance, but that you so do with an eye to the broader picture." And not troubling to open the file Jack had brought, the brigadier handed it back to him.

"Yes, sir." Jack rose to his feet, saluted, and left the room.

When he got back to his own office he locked the file safely away and tried Petra's phone number again. Again there was no reply.

Archie came in and thumped another pink-docketed report on his desk. "A British Gladiator took off without authorized clearance two hours ago," he said. "Seems there was an Egyptian at the controls and our radar had him heading straight for the German lines. Our blokes tried to shoot him down before he crossed them. They failed, but a stray German gunner did the job for them. What the pilot was up to is anybody's guess."

"Leave it with me. I'll send a report to Haigh in the morning. I understand you've got a hot date with Boo tonight?"

Archie grinned. "I have, but I've some paperwork to finish off first."

When Archie had begun pounding away on his battered typewriter Jack tried Petra's number again. This time the number didn't ring unanswered. This time it was unobtainable. For a phone to be out of order was a frequent occurrence in Cairo and controlling his impatience Jack said, "I'm off home, Archie. I'm in need of a stiff drink and a shower."

"Home," the flat he shared with two other officers, was only a five-minute walk away, but between setting off from Grey Pillars and arriving at his door, dusk fell, pale-yellow light turning fiery orange before plunging into deep-purple twilight.

He knew the instant he stepped into the narrow hallway that no one else was at home. Relieved, he made straight for the bathroom and turned on the creaky shower. The phone rang before he'd even had the chance to take off his shirt and certain it would be a fishing-fleet girl for one or other of his flatmates, he walked back out of the bathroom and into the hall to answer it.

"Thank God you're there, Jack." There was an edge to Archie's voice he'd never heard in it before. "Petra just showed up. She's very upset and said she had to see you. When I said you'd just left for the flat she asked for the address. I offered to escort her over, but she refused. She was nearly hysterical and so I thought it best to let her have her way."

"She left GHQ how long ago?"

"Two minutes. Maybe three."

"Stay by the phone in case I need you." He slammed the receiver down. Whatever the cause of Petra's distress, he knew it was something extremely serious. She'd been scared when she had spoken to him earlier and Petra wasn't the kind of woman who scared easily.

He strode into the bathroom and turned the shower off. As he did so the front doorbell rang.

He yanked the door open so fast that she half fell across the threshold.

To his stupefaction he saw she was clutching a battered German prayer book.

He put an arm around her, taking her weight.

"I have to talk to you, Jack . . ." She was gasping for breath. "I have to tell you—"

"Wait until you're sitting down with a brandy inside you," he said.

"No." She shook her head violently, her torrent of hair tumbling out of its pins. "There isn't time . . . I don't even know whether he's so injured he'll be there, or whether he'll be gone."

"He? Sholto?"

She nodded and, fighting hysteria, said, "He's a spy. I've

had suspicions for months, but when I found this . . ." Her fingers tightened on the prayer book. "When I found this, I was sure. So sure that I confronted him . . . He just laughed and then he lunged at me. We fought at the top of the stairs and I tripped him. He tumbled down and banged his head on the newel-post and that's where I left him, unconscious and bleeding. But when he comes around he'll come after me."

He didn't ask why she'd been suspicious of Sholto for months. He didn't ask what was in the prayer book.

He dialed his number at GHQ.

Archie answered.

"Our man is Sholto Monck," Jack said without explanation. "He's at 5 Sharia Aziz, Gezira Island. Go there directly with a squad of armed men. I want him taken into custody no matter what diplomatic immunity he claims. And I want him taken alive. I'll meet you there. Got it?"

"Got it," Archie said, stunned but unquestioning.

Jack took his Colt from its holster and strode into the bedroom. Tugging open a drawer, he took out a box of bullets and shook it open. As he began loading the revolver, Petra said unsteadily from the doorway, "Sholto isn't Anglo-Irish. He's German-Irish. I was looking for confirmation and I found this in a box of books which he brought with him to Cairo and never unpacked."

Jack put a handful of bullets into his top pocket, shoved his revolver into his holster, and took the dusty prayer book from her.

On the flyleaf, written in German, was a list of family birth dates. The last name on the list was Sholto's name and place of birth. Munich.

"What made you suspicious?" Jack demanded, taking fierce satisfaction from the fact that his suspicions where the embassy was concerned had been right.

"Lots of things."

Knowing the jeep would be with them within seconds she began speaking fast.

"He had so much money it was as if he was printing it—and I realized it was coming via a diplomat at the Romanian legation. He only met with Constantin when he thought no one would see. And Constantin's colleague at the Romanian legation was expelled for spying."

She took a deep shuddering breath and pushed her hair away from her face. "Then there's the contempt he has for Sir Miles and everyone else he works with at the embassy—though it's a contempt he keeps well hidden from everyone but me. I finally realized that he only married me so that he could gain contact with Ivor and Ivor's friends. When he drinks heavily and talks in his sleep he does so in German. In the early days he laughed it off by saying he'd been dreaming he was twenty-three again and studying for his Foreign Office exams."

The jeep screeched to a halt outside the flat.

He gripped her shoulders. "You're to stay here. If he's already left Sharia Aziz he'll be on the hunt for you. Don't go to Nile House. It's one of the first places he'll look. I doubt he knows this address, but I am going to leave an armed sergeant with you until I get back. Got it?"

She nodded. "Be careful," she said, her voice breaking. "I couldn't bear it if anything happened to you. It would kill me, Jack. Truly."

In the sudden knowledge that no matter what had gone wrong between them, she loved him still, he pulled her toward him, kissing her hard.

A minute later he was in the driver's seat, saying savagely to the officer he had ejected, "You're to let no one—*no one*—into this flat until I return. The woman in it is Lord Conisborough's daughter. You guard her with your life. Understand?"

"Yes, sir. Absolutely."

With a squeal of tires Jack careened away, heading for the

Kasr el-Nil Bridge, the palm of one hand slammed against the jeep's horn.

It was dark now and the streets were dimly lit to comply with halfhearted blackout restrictions. The bridge was as crowded as always and he fumed and swore as it took a seeming eternity to cross. Jack glanced at his watch. With luck, Archie and the squad of men would already be in Sharia Aziz.

As he swerved off the bridge onto the island he headed for the wealthy residential area favored by the embassy's diplomats. And then he saw the road to Zamalek and the handful of houseboats moored there.

He remembered how expertly Darius had hidden the fact that he was still anti-British. He remembered how the *Egyptian Queen* had been Sadat's first port of call when he returned to Cairo. He remembered how Constantin, who, according to Petra, was hand in glove with Sholto, had been with Darius the night Jack had first made contact with Darius—and of how speedily Constantin had disappeared when he had seen Jack's uniform. He remembered seeing Constantin with Sholto as the two of them entered a café off Kasr el-Nil Street.

If Darius was involved with Anwar Sadat, was he also involved in a quite different form of anti-British activity? Was Darius a German spy as Sholto Monck most definitely was?

Jack brought the jeep to a halt, perspiration beading his forehead. It was a possibility. As he looked at the fork in the road and realized just how very near to each other Darius and Sholto lived, he acted on gut instinct and slewed onto the road leading toward Zamalek, dreading what he might find.

The riverside road curved up the island past the Gezira Sporting Club. On the far side of the bridge the lights of restaurants and cafés glimmered. On the northeast side of the island there were only dense palm groves reaching down to the water.

Twenty yards away from the moorings he cut the engine

and rolled to a standstill. Making as little noise as possible, he walked toward the *Egyptian Queen*. The lights in the state-room were on, though the curtains were drawn. Darius's Mercedes was parked beneath the nearby date palms. There was no sign of any other car.

As he stepped onto the gangplank he could hear a woman crying.

With a hand resting on his revolver he crossed the deck and began to descend the ladder leading to the saloon. There was a sharp intake of breath and the crying stopped, but neither Darius nor Sholto challenged him.

They weren't there.

Only Zahra was in the cabin.

"What do you want?" she demanded, recognizing him at once. She knuckled away tears of fury. "If you've come to see your brother-in-law, he's gone. They've all gone."

The anger and bitterness in her voice was scorching.

"They?" he asked, as if it wasn't of much importance, knowing she would remember that as well as being Darius's brother-in-law, he was also a British officer. At the moment though, she was treating him as if he were a fellow conspirator.

"The Sholto man dragged me and Constantin here because he said his cover had been blown and he had to run, but first he needed Constantin to send a wireless message."

Jack's heart stopped. In one sentence she had confirmed there was a wireless transmitter aboard the *Egyptian Queen* and branded Darius a spy.

"What message did Constantin send?" he said tersely.

She shot him a withering look. "How do I know? He transmits in code. After he'd finished the row started."

"The row?" Precious minutes were ticking away, yet he knew he couldn't push her. To lose his temper would be fatal.

"Sholto said Darius and Constantin had to go with him and they didn't want to. Constantin said even if Sholto's cover was blown, his wasn't and the worst that could happen to him as a diplomat was that he would be sent back to Bucharest. And that if he was sent back, he would make sure I was able to join him there." Her voice shook with explosive fury. "But now that Sholto pig has taken him to Germany!"

"*Germany*?" Not all his long training in remaining ice-cool could keep him ice-cool now.

Zahra was too crazed with fury to register his stupefaction.

"Sholto said a plane would land at Malaqua and take them to Tripoli."

Jack had never heard of Malaqua, but if a German plane was to land there it had to be deep in the desert and presumably close to the German positions across the Libyan border. Which meant they were heading to an area that only a British army Long Range Desert patrol would be able to reach.

"Darius didn't want to go," Zahra was so angry at Constantin's betrayal in leaving her behind that she was happy to tell him everything, "but Sholto said he had to drive him and Constantin at least as far as El-Laban where he had a Bedouin contact who knew the route to Malaqua. And he said they had to take the transmitter with them so that they could keep in touch with the people sending the plane."

Jack knew El-Laban. It was a scattering of mud-brick houses set around an oasis thirty miles or so farther south than Saqqara. He'd been there years ago with Darius, but whether he could find his way alone, and at night, was another matter. He was, though, going to give it a hell of a try.

Knowing that he'd got all the information he could get and that what he was about to do could cost him his professional future—if not his life—he scrambled back up the ladder to the deck.

Ten minutes later he was driving fast across the English Bridge, heading for Giza. Even though it was night the road was still busy with carts and camels and military trucks. He tried to work out how much of a start Darius and the others had on him. Sholto must have recovered consciousness only minutes after Petra had fled from the house. He had then gone straight to the houseboat, picking up Constantin and Zahra en route. How long would that have taken? Fifteen minutes? Twenty?

He swerved past an armored car. At a rough estimate Darius, Sholto, and Constantin were a good fifteen minutes ahead of him. And if he didn't catch up with them before El-Laban, the race would be over. Only a Bedouin could travel the desert at night. Jack couldn't. He might not even be able to see the tracks of Sholto's car. And day or night, no one went into the Sahara unaccompanied. He had no emergency supply of water with him and no clothes to protect him from the crucifying cold.

Dark fields of sugarcane stretched out on either side of him and then, in the moonlight, the familiar shape of the pyramids reared blackly against the night sky.

The road to the Western Desert veered off one way. Another road, far narrower, led to Saqqara.

Within yards of racing down it he was stopped by two military policemen. He flashed his SIB card and they waved him on. Sholto's diplomatic identity card had, presumably, carried equal weight.

The road was one he knew well. Ever since he'd been a boy, he had hired a horse from the Mena House Hotel stables and ridden to the Step Pyramid, sometimes with Darius, sometimes with Davina.

Davina.

He couldn't even begin to imagine Davina's agony if Darius were to leave Egypt with Sholto and Constantin. And his leaving Egypt wasn't the worst scenario. The worst was that he would stay and be sentenced to a firing squad.

There were coils of barbed wire on both sides of the road and in the distance something that looked suspiciously like a skull and crossbones signaling a minefield. He kept to the middle of the road, mindful that the verges would be soft, deep sand. A motorbike zoomed out of the darkness toward him, the rider wearing the blue-and-white of the Signals Corps.

Jack was shivering with cold. What the devil was he actually going to do if Sholto's Chrysler came into view? He didn't want to draw his revolver on Darius, but what if they shot first?

Jack's stomach muscles tightened as in the brilliant moonlight he saw the Step Pyramid. From here, his only chance of catching Sholto was to pick up the Chrysler's wheel marks on the desert track.

As he covered mile after mile, with the Sahara stretching out on either side of him as vast as all eternity, his tension mounted. What if the tracks he was following weren't the Chrysler's? What if he lost sight of them or couldn't find them again?

After an hour or so he saw scrubby bushes in his headlamps and then he picked out the black silhouette of date palms. His relief was overpowering. Even if it wasn't El-Laban, it was at least an oasis—and an oasis meant water.

Minutes later he saw mud walls and knew that unless Sholto was still in the village making preparations with his Bedouin friend, his own journey had come to an abortive end.

There was no way that he could enter the oasis silently. In the desert the faintest sound carried for miles and El-Laban's inhabitants would have been aware of his jeep's approach for the last ten minutes. None of them, however, appeared to be curious.

As he cut his engine and stepped out of the jeep, there was no sign of any human movement. And no sign of a car.

In the starlight a skinny dog growled at him. From behind

one of the mud-brick houses a donkey brayed. In the center of the ramshackle collection of houses was the village well. Sitting on its waist-high wall was the dark outline of a familiar figure.

"Who," Darius asked conversationally, "is going to shoot first, Jack? Am I to shoot you? Or are you going to shoot me?"

THIRTY

Jack stopped. "Where's Monck?" he demanded.

"He's long gone. And there's no way you can catch up to him, Jack. Not without a Bedouin as a guide."

"I need a cigarette." He didn't want Darius thinking he was reaching for his Colt instead of a packet of Camels.

He took the cigarettes out of his shirt pocket. "Want one?" he asked.

The moonlight was bright enough for him to see Darius nod.

Not yet prepared to close the distance between them, he tossed a cigarette and his lighter to Darius.

"What is at Malaqua?"

Darius lit his cigarette. "An abandoned Italian airfield. Another six hours and Monck and Constantin will be in Tripoli."

"And how do you feel about that?"

"About Monck getting away?" Darius shrugged. "I'm indifferent. About Constantin? Constantin would be better off not getting on the damn plane. It's an option I doubt Monck will give him."

Jack inhaled deeply. "Tell me about Monck. For how long has he been Rommel's spy?"

"For as long as Rommel has been in North Africa. But he's not Rommel's spy, Jack. According to Constantin, Sholto has been spying for Ribbentrop since 1933. The payoff now is the promise that he'll be given a leading role in the future German government of Britain—assuming, of course, that Germany wins the war."

Jack was so stunned that it took him a moment or so to make sense of what Darius was telling him. He'd been a junior diplomat in the Foreign Office when Ribbentrop, as Hitler's special commissioner, had regularly visited London and met with Ramsay MacDonald, and with MacDonald's foreign secretary, Sir John Simon.

He'd met with a lot of other people too. When war with Germany was still six years away, Joachim von Ribbentrop had been a popular guest at many society dinner tables. Jack remembered Delia telling him of a dinner party where Ribbentrop and the Prince of Wales were both guests.

Had Ribbentrop's brief been to snare the Prince of Wales into friendship with Hitler so that when he became king, he would be king of a country Nazi Germany could count on as an ally? Not only did Edward have a host of German relatives, he also spoke German flawlessly. To Hitler, it would have seemed a viable possibility.

Ribbentrop had obviously set out to target other British aristocrats as well. He remembered seeing him with Lord Rothermere. When German intelligence unearthed the fact that Sholto had a German father, Ribbentrop must have thought he had struck gold.

"And Monck contacted Constantin, in order for Constantin to act as his radio operator?"

"That would seem to be about it."

"And did so from aboard the *Egyptian Queen*?"

"That would seem to be about it as well."

Jack drew in his breath. "The transmitter. Where the devil did you hide it?"

"Inside a radiogram. Below the turntable. All your men

did, when they searched the houseboat, was lift the lid. And now you know all that, Jack, what are you going to do about it? Because if you're thinking of taking me back to Cairo to be tried as a spy, I think it's only fair to tell you that I won't let you."

He moved his hand slightly and Jack heard the sound of metal grazing the top of the well wall. Whether it was a revolver or merely the cigarette lighter, Jack couldn't tell.

Determined to find out, he threw his cigarette away. "If that's what I wanted to do," he said, steel in his voice, "I'd have done it already. And it may come to that if you don't see sense."

Darius remained silent, the tip of his cigarette still gleaming red in the darkness.

"Why did you throw in your lot with the Germans, Darius? They're slaughtering Jews in their thousands and you're well educated enough to know that Arabs, too, are a Semitic people. You can't really believe that if Hitler wins the war, he will allow Egypt to govern itself."

"It's a possibility, and any possibility is better than none."

"There's another possibility I like far better."

"And what's that?"

"Throw me back the lighter and I'll tell you."

The lighter came winging through the darkness.

Jack caught it, hoping he wouldn't hear further sounds of metal scraping brick.

"Until tonight I didn't know about your involvement with Sholto. And I didn't know Constantin was his radio operator. But I did know that you had close links with the Free Officers Movement—and particularly close links with Anwar Sadat. The Americans know too, and are very interested."

"The Americans? Of what interest is Egypt to the Americans?"

"America will end up entering the war—and Egypt will be

of great importance to them. They are republicans and anti-imperialists, Darius. They will want to deal with a free Egypt without a monarchy, and without a British presence carrying the baggage of an imperialist past. Which is exactly what the Free Officers Movement wants as well."

Darius was again silent, but Jack knew he had his full attention.

"The government of an independent Egypt would be up for grabs. The Muslim Brotherhood have huge popular support. A mullah-led theocracy would not be the easiest for Western governments to work with. America prefers Nasser and his friends."

"Are you sure? Aren't you forgetting that Nasser and Sadat are both Muslims?"

"No, I'm not forgetting. What matters to the Americans is that they've never gone along with the extremism of the Muslim Brotherhood. And you are a Copt. American intelligence believes Nasser and Sadat have earmarked you for a role in any future government they might form. The Americans—always looking to the future—want to nurse you along as their main contact in that government."

"Which means they wouldn't want to see me shot as a spy?"

"Which means they very definitely wouldn't want to see you shot as a spy."

"Then that's just as well—for the British." Dry, dark humor entered Darius's voice. "The British wouldn't, after all, want to shoot an innocent man, would they?"

The silence that followed was so profound Jack could hear his heart beating.

"Run that past me again," he said, terrified he might have heard wrongly.

"I said that the British wouldn't want to shoot an innocent man."

"Are you innocent?" Jack felt giddy with hope. "Explain."

Darius flicked the ash from his cigarette. "I always knew Constantin gathered information for the Germans. It was all petty stuff. Things barbers, waiters, prostitutes overheard. And as far as I knew, all he did with it was report it to his superiors at the legation. Then he told me that a 'big fish' at the British embassy had contacted him. On the surface it was pretty startling information, but I didn't think the big fish was a serious spy. I reckoned Constantin was bragging. He never told me the name."

"So when did you know that it was Monck?"

"When he boarded the *Egyptian Queen* two hours or so ago with Constantin and Zahra and a revolver in his hand."

"It's a nice try, Darius, but it doesn't explain why the transmitter was aboard the *Egyptian Queen*—and why British intelligence picked up regular signals."

"That's easy." Darius tossed his cigarette stub into the darkness. "It was Constantin who introduced me to Sadat and, before you ask, I don't believe Sadat knew about Sholto, or that Sholto knew about Sadat. Constantin had many irons in the fire and kept them all separate. Sadat was mulling over whether an uprising within the Egyptian army—an uprising timed to help Rommel take Cairo—would be beneficial or not to Egypt. He didn't have faith in Germany's promise to give Egypt full independence. He'd drawn up a treaty. That was why Constantin brought the transmitter to the houseboat. So that Sadat—who is a signals officer—could make direct arrangements with Rommel for a member of the Free Officers Movement to fly to Libya with the treaty."

The dog, which had been quiet for a while, began barking again.

Jack thought of the British Gladiator that had been shot down over the German lines. Whatever arrangements Sadat had made with Rommel for his officer's safe arrival obviously hadn't filtered down to the gunners on the Libyan border who had inadvertently done Britain a big favor.

"Transmissions to Rommel about flying out an officer wouldn't account for the number of transmissions we picked up from the *Egyptian Queen*."

"No, probably not. Throw me another cigarette."

Jack lit one from his own cigarette, and walked close enough to Darius to hand it to him.

There was no gun, he noticed, either in Darius's hand or on the top of the wall.

"I think what happened," Darius said, "was that after Constantin's colleague was booted back to Bucharest on charges of spying, the legation, or wherever Constantin was transmitting from, became too hot. Once the transmitter was aboard the *Egyptian Queen* for Sadat's use, I think Constantin used it to transmit for Sholto. I once found him on board when I came home early from a party."

Jack not only wanted to believe him. He did believe him.

Turning around, he lifted himself up on the wall so that they were sitting companionably next to each other.

"Just out of curiosity," Darius said, pushing a lock of hair away from his brow, "how did you reconcile the idea of me being a British spy with my love for Davina? And before you answer that, you'd better let American intelligence know that I'm going to marry her."

"I don't think marrying Davina will queer your pitch with Nasser and Sadat. She's half American, for one thing. For another, her years of volunteer work among the fellahin is testimony of her loyalty to Egypt. Did anyone else think you were a spy, by the way? Did Petra?"

Darius grinned and shook his head. "No, though Petra's never liked me too much, mainly because she thought I was going to make Davina unhappy. When she knows differently,

I'm hoping our relationship will change. Fawzia assumes I'm a spy, though. And Fawzia will always assume I'm a spy. It's the reason I never wasted time trying to convince her otherwise. Just to cinch the fact that I'm not, I've got something for you. I pocketed it when Constantin was looking elsewhere."

From his back trouser pocket he withdrew a slim, dog-eared paperback book.

"It's Constantin's codebook," he said as he handed it over. "No transmitter, though. That's on its way to Tripoli."

As Jack's fingers closed on the book, he knew that Darius had provided all the commitment that American and British intelligence would need.

He thought of Sholto Monck.

"I would have liked," he said fiercely, "to have seen Monck before a firing squad."

Darius's mouth tugged into a wry smile. "He didn't much like you, either. On our drive out here he had quite a few choice things to say. One of them I should pass on to you." He took a long draw on his cigarette. "He told me that Petra is your father's daughter."

Jack chuckled. "No, she isn't. When I was five my father had mumps. It left him infertile. It's why I'm an only child. And there's a six-year age difference between Petra and me. You can work out the math for yourself."

"Then perhaps you should have a word with Petra. According to Sholto, your mother's husband, Theo Girlington, told her years ago that Jerome was her father. She's believed it ever since."

Jack ceased to breathe.

In one flashing moment, everything was clear.

He knew why Petra had fled London, and him, in such distress.

He knew why she had been terrified of having the slightest physical contact with him.

And he knew why Delia had so fiercely vetoed their love affair. She'd had suspicions; suspicions she had obviously never voiced to his father, suspicions she had kept a secret.

A secret that was now dust in the wind.

He sucked in air. The world revolved again.

"Come on," he said to Darius, joy roaring through his veins. "It's time the two of us got back to Cairo."

Together they walked across the village square to the jeep.

Jack slid behind the wheel. In Cairo Petra was waiting for him, just as Davina was waiting for Darius, and he knew now—had known from the moment he had seen the terror in her eyes when he had left her to hunt Sholto down—that she still loved him. That she had always loved him, just as he had always loved her.

He put the jeep into gear, and as he headed out of El-Laban, he began whistling "Dixie" as loudly and as jubilantly as his lungs would allow.

AUTHOR'S NOTE

In 1948 King Farouk divorced Queen Farida and married a commoner, Nariman Sadeq. In 1952 he was forced into exile in Italy in a revolution led by Gamal Abdel Nasser. In 1956 Nasser became president of Egypt and remained president until his death in 1970, when Anwar el-Sadat was then selected to succeed him. Sadat was assassinated by Muslim extremists in 1981.

READERS' GUIDE

1. When Ivor meets Delia in Virginia, he has been encouraged by Sylvia to find and marry a New York heiress. Why do you think he chooses Delia instead?

2. During her very first conversation with Jerome, Delia is reminded of her beloved cousin Beau and "instantly liked" the man she took to be a close friend of her husband. What do you imagine is Jerome's initial attitude toward her? Do you think he expects a friendship to grow between them?

3. Discuss the character of Sylvia. Upon first meeting Delia, Sylvia regards her with a patronizing smile, obviously confident in her own power over Ivor and the supposed inconsequence of his new wife. But after Delia saves her from drowning, Sylvia admits to an intense hatred for and jealousy of Delia. What has caused such a dramatic change? In your opinion, is it really Delia that Sylvia hates, or does her resentment belong more truly to Ivor, Jerome, herself, or her circumstances in general? How would you describe the balance of power in Sylvia and Ivor's relationship, and in Delia and Ivor's relationship, at this pivotal point?

4. What do you think of the division of the novel into character-focused sections? Does the order make sense to you? Does the choice of featured characters? Is there anyone else whose point of view you would have liked to see included?

5. When the Conisborough family arrives at their new home in Cairo, Delia reflects that she's happy with her choice of the young, pretty Kate Gunn as a nanny. Why do you think Delia likes Kate? Do you think she chooses her as much for Ivor as for the children, or is their affair an unintended consequence for Delia?

6. What role does Ivor play in his romantic relationships? How do his wants and needs change throughout the book? Discuss his progression from the commanding Sylvia, to the beautiful and haughty Olivia, to the magnetic and headstrong Delia, to the relatively unassuming Kate Gunn. What does each woman mean to him, and what role does he play in their lives?

7. Delia is often described as "unconventional." What exactly does this label mean to her? To what extent does she appreciate the power it holds, and how does this change throughout the novel? Does she become more unconventional as she gets older? Do you think she would have been seen this way if she had stayed in America?

8. Why doesn't Delia talk to Jerome directly about the possibility that Petra may be his child? Is there anything in Petra's character that leads you to believe that she could be? How did you interpret Delia's comment that Jerome was "most definitely not [Petra's] uncle"? Are there any other questions of paternity that occurred to you while reading *Palace Circle*?

9. As Jerome warns Delia soon after her arrival in London, infidelity among their social class is not only tolerated but to some degree expected. Do you think the same acceptance of

adultery carries on to the next generation? Why or why not? How aware are the children of their parents' affairs?

10. Though Delia has other reasons for gladly accepting a divorce from Ivor, she cites one main justification for the timing: Ivor and Kate are eager to have a child together—for Ivor, hopefully a son and heir. Do you think it's strange that Delia should support this, considering that her own daughters' inheritance is at stake? Is this decision in keeping with her personality? Is it in the best interest of her family?

11. What do you think of Ivor's character? Are his transgressions against his wife forgivable? How does his treatment of Delia change over the course of the novel? In your estimation, is he a good man?

12. Where does Davina get her seemingly boundless energy for community service and involvement with lower classes, as opposed to Petra, who remains happily focused on the activities of her own class? Is Davina's hands-on civic mindedness what Delia has in mind when she tells Petra that it is she, not Petra, who will "turn her father's hair white"? How do you think Ivor feels about his daughters' choices in activities?

13. Consider the importance of setting in *Palace Circle*. From Virginia to London to family homes in the British countryside to Cairo, places hold a great deal of meaning to the characters in this book. Who is linked with which places, and how does this inform the characters' interactions with one another as well as your reading of the novel?

14. In the final scene, were you surprised to find Darius (relatively) innocent of the charges Jack feared? Throughout the book, did you trust Darius? Did you like him? Why or why not?

15. Were you satisfied with the conclusion of *Palace Circle*? Why or why not?

16. Prior to reading this book, how much did you know about English and Egyptian history during this period of time? In what ways did the life stories of these characters illuminate aspects of the events and politics of World Wars I and II and English Colonialism in Egypt? Were you surprised by anything you learned?

For free supplementary materials, including information on book groups, suggestions for further reading, chances to win books, phone-in author appearances, and much more, e-mail broadwayreads@randomhouse.com.

Enjoy a preview of Rebecca Dean's next book,
ROYAL CIRCLE

ONE

May 1911

A slightly built, blond young man stood beneath Dartmouth Naval College's flamboyantly splendid portico. Hands deep in his pockets, he stared glumly across a broad terrace to where twin flights of steps led down to manicured gardens and beyond the gardens to a steeply sloping, tree-studded hillside.

At the foot of the hill lay the River Dart, thick with boats of all shapes and sizes. More than anything in the world he wished that, like many of the other cadets in his group, he were aboard one of them. While he hated the academic side of his training, he loved being out-of-doors and active. The time spent aboard a sailing cutter, with the wind of the estuary blowing against his face, was the only thing that made life at Dartmouth bearable.

His cadet captain strolled from the shaded recesses of the grand entrance hall and drew to a halt alongside him. "Off on a weekend's leave?" he asked affably.

David nodded, making an effort to look happier about it than he felt.

His captain hesitated slightly, as if about to say more. Then, thinking better of it, he merely nodded and, one hand hooked in the pocket of his naval uniform, went on his way.

David watched him, his eyes bleak. He knew very well that

his captain had been about to offer his usual good-bye to cadets going home on leave: "Give my best to your parents." Which, given David's unique circumstances, would have been a familiarity not at all appropriate.

It was for the same reason that the cadet had fudged calling him by name. He simply had too many of them. Seven, to be exact. Edward, after both his grandfather and an uncle who had died as a young man. Albert, after his great-grandfather. Christian, after one of his godfathers. George, after his father, or was it because George was the patron saint of England? He wasn't quite sure. Certainly Andrew was after the patron saint of Scotland, Patrick after the patron saint of Ireland, and David after the patron saint of Wales. With that little lot to choose from, it was no wonder people paused before addressing him.

Within his family circle he was known as David—and David was how he always thought of himself. If he'd had any close friends, it was the name he would have liked them to use—only he didn't have any close friends.

"It wouldn't be wise," his father had said grimly, hands clasped behind his back, legs astride. "Not in your position. That's why you're at Dartmouth and not Eton or Harrow. When you leave Dartmouth your former classmates will be pursuing careers at sea and you will rarely, if ever, see them. That wouldn't be the case at Eton or Harrow. Any friendships formed there would run the danger of continuing after your education and would become a burden to you. And you don't want that, David, do you?"

"No, sir," he'd replied dutifully, thinking there was nothing he'd like better than to have a couple of lifelong friends.

As if he had read his thoughts, his father's blue eyes had narrowed.

"If that is all, sir . . . ?" David had said, eager to be free of the familiar knot of fear forming in the pit of his stomach; eager to once again be on the other side of the library door.

Beneath the trim beard and waxed moustache, his father's mouth had tightened, but the expected explosion of temper hadn't come. He had merely made a sound in his throat that could have meant anything, and given a curt nod of dismissal.

As his cadet captain disappeared from view, David gave a heavy sigh, knowing all too well that in a few hours there would be a similar interview at the castle and that this time his father's ferocious temper might very well not be held in check.

He stepped from beneath the portico and began walking along the terrace fronting the college. Weekends at home were definitely not weekends he looked forward to, but they did have one redeeming feature. They gave him the opportunity to practice his driving. Slightly cheered, he rounded the building and strolled across the broad graveled drive to his Austro-Daimler.

As expected, Captain Piers Cullen was seated behind the wheel.

"No, Captain Cullen," he said pleasantly. "I'm doing the driving—at least until we're in sight of Windsor. Crank-start her up for me, there's a good chap."

Reluctantly, Piers Cullen stepped out of the open-topped car and, with even deeper reluctance, began cranking the engine.

David put on goggles and a pair of driving gauntlets. The car had been an early seventeenth-birthday present from his German first cousin once removed, Willy, and was the best present he could ever remember receiving. It had, of course, annoyed his father, who believed it had been chosen purely for that purpose. "Damn Willy's impudent cheek!" he had said explosively. "He's only sent it because the model is named Prinz Heinrich!"

David hadn't cared about Willy's motive. The motorcar went faster than he'd ever hoped a motorcar could go, and though his father had been led to believe that on public roads

Captain Cullen acted as his chauffeur, in reality he, David, drove it every opportunity he got.

As he drove out of Dartmouth and into the rolling green countryside, he saw with pleasure that Devon was looking its best. Even though it was nearly the end of May, primroses still massed the grassy verges of the country lanes and bluebells carpeted the floor of every wooded valley they passed.

He neared the market town of Totnes, wondering just what the weekend ahead held. His father would probably want to engage in what was commonly referred to as a "small shoot," and, as far as exercise was concerned, that would be it. For someone like himself, whose sense of well-being depended on a lot of physical activity, it wasn't going to be enough.

He thought again of the inevitable interview in the library and grimaced. His marks during the year had been nowhere near what his father expected of him, though God knows he had tried hard enough and had even come top out of fifty-nine in German and English. In history he had come second and in French third. It was maths—any form of maths—that let him down. "Forty-eighth in geometry and forty-fifth in trigonometry?" he could just hear his father bellowing. "Forty-eighth and forty-fifth?"

"Steady on the speed, sir," Piers said warningly when they were out in open country again. "That last corner was taken very wide . . ."

David made a noncommittal sound not very different from the one his father often made. Cullen was a killjoy, and having him alongside for a two-hundred-mile journey was tiresome, if unavoidable.

His low spirits worsened as they crossed the county border into Dorset. His younger brother, Bertie, wouldn't be home, as Bertie's leave from Dartmouth came much nearer the end of term. Which meant that there would only be his fourteen-year-old sister, Mary, for company, as Henry and Georgie were too young to really count, and his youngest brother, John, was locked away from sight in deepest Norfolk. And though he liked Mary a lot, finding something fun they could do together wouldn't be easy. Though Henry and Georgie's nursery could be raided for board games, his father always insisted such games be played with no uproarious laughter, which, to David, defeated their point. And they wouldn't be able to play cards, because there wouldn't be a pack to be found.

As Dorset merged into the airy uplands of Hampshire, the loneliness he always fought to keep at bay swept over him with such force he could hardly breathe. He had no one he could truly call a friend. Piers Cullen was too dour a Scotsman to be someone whose companionship he would voluntarily seek. And as far as Dartmouth was concerned, his father had never had to worry about friendships, for the boys he would have liked to have made friends with kept their distance and the others toadied up to him—and he hated toadies.

He was so deep in thought he didn't see the blind bend ahead until it was too late for him to slow down. As Piers Cullen gave a shout of alarm, he took it far too wide and far too fast.

Too late he saw what was in front of him. Too late he saw that short of a miracle, there was going to be an accident of tragic proportions.

He slammed his foot on the brake. Slewed the wheel to the left. And with a girl's screams, Cullen's desperate *"Jesus God!,"* and a horrendous barking ringing in his ears, he plummeted into a future beyond all his imaginings.